PRAISE FOR J. R. WARD AND HER BLACK DAGGER BROTHERHOOD SERIES

"Frighteningly addictive."

—*Publishers Weekly*

"J. R. Ward is the undisputed queen of her genre . . . Long live the queen."

—Steve Berry, *New York Times* bestselling author

"J. R. Ward is a master!"

—Gena Showalter, *New York Times* bestselling author

"Ward brings on the big feels."

—*Booklist*

"Fearless storytelling. A league all of her own."

—Kristen Ashley, *New York Times* bestselling author

"J. R. Ward is one of the finest writers out there—in any genre."

—Sarah J. Maas, #1 *New York Times* bestselling author

"Ward is a master of her o

J.R. WARD

MINE

◆ THE LAIR OF THE WOLVEN ◆

POCKET BOOKS

New York   London   Toronto   Sydney   New Delhi

Pocket Books
An Imprint of Simon & Schuster, Inc.
1230 Avenue of the Americas
New York, NY 10020

This book is a work of fiction. Any references to historical events, real people, or real places are used fictitiously. Other names, characters, places, and events are products of the author's imagination, and any resemblance to actual events or places or persons, living or dead, is entirely coincidental.

First Pocket Books paperback edition January 2024

POCKET and colophon are registered trademarks of Simon & Schuster, Inc.

Simon & Schuster: Celebrating 100 Years of Publishing in 2024

For information about special discounts for bulk purchases, please contact Simon & Schuster Special Sales at 1-866-506-1949 or business@simonandschuster.com.

The Simon & Schuster Speakers Bureau can bring authors to your live event. For more information or to book an event, contact the Simon & Schuster Speakers Bureau at 1-866-248-3049 or visit our website at www.simonspeakers.com.

Interior design by Davina Mock-Maniscalco

Manufactured in the United States of America

10 9 8 7 6 5 4 3 2 1

ISBN 978-1-9821-8023-2
ISBN 978-1-9821-8024-9 (ebook)

Dedicated to:
The two of you.
Personally, I think you make great houseguests.

Glossary of Terms and Proper Nouns

ahstrux nohtrum (n.) Private guard with license to kill who is granted his or her position by the King.

ahvenge (v.) Act of mortal retribution, carried out typically by a male loved one.

Black Dagger Brotherhood (pr. n.) Highly trained vampire warriors who protect their species against the Lessening Society. As a result of selective breeding within the race, Brothers possess immense physical and mental strength, as well as rapid healing capabilities. They are not siblings for the most part, and are inducted into the Brotherhood upon nomination by the Brothers. Aggressive, self-reliant, and secretive by nature, they are the subjects of legend and objects of reverence within the vampire world. They may be killed only by the most serious of wounds, e.g., a gunshot or stab to the heart, etc.

blood slave (n.) Male or female vampire who has been subjugated to serve the blood needs of another. The practice of keeping blood slaves has been outlawed.

the Chosen (pr. n.) Female vampires who had been bred to serve the Scribe Virgin. In the past, they were spiritually rather than temporally focused, but that changed with the ascendance of the final Primale, who freed them from the Sanctuary. With the Scribe Virgin removing herself from her role, they are completely autonomous and learning to live on earth. They do continue to meet the blood needs of unmated members of the Brotherhood, as well as Brothers who cannot feed from their *shellans* or injured fighters.

chrih (n.) Symbol of honorable death in the Old Language.

cohntehst (n.) Conflict between two males competing for the right to be a female's mate.

Dhunhd (pr. n.) Hell.

doggen (n.) Member of the servant class within the vampire world. *Doggen* have old, conservative traditions about service to their superiors, following a formal code of dress and behavior. They are able to go out during the day, but they age relatively quickly. Life expectancy is approximately five hundred years.

ehros (n.) A Chosen trained in the matter of sexual arts.

exhile dhoble (n.) The evil or cursed twin, the one born second.

the Fade (pr. n.) Non-temporal realm where the dead reunite with their loved ones and pass eternity.

First Family (pr. n.) The King and Queen of the vampires, and any children they may have.

ghardian (n.) Custodian of an individual. There are varying degrees of *ghardians*, with the most powerful being that of a *sehcluded* female.

glymera (n.) The social core of the aristocracy, roughly equivalent to Regency England's *ton*.

hellren (n.) Male vampire who has been mated to a female. Males may take more than one female as mate.

hyslop (n. or v.) Term referring to a lapse in judgment, typically resulting in the compromise of the mechanical operations of a vehicle or otherwise motorized conveyance of some kind. For example, leaving one's keys in one's car as it is parked outside the family home overnight, whereupon said vehicle is stolen.

leahdyre (n.) A person of power and influence.

leelan (adj. or n.) A term of endearment loosely translated as "dearest one."

Lessening Society (pr. n.) Order of slayers convened by the Omega for the purpose of eradicating the vampire species.

lesser (n.) De-souled human who targets vampires

for extermination as a member of the Lessening Society. *Lessers* must be stabbed through the chest in order to be killed; otherwise they are ageless. They do not eat or drink and are impotent. Over time, their hair, skin, and irises lose pigmentation until they are blond, blushless, and pale eyed. They smell like baby powder. Inducted into the society by the Omega, they retain a ceramic jar thereafter into which their heart was placed after it was removed.

lewlhen (n.) Gift.

lheage (n.) A term of respect used by a sexual submissive to refer to their dominant.

Lhenihan (pr. n.) A mythic beast renowned for its sexual prowess. In modern slang, refers to a male of preternatural size and sexual stamina.

lys (n.) Torture tool used to remove the eyes.

mahmen (n.) Mother. Used both as an identifier and a term of affection.

mhis (n.) The masking of a given physical environment; the creation of a field of illusion.

nalla (n., f.) or *nallum* (n., m.) Beloved.

needing period (n.) Female vampire's time of fertility, generally lasting for two days and accompanied by intense sexual cravings. Occurs approximately five years after a female's transition and then once a decade thereafter. All males respond to some degree if they are around a female in her need. It can be a dangerous time, with conflicts and fights breaking out between competing males, particularly if the female is not mated.

newling (n.) A virgin.

the Omega (pr. n.) Malevolent, mystical figure who once targeted the vampires for extinction out of resentment directed toward the Scribe Virgin. Existed in a non-temporal realm and had extensive powers, though not the power of creation. Now eradicated.

phearsom (adj.) Term referring to the potency of a male's sexual organs. Literal translation something close to "worthy of entering a female."

Princeps (pr. n.) Highest level of the vampire aristocracy, second only to members of the First Family or the Scribe Virgin's Chosen. Must be born to the title; it may not be conferred.

pyrocant (n.) Refers to a critical weakness in an individual. The weakness can be internal, such as an addiction, or external, such as a lover.

rahlman (n.) Savior.

rythe (n.) Ritual manner of asserting honor granted by one who has offended another. If accepted, the offended chooses a weapon and strikes the offender, who presents him- or herself without defenses.

the Scribe Virgin (pr. n.) Mystical force who previously was counselor to the King as well as the keeper of vampire archives and the dispenser of privileges. Existed in a non-temporal realm and had extensive powers, but has recently stepped down and given her station to another. Capable of a single act of creation, which she expended to bring the vampires into existence.

sehclusion (n.) Status conferred by the King upon a female of the aristocracy as a result of a petition by the female's family. Places the female under the sole direction of her *ghardian,* typically the eldest male in her household. Her *ghardian* then has the legal right to determine all manner of her life, restricting at will any and all interactions she has with the world.

shellan (n.) Female vampire who has been mated to a male. Females generally do not take more than one mate due to the highly territorial nature of bonded males.

symphath (n.) Subspecies within the vampire race characterized by the ability and desire to manipulate emotions in others (for the purposes of an energy exchange), among other traits. Historically, they have been discriminated against and, during certain eras, hunted by vampires. They are near extinction.

talhman (n.) The evil side of an individual. A dark stain on the soul that requires expression if it is not properly expunged.

the Tomb (pr. n.) Sacred vault of the Black Dagger Brotherhood. Used as a ceremonial site as well as a storage facility for the jars of *lessers.* Ceremonies performed there include inductions, funerals, and disciplinary actions against Brothers. No one may enter except for members of the Brotherhood, the Scribe Virgin, or candidates for induction.

trahyner (n.) Word used between males of mutual respect and affection. Translated loosely as "beloved friend."

transition (n.) Critical moment in a vampire's life when he or she transforms into an adult. Thereafter, he or she must drink the blood of the opposite sex to survive and is unable to withstand sunlight. Occurs generally in the mid-twenties. Some vampires do not survive their transitions, males in particular. Prior to their transitions, vampires are physically weak, sexually unaware and unresponsive, and unable to dematerialize.

vampire (n.) Member of a species separate from that of *Homo sapiens*. Vampires must drink the blood of the opposite sex to survive. Human blood will keep them alive, though the strength does not last long. Following their transitions, which occur in their mid-twenties, they are unable to go out into sunlight and must feed from the vein regularly. Vampires cannot "convert" humans through a bite or transfer of blood, though they are in rare cases able to breed with the other species. Vampires can dematerialize at will, though they must be able to calm themselves and concentrate to do so and may not carry anything heavy with them.

They are able to strip the memories of humans, provided such memories are short-term. Some vampires are able to read minds. Life expectancy is upward of a thousand years, or in some cases, even longer.

wahlker (n.) An individual who has died and returned to the living from the Fade. They are accorded great respect and are revered for their travails.

whard (n.) Equivalent of a godfather or godmother to an individual.

ONE

Exit 38S, The Northway (I-87)
Plattsburgh, New York

H IS DOCTOR, THE one who'd been keeping him alive, was dead.

As Daniel Joseph gunned his Harley up the Northway, he swerved around a semi, played hopscotch with a pair of sedans, and then eyed an upcoming break in the woods in the median and prayed there wasn't a cop hiding in the pine trees. He had bigger problems to worry about than speeding tickets and hey-where's-your-helmet citations: No weapon. No backup. No intel.

But hey, at least the woman he loved more than anything else on the planet was with him. Which was the precise offensive strategy you wanted when you were rushing into a crime scene that hadn't been cleared, that no one in conventional law enforcement could know about, and that you were bringing no weapons, no backup, and no intel to.

And it had started to fucking snow.

The shit that had begun to fall halfway through the rocket ship ride was only a non-issue, mid-

November squall in the morning—but that was if you were in a car or had a visor. As the flakes hit his face, they were shards of glass, on his cheeks, in his eyes, up his nose—

Thank God, he thought as their exit appeared and he pared off at the same speed he'd been going.

At the top of the ramp, he didn't slow down for the stop sign before merging onto NY 22S, and as he and the bike zoomed into the turn, Lydia Susi tightened her arms around his waist and ducked her head into his back. During the twenty-minute, breakneck roar from that apple orchard in Walters to this road leading into Plattsburgh, he had taken the brunt of the cold air, and he was feeling it. She was warmer, though.

He hoped she was warmer.

Goddamn it, he wished she weren't with him—

"We need Route Twenty-six," Lydia shouted in his ear over the din. "Toward the bay."

"Roger that." He turned his head to the side. "You okay?"

She gave him a squeeze. "Yes."

As he looked ahead of them again, all he could think was, *Don't do it. Don't ask back.*

She didn't.

Lydia was a master navigator, not that finding the condo development in question was all that hard, and once they were inside the ring-around of fifty or so white-sided, black-shuttered, Lego-like two-stories, the unit they were gunning for was easy to locate on the far side.

Pulling into the shallow driveway, he opened his mouth to tell her they had to stick together—

His woman ejected herself off the back of the Harley, landed on a lithe run, and raced up the front walk.

"Wait! Stop—" He tried to catch his breath. "Lydia—"

She all but attacked the door, twisting the knob, jerking, yanking. "Gus!"

Back at the bike, Daniel put his hand on his chest and tried to inflate his lungs, but for some reason, they weren't responding to the command. It was like he was suddenly breathing water—

"Around back," he wheezed as she pounded on the panels. "Go 'round . . ."

While an old guy from the unit next door stopped in the process of checking his mailbox, she took off again, jumping over some short-stack bushes, sprinting past the garage door, and disappearing around the far corner. The idea that she might find some bad news in the rear gave Daniel the energy he needed to dismount, but as he stumbled, he couldn't feel the asphalt beneath his boots.

"Everything okay?" the neighbor with the envelopes and the flyers in his hand called out.

Daniel coughed into a fist. "Oh, yeah." He cleared his throat so he could get more volume in his voice. "Cat on the loose."

"Dr. St. Claire doesn't have a cat."

Great. Just what he needed. "He was cat-sitting ours."

"Then why'd you come on a bike?"

Daniel narrowed his eyes, noting the cardigan, the reading glasses on the end of the nose, the salt-and-pepper gray hair trimmed *Father Knows Best* fifties style. For a split second, he almost asked whether the guy had seen anything suspicious around Gus's place. But then he thought of Lydia, and decided the well-preserved grandpa was a gossip grenade best kept with the pin in.

"Thanks for checking on us," Daniel said. Then in a lower tone, he muttered, "And if we need a hostage, I'm volunteering you."

Raising his hand in a little wave, he started off in the direction Lydia had gone—and holy fuck, he felt like he was dragging the Harley behind him: He was out of energy, a marathoner who had pushed too hard and was collapsing right before the finish line.

"Why don't I have a gun," he mumbled as he shambled his way along, batting away the gnat-like flakes. "Why am I unarmed . . ."

As he emerged onto the quilt-sized grass patch that passed for the backyard, he answered himself:

"Because you'd been about to pop the question. And who brings a—wait for me! Christ!"

Lydia was at the back sliding glass door and in the process of opening things. "This glass door is unlocked—"

No shit. "Hold on."

As she looked back at him, he grabbed the railing and hauled himself up onto the postage-stamp porch. He wanted to stop for a second to try to breathe again, but he knew her halt had a timer on it—

Bingo. She launched herself into the condo without him.

"Sonofa*bitch.*"

On his own entry, Daniel tripped the tip of his boot on the lip of the slider, and as he pitched forward into thin air, he had a quick impression of a messy, nothing-special kitchen: clutter on the granite counter, trash bin overflowing with crumpled take-out bags, a GE stove with the Home Depot plastic sticker on the front like the oven part had never been used—

He caught himself on an Ikea-like table, and the thing screeched over the tiled floor, his forward momentum transferring to the inanimate object and making it live for a good yard or so. After the bumpy ride, he stayed where he was, draped as a human doily, grunting through his open mouth.

"Be careful . . ." he said weakly. "Lydia, you gotta . . . be . . . careful."

Out in the front of the condo, she was racing from room to room, and he pictured her, so graceful, so strong, bouncing on the balls of her feet as she went around.

Holy hell, he loved her. With everything that he was, all that he had . . . and what little time he had left.

"There's blood here on the carpet . . ." she said off in the distance. "Here where the mail is. Oh, God . . ."

"Don't touch anything."

"Where is he?" More footsteps. "I'm going upstairs."

He opened his mouth to throw another *wait-stop-slow-down* onto the bonfire of good advice she was ignoring. But she was already halfway to the second floor—and with the drumbeat of her boots ascending, he followed her vertical example, pushing his chest up off the table. Getting to his full height was a process, and to give himself something to focus on other than how dizzy he was, he assessed the empty take-out containers and packets of sauce over by the refrigerator, and the empty Coke cans that were, well, everywhere.

Like Gus St. Claire had a breeding program for the damn things.

He glanced back at the four-top. Yes, the chairs were out of place, but he was the one who had messed them up—so this was normal living chaos he was looking at, not ransacked shit. And as he one-foot-after-the-other'd out toward the open living space, that opinion didn't change. The colorful collection of psychedelic concert posters from the late sixties and seventies were on the walls in their frames at right angles, none of the glass broken, nothing off-kilter. The TV was set properly on a low-slung table, the couch cushions were undisturbed—

As he tripped on something, he managed to catch his balance by flapping his arms, and when he saw what had caught his boot, he cut the bird stuff and frowned.

The stack of paperwork was fanned out around its staple, as if it had been dropped or thrown. And he might have ignored whatever it was except for the fact that he recognized one of the signatures on the last page with all the notary stuff.

His own.

As Lydia strode through the upper level, he gingerly lowered himself down to his knees. His hand was shaking as he reached out, and he made a mess of the pickup, the papers flip-flopping, fluttering, justifying their need for that staple.

As he started to go through the document, he couldn't believe what he was reading. So he went back to the beginning and gave it another shot. Because surely this wasn't what it looked like—

WHEREBY the party of the first part, Catherine Phillips Phalen, does intend to transfer the ownership of the compound "Vita-12b," its predecessors in development, and all relevant data to Dr. Augustus St. Claire . . .

"What the *fuck* . . ." His eyes continued to sift through the words, the operant meaning refusing to process. "What did you do, Phalen."

Was this what Gus had been taken for?

As if the condo itself could answer that question, he looked around—and saw what had caught Lydia's attention. In the midst of a messy pile of unopened mail on the floor by the front door, there was a pattern of dig-deeps in the wall-to-wall carpet and some bloodstains that were turning brown. So whatever had happened had gone down some time before. Like maybe twelve hours ago?

"He's not here."

Daniel was careful pivoting in his crouch toward the stairs. Lydia was halfway down them and finally stalled out, her hazel eyes wide, her cheeks windburned and bright red against a base of pasty white panic, her grown-out, blown-out, blond-streaked hair frazzled from the wild ride in. With her gray trail pants, and her black turtleneck and heavy fleece, she was wearing what he thought of as her uniform—and he wished she were covered head to toe in Kevlar.

"Where is he," she whispered in despair.

For a split second, silhouetted on that staircase, she was all he could see, all he could think about—even with the urgency of what certainly appeared to be a kidnapping at best, a beatdown-and-disappear-forever at worst.

Remember this moment, he told himself. *Imprint this and store it with the hoard.*

At the end, when things got really bad for him and he was just a flicker of consciousness trapped inside the husk of his body, he was going to need to remember what she looked like. Sounded like. Smelled like.

His beautiful wolven. An evolutionary master-piece, two sides inhabiting the same body, both human and lupine. A shifter that was very real, instead of some Halloween myth.

A miracle he still did not completely under-stand, but that he no longer questioned. How could beauty like hers be defined, anyway.

"Daniel . . . are you okay?"

I love you, he thought at her.

During the frantic ride in, with all his focus on getting them here, he'd slipped back into the black ops soldier he'd once been, and the return had landed him in such a familiar place that amnesia had wiped out reality. Everything was back now, though, from the rolling nausea in his gut to the god-awful wobble that dogged him—to the good-bye that was coming for them, sure as if they were stalked in the shadows, his killer closing in.

Fuck it, his killer was already here, inside of him.

He put up his palm as more alarm hit her face. "I'm fine. Don't worry."

Liar. And yet it was a truth. He was no more worse off than he had been, and when you had terminal cancer, no change was the new getting-better.

"What do we do?" she asked.

For a brief moment, a flare of intention reignited his body, purpose and sharp thinking tingling through him. But it was just a pilot light that flared and faded—

The sound of a vehicle screeching to a halt brought both their heads to the front door, and through a part in the drapes of the window seat, the blacked-out Suburban that had pulled in behind the bike was like a presidential detail rolling up.

He glanced back at Lydia and held out the documents. "I don't know where he is. But we may have the 'why' of all this right here—"

The loss of consciousness came with no warning. One moment, he was up on his granted-they-were-loose legs. The next, the carpet was coming at him like a rugby player who felt his momma had been insulted.

The last thing Daniel was aware of was the graceful wings of the paperwork as the legal document that transferred ownership of a potentially billion-dollar cancer drug rippled to the floor ahead of him.

Goddamn it, he needed Gus more than ever right now.

And someone had gone and killed his fucking oncologist.

TWO

L YDIA SUSI KNEW that Daniel was going
down a split second before the collapse
claimed him. Over the last six months, she'd devel-
oped a sixth sense about his passing out—or maybe
a change in his scent was the tip-off, her wolven
nose a barometer for the subtle shifts in his hor-
mones.

With a lunge and a swing of her legs, she vaulted
over the half-wall balustrade of the staircase, but
she didn't make it in time. Gravity was quicker than
she was, and Daniel's fragile body landed in a heap
on the carpet, his arms flopping when he didn't
even try to brace himself against the impact, his
head bouncing in an alarming recoil thanks to the
face-first digger.

As she threw herself down beside him, the tile in
the kitchen registered out of the corner of her eye.
At least he hadn't been in there when he'd—

"Daniel," she said hoarsely. "*Daniel . . .*"

With gentle hands, she rolled him over, and the

way his skull lolled to the side made her send up a plea to her dead grandfather. But like that Finnish specter ever did anything to help? And why hadn't she thought more about Daniel on the ride over here? She should have known that he didn't have the strength for that roaring trip, much less for what was waiting for them.

Gathering herself, she tried to calm down. "We just need Gus to have a look at you—"

Except there was no Gus. Anywhere. That was why they'd come.

Fine, someone else, then. Back at C.P. Phalen's hidden lab. Where a possible cure that Daniel was refusing to try was still waiting for its first patient.

"Daniel, can you hear me?"

As she waited for a response, she pictured the love of her life as she had first seen him, coming into her office at the Wolf Study Project, knocking her off her feet even though she'd been sitting down. Candy, the receptionist, had given her a heads-up, but she hadn't been prepared: Daniel's face had imprinted on her brain before his features had even registered, and the sheer size of him, his big shoulders, his strong legs, his muscled arms, had made her aware of her own body from across the room in ways that should have gotten her written up for an HR violation.

"Daniel?"

Six months later, he was a fragile echo of that

previous man. He was down fifty pounds, maybe sixty. After chemo, his hair was nothing but a shadow of new, lighter-colored growth on his head. His skin was sallow, and his eyes, which were a logy half-mast at the moment, had sunken into his cheekbones.

"*Daniel—*"

The door in from the garage flew open, and the woman who burst into the kitchen was another exercise in past-present, compare-contrast: C.P. Phalen, the corporate battle-ax, as Daniel called her, had downshifted from her black suits, stilettos, and precisely waved cap of blond hair, to sweatpants, sneakers, and all kinds of flyaway pinned down by a cheap barrette. She was going by Cathy now—not that Lydia had been able to make the name switch in her head.

Something about the woman screamed authority, even when she was in that fleece she seemed to wear all the time now.

Gus's fleece.

"Oh, shit," the woman said as she stopped short. "Is he dead?"

Can we not *use that word*, Lydia thought.

"No," she replied in a croak. Not yet.

"Thank God. I'll call Gus—"

C.P. shoved her hand into a pocket, but as the knee-jerk impulse went no farther—just as Lydia's hadn't—those cool blue eyes shot to the bloodstains on the carpet. As all the color in her face drained out, a twitch started to spasm in her left eyebrow.

"He's not here," Lydia croaked unnecessarily. "I even checked under the bed."

As more SUVs pulled up outside, there was a long, tense moment while C.P. blinked fast. Then her expression tightened into a mask of composure and she followed through on taking out her phone.

"I'll get Lipsitz for him, then," she said under her breath. "The man's got a bedside manner like a toaster, but he's an excellent doctor."

Not as good as Gus, Lydia thought as she refocused on Daniel. He was still breathing, thank God, and she told herself the fact that his lids were partially open was good. Even though it probably didn't mean anything.

"Wake up," she whispered. "Come back to me . . ."

She was so consumed by measuring his every inhale and exhale, she didn't notice the men who entered through the garage until they filed past her. The heavily armed guards were in black uniforms without any state, local, or military insignia, and they wasted no time fanning out and going through the rooms. She wasn't going to bother to argue that she'd already looked around. They wouldn't take her word for it.

Glancing up at C.P., she said, "I need help getting him back to the lab—we came on the bike—"

"We'll put him in the Suburban—"

"I'm *not* leaving my Harley here."

At the mumbled words, both of them looked down at Daniel. His eyes were open and his stare was more aware, though nothing much else had improved. His body was still in an awkward tangle and he didn't seem to have the energy to straighten himself out.

But she'd take the consciousness.

"We're not going to worry about that." She smoothed a gentle palm over his brush of new-growth hair. "Let's take care of you."

As C.P. barked orders into her phone, Daniel tried to sit up—and of course, he fought the help that was offered, pushing Lydia's hands away. When he finally managed to brace his upper body against his elbows, Lydia gave him some space and tried not to stare at him like she was searching for evidence that he was about to die. Right in front of her. On the pale wall-to-wall condo carpet. With there being nothing she could do to stop the Grim Reaper's robbery.

A familiar helplessness settled on her shoulders like a pair of heavy claws, a crushing sense of inevitability causing her to collapse on the inside.

"I'm not leaving the bike," he repeated with exhaustion.

"We have other problems—"

"Well, *I* have that problem. And it's going to be solved before I go anywhere."

His voice was sharp and she opened her mouth to argue. Except he didn't have the strength for a heated exchange, and frankly, neither did she.

"We'll come back for it."

"No." He shook his head, then swallowed like he was trying not to throw up. "I want you to take it back. They can load me into that SUV like luggage. You'll be on my bike. That's how it's going to go."

Who gives a shit *about the Harley*, she wanted to scream at him.

But she tried to put herself in his position. When easy options were impossibles, you thought in different ways. You put out demands because you had no choice. You dug your heels in on things that felt arbitrary and insignificant to other people because that was all you had.

"Okay."

"Thank you," he said roughly.

"They're waiting for us back at the lab." C.P. ended her call. "Let's get you moving. My men will process this scene and I'll drive you myself—"

"Why the hell did you do that to him," Daniel cut in.

The other woman's eyes narrowed, and instantly, the cold calculation Lydia had associated with C.P.

Phalen at first entered that stare. Gone was the friend she had become.

"Excuse me."

"You gave him . . . Vita-12b." Daniel pulled over the paperwork he'd been holding and had dropped. As he held up the pages, they shook like they were in a breeze because his hand trembled so badly. "That's what I signed in your office, when you asked me to witness your signature. You gave him the rights to the compound and you made him a target."

"I'm not going to dignify that with a response." The woman shoved her phone back in her pocket. "Can you stand? Or are we carrying you out of here—"

"You put him . . . in the crosshairs. You live with . . . an entire platoon of those rent-a-guns—and you gave him . . . the drug that requires all that security—"

"Right, we're moving you." C.P. motioned at the men who were coming down the stairs. "Pick him up and put him in my car. He's going back to the lab right now—"

"*Fuck off.*"

Daniel grunted and heaved himself to his feet. As he lurched to the side, he threw his hands out for balance and before she could stop herself, Lydia jumped up and steadied him. When she realized what she'd done, she braced herself for more arguments—and as none came, she was grateful. But also more scared than ever.

"Come on," she said in what almost passed as a level voice. "I'm sure we'll get updates soon."

She shot a meaningful look to C.P., and the woman nodded sharply in return. "As soon as I know anything, I'll pass it along."

With that settled, Lydia started leading Daniel slowly through the kitchen to the garage door. As they went along, he did lean on her strength, but his back was straight and he seemed determined to go out on his own two feet. He hadn't been using his cane for the last couple of days, and as he struggled now, the pit in her stomach was a spotlight on how much she had internalized the relative improvement after his immunotherapy had ended. With all its side effects winding down after the infusions had been stopped, the rebound was real, but temporary.

The Keytruda hadn't worked. Just like the conventional chemo hadn't.

This was the problem with smoking. Some people got away with it—and some did not. And you didn't know which group you were in until it was too late. Meanwhile, Daniel's terminal cancer was a bomb in her own life, blowing apart everything, laying ruin to her present and her future, but also taking her past, all those beautiful memories from the spring buried in a toxic swill of flashbacks featuring crash carts, and treatments that hadn't worked, and scans that had spelled out more and more bad news.

"Here, let me get the—"

"I'll get the door," Daniel said firmly.

She stopped and waited for him to slowly move ahead of her, open things, and hold the panel wide. As she passed by him, his eyes stayed down on the tile, his dignity as a man ravaged by a cruel disease.

"Thank you," she said quietly.

Emerging into the garage, the motion-activated lights came on and she glanced at Gus's Tesla, thinking of the gas-guzzling Harley. How was it possible that they'd just been together in that apple orchard? The quiet moment they'd shared seemed like something that had happened months ago, and she missed that time like it was a friend she hadn't seen for years. Then again, for a short shining moment, she'd felt as though they had stepped off to the side of their situation and been what they'd been before.

Two people without a disease.

But like all vacations, you had to return to your real life. Even if it was a nightmare.

"Can you make it to the SUV," she asked as she looked past a set of rolling trash bins to the pedestrian door on the far side of the space.

"Yes," he answered roughly. "I can."

Lydia took his arm anyway.

I love you, she thought at him. *Now and forever, you're mine.*

"We're going to find Gus," Daniel vowed as they shuffled along. "And if it's the last thing I do, I'm going to make this right."

She didn't know how to respond to the vow.

No, wait. She did.

Reality was cruel, however, and reminding him of all he was limited by was mean. Besides, he knew the truth.

That was why he was drawing such a hard line.

This time, when they came up to a portal, she was the one who had to open it for them. Just the short distance from the kitchen had drained him of energy, and it was funny how you could miss arguing with your partner.

Not funny at all, actually.

THREE

I HAVE SOMETHING MORE for you. Do you re-member what it is?"

As the question was put out there, it was a tough call what language the words were in. The syllables were from a Romance-based system of communication, sure, but other than that—

"I asked you a question, Dr. St. Claire. Can you guess what it is?"

No, the shit was English. Just with an accent.

Gus opened his eyes. Or tried to—unless, wait . . . no. His eyes were open, it was his vision that was fucked. And what do you know, he didn't need his HMS diploma to know blindness, in a person who had been sighted, was bad news—

"What do you want, man," he said through lips that were swollen from bruising.

When the hell had he been punched? Where the hell was he? As he sent the questions upstairs to his gray matter, his brain was sluggish, his memory patchy. Likewise, the sensations in his body were distilled through a filter of numbness, nothing but echoes of aches and pains registering. Which given how fucked he felt was probably a good thing—

"You gave me something," he mumbled.

"Sodium pentothal," said the male voice.

Truth serum? What the *fuck*.

From out of his sensory swamp, he babbled, "Is this a Jean-Claude Van Damme movie? And it's sodium thiopental. So you really are European, huh."

"My accent betrays me."

"That and the fact that the compound was outlawed for production in the U.S. in January of 2011 and there can be no official importation from European sources, either." He frowned—and promptly cut that out because it made his eye sockets throb even more. "Then again . . . you don't worry about the law, do ya."

There was a pause. "I'm afraid you're rather strong-willed, Dr. St. Claire."

"Been called worse."

"Indeed. Well, we are going to have to provide you with a secondary dose."

Gus laughed in a burst—and then grimaced as his ribs hurt. "Careful," he grunted. "You might kill me."

"I shall be of great care."

When he felt fingers brush the inside of his forearm, he swung his face down.

"Wait, no rubbing alcohol? You managed to get truth serum, but can't go to a Walgreens and buy some—ow!"

When he went to massage away the pinch at the crook of his elbow, he discovered that both arms were bent at a forty-five-degree angle and tied down at the wrist—and this brought into focus that he was sitting up in a high-backed, hard-seated chair. His legs were likewise restrained at his ankles.

Like he was a prisoner in an old school electric chair.

And yet, there was something soft behind his head, as if a pillow had been tucked into the nape of his neck for comfort.

"Forgive me," the voice said. "I am not formally trained in matters of infection. Such as yourself."

"So drugging people is more a hobby for you." Gus tried to lick his dry lips, but his tongue was sandpaper. "You wouldn't happen to have any Coke around . . . and I'm talking about the soda kind, not the nose—*whoa*. That shit is fast-acting, isn't it."

"Perhaps we have finally reached the proper dose for you."

With a fresh wave of woozy cresting over his consciousness, Gus abruptly remembered being back at his condo. He'd walked in from the garage after having quit Phalen's lab . . . found some crazy paperwork in an envelope on his doormat . . . and then discovered he wasn't alone. A male figure in black had pointed a gun at him and shot him in the chest— but not with a bullet. A dart. And just as his brain had started making connections, he'd fallen forward and landed on his—

Face. Which explained the mouth.

Shit, he thought. He needed to stall. Maybe someone would be looking for him. Maybe he'd been missed—nah, that was wishful thinking. He lived alone and he'd just quit his fucking job and his new one didn't start for two weeks. And the one person who might have missed him now hated him because he—

"You're not following the script," he mumbled.

"I beg your pardon?"

"The script. You know, as in a movie?"

"On the contrary," the accented voice said. "Everything has gone right to my plan. Which makes me the writer, does it not."

Aware that he was going in circles in his head, Gus tried to get with the program. What the hell had he been—

"No, no, no, if this were an eighties action movie . . ." His tongue clicked inside his desert mouth. ". . . the stakes would be higher. We'd be hanging off the side of a building . . . instead of wherever we are. Where did you say we . . . were?"

"I did not," came the haughty response.

As another wave of *whoaaaa* hit him, it was like he'd been injected a third time. "Wow. DIY tip— if you ever do this yourself, get ready for the chaser. It's a dooooooooooozy . . ."

"I suspect the tranquilizer has not completely worn off yet."

"Which one did you use?"

"Does it matter?"

Keep talking, he had to . . . "No, it doesn't— hey, where are we? I can't see a thing."

"You have an eye mask on."

"Ohhh, that explains it." Gus swallowed hard as his saliva glands started to tingle like his stomach was considering an evacuation. "You know . . . I think I might be sick."

"Oh, good. We are where we need to be. Worry not, that will pass."

"So you've done this before, huh." Coughing a little, he told his goiter reflex to calm the hell down. "I need a drink, my man . . . my mouth is a dessert. Wait, I think that's the wrong word."

As his head listed off to the side, it was promptly reangled with gentle hands, the strain in his neck relieved, the pillow likewise rearranged with comfort in mind.

"Thanks," he murmured. "You know . . . this whole kidnapping thing doesn't work . . . out, you have a future in the hospitality . . . industry."

"Why thank you, Dr. St. Claire."

"You're welcome. You can anticipate a good review ... on Goodly ... Google, I mean ..."

"Yes, I believe we are ready, Dr. St. Claire."

"Yeah, you better ..." See, this was the problem with the thiopental. It made you too agreeable. "... get the questions done. I'm running out of time before I lose ... consciousness."

He should probably be more scared. It was doubtful he was coming out of this conversation alive, and he didn't think anybody was going to find his body—

"I need to know how to get into C.P. Phalen's house, Dr. St. Claire."

Annnnnnnnnnnnd there it was. No surprise.

"You try Zillow?" Gus laughed a little, then had to cough his throat clear. "Have you seen the *SNL* ... skit they did on Zillow—"

"You are going to tell me the code to the entrances. And then we can be finished with our business."

Gus's scrambled-egg brain spit out an image of the blond woman in question, so tall in those heels she always wore, the black suits tailored onto her body, her hair all camera-ready. Fucking Phalen. She'd been too important to him from the second he'd first met her—and then things had gotten so much deeper that he'd had to quit her underground lab and defect to her biggest competitor. And the punchline? In the law of unintended consequences, it appeared he was taking Vita-12b with him thanks to her paperwork.

Not that he was going to be alive much longer.

Their goodbye had sucked, he thought. His and fucking Phalen's, that was.

But how was it ever going to be a good one? He was in love with her.

"Oh, Hans," he said sadly. "I think this is the end of the best part of our relationship."

There was another pause. "My name is not Hans."

"I've Gruber'd you in my head. Just so you know."

"I'm complimented. Ivan Reitman is one of my favorite actors."

"Alan Rickman, you mean. Reitman did *Ghost-busters* as a producer."

A soft chuckle was almost a purr. "You are very smart, Dr. St. Claire. And the time for obfuscation is over."

"Big word, there, Hans—and it's too bad. I was enjoying our back-and-forth. The initial stupor is receding and I'm feeling quite chatty now."

"Good. For you."

As some kind of second phase ramped up, tremors began to go through his body, a buzzy energy making his teeth rattle.

Seizure coming? he wondered.

"Not that you care," he chattered, "but I hate the fact that Alan Rickman died so young. And you know another thing that's always bothered me? Alex Trebek. Which then makes me think of Patrick Swayze . . . Michael Landon. John Hurt. Do you know what those five have in common?"

"Dr. St. Claire, we are off track—"

"Pancreatic cancer." Gus shook his head and felt the facial mask move, the band around his ears shifting. "Silent killer, most don't find out until it's too late, and then it's a fucking bitch with conventional treatments—and even if you do the Whipple procedure, the five-year survival rate is only twenty percent. We need to do better with so—"

A sharp, thin line of pressure across the front of his neck stopped him.

"The codes, Dr. St. Claire."

Gus swallowed, and felt the blade cut into his Adam's apple. "Is that a knife, Hans?"

"It is not a pencil."

"Look at you, quite the jokester."

Abruptly, another image of C.P. Phalen came to the forefront of his mind. No suit or stillies this time, and her pale hair was all frazzled, her face younger without the makeup. She was wearing one of his fleeces, the soft folds of navy blue fabric billowing around her upper body, and sitting on a hospital bed down in the lab. She had been scared and keeping a lid on the fear as best she could, just like all the other patients he'd ever had.

She was just like that Daniel Joseph. Stage four.

Different kind of cancer, though, not that that mattered because hers couldn't be treated anymore, either.

God, he hated that woman.

Fine. He just *wished* he could hate her. And on that note . . .

"You might as well use that knife now, Hans," Gus said softly. "Because I'll die before I help you hurt that woman."

FOUR

S O WHY'D YOU give Vita to Gus."

As Catherine Phillips Phalen glanced over her shoulder to the Suburban's middle row of seats, two things occurred to her. One, given the angle of her view, apparently she was driving. This was a news flash that shouldn't have been a surprise— and probably a contraindication for her being behind any wheel. Secondly, with the way Daniel was propped up against the rear door's blacked-out window, his shoulders collapsed into his chest, his mostly bald head at a bad slant, one arm lying dead across his lap, she probably should have laid him out flat in the back-back.

"We're almost home," she heard herself say as the great stone wall marking her acreage started to run beside them on the shoulder of the rural road. "Less than a mile."

The guard next to her nodded, but didn't look up from his phone. His role in this fast-track back to her estate was monitoring an overhead drone feed. Meanwhile, his assigned partner for this shift was in the rear bench seat and on a constant pivot, his eyes swiveling an owl-worthy three-sixty. The other two she'd brought with her were still in Plattsburgh going through Gus St. Claire's condo, looking for what she was willing to bet they would not find: fingerprints, footprints . . . hair and fiber samples that were not the doctor's.

Her hand went to rest on her abdomen. *Gus. I'm going to find you, I swear.*

As she looked down, like she intended to make the vow or prayer or whatever it was stick, it was as if the child she was carrying were God or something.

Which would make her the Virgin Mary. Or the Virgin Catherine, as it were—

Okay. It was official. She'd lost her mind.

Daniel spoke up again. "You might as well have put a target on the man's back. He's not like you and me."

That's right on too many levels to count, she thought.

Gus was the finest oncologist, researcher, and doctor she'd ever met—but he was also a prince among men, an Afro-sporting counterculture rebel with a Nobel Peace Prize brain, the moral compass of a saint, and an inexplicable, yet somehow charming, penchant for concert t-shirts from the seventies. He also liked basketball. Coke from a can.

What was she, his eHarmony profile?

"Why didn't you tell me?" Daniel demanded.

"About what," she said with a low warning.

Which naturally went ignored: "That you were going to give that drug away."

"You decided you weren't going to be our patient one. So why do you care." When there was no response, she glanced up into the rear view. "Funny, how when something is out of reach, its value to us becomes more clear, isn't it."

Wow. She was an asshole saying that to a terminal patient. But the shit applied to her as well.

And she missed the man just as much as Daniel did.

"Gus was your doctor," she continued—because she always doubled down when it hurt and she was talking to herself at the same time. "Not your family, not your friend, not one of your black ops clients. Besides, when you witnessed my signature, you told me it didn't matter what you were signing, remember?"

"I worked for the government, *remember*—so I didn't have clients. And you lied to me. You told me it was a healthcare proxy or some shit."

She glanced back at him again. "Considering all you kept from people at the beginning of your little adventure here in Walters, I wouldn't throw stones in that glass house, if I were you—"

"He could have lived with you. Jesus, these interchangeable rent-a-guns you stack the house with would have protected him, too. Or maybe you could have spared one or two out of your hundred or so and had him watched—"

"I am *not* going to debate this issue with you."

"Was it your last-ditch effort to try and get him to stay? Giving him the drug?"

"Here we are." As the front gates to her property appeared up ahead, they were the only break in that twenty-foot-tall stone wall, and she snapped the turning signal upward even though there was no one behind them. "We have medical staff on standby for me—I mean you. You."

"Well, I don't need them."

"And neither do I."

Hey, two could play at being defensive.

Hitting the brakes in front of the security checkpoint, she was ready to crash through the iron bars as a way to release some tension. So she twisted around, popped an eyebrow, and continued to pick fights.

"You sound like a toddler being asked to eat his veggies."

"Fuck you, Phalen."

"Back at you, Joseph."

As the gates began to open, she refocused on the steering wheel and didn't wait until the two halves were fully wide before hitting the gas. On the far side, the allée of trees that had been planted by the property's previous owner was a green chute directly to her sprawling stone fortress's front entrance, and as she stopped under the porte cochere, people in white coats and surgical scrubs streamed out into the gray daylight. The flow of doctors and nurses swamped the SUV, and the guard next to her got out and opened Daniel's door like he was a bellhop.

Conversation layered up as the medical staff clustered around Daniel like he was liable to go into cardiac arrest at any moment. And naturally, the worst patient in the world refused to cooperate—especially as a wheelchair was brought out.

Batting at his own personal 911 medical response, the man's mouth started running. Because of course, fight with an offer of help: "Get off me, I don't need that, where is—"

"Lydia's right behind us," C.P. cut in over her shoulder. "Relax."

At the sound of her voice, everybody paused—which was what happened when you were paying all the bills: People listened to you, did what you told them, and went where you ordered them to go. She liked that part of her life.

Gus had been the only one who hadn't marched to her tune.

As her hand went to her lower abdomen again, she forced her palm back onto the wheel. Why the hell did she always do that whenever she thought of him? It wasn't his baby, after all—

The Harley's deep-throated growl grew louder as the motorcycle was piloted through the allée— and then there the wolven was, no helmet, hair streaked back, eyes keen on the chaos convention at the front door, looking for the man she loved.

For a split second, C.P. renewed her appreciation for the woman. Wolf. Whatever the hell she was.

Nothing was going to keep her from her man.

"Mr. Joseph, I'm going to have to insist—"

"If you would just let us assess you—"

"Let's get you into the wheelchair—"

The volume on the medical chatter got turned up again, and she rolled her eyes. "He's not going to fight you people anymore. He has what he needs now."

Although Lydia had maintained she'd never driven a bike before, she handled the halting like a pro, pulling up in front of the SUV, hitting the brakes, killing the engine. After she kicked out the stand and put it in a lean, she took the keys with her as she dismounted—and by way of greeting, she stepped through the sea of staff and gave them over to Daniel.

As her eyes searched his face, he did the same to her, like the pair of them had been away from each other for years.

"How'd you like it?" he asked weakly.

"Now I understand." The wolven brushed his face. "The bike is freedom."

"Yes." He closed his eyes and sank into the SUV's seat. "That's right."

"He doesn't want that," Lydia said to the nurse with the wheelchair. "He's going to walk into the house himself. Aren't you."

As Daniel nodded and put out his hand for Lydia to help him, the medical staff didn't force the issue—then again, they'd been dealing with him for how long? Six months now? They knew what the angle of his chin meant.

Well, and then he had his woman.

Wolven, rather.

"We going back to Plattsburgh now?"

The male voice in C.P.'s ear was a confusing interruption. But then she shook her head to clear it and glanced at the guard, who had leaned back into the interior.

Was that what she wanted to do? In a quick sequence, she replayed pulling up to Gus's house. She'd been frantic. Distracted. But she knew she was never going to forget the bike in that short driveway, or the way the snow fell in lazy circles, or how neat and tidy everything had appeared from the outside, given what had happened in the interior. If she hadn't known better, she would have— like anybody else—assumed all was well.

The residence should have been stained with smoke, or pitted with bomb holes, or rotted and decayed and about to fall in on itself.

As she'd gotten out, she had barked at the two guards with her that she was going first—which in retrospect had been more about her need to take control than any rational thinking. But she had wanted to be the one to go over and punch in the code to lift the garage door. Gus had given her the six digits for the keypad on his first day in the new lab site, when she'd asked him about an emergency contact.

God, she could still picture him in her office, sitting on the other side of her glass-topped desk, wearing a pair of blue jeans with a hole open on one knee and a Led Zeppelin t-shirt for some concert that had been held on April 19, 1977, in Cincinnati, OH.

Funny, how she could remember details like that about him. And forget so much about so many others.

1-1-2-7-4-2.

She'd written the random sequence down, and when he'd gone to leave her office, she'd reminded him that he still hadn't given her an emergency contact.

He'd looked over his shoulder at her, wagged his eyebrows, and said, *Looks like you're it.*

So she'd gotten that garage door open—and

the instant the panels had risen and revealed his Tesla, an alarm bell had gone off in the back of her mind.

It was still ringing. And she still couldn't figure out what it was trying to tell her—

"Ms. Phalen?"

With an odd disassociation, she focused on the guard. The man's pose, as he leaned in, was dynamic, his well-trained body poised on an off-balance that he could have held for hours if he'd had to. For a moment, his features and hair color distorted. No longer dark-haired and dark-eyed, he became blond and baby-blue'd. Then, between one blink and the next, she saw a dead body out on her lawn where her helicopter landed and took off from. The skin of the handsome face was gray, the stare sightless, those bright spring-sky eyes no longer lit with consciousness.

Her hand went back to her stomach, and this time, she let it stay put.

"You go back," she heard herself say.

With jerky movements, she opened the driver's door and jumped to the ground. "Check the Tesla and see if it was left on sentry mode. If there are any PINs to access the car or its computer for the camera feeds, use one-one-two-seven-four-two. I don't know exactly how those fucking iPhones with wheels work."

The guard nodded. "Can you repeat that—"

"Jimi Hendrix's birthday," the man in the rear announced as he crabwalked forward. "I've got it."

Well, that explained the sequence, didn't it. Gus's favorite musician of all time.

And as for Teslas, her security detail had told her back in 2017 that she could never own one because they recorded everything if you weren't careful. No worry there. She liked her cars with gas engines that sounded like something. But if Gus's goddamn Tinkertoy had managed to catch the break-in? She promised never to take the company's name in vain again.

As C.P. headed for her mansion's threshold, she cut past the remaining white coats who were lingering in a disapproving kibitz, and the moment she stepped inside, her eyes went to the left. Lydia and Daniel were slowly making their way across her acre-sized black-and-white foyer, heading for their bedroom in the rear of the house.

Her own purposeful momentum was lost as she watched them go.

Envying them was faulty reasoning on her part because no one would want what they were dealing with.

And yet she couldn't keep going until they had disappeared down the hallway and through the door to the bedroom suite she had given to them a hundred years ago. Or maybe it was two hundred.

Fine, it was only back in April that they'd moved

in, after truths had come out, and Daniel had been shot, and his stage four cancer diagnosis had blown his life apart as all terminal illnesses did when they finally made their presences known.

Snapping back to attention, C.P. followed in the couple's footsteps for half of the way, and as she got to her study's closed door, she thought of people who entered places without knocking. And saw things they shouldn't have. And jumped to conclusions that were correct.

Gus had left her and her business for all the right reasons. But his greener pasture was not just full of weeds—he was going to be buried in it.

As her stomach rolled, she shoved her way in and went right to her desk. Sitting down, she stared across the empty, glossy surface. It was like a mirror and the last thing she wanted was to look at herself, so she triggered the phone compartment release: Off to one side, a panel retracted, and a platform raised up, presenting her with an encrypted land-line.

She dialed from memory and sat back. As the ringing commenced, she pulled the fleece she had on closer and turned her face into the top of the collar. The cologne or aftershave or soap Gus always used was fading, but she could still smell him.

Or maybe she was imagining things. Either way, it worked . . . she saw Gus as clearly as if he were standing in front of her, his presence summoned—

"Catherine, what a pleasant surprise."

The way Gunnar Rhobes rolled his *r*'s made her want to slam the receiver down four or five times, right in his supercilious ear.

"What did you do to Gus," she demanded.

"I beg your pardon?"

"Spare me the pseudo-polite bullshit." She swiveled around to face the floor-to-ceiling windows that looked out into the back field. "Where is he."

"If you recall, *I* was the one who notified you that he could not be located—"

"What better way to divert attention away from yourself? And do *not* pretend you don't think like that. You're capable of anything, Rhobes."

"Why, thank you," the man said dryly. "I am complimented in the midst of your insults—"

"You lied, Gunnar."

"About what."

"His car was in the garage." She shook her head. "When you called me an hour ago, you told me that it was in the driveway. That's a pretty big discrepancy, dontcha think."

There was a moment of silence that could have been interpreted in a variety of ways. Then her chief business rival said: "You're accusing me of having no honor, over a detail like that?"

"In. The. Garage." At the edge of the forest, a doe soft-walked into view, nearly invisible against the pale brown rushes that had died back in October. "You expect me to believe that a man who runs an empire like yours is going to forget something like that?"

"I did not go to his abode. One of my associates did."

"Associates. Is that what you call them?"

"Do you refer to your hired mercenaries as something else? And are we really arguing about this, considering the single most significant brain in medical science today has gone missing?"

The doe proceeded forward, seeming to place each hoof down at a precisely chosen spot, so careful, so hyperaware. And then there was a sound that brought the animal's head up, her radar-cup ears sweeping as her tail twitched, her haunches vibrating as if she were ready to bolt.

Funny how survival of the fittest dictated that the paranoid tended to live long enough to reproduce—and keep their offspring alive. So anxious genes prevailed.

"I don't get it," she said tightly. "He works for you now. You won. Why do you have to pretend—"

"I called you in good faith," Rhobes snapped. "I do not like you, you do not like me. We are not just competitors, we are enemies—and you are correct. I did win and he does work for me now—which is why I wish to discern his *goddamn* location."

The deer bolted back into the trees, as if the vitriol was what had spooked her, and C.P. pivoted back around to her desk. With an objective eye, she regarded the restrained decor she had chosen, the furniture modern and monochromatic, the art on the walls abstract and worth a fortune, the bound rug a vanilla lawn cropped close as the green around a golf hole.

Eyeing the Rothko across the way, she did some quick math on all her debts and wondered what kind of seller's cut Sotheby's down in NYC would take if she sold the thing. Then she remembered she didn't have to think like that. Her time was running out way faster than her cash position.

"I've never heard you swear before," she commented absently.

Rhobes exhaled like he was exhausted. "There are plenty of other words to choose from. Especially when one speaks five languages."

"Aren't you a good little student." She closed her eyes and pictured the man in one of his European-cut suits with the slim slacks and the double-vented, double-breasted jacket. "Where do you keep all those merit badges."

"In my downstairs bathroom so the guests can admire them, of course." There was a silence. "You could have just sold me Vita-12b, Catherine. It would have avoided much unpleasantness."

"I told you to make an offer. Instead, you raided my scientist."

"You would have done the same in my position. Gus St. Claire is worth more than that one particular cancer drug. He's a pipeline in and of himself, so you can keep your drug, Catherine. I hope it replenishes your dwindling accounts."

You don't know, she thought as she almost laughed. *It's Gus's now.*

"Hello?" Rhobes said. "Have I lost you?"

The paperwork turning Vita-12b over to Gus had been delivered the day before by one of her guards—and even though there had been a raft of unopened mail on the carpet underneath the postal slot in the front door, Daniel had found the document out of its envelope. So Gus had clearly read it. And he would have brought his ownership position up with Rhobes as soon as he could, because it made them no longer employer/employee. They were partners.

But that conversation had evidently not occurred.

C.P. rubbed the back of her neck. Why would Rhobes kidnap the very man he had hired?

Maybe she'd heard the man wrong about the Tesla's location.

And if Gus's abductor had known what that paperwork was, surely the document would have been taken with them?

"When I call you," she said, "you answer your phone."

"I picked up this time, did I not."

"Every time. You answer my fucking calls, Gunnar."

The chuckle that came over the connection was almost affectionate. "So crass for a woman of your stature."

C.P. ran her hand down the fleece. "I'm not worried about stature anymore."

"How fortunate for you. It will make your reversal of fortune an easier adjustment."

"You know, Rhobes, I was almost not despising you for a moment there."

"Oh? Why was that?"

"I was enjoying how much you don't know about things. But then you had to go and remind me who I was talking to."

"Reality is what it is, no matter who is commenting upon it."

"Just answer my call."

She hung up on him as she'd wanted to, a solid crack sounding out loudly as the receiver hit the cradle. Imagining the supercilious bastard sitting in his skyscraper office in Houston and ripping a cell phone away from the side of his head made her smile a little. She hoped the ringing in his ear lasted awhile.

Turning back to the windows, she searched the forest line for the doe. The tender-footed sweetheart had not made another reappearance, and as C.P. considered what kind of predators could be lurking in the pines and maples, the bucolic acreage loomed like a threat rather than a haven for the delicate animal to seek protection in.

The cold winter was coming. Where would she find enough food?

C.P. felt the weight of her palm on her abdomen, thought of Gus St. Claire . . . and could no longer fight the realization that had been growing on her for the last day or two.

The reason she always found herself resting a hand there when she thought of him?

She wished the baby were his.

There. She'd said it.

Thought it.

Whatever.

She reached out for the phone before she was conscious of wanting to pick the receiver up again. Dialing a shortcut, there was only one ring before her guard answered.

"What did you find," she barked as she put her hand back on her lower stomach. "Where is my doctor."

FIVE

"Are they all outta here?"

As Daniel spoke up from his recline against the pillows, Lydia had an urge to pull some covers to his chin. Bring him chicken noodle soup. Go for the Tylenol and maybe the Nyquil. The way he was lying there, so still, his breathing shallow and uneven, suggested he was uncomfortable and determined not to give in to how bad he was feeling.

How she wished this were only a cold. The flu. Food poisoning.

"Yes, they're gone." She hesitated at the foot of the bed, wondering if she should shift the duvet over his legs. "Do you want to eat—"

"You'd have thought the closed door would have stemmed the tide."

"The doctors are just trying to help."

Sitting down next to him, she took his cold hand and rubbed it in her own as she glanced around the bedroom suite they'd been sharing since the spring.

The accommodations were slick and luxurious, but they were a hotel room, really, nothing personal anywhere, the sophisticated, but stark, decor nothing she would have chosen, nothing she could have afforded. She wished they had a proper home, filled with things collected over time, and permanently placed because the two of them had no intention of moving. Rocking chairs that creaked by the fire. Quilts that had been handmade to curl into on cold nights. Copper pans in the kitchen, braided rugs to cushion the feet, plants nurtured in sunny spots flaring green and lush.

And yet this austere four walls and a ceiling had become a safety blanket of sorts.

When they were here, if something happened medically, there were people who could help, ready at a moment's notice.

Who needed 911 when you had an entire team and a state-of-the-art medical facility thirty feet underneath you.

"Do you want something to eat?" she asked again.

Daniel's lean face scrunched up with distaste, his half-mast eyes nearly disappearing. "God, no."

On reflex, she measured the distance to the marble bathroom. As they'd come in, getting him to lie down had been the most important thing, so he was on her closer-to-the-door side of things. But if he was going to be sick? The trip around the base of the mattress to get to the loo was going to add a couple of yards. Which was no big deal. For most people.

For Daniel? It might as well have been a fifty-mile trek uphill at a dead run.

Fear crept up her spine and tightened the base of her neck. "I can get Dr. Lipsitz back if you're going to throw up? You can have a—what do they call it?"

God, her brain was just shorting out all over the place.

"Antiemetic. And no, thanks." Daniel stretched his opposite arm over his head and arched his back, as if he were trying to make room for the nausea in his abdominal cavity. Like it was a tangible object he'd swallowed. "I've had it with the poke-and-prodding—hey, you know what C.P. needs to make next?"

"What."

"That scanner thing Bones had on *Star Trek*. He'd just move it up and down over the person and know everything." He resettled the limb at his side and closed his eyes completely. "I still remember the little electronic whirring sound it made. I can't tell you how much I'm into noninvasive now. Did you ever watch *Star Trek*?"

She traced his gaunt face with her eyes, and was relieved that there was a little color in his cheeks—until she remembered the ride up the Northway and the squall of snowflakes. It was likely windburn.

"Is that the one with Darth Vader?" she mumbled as she told herself to stop counting his frailties.

"No, Captain Kirk. James Tiberius. The starship *Enterprise*? Does that ring a bell?"

When the doctors and nurses had been examining him, they'd made him take off his jacket, sweatshirt, and t-shirt, and there were so many bones showing through such thin skin—and then there was the bruising and the puckered scar from his Hickman line's removal on his upper pec. They'd taken the access out how long ago? After the chemo didn't work? Things should have healed by now.

"My grandfather didn't have a TV in our house," she said numbly. "And C.P. goes by Cathy now, I think."

"She's still C.P. to me."

"Me, too."

There was a long period of silence. Then he squeezed her hand. "Lydia."

"Yes?" She was afraid to meet his stare for fear everything she was thinking was in her eyes. "Are you going to be sick—"

"You know they're not going to find anything at that condo."

Oh, what a great change of subject. Something to lighten the mood.

"Well, maybe they can call . . ." She let her voice drift off. "Of course they're not going to call the police, are they."

"No, and C.P.'s guards have better forensic training than local law enforcement up around here anyway. Still, no matter how hard they look, they won't
get anywhere. That was a professional job."

As her throat tightened like a fist, she choked
out, "Is Gus dead?"

Funny, how that rhetorical could come out as a
question. And how unfair. As if Daniel could dis-
pel the sole rational conclusion to all that had happened.

"You need to go to the mountain tonight."

Lydia frowned and immediately shook her head.
"I'm staying with you—"

"Blade will be up there—and as much as I hate
you being anywhere around him, you need to go
find him. He's the only one who can help us right
now, if Gus is going to have any chance at all."

Even though she fought it, the image of a powerful male in red robes, lurking in the shadows of
the summit, staring at her, talking at her, would
not be denied. He had seemed to understand instinctively that she was of two things, both tame
and wild—and that moment between them hadn't
lasted. The attack had come from out of nowhere,
gunshots ringing out, some kind of cyborg nightmare that made no sense nearly killing them both.
Blade had been injured, and she had helped him—
and his sister.

The next day, Daniel had jumped to conclusions that had made sense only on a surface level, and everything had fallen apart for her. For the two of them.

She had not, and would not, ever be with Blade.

His attraction, his obsession, with her was a one-sided figment.

Lydia shook her head and got to her feet. Even though the last thing she was going to do was leave the room. "I'm not in a big hurry to see that man— or whatever he is—ever again."

Symphath. That was what his kind were called.

With a grunt, Daniel pushed himself up on the pillows, and as he swept his hand over his head, it was a familiar gesture that reminded her of when he'd had such thick, beautiful hair.

"I would do it if I could—"

"Do what." She crossed her arms over her chest. "You already said there'll be no evidence at Gus's—"

"—so Blade is where we have to go. My former boss is—"

"Totally untrustworthy. You said that yourself—"

"I tried calling him." He nodded at the door as if he weren't hearing her at all. "When you walked the medical types out and talked to them in the hall. He didn't answer—maybe he killed that number."

She thought about being in that cave up on the mountain, where Blade had been recovering after he'd been shot. The memory of Daniel walking in on them was not a good one.

"Lydia, if we want to help Gus, we need him."

"Even if I could find that male, what makes you think he'll help us—"

"He's in love with you. He'll do anything you ask him to." As she opened her mouth, Daniel put his palm up and continued in a bleak tone. "I'm still sorry I was such an asshole when I saw the two of you together. I was wrong. Utterly wrong. And as for how dangerous he is, I know you can take care of yourself, especially up there with all those wolves protecting you. If there was another way . . . but we need everything we've got right now."

Daniel's defeat was in the lines of his face, the grooves at the sides of his mouth making him seem closer to eighty than twenty.

"I would do it myself, Lydia. If I could."

"If C.P. Phalen's squadron of guards can't find anything, what makes you think Blade can?"

"I have a lead. I found it when I back-doored into the FBG server after that guard was killed on the front lawn here. Maybe it isn't anything, but Blade will know. The bastard knows more than even I do about the hidden labs in this country—and who the fuck else would take someone like Gus."

FBG. The Federal Bureau of Genetics. A supposed covert arm of the U.S. government tasked with protecting and defending the integrity of the human genome. Daniel's former "employer." Which in actuality had just been a front so Blade could go around bombing the underground labs that were just like C.P. Phalen's.

Daniel had lied to her when he had first come into her life. But she had lied to him, too. And yes, two wrongs didn't make a right, however they'd both had their reasons.

Lydia went over to the tall windows that overlooked the field that went all the way back to a forest line. Underneath her skin, the wolf in her stalked its cage of DNA, ready to run. Demanding freedom.

Daniel's mission had been to destroy C.P. Phalen's secret facility, but instead of getting to that goal, he had become a patient in it—and, for a time, the first person intended to test Vita-12b. But after so many conventional treatments had failed? Who needed another medication gauntlet, especially one that had never been in a human before.

Gus St. Claire had understood that, even better than Lydia had. The man had devoted his life's work to trying to help patients like Daniel, as well as family members and loved ones like her, who were suffering alongside.

There was nothing she wouldn't do for him.

"If there was something, anything else," Daniel muttered, "I'd be pursuing it. Especially because Gus may already be dead. But that man believed in miracles, and there are times you have to engineer your own."

Lydia looked over her shoulder. Her man seemed so frail as he lay there, his heavy-lidded eyes bloodshot, those too-bright cheeks now making her worried he had a fever—except surely all those medical degrees in white coats had checked that?

Had she seen them take his temperature?

God, she was tired of playing nurse.

On that note, if she left Daniel to go on some wild-goose chase, and he had an acute event—which they had been warned could happen at any moment either because of all the treatments he'd had or be-cause of the fucking cancer—she would never forgive herself.

But if she didn't go up the mountain and try to find Blade, she'd feel responsible for Gus's death. Or at least complicit in it. And she would never forgive herself.

As she teetered, she heard Gus's voice:

Call me anytime, my phone is always on.

The words came to her through the dualities of her exhaustion and panic—she couldn't count the number of times he'd said that to them. And he'd meant it, too. The other thing that he'd always said?

Why didn't you call me if you were this worried?

He had always put his patients first—

The coughing spell started as they all did, a little throat-clear that Daniel tried to hide. But like the most recent ones, the spasms in his lungs were a deadly locomotive that refused to be slowed down or derailed.

The hacking brought him up off the pillows, his hands punching into the mattress as he jacked himself forward and bent his knees to triangulate into a pose that gave his poor lungs the best chance to inhale fully. Desperate to breathe, his mouth opened wide and his eyes bulged as sweat broke out across his chest and forehead, his flush an ugly purple as he desperately attempted to haul oxygen in.

She grabbed a towel on the way to him, yanking it off the top of the bureau. Idiotically, she noted it was still damp from when they'd showered together earlier—

Too late. The blood speckles, bright as ink, marked up the covers underneath him.

As he grabbed the terrycloth, she lunged for the bedside table, knocking bottles of pills onto the floor as she went for the inhaler. Shoving it into his open mouth, she pushed hard on the cylinder, but he couldn't breathe anything in—

"Work with me," she said. "Calm yourself—work with me—"

Lydia had no idea what she was saying. No clue whether the medicine was getting into his bronchial tubes. No prayer left to offer up to anything or anybody. With tears spearing into her eyes, and her own chest turning into a block of ice-cold terror, she couldn't do this anymore. She couldn't live like this for one more day, one more night. She couldn't bear to hear the staccato, snare drum beat of the cough—

The tide began to turn subtly, a little more air getting down and carrying the spray into Daniel's throat. Then the coughing took a pause of a second. Then two. Then three . . . seconds.

"One more," she said over the wheezing as she punched the top of the cylinder again. Even though she'd been told to only give him a single dose in a rescue situation.

Like anything had gotten into him, though?

When Daniel finally sagged in relief, his head dropping between his knobby knees, her own legs went out from under her and she sank down onto the floor at his bedside. With shaking hands, he moved the towel away from his lips.

There was so much red on it, the thing looked like it had been died.

Dyed, she corrected.

"I'm calling the doctors back to us," she said as she reached for the phone. "Right now—"

Daniel grabbed her arm. Desperate eyes locked on her own. "Find Blade. Help Gus. It's what he would do for you and me."

SIX

A S A CELL phone went off like a car alarm two feet from her head, Xhex, mated of the Black Dagger Brother John Matthew, had two thoughts: One, she was actually sleeping—and this was good news. Number two? If the fucker who was reaching out and trying to touch her was a telemarketer, she was going to reach through her fucking Samsung and let her fingers walk all over them.

Throwing her hand out into the darkness, her speed was better than her grab-accuracy, and instead of palming the Samsung, the thing went eight ball in the corner pocket.

Except she didn't sleep next to a pool table, so it shot off into thin air.

"Sonofa—"

Beside her, her mate came alive, jumping out of the bed and landing buck naked in an attack crouch. In his dagger hand? A black, finely honed blade capable of gutting anything that lived and breathed. In the other, a nine millimeter, the laser sight of which was trained on the door that opened out into the hall. Then into the dim marble confines of the bathroom. Then at the panels of their walk-in closet.

"It's okay," she said as she stretched out her arm. "I just knocked the phone off trying to answer it."

As if the Samsung didn't want any of that smoke, it rang again to remind everybody why it was in the room—and the electronic bell was enough to get John off the boil. That black dagger slowly lowered as Xhex reached down to find . . .

In the dim light from the bathroom, her mate's naked body was illuminated with a lover's touch, his broad shoulders and tight pecs, his ribbed abs and winged hips, his heavy thighs and strong calves thrown into relief with shadows cast by the contours of his power and strength—

The third ring cattle-prodded her back into focus. Cursing, she promptly over-extended herself, slipped off the side of the mattress, and dropped from the waist-high antique bed frame. As gravity got greedy and snatched her in a hard hold, she tried to catch herself before she face-planted—

The electrical cord to the lamp somehow got tangled in her carpet fend-off, and she managed to pull the heavy crystal block and its hot-air-balloon-sized shade onto herself. Fortunately, the top half was what hit her top half, so things were cushioned. Unfortunately, her hips and legs followed.

It was like being in a car crash without the bumpers and the airbags.

As John willed the overhead fixture on, there was a blazing light, sure as if the Scribe Virgin were still around and had decided to check on all the commotion.

"*Fuck . . .*" Blinded, Xhex covered her eyes with the crook of her elbow. Which was easy to do considering she'd nearly knocked herself out with the damned thing. "And who the hell is calling us at this hour?"

It had to be, what, three in the afternoon? Fine and dandy if you were a human, an absolute ungodly interruption when you were a vampire.

As the fourth ring registered, and John Matthew came around the base of the bed, she pushed a hand under the inlaid three-drawer stand—and finally, her phone was ready to be found. Snagging the thing, she answered it on the way to her ear.

"*What.*" If this was some asshole talking about buying a piece of property she didn't own, a car warranty she didn't have, or school loans that she— "You better start talking or I will reverse-search this bitch and find you—"

The female voice was instantly recognizable. But the torrent of words that came through the connection was nearly indecipherable.

"Whoa, whoa—slow down. What . . . ?"

Shoving herself up, Xhex leaned back against the

horizontal rail of the bed frame. As John Matthew knelt beside her, she switched to speaker.

"You need to slow down," she said to the phone. "What's going on?"

In a tinny tone, Lydia Susi announced: "I need to get in touch with your brother."

Xhex closed her eyes. The wolven might as well have asked to hold a grenade with the pin out in her palm.

"Mind if I ask why?" Or, more bluntly: *Are you fucking insane?*

The story rolled out as most drama did: A good guy in a bad situation with no better options. Except throwing Blade into anything other than a bonfire was guaranteed to make things go totally tits up.

"Lydia, I don't know what to tell you." Well, she had a list of dumb-idea expletives. But what was that thing—is it useful, is it kind? "Other than you need to look for another solution."

As she tossed out the advice, she glanced at her *hellren*. When John Matthew motioned back and forth between them, she shook her head.

No way did they need to volunteer for the complications.

"Gus is our doctor." The female cleared her throat. "But more than that, he's a good man. He doesn't deserve to be hurt or—worse. *Please.* Can you ask your brother to meet me up on the mountain?"

Xhex closed her eyes. "You don't want to do this."

"I agree. But none of us want to be in this situation, and the only thing that's worse is sitting around, doing nothing."

"I can respect that, but why would you think Blade can do—"

"He was Daniel's boss. They used to work together, and Daniel has a lead that Blade may know what to do with."

Xhex cursed under her breath. Fucking Blade. Of course shit was more entangled than she'd known.

"What exactly did Daniel used to do?" she asked grimly.

"He worked for what he thought was a clandestine arm of the U.S. government."

And why hasn't this come up before? Xhex wondered. But at least that was one question she could answer: Because her brother was a lying, manipulative, dangerous sack of shit. That was why. God only knew what he had done with a bunch of humans like Daniel Joseph at his disposal. The only thing she could be sure of was that it probably made money and definitely wasn't a crocheting circle with an Etsy shop attached.

"Look," she said, "it's not my business to tell you what to do—"

"So please have him meet me—"

"—but my brother is no savior you want."

"—up at the summit tonight."

The two of them talked over each other, but ended at the same time, like a pair of dancers pirouetting around separately to harmonizing chords.

"You're *not* safe around him." Xhex did nothing to hide her don't-be-a-dumbass tone. "And yeah, I know you're a wolven, and I don't doubt you're deadly when you want to be, but he's deadly *all* the time."

"I'm not afraid of him."

"You should be."

"So is this a no?" the female demanded. "Are you telling me you won't reach out to him?"

Xhex looked at her *hellren*'s chest and focused on the star-shaped pattern that marked his pec. The symbol of the Black Dagger Brotherhood was embedded in his flesh, the marking that was given to each Brother during induction somehow something he had been born with.

"Hello?" the wolven prompted. "Have you hung up on me?"

Xhex pictured her brother, from his gleaming black eyes to his coldly beautiful face to the black hair that was so like her own—

Her past rushed up at her, just like the floor had, and the impact was as pleasant as the rug burn on her shoulder: Instantly, she was back over twenty years before, bound and gagged, being dragged into a van up at the *symphath* colony. She hadn't known where she was going to end up, but she'd been certain of three things: She was being punished. She was not going to survive this.

And her brother had been the one to lure her back to the Colony and turn her in to her family.

Blade's face was the last thing she'd seen before the bag was put over her head, and there had been no emotion on it whatsoever. As if she'd been lower than a stranger. As if she had been a dog to be put down.

After that? Off to the lab she had gone. Where she'd been experimented on by humans . . . tortured, really—

"*No*," she blurted roughly.

"No, you haven't hung up?" the wolven said.

"No, I'm not going to get in touch with my brother on your behalf."

The wolven expelled a frustrated breath. "You could be sentencing a good man to die. Or letting his murderer go free."

Absently, Xhex realized her free hand was shaking, so she tucked it under her hip. "But I'm definitely keeping a good female alive. My conscience is clear, believe me."

"I don't need you protecting me."

Xhex shook her head slowly. "You have no idea what you're dealing with or what you're suggesting. Even if Blade helps you, it will cost you your life. You do not want to be in debt to a *symphath* like him."

"Please—"

"No, I'm sorry—that's my final answer. I'm ending this call now."

As she cut the connection, she put the cell face-down on the carpet. "*Fuck.*"

Next to her, John Matthew tucked his dagger under his arm. Then he signed, *You're doing the right thing.*

"Yeah. I know am. It just feels wrong."

A vibration of stress rode up the column of her throat and made her clench her teeth. But instead of screaming the energy out, she wrapped her arms around her naked torso. For a split second, she was cold . . . but then the heat of deep-seated fury started to warm her blood.

Boiled it.

"God, I fucking *hate* my brother," she heard herself say.

SEVEN

Deer Mountain
Walters, New York

U PON THE FALL of night, after the velvet darkness claimed the whole of the sky and the snow clouds departed to reveal a pinprick pattern of stars, the lone male emerged upon the summit of the mountain called Deer and came to stand at the keyhole view of the valley below. With the keen eyes of his vampire kin, he regarded the undulations of the topography, the acreage so vast, it deserved a poetic appreciation of its breadth and beauty.

Pity he was mostly a *symphath*. Things of beauty were wasted upon entities such as himself. After all, what leverage could one bring with a vista that merely pleased the eye?

Outside of a real estate transaction.

On that note, his calculating stare focused on the hotel site that had been carved out of the mountain across the valley. Lights twinkled in its many-roomed sprawl, a sign that the establishment was nearing an opening date—or mayhap it was already servicing its intended demographic of wealthy spa-goers looking to be one with nature in a completely climate-controlled environment that included on-demand facials as well as feather beds and Michelin-star-ranked food.

Frankly, he would rather camp with no gear. In frigid January. Out with the wolves.

Or . . . one wolf in particular.

Wolven, rather.

As melancholy washed over him anew, he erased the human-made eyesore with his ailing mind and imagined what the sunset might have looked like as the storm clouds of the afternoon began their departure unto the east, just as the last rays of daylight illumination funneled into the western juncture of evergreens on the far side of the silver sliver of lake. Thanks to his half-breed pretransition youth, he could paint quite clearly the gathering intensity of peach and pink as the sun died, a flare of vibrant red tickling the undersides of the clouds, a last gasp before darkness claimed the heavens.

Things were always most vivid just before death. And as he considered his turbulent emotions, he put his hand over the ache upon his heart and certainly felt as though he were dying. Yet he couldn't remember ever being this alive.

"Messy business, this bonding . . ."

At the sound of a stick breaking behind him, his breath caught and he twisted around, hope bursting through the storm clouds of his pessimism, a brilliant color in the midst of his gray numbness—

Though his visitor remained within the shadows, his *symphath* side recognized their calling card.

The deflation was immediate. This was not the female who haunted him night and day, stalking his equilibrium through the alleys of his conscious purpose and distractions, hunting his sense of superiority as a male who was not to be toyed with, killing his coldness with a heat that came from sexual need and soul-deep yearning.

"To what do I owe this honor," he drawled in a slow cadence. "I rather thought our paths would not cross again, given your distaste of me."

There was a pause. And then Xhexania, his blooded, estranged sister, stepped out into the clearing. She was dressed head to foot in black leather, a gun holster around her hips, an ammo belt running across her torso, a knife strapped on her thigh. With her short hair and her hard gray eyes, one might have mistaken her for a Brother.

"I'm surprised you knew it was me," she said. "I'm downwind."

He motioned above his own head. "Your grid."

Her cold stare narrowed on him, as if she were offended that he could read her emotions in the manner of their kind. But come now. In this, at least, he was not being deliberately offensive. All *symphaths* saw the inner components of all sentient beings, their anger, sadness, joy, and fear, among other whims of feeling, depicted in a three-dimensional grid that followed them around like a comic strip thought bubble.

Hers . . . was obvious as well as alarming.

And then there was the fact that clearly she no longer had the ability to block others from reading the thing.

"Must you," she muttered.

Blade waved his hand in a dismissal. "You already know your grid is collapsing. Not that you like to dwell upon such a truth. No, no, you shall just go along, hoping it fixes itself, ignoring what Rehvenge no doubt has hammered you about, seducing yourself into a false sense of security that just because you're sleeping again, somehow what you wish to be true is actually happening—"

"I didn't come here for this bullshit," she snapped.

"Of that I'm quite sure." He turned toward the view once again, offering her an undefended position. "But you did come in search of me—and having found me, can you truly be surprised at what greeting you receive?"

Her voice lowered to a growl. "You shouldn't offer me your back like that. Not in my current mood, at any rate."

On the contrary, she would be doing him such a favor if she killed him. No Fade for those who escorted themselves unto their own grave, so he was a bit trapped. And it was funny. The afterlife had never interested him, but since meeting his wolven, he had found a strange preoccupation with what came next.

Perhaps in their next life, however it presented itself, they would meet again, and this time, they could . . .

Except he had been a wicked male. All the nights of his life. Or most of them, at any rate. Therefore, no Fade for him anyway.

"So what say you." He did not bother to keep the exhaustion out of his voice. "Why seek me out? I have kept our bargain." Or was it more a vow? Yes, a vow it had been. "I have not seen the wolven called Lydia Susi, as you requested. Am I not a good boy? I want a cookie. Or perhaps a merit badge."

Dear God, would this pain in his chest never cease, he wondered.

"You didn't tell me about Daniel and you," Xhex said.

The wind sustained a sudden increase in strength, and as the cold made his cheeks and nose burn, his blood-red robes undulated around his body. Following their twisting agitation, he turned unto his sister.

Blade cocked a brow. "You did not know that Daniel walked in upon myself and the wolven you have taken so much interest in? Quite a scene. The man was very offended. He does not share well, evidently, not that she had offered me aught."

"Lydia doesn't want you."

"Oh, she made that very clear." He smiled in a nasty fashion. "Thank you for reminding me of the fact. How kind of you."

Could his sister read his heartbreak? he wondered. If she was able to, no doubt she would assume he was projecting the agony onto his grid as a way to distract her or play with her. There was no way she would believe how awful he felt.

He didn't believe how awful he felt.

Xhex took a step closer. Unlike him, her clothes were intended for fighting, so there was nothing loose upon her for the wind to grab hold over: She was a solid block of menace, all those weapons at rest, but on the verge should she decide to use them.

"You didn't tell me that you and Daniel had worked together."

Instantly, Blade shut down his grid, clapping shut his mind and emotions, something he should have done the instant she arrived. "You seemed to care primarily about keeping me away from her. Not her mate. What does my history with him matter?"

Those gray eyes narrowed even further, as if, in her mind, she was maiming him in some inventive manner.

"Daniel told Lydia you were his boss. What did he do for you?"

Memories stirred under his lockdown, images of that man, so capable and aggressive, yet so logical and in control, crystal clear. Daniel Joseph had been a rare find indeed, eager to fight, but no wild card with his firepower, his path of self-destruction requiring precisely the kinds of targets Blade's ultimate goal had been able to provide. The U.S. Federal Bureau of Genetics. What a jolly good lie, the perfect camouflage for Blade's purposes, a mental placeholder he had inserted in his operatives' minds, to give them a context for their missions that made sense for their version of the world. If he had attempted to hire them to work for a half vampire, half *symphath*, to destroy the labs that had injured his sister so grievously, as a way of expunging his limitless self-loathing? Well, that would have been a hard sell, wouldn't it.

He had engineered what he'd needed. As usual.

"He no longer works for me," he murmured.

"That isn't what I asked you."

"That is all that is relevant for our purposes. His and mine. Yours and mine."

The final lab that he had been able to locate was in fact under his feet as they spoke. But he had it on good authority—Daniel and Lydia's—that there were no experiments being conducted therein on vampires, no torturous protocols, no exploratory surgeries, pregnancies, disease transmissions. Therefore he had no business with the enterprise and thus had let it stand.

And now he was retired.

Mayhap that was why he had cleaved to the wolven so. A new purpose.

"You know something," he heard himself say. "It is occurring to me that I have lied to you."

"Ask me if I'm surprised."

Inclining his head in deference, he continued, "When I told you I would not be in the presence of the wolven, I meant as long as her mate is alive. As soon as he is gone—"

"Don't you *dare* go after him," Xhex growled.

"Oh, relax. That disease of his is going to do the job, not me." Blade shrugged. "And before you accuse me of human engineering, I had nothing to do with his cancer. You can thank the Marlboro man for that—"

"What did he do for you." The sound of a blade unsheathing was a musical note that seemed fitting in the icy air. "And I'm not asking again."

Blade glanced down at the weapon in his sister's hand. The silver dagger gleamed in the darkness, just like the valley's lake did.

"Just what do you intend to do with that?" he inquired. "And before you answer, I will remind you that making threats against a *symphath* is a dangerous waste of time—"

She moved just as fast as he imagined she would: One second, she was before him. The next, she was on him, grabbing him by the throat and pressing the tip of the blade to his abdomen.

Her eyes were clear as the night sky. And just as cold. "Even after Daniel is dead, you're staying away from that female."

Blade drew air in with difficulty. Which was a pleasant distraction from his heartache. "Why do you care, sister mine," he choked out. "She is not kin to you. You didn't even know her before this interlude—she told me herself."

"You ruined my life," came the harsh reply. "You killed me on the inside when you put me into that lab twenty years ago, and I won't let your casual cruelty enjoy another chew toy. She doesn't deserve that—especially after the way fate is already fucking her mate."

Opening his mouth to respond, he had some kind of intention to utter some kind of denial. But then the strangest thing happened: Tears welled in his eyes—and as Xhex's face registered shock, she obviously noticed them, too.

As a single, blood-red drop fell onto his cheek, he would have wiped it away, but really, trying to hide that which was already obvious was a waste of effort.

"I am so sorry," he said in a hoarse voice. "That I hurt you."

Xhex blinked once. Twice. Then she recoiled as if he had slapped her, her hold on his throat releasing even as that blade stayed right where it was.

"You sick *fuck*." She shook her head in disbelief. "You really think crocodile tears are gonna work with me?"

"Is that what they are," he whispered as a wolf howled off in the distance.

Well, was this not irony at work. The one time he showed himself truly unto his blood, his credibility was picked from his pocket by the past—

"No!" someone shouted. "Don't kill him!"

EIGHT

Back at the Phalen house, Daniel was arching over his female on their bed, going for her mouth, kissing her deep and slow. The sensations were hot as fuck, and in the core of his consciousness, he recognized that it had been a long, long time since he'd felt the heat and the anticipation this clearly ... except wait, that didn't make sense?

It hadn't been long, at all. They'd had a shower together before they'd gone to the apple orchard. And even though his side of things didn't work anymore, that didn't stop him from thoroughly enjoying the pleasure he could give her—

Looking down between their bodies, he was astonished. For months and months, he had been impotent, the treatments robbing him of any kind of erection.

Holy shit, he was *hard*.

How the hell was this happening—

Whatever, he wasn't wasting time on questions.

You didn't ask the lottery to double check if you won Mega Millions.

As his cock throbbed at the front of his hips, he was acutely aware that his woman was totally naked underneath him, her thighs split wide to accommodate him, her breath ragged from what he was doing to her, her nipples brushing his pecs, her hands grabbing his back.

I got you, he told her as he restarted the kissing.

Swallowing her moans, he was beyond ready for what was coming next, the penetration, the pumping, the orgasm when he came inside of—

This is not real.

The conviction slammed into him with the impact of a physical assault, and he broke off their mouths to glance around for a flesh-and-blood intruder. There was none.

Daniel? Don't stop.

As his wolven's voice resonated in his ear, it all felt real . . . yet the nagging sense that reality had morphed on him somehow persisted. To try and ground himself, he noted that everything in the bedroom was where it was supposed to be, the bureaus, mirror, and pictures in the same places, the windows that looked over the back meadow in the correct position, the door to the marble bathroom partially open and letting a little light in, as it always did when they went to sleep.

There was just one thing that made him uneasy. Down on the floor, right by the bed, there was a pile of his clothes: a shirt, a sweatshirt, a jacket. Vaguely, he remembered taking them off—but no. Someone else had removed them from his upper body. Some*ones*, actually—

Please don't stop, Daniel . . .

He refocused on his female, and told himself that he needed to chill. Why the hell was he ruining this chance to be with her properly? Especially when he didn't know when it would come again—

Daniel, she said as she stroked the flop of his hair back from his face. *Oh, God . . . I need you. I ache.*

I know, he told her. *And I'm going to take care of you so good.*

Back when he'd rolled over on top of her, he'd had plans to make them both wait. It had been so fucking long, too long, and he wanted it to be perfect, this reunion. Finally, after all these months, he was going to—

Why was his hair in his eyes?

Daniel, now. Please. I just want to feel you inside.

Fuck, yes, he forced himself to respond. *I'ma make it good for you.*

Kicking all the weird thinking away, he leaned on one elbow, and reached down to his hips. It was the most natural thing in the world, to go for his cock so he could get it positioned right for the thrust in—

The moment the thick, hard length hit his palm, he halted.

Daniel . . . she choked out. *I've missed you—*

Don't cry, I'm right here . . .

No, this was not right at all, he thought with despair as a tear rolled down her cheek and onto the white pillow underneath her head.

Where have you been? she asked.

I don't know . . .

Straining his neck, he looked down between them again, seeing her breasts with their tight tips, and her belly, and her graceful hips.

And in his hand, an erection that he knew didn't make sense—

Make me yours, Lydia said through her tears. *I've missed you.*

A sense of impending doom made his body shake: He was running out of time. If he wanted to be with her, he had to move fast.

I love you, he told her.

Bringing the head of his—

◆　◆　◆

Daniel didn't so much wake up as he was kicked out of the dream, and sure as if someone had nailed him in the back of the skull with a size twelve, his torso shot up to the vertical. Panting like he'd been racing from an assailant, he glanced around the dim contours of the bedroom. Then he threw his hand out to the space beside him on the bed.

Lydia wasn't next to him. And through the crack

left open by the door into the bath, he could see that she wasn't in there, either.

Just as he was getting a proper flip-out on, he saw the note on the bedside table. Grabbing for it, he read her precise cursive handwriting twice. The mountain. She loved him—and she had gone to the mountain.

Just as he had asked her to.

"Fucking hell."

But what choice did they have? Phalen had checked in, just as she'd promised, and nothing forensic had been found inside Gus's condo: No human hairs of note. No fingerprints. No mistakes. Except he'd already known that was going to be the result: A human hadn't done the abduction. And neither had a vampire or a wolven, for that matter. It was one of those fucking cyborgs.

And just their luck, the Tesla in the garage hadn't been spying on its surroundings. As for the development's security cameras that were located in the common area in the center? They had to be hacked into and that was going to take time—but he wouldn't be shocked if they, too, came up with a big, fat goose egg.

Rubbing his eyes, he worried about sending Lydia up that mountain. She wouldn't be alone, though. At least her kind would watch over her. Even though she was, as she termed it, a half-breed, she was embraced among the wolves who lived on the preserve as one of their own.

It should have been him. He should have gone up with her.

Goddamn it. If he weren't so busy fucking dying . . . they wouldn't have had the conversation in the first place.

There was so much shit he wished he could do.

Shoving the covers off himself, he glanced at his lower body. Then he put his palm on his flaccid dick.

There were things, *so* many things, about cancer to get terrified over; the what-ifs, the maybe-nevers, the blind corners crushing your hopes and dreams for the future just in time for the actual bad news to crater your present. And then there was the stuff that hurt, and the surgeries and the tests, and all of the side effects of the treatments. There were also the indignities of strangers seeing you naked, the concessions to weakness like needing his cane to walk and his inability to hold peas on a fork anymore, and the loss of hair.

But he couldn't say any of all that made him feel . . . small.

The fact that he couldn't get it up anymore?

Daniel covered himself back up with the duvet. Layer by layer, what had made him a man, a person . . . *himself* . . . was being stripped away. No hair. His muscles gone. Hard to feed himself. Hard to walk. Hard to sleep.

No longer hard down below.

And it was just going to get worse.

Sadness crept into his marrow as he remembered Lydia pushing a towel into his hands as he coughed up blood, terror on her face. One day—or maybe night—that fear would be well founded. It would be his end—

"But not this evening," he muttered. "Get your shit together, Joseph. Get your *fucking* shit together."

He had to pull out of the spiral and be where he was right now: No medical emergency. No one pounding his chest to resuscitate him. No one hooking him up to a battery charge and shocking him back to life. No one bagging his lungs, or inserting a feeding tube, or coming up with another test or IV or drug or anything.

"I got time left," he said out loud. You know, in case He was listening. Or She. Or Whoever was up there.

How stupid was he going to feel if it turned out that he had six months . . . and he spent them all sitting in this bed, staring off into the darkness, waiting for the Grim Reaper to remember where he lived?

And as for sex? Yeah, sure, his cock didn't work, but his fingers sure did.

His tongue most certainly did.

Giving his Lydia pleasure was pleasure to him, and that was a helluva lot more than some cancer patients had or could do tonight.

Easing his hips to the side, he pushed his numb hand into the front pocket of his jeans. The zip tie with its trimmed end was about as romantic as a monkey wrench, but it was the only stand-in for a ring that he could find in the house without asking anyone. He'd intended to put it on Lydia's finger in that apple orchard, and then go with her to find something more proper. Fate, that fucker, had had other ideas, but two could play at that game—

Tap, tap, tap.

On his shoulder.

Daniel jerked around, expecting to see Lydia—

Nobody was at the bedside. No . . . that wasn't true. He could sense someone's presence.

"Hello?" he called out. In case somebody had knocked on the closed door. "Come in?"

Although if it was a white coat with a tray of needles and bright ideas, he was going to regret—

Shouting. Someone was shouting.

Out in the hall.

Even though it was the last thing he needed to do, he put the zip tie aside and gingerly got off the mattress. When his legs supported his weight on his numb feet, he picked up his sweatshirt and yanked it on. Then he took out his snub-nosed nine millimeter from a drawer in the bedside table and slipped the small gun into the front pocket of the jeans where the zip tie had been and headed for the door.

Old training and too much relevant experience

had him back-flatting by the exit. Holding his breath, he listened for a heartbeat or two, and then slipped out into the hallway.

In his bare feet, he made no noise at all as he walked slowly toward the sounds.

No more shouting now. Just muffled mumbling, as if he were in a game of reverse Marco Polo, with the closer he got, the quieter the target became.

It was a woman.

Phalen?

Where are the guards? he thought as he zeroed in on the woman's study. Surely they'd heard it, too?

Unless this was another dream . . .

The door to her inner sanctum was closed, and he put his ear to the cool panel. When there was only silence, he knocked.

"C.P.?" *Knock-knock.* "Hello?"

After a moment, a dim response: "I'm all right."

Daniel frowned and spoke to the door. "You don't sound all right. Was that you yelling?"

When there was no response, he put his ear flat to the panels again. Then he knocked once more. "What's up, Phalen."

No response.

Stepping back, he ran his palm over the new-growth on his skull and reminded himself that though he was a guest in her fortified house, her life was none of his business, and if she wasn't answering him? See the previous operant statement—

Tap, tap, tap—

Daniel wheeled around, and as he lost his balance, he grabbed on to the molding at the jamb. "What. What do you want?"

Yes, he was talking into the air, but something was absolutely standing beside him, and this was clearly another dream, and—

Was that lavender? Why was he smelling lavender . . . ?

The weeping was so soft that at first he figured it was his own wheezy respiration, but when he held his breath and the quiet sorrow persisted, he knew the rhythmic, heartbreaking stuff wasn't him.

"Fuck it." He grabbed the handle and announced loudly, "I'm coming in."

Pushing things wide, he looked to the glossy desk to the left. No one was in the chair that had been turned away to the side. Checking out the seating arrangement on the right—

In the open doorway to the half bath, C.P. Phalen appeared, her face white, one arm around her chest, the other extended down her body.

So that she could attempt to cover the enormous bloodstain between her legs with her hand.

"I think I'm losing the baby," she choked out.

NINE

"STOP! DON'T HURT him!"

As Lydia jumped into the summit's clearing, her arms were out, her hands ready to do something, anything. Meanwhile, in front of the mountain's best view, the vampire Xhex had a vicious-looking dagger right at Blade's gut—and if the female followed through on her facial expression?

That brother of hers was not just going to end up with one hell of an ouchie, his entire digestive system was going to roll out and land at his feet.

And then where was Gus St. Claire going to be?

"I need him!" Lydia exclaimed as the two of them looked over at her.

Well, Xhex turned her head. Blade's gleaming eyes were all that moved in his case, and he quickly wiped at them with his hands. Then he stared off at the view, stony and stoic, his red robes swirling around him in the gusts that rode up the elevation's western side.

"Please," Lydia begged as the wind cut through her clothes, its cold claws making her shiver. "I have to talk to him."

Xhex's cursing was so low, she couldn't catch the words. But when the female stepped off and took her dagger with her, at least there was a reprieve.

"Thank you," Lydia whispered.

"You're fucking crazy," Xhex responded tersely.

And then Blade looked at her.

In the tense silence that followed, Lydia was glad she'd taken one of the SUVs up the big trail and jogged the rest of the way to the cave where he had been staying. Her wolf side had wanted to run, but she was not about to be naked in front of the male again—even though it meant nothing to her.

"Good evening, wolven," he said in a low, seductive voice. "You came all the way up here to find me? I am quite popular this evening, it appears."

"I need you," she told him.

"Do you *ever* listen to good advice?" Xhex bitched. "No, of course not—"

"I *have* to talk to you."

"I am, as ever, at your disposal." Blade bowed low and then pointedly glanced at his sister. "Although I must say, dear Lydia, that I did not expect to see you again."

As some of her kin howled off in the distance, she'd had enough with the pleasantries. "A friend of ours has been abducted. And Daniel says that you can help us—"

As he put up his hand, she stopped. "Will you excuse us," he said to his sister. "We do not require a chaperone the now."

"Too bad. I'm not leaving."

Yeah, okay, enough with the sibling conflict, as well. "Daniel says he has a lead from when he worked for you. About a—"

"I am out of that line of business." The male took a step back. "So I'm afraid that you will have to solve the problem with your friend on your own. Is there anything else about which I may be of service?"

"But Daniel told me—"

"I cannot help you."

Another gust of wind swirled around the male, sure as if his essence was calling the restless energy of the night to him, and as if in response, more howls from her kin echoed and weaved through the shadows.

The clans were reassuring her she was not alone, and she loved them for it.

"Is that all?" Blade asked as he stared at her. "And do take your time, I am enjoying the view."

"Will you *cut* the bullshit," Xhex snapped.

"You should feel honored, my lovely wolf, that this one"—he inclined his head in his sister's direction—"cares for you so deeply. Usually, she is much more reserved with her affections."

"Kurtis Joel," Lydia announced, loud and clear. "Daniel says you know where to find him."

Blade's facial expression did not change in any way: There wasn't a twitch of an eyebrow or a shift of the lip, not a tic or a frown. So he knew exactly who she was talking about. The ironclad composure was a dead giveaway.

"Don't lie to me." She stepped toward him. "There's an innocent man's life in the balance and Daniel—"

"I am terribly sorry to inform you that your intended is wrong." A shoulder lifted in casual disregard. "I cannot help you. Now, if there is nothing further, you must excuse me . . ."

As the male turned away, she pictured Gus, clear as if he were standing before her, from his Afro to the H.R. Pufnstuf t-shirt he liked so much to the faded, well-worn jeans he always wore.

"You're our only hope. *Please.*"

Blade froze. And then turned back around. For a moment, there was a glow of menace about him, and she recognized what it was: A predator on the hunt. She knew the feeling from her wolven form.

"What exactly are you offering," he said in a deep voice.

"You know what?" Xhex pointed to Lydia with a jab of her forefinger. "I'm done warning you. If you know what's good for you, you'll walk the hell away from him right now; otherwise you're going to live with the consequences. Either way, I'm out."

The vampire dematerialized, leaving behind a string of curse words that were consumed by the wind. And then Lydia was alone with the male, the night somehow growing darker, the air getting even colder. As she tried to keep calm, she realized his sister was right. This was not a male you wanted to show weakness around.

And sure enough, like he could read her discomfort, Blade lowered his head and looked at her from under hooded lids. "What exactly are you offering me in return for my aid?"

"I can pay you," she blurted.

"I already have money, but perhaps something else then. What else are you willing to pledge, female?"

"I don't know what you're implying—"

"The hell you don't." His voice practically vibrated with a distinctly masculine intention. "There is only one thing I want from you and you know precisely what that is."

"I am in *love* with Daniel," she said with force.

"Oh, yes, I know." He tilted his head to the side, his stare gleaming. "But let us consider your situation, shall we? If I help you with this problem concerning your friend, if I handle things on your behalf—and I believe we both know what you want me to do—then you will owe a payment—"

"I am *not* sleeping with you—"

He put a hand to the center of his chest, as if offended. "Not now, of course. Not whilst your Daniel still lives. I am not a total savage, you realize."

Lydia's heart started to pound so hard, her hearing was affected by the rushing noise.

"Ah, if you could only see the expression on your face," he said with a smile. "And yet I do not understand the shock. You need something I have. I want something you have. This is a negotiation— and I am willing to delay my resolution so that your conscience is clear. Quite a sacrifice to your benefit."

In a bald voice, she said, "I do not want you."

"I know that. Yet it does not bother me."

"And in any event, I can't trust you."

"Actually, you can, in this situation. It will be amply clear whether or not I live up to my side of the bargain—and it goes without saying that what you are looking for is something I can provide. I am uniquely suited to this mission of recovery of the remains and revenge. After which, I will wait for however long is required so that your mate is not betrayed by our little arrangement. Indeed, he need never know."

She recoiled. "I am not going to lie to Daniel."

Blade's shrug was nonplussed, as if they were discussing nothing more than a lunch date between friends. "I do not care whether you do or don't. That is your business."

When she just stood there, he put his palm out for a shaking. "Do we have a deal? Do you want your revenge or not."

"Gus could still be alive," she said in a numb way. Mostly to herself.

"Not if he is in Kurtis's hands. If that is who has your friend? He was dead within the hour—if he was lucky."

◆   ◆   ◆

As Blade read the wolf's grid, he attempted to regard her pain, fear, and helplessness with the detachment so characteristic of the psychopathy that defined him: On the surface, her upset was a consummate win and amusement for his *symphath* core, this forcing of a female of worth to give herself to him, in the midst of her mourning, when she had absolutely no interest in having sex with him, because she was trying to avenge the wrongful killing of someone who evidently was important to her, a tasty meal of distress.

Such a delicious tangle of toxic emotions. For her.

Oh, and the chaser? Underlying all of it was the fact that her beloved Daniel, once so strong, so capable, so well-trained, could have gone after "Kurtis Joel" himself, had he been physically able to do the job. But he was dying, and his disease had made it such that he'd had to send his female up here, to ask his sworn enemy to do something he would have completed quite easily just half a year ago.

The duality of the cruelty was delicious. A two-for-one feast.

And Blade was such a glutton.

Under normal situations.

"So," he forced himself to prompt as he deliberately regarded his extended hand. "Whatever are you going to do?"

Crossing her arms over her chest, she lifted her chin. "Just tell me what you know."

"I'm sorry?"

"I'll take care of it myself." Her golden stare was unblinking. "You're right, we both know what I'm looking for and I don't need you to do my work for me. Tell me where the man is, that's all I need from you."

As she regarded him down the bridge of her nose, he recalled her riveting transformation, that which was lupine becoming human in appearance not with some ghastly series of cracks and pops and drooling à la eighties horror films, but rather with a graceful shift that was molecular ballet as opposed to anatomical car crash.

His sex stirred beneath his robing, thickening.

How could he be erect, though? He did not favor females. And he certainly had never tiptoed into the quicksand of obsession over something as transitory and unimportant as an orgasm. Or twelve. Or twenty.

Be a hero, he told himself. *Give her what she—*

Blade shook his head. "No."

"Why are you so heartless?"

"It is my nature," he heard himself reply. "I am what I am."

"Well, that's true for me as well." She glared at his palm. "And my answer is no. We do not have a deal."

A blaze of pain went through him, and he found himself swallowing a gasp with a grim surge of masochism.

Naturally, his unparalleled reactions merely piqued his interest further.

He was not a male to whom people said no.

Well, not unless they were answering the question *Would you like to die under mine hand this night?*

"What are you going to do about your friend," he asked softly as he lowered his arm. "Let him go?"

"You don't have to worry about that, do you. And now you're right. You are never going to see me again."

As she turned away, he bit out, "Daniel doesn't know what I do about dear old Kurtis."

The wolf glanced over her shoulder, her whiskey-colored eyes as cold as January. "My husband can find everything out. He's very resourceful."

"He told me that you were not mated—forgive me, I believe 'married' is the word."

"He *is* my husband—and we will take care of ourselves. I'd thank you for the kind offer, but it wasn't kind and I am never going to thank you for anything."

"Do not go after Kurtis Joel yourself," he said grimly.

"Goodbye—"

"If you want to live long enough to see your husband die, do *not* go after him."

The female stared at him for a minute. Then she took three steps forward until they were face to face. She was tall enough so that she didn't have to tilt back to meet his eyes, and as her upper lip pulled up off her canines on one side, he could sense her wolf coming to the fore, just under her skin.

"You have no idea who I am," she growled. "And no clue what I will do to protect what is mine."

Blade's own fangs descended as his cock positively pounded with need under the drapes of red. "I pray you do not find him."

"Pray for him, not me."

With that, she ran off without a sound, ducking into the pines, moving with the kind of coordination that one rarely saw in humans, but that was true of every nimble animal of the forest. In her absence, he exhaled and fought a wave of mourning so great, he felt certain it would knock him off his summit perch and send him tumbling to his death in the valley far, far below.

As devastating as it was to think he would never see her again, there was something worse.

For the first time in his life, he hated that someone thought he was an asshole.

TEN

L YDIA PULLED THE SUV she'd borrowed
under the porte cochere and parked it at the
stone mansion's front door again. After cutting the
engine, she left the blacked-out box where she'd
found it. As she jogged up to the fortified entrance,
she was pissed off and still talking to that *symphath*
in her head.

Who knew there were so many different ways to
use the word "asshole."

Courtesy of C.P. Phalen's state-of-the-art security
monitoring, her entry into the house was facilitated
by one of the guards, and as he unlocked the bolting
mechanism and opened things, she ripped by him—
and his frozen, expressionless face reminded her of
Blade's rankling superiority. Which made her want
to punch something—

Lydia stopped dead two strides into the black-
and-white foyer.

The scent of blood was precisely the kind of
crappy news flash that the night seemed determined

to keep providing, and the air was so saturated with copper that she expected to see a decapitated body down on the marble-tiled floor. Glancing back at the guard, the man was shutting the door, and then he returned to his sentry spot by the archway into the library that looked out over the back acreage. It was on her tongue to ask him if he smelled it, too, but then he probably didn't. She sometimes forgot how much better her nose was.

The guard swiveled his head toward her, like he was remote-controlled. "You forget something out-side?"

"Ah, no. Thanks."

He nodded and resumed his forward-facing stance, his eyes staring into the middle distance. Standing there in that little alcove—which must have been built specifically for a statue—he was like part of a chessboard, the knight come to life.

Tracking the scent, she went down the hall to-ward her and Daniel's bedroom, but thank God the blood wasn't his—

The study was wide open, which wasn't normal, and as Lydia closed in on the floor-to-ceiling aper-ture, the scent exploded in her nose.

Oh, God. C.P.

She spoke up. "Hello, is everything all right—"

Across the austere space, a door into a private half bath was thrown wide, and the red pool on the white marble floor gleamed in an evil way.

"*No!*"

She bolted across and swung around the door-jamb without entering because she didn't want to step in the puddle. The toilet hadn't been flushed, and the white bowl was bright—

"She's okay."

Lydia spun back. Daniel had entered the study, and the sight of him in his sweatshirt, with his jeans hanging off his hips, his feet bare, and his cane angled to support his weight, made her want to cry. As she ran to him, she was babbling all kinds of things, but then she was up against him and just trying not to faint.

"Is it the baby?" she mumbled into his shoulder.

"You knew?"

Lydia pulled back and nodded. "But it wasn't my story to tell. I caught the change in her scent, and then I—I didn't keep anything from you, I swear—"

"Shh. It's okay." He stroked her arms. "She's medically stable. There was nothing anybody could—whoa, take a deep breath."

Such good advice. That she tried to take. "She wanted that pregnancy. I am so sorry—where is she—"

"Upstairs."

"Can I see her?"

"Yeah. No doubt she'd like that. It's been . . . a helluva day."

As his eyes searched her face, she knew what

he was looking for, and shook her head. "He's not going to help us. I saw him up there, and that *asshole* is not going to help us."

Daniel's jaw locked for a moment. "We'll find another way. Somehow—"

"How can he be so cruel?" Releasing his shoulders, she tangled her fingers in her hair. "I don't understand how anybody can be like that. He's a monster, an absolute—"

Daniel urged her arms down. "Hey, hey, let's move on from him. Just breathe with me, okay?"

Lydia nodded. Nodded some more. Then she replayed the exchange up on the mountain—and got stuck in a memory loop with the *symphath*'s sadistic detachment.

"You're right," she muttered. "We don't ever need to see that man—male, whatever he is—again. But, God, I can't get over how ruthless he is."

Daniel's eyes narrowed. "What did he say to you?"

"Nothing that bears repeating," she shot back with strength. "I just hope he rots in hell—and you're right, we're going to have to help Gus on our own. We can find that Kurtis Joel guy ourselves."

"Yeah, well, that might be a problem." Daniel ran his hand over his skull a couple of times, like he was trying to rub his brain so it worked better. "I have no idea who the guy is, where he is—why he's in the file system. The name appeared twice in the old FBG database, and it stood out to me because it was the only entry in the whole goddamn thing with no larger context. No detailed biography. No company ties. No notes. There were just two words, each time—'*apparatus occisio*.'"

Lydia frowned. "Is that Latin?"

"Yup. 'Killing machine.'"

She thought back to when she had first met Blade—and that enemy soldier had come out of nowhere. The thing hadn't been human at all. And then she went back further, to the spring . . . when she and Daniel had been tracked through the woods by what she thought was a man, but hadn't been. At all.

"The scene at Gus's was totally clean," Daniel said. "No hair, no fibers—and the blood was Gus's only. That's what made me think of the entries. A killing machine. It has to be what broke into the condo, and that database was maintained by Blade. He made the notations and he knows something— I can feel it."

"I agree, but working with him is *not* going to be an option."

Daniel's eyes flared with a nasty gleam. "What did he want in return."

"Nothing I was willing to give him."

"Fucking *bastard*—" Daniel walked off, relying on his cane, moving around in a circle. "I shouldn't have sent you up there—"

"We had to try and we did. Now we move on to the next thing."

She focused on that cane, and didn't want to ask him why he was suddenly using it again. But maybe he'd helped with their hostess's medical emergency.

Switching gears, she said, "I do have an idea. Are you strong enough to—"

"Yes." He squared off at her. "Whatever it is, the answer is yes."

✦ ✦ ✦

No more than five minutes later, Daniel was back in the SUV, but considering he was sitting properly in the front passenger seat, instead of slumped like a drunk in the back, negotiating with his ability to stay conscious?

It proved the whole night wasn't going to shit—even if that was the overwhelming trend.

He should have known what the outcome would be of telling Lydia to go see his old boss—but he'd been desperate, and desperate people did stupid things as they argued with reality.

And he could well guess what the sonofabitch had wanted in return.

As Lydia drove them off from the Phalen estate, night had come solidly, the darkness consuming the rural landscape. Courtesy of Walters being nothing but a little mill town, there were no other cars on the road, and the few houses that dotted the shoulder were set so far back that their lights seemed as distant as the stars overhead.

Glancing over at Lydia, he studied her face in the glow of the instrument panel. Her brows were down low and her lips were a tight line of intention—and goddamn, she was beautiful. Then again, she was always that way to him, no matter her mood, no matter the circumstance—which was a consequence of loving someone deeply, wasn't it.

As his eyes drifted across her upper body, he thought of his dream.

"What are you looking at?" she murmured.

"Now isn't the time." He shifted in his seat and went back to looking out the window. "Where are we going, by the way?"

He hadn't asked when they'd left. He'd just been determined not to sit on the sidelines of chaos for one fucking moment longer. And now, as she answered him, he found himself less interested in the words she was speaking, and more into how much he liked the way her mouth moved as she enunciated the syllables—

"You're staring again." She glanced away from the headlight-lit road. "Penny for your thoughts?"

Letting his head fall back on the rest, he muttered, "Knock knock."

Lydia laughed in a short burst. "Who's there?"

"Warrior."

"Warrior who?"

"War'ya been all my life?" As she grinned like the joke had been any good at all, he shook his head. "I'm still not funny, and yet you giggle."

"Ah, but you're funny enough for me." She hit the turn signal, then slowed them down. "And you know what I like about you?"

"Just one thing? I gotta do better."

Lydia laughed some more. "See? You do have a sense of humor."

"And you're biased."

"Completely biased." Easing them off the county road and onto a long driveway, she glanced at him and got serious. "I like that you didn't even ask where we're going. You just jumped in right beside me."

"Well, for one, your idea *has* to be better than mine," he muttered. He was never going to forgive himself for sending her on that fucking goose chase. "And as long as we're together? I'm good. I'm sooooo good."

"Me, too."

They leaned in over the center console at the same time, their lips meeting briefly, and as he closed his eyes, he cursed the destiny or fate—or whatever the hell it was—that doled out the good and the bad. Surely there had been a mistake when it came to the pair of them.

Too much on the—

Reopening his lids, a farmhouse was in view, and

when he recognized its modest lines, what she'd told him decoded, the reply finally resonating, her idea crystallizing for him.

"Eastwind," he said.

"He's more than a sheriff. He just pretends . . . he's normal."

Daniel nodded, even though he wasn't sure what she meant—or whether this was such a great idea. One thing that was clear? The guy could keep up a property. Everything from the black shutters to the white siding and the wraparound porch was freshly painted, and the yard was free of downed branches and dead bushes, the detached garage a satellite that was similarly spick-and-span'd. Likewise, the barn and the fenced-in meadow in the back were ready for animals to graze, although there didn't seem to be any around.

Lydia brought them to a halt and put the Suburban in park. "Do you want to come in with me?"

"Hold up a sec." He put his hand on her shoulder as she reached for her door latch. "Let's think this through. Do we really want law enforcement involved? What happens if we figure out who took Gus? Do you want whoever's responsible to go through the human legal system? No, you don't. You want proper revenge. If you head down this path with Eastwind, solving things on our own could get complicated."

"I'm not here because he's a sheriff."

Daniel frowned. "Then why—"

"We just need to find Kurtis Joel. Then we can take care of it our way." As she looked over, the predator in her was out and about, even as she stayed in her human skin. "I'm very familiar with operating outside of normal channels. And so are you."

"Exactly. Tipping them off to the problem begs for trouble. You know this."

Lydia turned her head toward the house. After a moment, she shook her head. "Eastwind's not normal channels, either, Daniel. You gotta trust me on this—"

"If you mean that he's a small-town lawman who bends rules here and there inside his jurisdiction? I'm sure that's true. But if you tell him Gus is missing— and there was plenty of blood at the scene? He'll be required to notify the Plattsburgh police, and probably the New York Staties. Maybe even the FBI if there's a concern that Gus has been taken over state lines."

When she didn't say anything, he cursed softly. "Hello? Did you hear me—"

A dim porch light flared to life, and a second later, the front door opened. Sheriff Eastwind stepped out onto his stoop while in the process of wrapping a navy bathrobe around himself. The way he tied the thing with a jab of his hand was the extent of any annoyance that a vehicle had shown up on his property at—

Absently, Daniel glanced at the dash. Midnight. Past midnight.

Lydia popped her door and looked back. "Trust me."

Like his plan had been better? he reminded himself. "Roger that."

Daniel got out as well, and he hated that he took his cane with him. Helping Phalen had cost him, but he refused to give in to the aching.

By way of distraction—and also because he now had a gun in the center pocket of his sweatshirt—he focused on Eastwind. The sheriff was standing calmly as his visitors approached, like people disturbing him at strange hours was something that happened often.

"Long time no see," the man said as he moved his thick braid of black hair back over his shoulder.

"Sorry we're here so late." Lydia waited for Daniel to join her before walking up the steps. "But it couldn't wait."

"Okay."

As they reached the porch, Eastwind stepped aside. "It's cold out. C'mon in."

"Thanks." Lydia slipped by him. "We appreciate it."

When Daniel went to step inside, Eastwind's dark eyes did an up-and-down. "How we doin'?"

Daniel offered his hand for a shake. "Fine and dandy. You?"

There was a curt incline of the head, and then what was offered was shaken. Like the guy was perfectly prepared to drop the subject of exactly how not fine-and-dandy Daniel obviously was.

"Yup," the sheriff said. "Good."

And then they were in a living room that had almost no furniture, but an incredible collection of Native American blankets hanging on the walls. The handwoven masterpieces were secured at the tops with padded holders, and the saturated colors of red and blue and yellow, as well as the geometric patterns, were a feast for the eyes.

"So what've we got going on," Eastwind said as he lumbered over to an easy chair and let himself fall into the thing like it was a baseball glove made specifically for the contours of his ass.

"Do you mind if I sit?" Daniel said as he glanced at the sofa.

"G'head." Eastwind reached down and pulled a lever so that a padded leg support popped up under his calves. "Sorry, Lydia, you're going to have to share with your man. I don't have houseguests ever, so I don't need any other chairs. Come to think of it, I don't need that couch, either, but I guess I'm too cheap to throw it out."

This was all said like he wished the pair of them had adhered to his no-houseguest rule, but he wasn't going to be rude about it. And as Daniel lowered himself onto the sofa, the sheriff linked his hands, settled them over the lapels of his fleece robe, and let his head ease back against the rest. Like the guy could go to sleep in the chair perfectly happily.

Or maybe he was just wishing he was still upstairs in his bed.

"We need your help." Lydia began pacing around the braided-rug area. "And before I tell you everything, I need you to—"

"I don't know where your scientist is."

She stopped dead. Pivoted slowly to the sheriff. "How did you know Gus was gone?" When Eastwind just shrugged, she cursed. "Not good enough. How?"

"Your grandfather ever teach you not to sass your elders? And I told you way before, nothing happens on the mountain without me knowing it."

"You can help us," she said urgently. "If you know he's gone, you know even more—"

"I didn't say that."

"You don't have to. C.P. Phalen's house is a vault, and the abduction happened in Plattsburgh. If you know about it at all, you—"

"Maybe I just saw a lineup of SUVs with blacked-out windows speeding onto the Northway, one after the other, while I was sitting in the bushes looking for people going eighty in a sixty-five. Phalen's Fleet is what we call them at HQ. And you're right, they were headed to Plattsburgh, and that doctor of yours lives there. He told me himself when I was allowed to come see you, before the chemo crashed your man's immunity and he couldn't have any more visitors."

"Maybe those Suburbans were driving to Montreal."

"I followed them. They were going a hundred. I was going to get a bonus from our governor, you know. If I'd pulled them over."

As Lydia and Eastwind went back and forth, Daniel studied the man, looking for his tells, falling back into an old, familiar role of lie detector machine. He didn't get much of anything. Eastwind's eyelids were low, like the conversation was boring him, but he was calmly focused on Lydia—his facial features, so bold, so carved, were neutral.

Then again, he was a professional. Professional what . . . though.

"I don't buy that story," Lydia said. "And we did not come here to argue with you."

"What a relief," Eastwind said dryly. "I'm also hoping you don't expect food. I eat at the diner for breakfast, lunch, and dinner. The only thing in my fridge is old ketchup and some milk that I'm sure is a solid now—"

"I've already been lied to once tonight," Lydia announced in a grim voice. "It's not happening again."

"Aren't you a force to be reckoned with."

"I know the truth about you," she cut in.

"Do you."

The way she was standing there over the lounger, taking control of the conversation, aggression banked, but right under the surface, Daniel felt a flush of pride—and then an aching, bittersweet relief. When his wolven said she could handle things, it was very clear she could. She was going to be okay without him in the big bad world.

She really was.

"Back in the spring," she said, "I had to go to the high school to use the computer lab. I went by the display of trophies, the one in front by the office. All those trophies on those shelves . . . lot of team pictures with them, going back for years. I know you know the ones. Don't you."

It was subtle, but Eastwind's energy changed even as his body remained right where it was, his ankles crossed, his brown leather slippers knocking together in a rhythm that was like a heartbeat.

His vibe just was different.

"You know those images," Lydia said, "because you're in one. From nineteen eighty. And here's the funny thing. You want to talk about magic? You look *exactly* the same as you do now."

There was a stretch of silence.

"Plastic surgery is good these days." Lydia shook her head slowly. "But it's not that good. So no, I don't think you were waiting in a speed trap, and I don't think you saw those vehicles, and I do not believe you followed them to Plattsburgh. You know what kind of doctor, what kind of man, Gus St. Claire is. If you were in his position, he would help find you if he could. I expect you to do the same."

Daniel passed a hand down his face as he remembered the hours Gus had spent talking with him, explaining symptoms and test results and drug therapies. And sometimes just shooting the shit, particularly when Daniel was getting infusions.

"Come on, Eastwind," he spoke up. "The man's probably dead, but that can't be how this ends, if you know what I mean. Help us do what's right."

Eastwind's slippers stopped tapping. "Something tells me you're not talking about jail time, and I'm going to give you a little tip. If you're considering homicide, I'm not the one you need to come to. Remember, I am an officer of the law."

"That's not all you are," Lydia intoned. "Not by a long shot."

ELEVEN

G US WAS NOT feeling so hot.

As he resurfaced to some muddy version of consciousness, he was surprised he was still alive. For one thing, his wheezing woke him up. For another, there was a dripping sound that he had a feeling was his own blood. And God, his stomach hurt. Actually, he didn't need his medical degree to know that *everything* hurt—

"You're awake again."

The sound of that oddly accented voice activated his adrenal system like nothing ever had. As his body began to shake uncontrollably, his heart pounded and knocked out his hearing—

But wait, he could see now.

His vision was blurry, and he couldn't lift his slumped head to look around much—but the mask was off his face so he got an eyeful of the pool of blood that was congealing on the concrete floor beneath a wooden chair leg. Lot of blood. Pints of it.

Shit.

Shifting his eyes off to the side, he could see nothing beyond the bright beam of interrogation light that was shining down on him. Everything was darkness, and he gave up trying to penetrate the illumination shield. As his lids fluttered, bits and pieces of what had been done to him over the course of hours came back to him, and he started to choke, his throat spasming, his lungs pulling down bodily fluids instead of air—

"Now, now, let us not get agitated."

Gus moaned as his head was gently repositioned on the pillow that was now damp. With his airway straightened out, his respiration got a little easier, but a rolling dizziness made the darkness around him spin.

"I . . ."

"You are what, Dr. St. Claire?"

His eyes tracked the inquiry to the right and he blinked in an attempt to get his pupils to function better. The man who had worked on him was just a dim shape on the edge of the light, looming as a promise of more pain.

"Done . . ." Gus coughed weakly. "I am done."

"I would imagine you feel that way. And I must tell you that I, too, am almost finished with you. Indeed, you will find that I am a male who must complete things."

There was a soft crackling, like a fire made with damp wood, and even though Gus's consciousness didn't immediately identify what it was, his body knew. His body spoke.

"No . . . God, no . . ."

"There are ways to make this easier on you, my friend."

Gus forced his protest out through teeth that chattered. "No . . . just kill me . . ."

"It is better that you die naturally. As a physician, surely you understand the ethics of it all. And I think you're close. I have not had the formal training you have, but experience tells me much."

A flickering of blue entered his sightline, the charge of electricity dancing in between two contacts on a handheld device, the energy eager to be set free along different channels.

Like the water molecules inside a human being.

Tears burned in Gus's eyes and stung the open wounds on his face as he started to weep. He was so exhausted that the agony in his body wasn't something he felt, it was all that he was. No more skin, muscle, and bones, no blood, no marrow. Just the terrible pain.

"Now tell me about that house. How do you get in."

It was the same question. For hours. Six words. Followed by five words. And he had answered, God save them all, he had—

"I . . . told . . . you everything."

"Yes, you have."

"Why . . . are you still doing this—"

"I like to be sure."

No, the man liked to inflict pain. It was as if he snorted suffering as a drug. Even now, Gus could feel something transpiring between them, a draw. A sucking—

"The card . . . is in my . . . wallet—"

Every time he answered, with each instance of capitulation, he lost another part of who he was: Even though his reply was the same, the concession was an endless pit, the shame a new slice on flesh that had yet to be breached.

"Yes, the card. Tell me more."

The Taser, or whatever the hell it was, was applied to the thick meat of his upper thigh, and Gus screamed as the biggest muscles in his body contracted, the locking-up so vicious he knew for sure his leg was going to snap in half—

"There, there, Dr. St. Claire."

As that voice registered once again, he realized that the weapon had been removed from his quadriceps. The pain remained.

"Tell. Me. More."

Gus prayed his flickering heart would finally stop. If his captor could just shock him on the neck, on the vagus nerve, maybe it would finally—

"Why," he mumbled. "Why are you doing this . . ."

"You are a fine meal," came the remote response. "A strong will broken is the best sustenance for what I am, so let us enjoy our time together some more. Tell me how to get into that—"

A brisk knocking dimmed the crackling sound of the Taser, and his captor pivoted around.

"Enter."

The creaking was of the metal-on-metal variety, as if a vault door were being pushed wide. And then another voice, also male, spoke urgently, a conversation back-and-forthing. The language was not one Gus recognized. Then again, he didn't have the energy to care about linguistics.

Shuffling now, as if objects were being gathered up quickly. Then rattling, like they were being dumped into a bag.

"I must go, Dr. St. Claire. I shall trust nature to finish this job—not a preferable conclusion as I never leave things hanging, but for reasons of my own, I must depart with alacrity. Worry not, the party who is imminently arriving is not interested in you. It is I whom he seeks, but now is not the time or place for that." There was a pause. "This has been . . . exquisite for me. You are a rare find, and I wish we had met under different circumstances. And now, I will leave you with this."

His captor leaned into the light, but Gus's vision was blurry so all he got was the impression of dark hair that was precisely styled in a side part and pale skin. The eyes were just a pair of pupils, pits of black. The smell, though, was unforgettable.

Dark . . . spices. Like expensive cologne, although no brand that was immediately identifiable.

"You have been a revelation. Thank you."

A chaste kiss was pressed to Gus's forehead, as if they had had dirty sex that had been satisfying on a spiritual level.

As his captor straightened, Gus felt two cool points on the side of his throat, right over his jugular vein.

The Taser, he thought. *Finally*—

"Goodbye, Dr. St. Claire."

The electrical volts rocked through Gus's body, throwing him into a seizure that stiffened his limbs and threw his head back and locked his molars.

No more vision.

No more hearing.

No more copper smell.

Nothing. And unlike the other times, not even . . . any last thoughts.

◆ ◆ ◆

"Come back in forty-eight hours."

As Lydia stood over a laconic, recumbent, navy-robed Sheriff Eastwind, she shook her head. Which was better than cursing or throwing something in frustration. "Why."

"Because I said so."

To keep herself from losing it, she glanced around, noting the First Nations' woven textiles on the walls, the pottery lamp that was glowing next to Eastwind's recliner, the fireplace that was set with hardwood logs and fresh newspaper. Through an archway, the dim contours of a kitchen were visible, and there was no table or set of chairs in there. No clutter on the countertops or on the top of the old-fashioned stove, either.

"And what's going to be different," she demanded.

"It's going to be forty-eight hours from now." The man cocked an eyebrow. "That's two days, FYI."

"I can count."

"Clever girl."

Lydia glanced over at Daniel, who just shrugged. "And then what," she snapped. "What happens."

"That's my offer." Eastwind reached down the side of his chair, pulled on the lever, and was propelled into a sitting position. "Now, if you'll excuse me, I'm going back to bed—"

"No." She stamped her foot on the rug. "This is not good enough—"

"Plattsburgh is not my jurisdiction." Eastwind paused in the process of getting up, his broad palms planted on the padded sides of the chair, his arms bowed out at the elbows. "I have no power there in the big city. And before you point out that Gus St. Claire works here in Walters, the crime happened at his home, not Ms. Phalen's lab. Now I'm going to say goodnight. Goodnight."

Finishing the job with the vertical stuff, he nodded at Daniel. "Hope you still do okay."

Then he nodded at Lydia, and went to the stairs like he didn't care if they camped out underneath him, or left without closing things behind themselves. As the sound of his footfalls ascended and then crossed above, all she could do was look to the farmhouse's ceiling and track the progress in disbelief.

"Are you kidding me," she muttered as bedsprings squeaked under a heavy weight. "And he didn't even show us to the door."

From above, a muffled voice: "If you can't find it, you need more help than you asked for."

Daniel eased his way up to his feet, catching himself on the arm of the couch as he wobbled. "Let's go."

Lydia looked around one more time. "I hate this."

The state of being out of control felt like it had consumed her life, and she missed the sense that she could make decisions, take action, effect change. Lately, everything had been about adapting to situations she despised and was trapped in, iron bars everywhere.

Daniel touched her shoulder. "There's nothing for us here."

Even though she wanted to argue with that, she let herself be led over to the door—and as she stepped out into the night, she had the urge to slam the thing. Like a dozen times.

Instead, she drifted over to the SUV on a cloud of distraction, the cold, damp air tingling in her sinuses, her body shivering, even though she wouldn't have said she had a chill. As she hauled herself into the vehicle, she glanced back at the house—and a strange premonition crept up her spine.

She was going to see this place again, she thought.

Then again, of course she would. She was damn well coming back in two frickin' days.

The intention resonated all the way through her as she drew the seatbelt across her heart and clicked it into place. Starting the engine, she put her hands on the wheel, fully intending to get herself and Daniel into reverse and take them back up to the county road.

Except she just sat there, staring out over the dashboard at Eastwind's garage.

On the other side of the Suburban, Daniel opened the passenger door and got in with the help of his cane. "You okay?"

"No, I'm not. But I just need to take us home." She glanced back at the farmhouse. "I mean, to Phalen's."

She and Daniel didn't have a home.

"I want to go to the FBI," she heard herself say as

she K-turned and then hit the gas. "The CIA. Every newspaper and TV channel. I want . . . all kinds of things."

"This timing just sucks."

She glanced over. "Is it ever good to get kidnapped?"

"That's not what I mean."

She intended to ask him to clarify, but her mind got tangled in frustration and she let it go. Meanwhile, the trip back to the Phalen property took a hundred years, but also seemed to happen in the blink of an eye, and after she piloted them under the porte cochere, Daniel was the one who turned off the engine. He also had to come around and open her door.

"It's bad timing because we need to go talk to Phalen," he said.

She blinked stupidly. Then made the connection. "Oh, God. No, not after what happened to her—"

"What choice do we have? We're running out of time. Maybe she knows about this Kurtis Joel guy."

Lydia wanted to argue. But in the same way nocontrol had become her standard operating procedure, balancing two bad options was her perennial crossroads.

So she just followed him into the foyer and up the stairs to the second floor. As they reached the open area at the top, she glanced to the right. When

Daniel had been injured and first diagnosed, they had been given a bedroom here on the upper level. Chemo had knocked him hard, however, and to keep him from having to deal with the steps, they'd moved into the suite they were in now.

A lifetime ago, she thought as they went over to a set of double doors that were closed. Just as Daniel curled up a fist and went to knock, the entryway opened on its own.

Across a white carpet the size of most people's front lawns, C.P. pushed herself up higher on a king-sized bed that was draped with a monogrammed duvet. The parallels to a luxury hotel ended there. At the headboard, padded panels had dropped away to expose hospital-grade monitoring equipment, and surrounded by all the hi-tech machinery, the woman seemed tiny. And very fragile.

Her voice was steady as ever, though: "You want to tell me where you went?" she said briskly. "And Lydia, please don't look at me like that. I appreciate the sympathy, but I can't deal with it right now, I really can't."

Lydia cleared her throat and brushed a stray hair out of her eye. "Of course. I'm sorry— I mean . . ."

Daniel stepped forward—and had to take Lydia's hand before she was willing to follow him. As they approached their hostess, those doors eased closed with a whisper that only Lydia's wolven ears picked up on.

At least she assumed neither of the humans with her could hear the quiet sound.

When they reached the foot of the bed, she tried not to stare—and failed. C.P. was pale as her floor and walls, but her hair was freshly washed, and for once, she wasn't wearing Gus's fleece. A silk dressing robe was wrapped up tight to the base of her throat, and her hand played with the lace lapels, the nervous twining more desperate trembling than any conscious movement.

That fleece was next to her on the bed, though. Folded precisely on the monogrammed pillowcase.

"We need to ask you about something," Daniel said. "Privately."

C.P.'s busy hand stilled. Then she called out, "Georgina, give us a minute. Would you."

From around a corner, a red-haired nurse Lydia recognized leaned in and gave a wave. "I'll just be in the back. Hit the button if you need me."

"Thank you."

The nurse ducked away, and then a door closed sharply, like she wanted to announce her departure to all involved. After that, C.P. stared up with a professional composure, as if they were in her office or her boardroom—

"I'm so sorry," Lydia blurted. "About the baby."

As C.P. flinched, Lydia realized what she'd said and slapped a hand over her mouth. But before she could apologize again, and likely mess things up further, the other woman shook her head.

"It's all right," she whispered. "Miracles come . . . and miracles go. Don't they."

Abruptly, Lydia glanced over at Daniel. As he switched his cane to his other hand, he looked utterly spent.

"Yes," she heard herself reply. "They do."

TWELVE

As music bumped, loud as bombs being dropped in sequence, and a herd of humans milled around the alcohol trough of the bar, Xhex spotted tonight's problem through the shifting bodies. It wasn't that the man was pushing at people or grinding on them without permission. He wasn't drunk or twitchy from coke or meth. And in his black sweatshirt and black jeans, he might have been a little casual and covered up, but he wasn't dressed in a particularly standout fashion.

It was the way the guy stood alone on the periphery of the other patrons, a statue by the hall to the bathrooms.

As the head of security for the club, with years of being in charge of all kinds of venues under her belt, Xhex had a radar for trouble—and that was before you threw in her *symphath* shit.

The fact that he didn't move from his position was what had first gotten her attention and made her assess him. He wasn't that tall, he wasn't that broad, and with his brush-cut hair and stubble, he was very forgettable—in a calculated way. Like he wanted to project an image of being just another twenty-ish man in a part of the city where there were thousands of them.

Even so, she might have dismissed him—if it hadn't been for the way he was looking around with such a pointed lack of emotion. If somebody was searching for someone specific, like if they'd lost the buddy or the date they'd come with, they got frustrated after a while. If a person was after sex, they were greedy as they focused on the objects of their desire. If they were giving up because they'd been ghosted or nobody wanted them, they were depressed.

Not this guy. He was like radar, sweeping back and forth with only his eyes moving, as if he didn't want anyone to know who he was focusing on. Law enforcement undercover? No. They checked in with her as a courtesy—and anyway, his attention was too diffused, even in its intensity. He was searching for a type, not an individual. A vibe. Something that was inside of him sparked by someone outside of him.

He would know it when he saw it.

The way any predator can pick out the weakling in any group.

And when he found what he wanted to take, then he would move. He would start to track—

A couple who were arm-in-arm passed by her, cutting off her field of vision. As soon as they were clear, she looked back to see if the man was still—

"Of course you're right there," she muttered under her breath.

Read him, a dark part of her demanded. *Read him and see the truth your instincts know for a fact.*

"Yeah, and then what," she said.

You know what you want to do.

Xhex laughed. "Far as I'm aware, I'm at work and perfectly happy overseeing my staff and watching the crowd. So what I *want* to do is my fucking job—"

If you read him, you are free to do what you want.

In the recesses of her mind, she was aware that the back-and-forth was taking "talking to yourself" to a level that should probably be professionally assessed, but it was fine. She was fine.

Everything was fine—

"I'm free now." She looked away from the man to prove the point. "Free as a bird."

Read him.

"Will you leave me the *fuck* alone—"

"Sorry, I'm just following up on the text you sent earlier?"

With a jump, Xhex focused on her second-in-command. T'Marcus Jones was pointing to his iPhone as if to prove he wasn't wasting her time. Not that the former Marine ever wasted anything.

He was a consummate professional, always in control of himself and anyone around him. His black shirt might have had STAFF on the back in big letters, but like he'd be confused for anything other than BADASS?

What the hell had she asked him to do?

To cover her confusion, she waved his arm down. "Yeah, yeah. Good. What's the answer?"

His brows went up. "Ah, I did it?"

"What?"

"I set the schedule for next week and sent it out to everyone?" When she just blinked at him, T'Marcus leaned in, like maybe if they were closer together she'd understand what he was talking about better. "You told me you were coming in late tonight and asked me to take care of it first thing. Bobby, the new hire, is covering for Mike while he's on vacation, and the rest of us are splitting Bobby's night off on Wednesday. S'all good."

"Oh. Right." She cleared her throat. "Thanks."

"You need something else?"

"I'm fine." Making a show of checking her watch, she said, "Is it me or is this night crawling?"

T'Marcus nodded and asked her something she didn't track. As she nodded to whatever it was, what she was really concentrating on was the flare of panic kindling in her brain stem—and when he walked off, she told herself to get her shit together.

This time, the voice in her head wasn't some

version of her own, but Rehvenge's: *Your grid is still collapsing.*

Rubbing her bloodshot eyes, she said, "No, it isn't."

As she answered yet another disembodied opinion, and then resolutely blocked out Blade's second opinion on the subject, she looked back for the man in the hoodie—

He was gone.

Her senses came alive, and she moved without being aware of deciding to. Her body ambulated on its own, striding forward, shuffling through the humans getting their good time on. Tracking her prey—

Black sweatshirt was *not* prey, she reminded herself. No, she was just going to talk to him. Get him to leave peacefully.

Go on about his business before he got hurt.

Moving along, her eyes sharpened on the heads around her, weeding out the blond and red-haired, the long-haired, the mullet, and the braided. No hoodie thickening the nape of a patron, anywhere. But she hadn't been talking long. He couldn't have gone far—

Down at her waist, her hand snuck into her front pocket. The switchblade she carried with her came to her palm like it was answering a call, and her thumb searched for the knife's release. Except she wasn't going to do anything to him.

She wasn't ... going ... to ...

A strange pall came over her, her mind going numb to the point where her thoughts disintegrated as soon as she had them, threads of consciousness fraying until she couldn't remember why she was here in the sea of humans, or what she was doing—

No, she *knew* what she was doing. She was going to take out that human in black.

"I'm protecting the patrons," she said. "I'm supposed to protect them ..."

Zeroing in on the hallway to the bathrooms, she made the turn and—

There he was. Her target. The man with the brush cut, and the stubble, and the eyes that moved over the stupid innocents getting drunk and high like he was at a buffet.

Except she stopped short as she recognized the big human standing with him.

T'Marcus.

And then they both looked over at her with expectation. Like they wanted her to say something. Do something—just not with a switchblade.

"Hey, boss," the man in black said. "How'm I doing?"

Xhex glanced over her shoulder and got braced to see someone else standing behind her, someone who had hired the—

Abruptly, her mind sputtered and coughed, her

memory engine coming back online. Turning to the men once again, she felt a stone-cold chill go through her—

The new hire. Bobby, the new hire.

She'd interviewed him two weeks ago. He and T'Marcus had served together in the Corps.

Bobby glanced at his friend like he was worried he'd done something wrong. "Ah . . . did I do something wrong?"

Xhex told her hand to release the switchblade and remove itself from her pocket. And in a feat of parallel processing, she also managed to reply to the question with some kind of word salad. She must have gotten the syllables right, too, because the guy smiled, and T'Marcus nodded with satisfaction.

"I'm taking a break for ten." She made a show of checking her watch. "You're in charge, T."

The guy touched his right brow in a shadow of the salutes he'd no doubt given all his years in the military. "You got it, boss."

Nodding like she had a clue what she was doing, she headed for her office and was glad it wasn't far. Stepping into the concrete cell, she couldn't wait to shut the door—and God, you'd have sworn the little box with its old-fashioned, elementary-school-marm desk and the black rolling chair she'd gotten from Home Depot was a deluxe spa. Not that the bass line of the music was dimmed much—that shit was running all the way down to the foundation and all the way up into the rafters of the low ceiling.

But she was by herself. So that cut the volume on all kinds of things.

Sitting in her chair, she stared at the lock screen of her laptop. Lasers of pink and yellow, blue and lime green shot through a black background, and as she traced them with her eyes, she wondered what the cutoff was for seizure triggers. If the linear extensions were faster? Brighter?

Probably both.

And why in the hell was she thinking about that kind of thing anyway—

Well, considering she had been talking to herself, and playing spot-the-serial-killer with an honorable discharge who'd filled out a job application she herself had reviewed? Why not wonder about neurological hiccups.

Closing her eyes, she let her head fall back and thought of Blade. No wonder she was homicidal. Seeing him had scrambled her, and just because she was a little confused, and had just jumped to a minor conclusion—

"My grid is fine—"

A sudden burst of shouting percolated through the dull thump of the music, and as the discord registered, she groaned. It was the kind of thing that a human in her office, behind her desk, in her chair, wouldn't have heard. But thanks to her keen ears, the Houston-we-have-a-problem was as obvious as a holler.

Whatever. T'Marcus and the new guy were going to have to deal with it.

It was why she'd hired them. Both.

As her head started to pound, she went to rub her face . . .

And froze as only her left hand came up to do the duty.

Glancing down, she saw that her right one was still in her pocket. Still locked on that switchblade.

"Let go," she whispered. "You let go . . . right now."

Instead of releasing her grip, her arm moved on its own, slowly retracting to reveal what was in her hand.

It was not a switchblade.

The tool was about five inches long, with an end like a melon baller. A *lys*. An ancient artifact that was used to remove the eyes of the dead.

Or the living that was soon to be dead.

Xhex's heart began to skip beats. The old weapons weren't seen much anymore, but she was well familiar with them.

And this one had blood on it. That was dried, but still red.

Lungs burning, she dropped the length with hor-

ror on the desk next to the light-show laptop, and
the way it clanged made the hairs on the back of her
neck stand up.

"Calm down . . . fucking calm . . . down . . . —"

In slow motion, she watched from a distance
as she reached out and pulled open the thin
drawer underneath the desktop. The key that she
didn't want to use was in the way back, on the
right, behind blank envelopes that would never
be put in the mail, brochures from the furniture
company they'd used to kit out the VIP section
with booths, and miscellaneous scissors, paper
clips, and pens that were running low on ink, but
not completely out.

A copper key.

Her feet gave herself a quarter turn on the chair's
rollers. There was a set of drawers off to the side,
and the one on the left on the bottom had a tar-
nished circle under the stainless handle.

The trembling was bad as she went to put the
key in its slot, and it was a while before the copper
found home.

The lock turned easily.

Xhex pulled the drawer out a little, and the
darkness that was revealed was an abyss that had
no end.

A little farther out.

A little more.

Come on, she told herself. There was nothing

in there, just an empty gray interior to match the cheap exterior—

The lidded glass jar was all the way in the back, not making an appearance until there was no more left to pull.

And for a moment—for a split second—Xhex thought there were marbles in the squat, transparent container. Big ones. Aggies—

Gagging, she wrenched away and pulled the wastepaper basket over.

The dinner that Fritz and his staff had pulled together with such gourmet aplomb came up quick. After that . . . there was only dry heaving.

The eyes have it, the voice in her head said.

"Shut the fuck up."

Squeamish? Really? You were the one who wanted to start a collection. Come to think of it, you have something to add to it, don't you.

As she straightened and wiped her mouth on the back of her hand, the argument between patrons was still going on outside her door, but fuck that. She had bigger problems—and they were just about to go nuclear.

With a sense of dread, she reached into the left pocket of her jacket—which she hadn't been aware of having on.

The bundle she took out was fit-in-the-palm size, a red bandana loosely wrapped around something that didn't weigh much.

She told herself to just throw it away. And not under her desk. She needed to go to the dumpster behind the staff entrance. Or maybe head a couple of blocks down to an alley—

The bandana unwrapped itself.

And inside . . . a pair of baby blues.

THIRTEEN

SOMETIMES ALL YOU could do for someone was just be with them. Yes, you wanted to do some heavy lifting with your conversation, make sweeping declarations that framed suffering in a way that made it more bearable. Or maybe you wanted to try a little A-level distraction by telling hot gossip or reliving shared memories. Dumb memes. Recipes.

Sports.

As Lydia sat next to C.P. Phalen's cumulous cloud of a bed, she was drawing blanks on everything. The inspirational stuff. The pseudo-psychology. Definitely the gossip, because she had none, because she knew nobody. She also was never on the Internet and she didn't cook, and sportsball season started when?

And as for any in-common things? Professionally, there was no crossover between the pair of them anymore. Back during the Wolf Study Project era, C.P. Phalen had been the chair of the board, and Lydia, as a biologist specializing in wolf populations, had had some contact with the woman. But the nonprofit had shut down months ago.

Which was what had to happen after the executive director and the head vet died in the process of playing on the dark side of science and money.

On the personal level? Given everything that was going on for C.P., who needed to talk about Daniel's latest bad-news PET scan.

"Thank you," C.P. murmured.

Lydia jerked to attention. "For what?"

"Just being here."

"I've been feeling useless about so much. But the idea I could be any kind of comfort to you helps me."

"Silence can be therapeutic. When you're in good company." C.P. shrugged awkwardly. Then pulled the fleece into her lap, up to her nose. "I tell myself I can still smell him. I wish I had your nose."

As she stroked the navy blue folds, Lydia murmured, "How long have you been in love with him."

"Since the moment I met him, if I'm honest with myself. Naturally, I fought it as long as I could . . . because I was scared of what I felt." A lopsided smile flared and disappeared. "I like control, in case you haven't noticed."

Lydia laughed a little, and motioned around the white room. "I mean, this chaotic color, these patterns. And it's all over the house, too."

"That's me. The chintz queen." C.P. grew serious and then tapped her temple. "He was smart, though. Well, I suppose Gus's IQ speaks for itself. But he didn't want me. He knew . . ."

"Did you tell him how you felt?"

"In a roundabout way. He kept things professional when I would have taken them in a different direction. He was too good for me—"

"Don't say that."

"Oh, but it's true. Just because reality hurts, doesn't mean you should ignore it. In fact, self-preservation is often unpleasant, and when you don't have a lot of time, like I do, you can't afford to waste a moment in delusion."

Lydia wanted to say something along the lines of "We'll find him," but she kept that to herself. Gus's body was what was going to turn up, if anything did, and who needed to be reminded of that?

"Anyway . . ." C.P. yawned in what seemed like an exaggerated way. "I think your man might have the right idea. It's late."

Indeed, Daniel had excused himself an hour ago. Or was it two hours ago? Who the hell knew. He'd been doing his best to hang out in the other super-soft armchair they'd pulled over to the bedside, but after a while, he'd no longer been able to hide the fact that he was falling asleep sitting up.

Lydia shifted her legs out of the tuck they were in. "Do you need anything? Should I call Georgina for you?"

"No, she'll come out the second you're gone. There's a sensor back there that's tied to the door."

"Oh, okay."

"Thanks, though."

After a moment, Lydia nodded, got to her feet, and turned away. At the door, she hesitated again and wasn't sure why. Then again, she could really smell the cancer inside the woman now, and she felt like she should acknowledge that in some way. As with the pregnancy, she had been too distracted at first by what was going on in her own life to notice the subtle changes in scent. But the disease was becoming more and more obvious, almost by the hour.

"The answer is, I don't know."

Lydia jumped and looked back around. "I'm sorry?"

C.P. stared down her fragile body and across the grand bedroom. "I don't know whether I'll try Vita-12b. Funny, it felt safer if Gus was the one giving it to me, which is illogical. The drug doesn't care who is doing its administration. Then again, he would take care of me . . . if something went wrong. Would have, I mean."

During their marathon of silence, Lydia had wondered about that, but how could she ask? Talk about insensitive: *Hey, so you've lost your baby, how 'bout you try that novel agent you cooked up in your lab—if only because maybe it'll help Daniel to take the drug, too. And then my life won't be ruined if it works.*

"That's a decision only you can make," Lydia said. "Get some rest. I'll check in on you later."

What a generic goodbye, she thought as she slipped out.

The kind of thing that took for granted you'd see the person again.

The stairs down to the foyer seemed as long as a trail descending a mountain, and when she got to the bottom, she went over to the guard standing sentry in his alcove.

"I'm just going to get something from the car," she said.

He nodded curtly, and triggered his shoulder-mounted communicator. By the time she reached the heavy door, the lock was sliding free, and as she gripped the wrought iron handle, she sank down into her thighs and put her back into it—except there was no need for the muscle show. The bank-vault-like panel, which was easily as thick as her leg, opened as if it was nothing more than the lid to a bread box.

Outside, she took a deep breath, descended the shallow steps, and proceeded down the passenger side of the Suburban. As she came to the rear hatch, she stopped and stared at the glowing Chevy symbol on the asphalt, a false moon.

Shoving her hand in the pocket of her pants, she took out the key. She'd forgotten she'd had the fob with her.

She'd lied to the guard. There wasn't anything she needed inside the SUV.

Wandering out from under the porte cochere, she looked over the front acreage that skirted the allée of trees guarding the driveway. In the nicer months, the lawn was mowed to golf course precision, the smooth, green nature-made carpet undulating out to the stone wall that ran along the roadside edge of the property. Currently, the landscape was draped in moonlight, everything in shades of blue, from the dull French gray of the ground cover, now dead, to the icy bright, skeletal branches, and the sapphire shadows thrown by the big trunked maples down by the road. This nocturnal palette wasn't going to last long. Over to the east, along the horizon, a glow was just beginning to appear—

The flare of light came with such intensity that she was not just blinded, but assaulted by the burst of illumination.

Throwing both arms up to cover her eyes, she got nowhere with the blocking, her retinas continuing to burn in spite of the barriers.

Then again, what she was seeing had nothing to do with the coming sun, or anything that was part of the real world.

"No . . ." she moaned. "Oh, God . . . no—"

Stumbling back, she squeezed her lids shut behind the double bars of her forearms—and though she knew there was no fighting against what had come and found her, she turned away from what she was being forced to see.

For the second time.

"It's not Blade. It's not him. It's not . . ."

As she repeated the denial over and over again, there was no forgetting what her superstitious Finnish grandfather had always told her, no denying the truth that had already come to her once: According to the ancient traditions, if you wanted to see your past, you went out into the gloaming, that sacred time between sunset and true darkness, and waited for the light to find you.

And if it was your future that you were seeking, the moment right before the dawn was the time—

"I am not seeking anything!" she called out. "I don't care about the future—I don't want the future!"

She had already seen Blade surrounded by the illumination.

He . . . was her future. And unless the universe had changed its mind, the *symphath* tormenter was somehow on the property again—

Lydia started back for the house's entry in a blind sprint.

She did not get far.

When the wind abruptly changed directions, the scent of fresh blood speared through the chaos and panic of her mind, and yanked her body to a halt. The illumination was still there, still blinding her— even though she was no longer facing the source—

and she could sense the *symphath*'s presence, looming in her wake. The blood, though . . .

"*Gus?*" she gasped as she wheeled back around.

Lowering her arms, she blinked fiercely—and could not comprehend what was coming toward her across the frost on the ground.

In the midst of the brilliance that threw no shadows and carried not one inch into the lunar-lit landscape, Blade's body and red robes were an unmistakable black silhouette in the center of the halo. But unlike before, he was not alone.

In his arms . . . he carried a lifeless body.

"Gus!" she screamed as she started to run.

The *symphath* was still a good distance off, a hundred yards at least. And the instant she called out and started racing toward him, toward the light, he stopped and stared at her.

As she closed in, his face became clearer to her, his expression locked into a mask that gave nothing away. And then, without a word, he bent down and laid out the remains on the lawn.

There was so much blood on Gus's corpse that it glistened.

Blade straightened, looked at her one last time—and then he seemed to bow to her. After that, he was gone. Into thin air.

And he took the strange, holy light with him.

"*Gus,*" she choked out as she skidded up to the body.

Falling to her knees, her breath coming out in cloud bursts, she pulled Gus into her lap. With tears falling, she arched over him and wept for so much more than the death of a compassionate healer—

The cough wasn't much. And at first, she thought she was the one who'd made the sound. But when it happened again and she realized it wasn't her, she straightened a little.

Gus's head had fallen back on her arm, and for a split second, the sight of his bruised and battered face was so horrific, she couldn't think of what had gotten her attention.

But then his mouth, slack and open, clicked. As if his tongue had moved.

Lydia looked down at his bare, blood-slicked chest. By some miracle . . . the ribs expanded and contracted weakly.

"You're alive?" Disbelief warred with confusion. But then she snapped to attention, whipped her head up, and screamed, "Heeeeeeeelp! Help me! Heeelp—!"

Whether it was from security monitoring, or her yelling, a guard came bolting out of the house, his hand locked on his communicator as he appeared to be barking orders into it.

"He's alive!" she hollered. "He's *alive* . . ."

◆ ◆ ◆

Lying in bed, Daniel heard the commotion out in the front of the house, and the scramble and voices were so loud, there was no mistaking that something was happening—and anyway, he'd been waiting for another dramatic interruption. After he'd left Lydia and C.P. up in that bedroom-oh-wait-maybe-it's-an-ICU, he'd come down to find some sleep, but that hadn't gone far. The sense that another shoe was about to drop had been like a prowler in the room with him.

And here it is, he thought, as he shuffled to his feet and went for his cane.

The magnitude of what was going on became apparent as soon as he opened the door: There was what sounded like a squadron of guards moving around out by the front entrance. But no alarms. No shooting.

So it wasn't an attack. Or at least . . . not one that had reached the interior of the house yet.

In the foyer, the front door was open and four guards were standing in it, with guns drawn. As he came up to them, he expected an argument when went outside, but they just let him pass—and the lack of attention they paid to him was a loud-and-clear that he was too slow and infirm to be a concern. If they needed him out of the way, they'd move him. If they wanted him to stop, they'd hook his arm. If he got hurt? He was dying anyway.

Now he knew what being an eighty-year-old was like.

Heading under the overhang, he worked his way around the SUV and—

Lydia and a guard were closing in at a fast pace, and they were sharing a load: A body was strung between their arms.

Gus.

But why were they rushing? Dead bodies had no timeline to worry about—

"Excuse me," someone said as they brushed him aside.

He barely caught his balance before he was hit by another person hurrying by him. This time, it was a nurse in scrubs—Georgina, the redhead from upstairs.

"In the house," he heard someone order. "Right on the floor."

All he could do was get out of the way, and he met Lydia's eyes as she shot by him, the medical types hovering around, molecules circling a gravely damaged nucleus. As he watched helplessly, he had a thought that the guard was clearly strong enough to carry the load on his own, but Lydia wasn't letting go of Gus's shoulders—and she stayed with him as they followed orders, putting him out flat on the black-and-white marble tile.

Hitching up his strength, Daniel doubled back

into the house, but he had to pause on the threshold to catch his breath.

It seemed fitting that he watched the assessment happen from the periphery, and as a stethoscope was pressed around the bloody chest, Daniel did his own review of the injuries. Gus had been beaten in the face and head, and there were two-pronged burn marks on the side of his neck, across his abdomen, and along his thighs.

"He's coding—I'm using the defibrillator."

The statement was calm, the doctor who was in charge moving quickly but with deliberation as he pulled over a small red box logo'd with a white heart and an electrical charge symbol.

More duffle bags were brought to the resuscitation as the chest was cleaned quickly by C.P. Phalen's nurse, and pads were stuck to the skin up high by the collarbone and down under the pec. Oddly, the discarded, bloodstained gauze bundles were what came into sharpest focus. They were like blooms fallen from some demonic bouquet, and depending on what square of marble they landed on, they were either offset by a loud white background or consumed by a black one.

"Clear," the doctor said firmly.

All hands were raised, including Lydia's, and there was a little whine as the charge was gathered—then the torso jumped as the electric shock was delivered.

Daniel looked at Lydia. She had been forced to

the sidelines, too, but she wasn't going far. Sitting on her knees, her bloodstained hands were palms-up on her thighs, as if in prayer, and her mouth was parted as she breathed hard. In her pose, she reminded him of the saints in the Catholic tradition, suffering in their piety, sending up an entreaty for aid in their crisis—

"You in or out?"

As the question was presented, Daniel glanced to his left. The guard who'd come up to him was his own height, but had seventy-five pounds of muscle on him, easy. With a square jaw and confrontational stare, it was like he'd been ordered out of the Military Stud handbook.

"I used to be you," Daniel said numbly.

"What the hell are you talking about?"

"Enjoy your health while you have it." Daniel moved himself forward. "And I'll be going in, thanks."

As the door was shut behind him, he noted the whirring sound of the lock being engaged, and then the clapping sound of footfalls on the stairs made him look up. C.P. was racing her descent, her face as white as her sculptures, Gus's fleece like a part of her as opposed to a piece of clothing as she clutched it to her silk dressing gown—

Later, Daniel would wonder what made him do what he did. Maybe it was the impotence that was riding him, the urge of a former operative to come out of involuntary retirement and insert himself as a way to be relevant—but he liked to believe his actions were because he wanted to do good, and for sure that was part of it.

Moving faster than he should have been able to, he rushed over and snagged the woman's arm at the base of the steps, forcing her to stop.

Phalen yanked so hard, she nearly took them both off their feet. "Let me go—"

He leaned in and spoke with urgency. "You gotta change the lock coding system."

"What?"

"To this place and the lab. Everything." He squeezed her forearm because his voice was not as strong as he wanted and he didn't know how else to communicate the importance of what he was saying. "Even if you have a system in place that cycles in new numerical sequences, you need to switch it immediately, and cancel all the pass cards—better yet, just lock us all down."

"What are you—"

He lowered his tone. "Gus was interrogated. And there is no way he didn't give things up. It's not about willpower or allegiance or how strong his mind was. No civilian can withstand that kind of sensory assault, and he was worked on for hours."

C.P. opened her mouth. Closed it.

"Trust me," Daniel said softly as a tear escaped

her eye. "Maybe your men are already working on it, but you need to assume that this property and the lab are no longer secure. I know that you are worried about Gus, I get it. But he's under this roof now, too. You want to give him the best chance to survive? Make sure that nobody—or nothing—gets in here."

There was a long pause—or perhaps it was just a nanosecond.

"Fucking hell," C.P. whispered.

Without another word, she changed her trajectory and went over to her guards, bypassing the medical event in the center of the space.

Absently, Daniel noted the way the diaphanous skirt of her robe moved like mist around her bare ankles and feet.

And then he wasn't thinking about her.

He was going to Lydia, easing himself down beside her on the cold, hard floor . . . and taking her hand.

"Is he going to be okay," she mumbled as Gus's heart was hit with a second charge.

While the man's palms clapped on the marble, Daniel focused on the black-and-red burn mark on the side of that neck. Instead of answering her, he let his mind go, the wheels of intention starting to turn.

He might not be physically strong. But as he regarded the battered body of his dear friend and doctor—and did the math on how long and how much Gus had suffered?

There was a clear mission: Daniel was going to figure out how to get to the person who did this.

And if he couldn't deal with them, he was going to make sure someone else did.

FOURTEEN

CATHY STAYED WITH Gus through everything: The resuscitation on her foyer floor. The trip on the gurney down into the lab. The assessment in the main examination room, and the running of various drugs, the names of which were familiar to her, the precise mechanisms of their molecular makeup unknown to her. After that? The waiting. The endless waiting...

To see if the efforts to support his heart rate, oxygenation, blood volume, and blood pressure worked.

Beep. Beep. Beep . . .

The sound of the monitor counting cardiac compressions was the only sound in the room, assuming the soft whistling of the HVAC vent overhead didn't count. Finally, after such flurries of activity, she and Gus were alone, even if just for a moment. The doctors and nurses would be back soon enough, and it was a toss-up whether she wanted them around or not. If they were in the room? He could get help in seconds if his heart stopped again. But like anybody was all that far?

She glanced at the monitor by his head. Measured the fluid in the bag that was draining into his vein. Tried not to look at his face, because it was just too hard.

The litany of injuries was extensive and gruesome: Broken nose, broken ribs, broken fingers. Burn marks that suggested he had been tased in the legs, torso, and the side of the neck. His back, calves, and under his forearms were the only places that hadn't been touched, and that made her think he'd been tied to a chair, sitting up while he'd been tortured.

Gus was interrogated. And there is no way he didn't give things up.

Squeezing her lids shut, she couldn't block the image of his swollen eye sockets or the raw scrape at his temple or his bruised mouth. And when she started to panic, she tried to focus on something, anything else—

The chair under her was hard.

There. That was as much as she could do.

Beneath her bony ass, the seat might as well have been made of granite, and in a pathetic attempt to regain a sense of order and control, she made a mental note to upgrade the furniture accessories in the four patient rooms.

Except then she remembered all the reasons she wasn't going to change a goddamn thing.

How has it all come to this, she wondered as she reached out and took Gus's bandaged hand.

"This was not how we were going to end up, you and me." She gently rubbed her thumb back and forth over the white wrap. "We were going to cure cancer. We were going to . . . change the world. We were going to . . ."

Save my life, she thought.

Considering where she was now—out of money, out of hope, out of time on so many levels—she had to marvel at the sheer arrogance she'd been sporting as she'd moved her underground operation to the property here in Walters, and started working with that vet at the Wolf Study Project. Back then, in what she now thought of as her previous life, she'd been a big swinging dick in the pharmaceutical world, making waves, aware that the Grim Reaper was hot on her trail, but determined to outrun him with Gus's magic drug.

Their Vita-12b.

Twelve versions to get it right. Twelve and a half, actually.

"But you're alive." She put her other hand on her stomach. "And so am I . . ."

For now, she tacked on to herself. And given the cramping in her uterus, her own blood loss, and all the cancer cells in her body, she supposed that was a sliding scale with a steep slope into her grave.

"You know something," she whispered. "That wolven is right. I am in love with you."

Her eyes shot up to Gus's battered face, but he remained unconscious, and she wondered where he was, where that beautiful mind of his had gone to. Was it still in the husk that had been so sorely abused? Or was the damage so great that he was gone, even as his body lived on?

Tears came to her eyes, making the vision of him in the hospital bed go wavy.

"Do you remember where we first met?" She wiped her cheeks and sniffled. "I do. I can recall exactly where we were."

As she spoke softly, she wanted to reach up and caress his face, but that seemed like an invasion of his privacy since she'd never touched him like that when he'd been awake. The closest they'd ever gotten to that kind of line-crossing had been that one time they'd been about to kiss, when she'd finally finished fighting her attraction and he'd looked at her as a woman.

He'd stepped back, though. Stepped away. Stopped . . . everything.

"You were speaking at that symposium on immunology at Stanford." She smiled at the memory, and it felt good to go to a lighter place, back when they'd both been stronger. "All those clinicians and researchers in their ties and jackets, with their somber PowerPoints. And then you took the podium."

She had to wipe her eyes again, and as she drew in a shuddering breath, she smiled through the sadness. "God, I can just picture you taking that stage. You were wearing blue jeans and Converse hightops. You had on a Led Zeppelin t-shirt, with that blimp on it. Those tight-ass bastards were twitching in their seats, whispering under their breath— and you just stood there in those lights, with a half smile on your face because you knew you were smarter than all of them. You didn't care what they thought of you or how much they disapproved of you for all the wrong reasons. You had the mic— and you blew them away. Right out of the water. Your ideas were groundbreaking, your research in its infancy, your career about to begin. I knew then and there . . . I *had* to work with you. I knew you were the one."

Lowering her eyes, she shook her head. "And then you came here. I never expected to be afraid of a living soul, but you rattled me. You, with your concert t-shirts of bands I'd never heard of and your cans of Coke. Everyone looked up to you in the lab. Worshipped you, really. I worshipped you—and I tried distracting myself. I did."

Glancing down at her stomach, she thought of the blond guard she'd slept with for a couple of

months. Who'd then been killed. The pregnancy
had been an impossibility, something that never
should have happened after chemo had cooked her
ovaries.

Something she had never been able to tell the
man about before he'd been murdered on her lawn.

Gus had told her about the baby. The screening
tests for her trial of Vita-12b had revealed everything, and almost instantly, she'd been determined to
keep it—even though that meant she couldn't be patient one for their drug. She'd told herself that a child
would be her legacy, and she'd decided to leave the
baby to Lydia to raise as soon as the cancer got too
far advanced.

Lydia was going to be a great mother someday.
And her broken heart was going to need something
to live for.

Deep down, though, she'd known the pregnancy
couldn't last. She wasn't a genetics expert, but the
chromosomes she'd put into the mix had to be de-
ficient. They just had to be. And . . . they had been.
The miscarriage was all very logical from a medical point of view. The human side of things? That
was proving difficult. For someone who had never
wanted to be pregnant, who wouldn't know what to
do with an infant if she were handed one for just a
hi-hello, she was shocked by the sadness.

She glanced back at Gus's bruised face. "The
baby's gone. If I lose you, too, I'm done . . . I'm

not going out fighting, there's going to be no great show of courage. I'm just going to head up to that bed and lie down and let my cancer take me."

Beep-beep-beep . . .

The heart monitor kept a steady metronome that, instead of reassuring her, just made her anxious for the moment it missed a beat. Like her losing her baby, surely that was going to be the outcome.

"Just so you know," she murmured, "my lawyer insisted I put a reversion clause in that contract giving you Vita. So if you die, she comes back to me. And when I die . . . she's going to disappear with me."

Like the baby. A spark of life, and then gone.

It was a crazy idea anyway. Curing cancer.

What the hell had they been thinking.

"Anyway, I just wanted to say it all out loud once." She laughed in a short burst. "Deathbed confession, really. I love you, Gus. You're the best man I ever met. And in another life, in another time . . . I really think we would have been great together."

◆   ◆   ◆

Up in the first-floor guest suite, Lydia stood in the shower, her head back, the hot jets of water spearing through her hair, the suds of her shampoo running down her spine and puddling on the tile under her feet. On a lot of levels, it seemed inconceivable that she was doing something as normal as having a wash.

She also felt like it was an impermissible self-indulgence.

There was this need to be clean, however . . . as if soaping herself up and having a good rinse could somehow wipe away the images she saw on the backs of her eyelids every time she blinked. Or at least maybe the cleansing would dim the memory of what Gus had looked like, bloodied, bleeding, going into cardiac arrest, on the black-and-white marble floor of the foyer.

The amnesia strategy wasn't working, unfortunately. But her aching body was loosening up so she lingered in the neither-here-nor-there of the warmth and the steam and the scents of sweet-smelling products that were familiar to her.

Which were nice things to focus on. As opposed to whether Gus would live, and how Daniel was doing . . . and the light she had seen around Blade—

Cranking the faucet off with a jerk, she stepped out.

"Towel?" Daniel said as he held one out.

"Thank you."

Instead of giving the terrycloth to her, he stepped forward and wrapped her up, not just in the softness, but in his arms. And what do you know. As she leaned into him, she didn't care about drying off.

This time, as she closed her eyes and breathed in deep, she saw nothing. She was too busy feeling him.

"I need to stop thinking," she whispered. "I really . . . want to be with you. Make love to me?"

"Always."

Tucking the towel around her, he took her hand and led her into the bedroom. They hadn't turned the lamps or the overhead fixture on, and with the glow from the bath, things were almost candlelit. When they got to the bed, he unwrapped her body and patted the duvet.

"My hair is all wet."

"And I'm going to take care of that."

As she sat down, she looked up at him. His expression was rapt as he brought the towel to her head and began to massage her still-dripping waves. The motion was hypnotic and she swayed as his big hands went back and forth, back and forth, her breasts following the movement, the tightening tips brushing against the waistband of his jeans.

Thinking of what was behind his fly, she ached for what he once had, but she couldn't let that sadness take over.

Here and now, she reminded herself. This was what they had.

And it was good.

Daniel dropped the towel to the floor and stared down at her. He had a slight smile to his mouth, one that was anticipation wrapped up in a tilt to the lips, and as he bent to kiss her on the forehead, she put her hands on his hips.

"It's okay to stop thinking." He brushed his fingers through her damp hair, capturing it and twisting the weight into a rope that he laid down on her spine. "The crisis will be there in the morning. It doesn't mean you don't care about what happens to him."

"You always know what to say to me, don't you."

Holding on to the bedside table for balance, he lowered himself to his knees. "Close your eyes."

She followed the command, and took a deep breath.

"When was the last time I told you how beautiful you are?"

Lydia laughed a little and looked at him again. "It's pretty often. You spoil me."

"Just speaking my truth. Now shut those eyes . . . and feel me."

The first thing she was rewarded with was a brush on her cheek. His fingertip. And then it traveled slowly to her jaw and followed around to her lower lip. Back and forth the caress went, as a kiss would, until her mouth parted when she gasped— and as if she'd given him the response he'd been waiting for, the touch continued on. Now . . . it was on the side of her throat, moving to her collarbone. Oh, God, she knew where he was heading and her nipples peaked even further—

Except he went between her breasts, that hovering touch tracing her sternum.

"I'm such a lucky man," he said hoarsely.

Her lids flipped open; she couldn't help herself. It was the hunger in his voice, and sure enough, he was staring at her body with his eyes at half-mast, a very masculine expression of need on his face.

"Look at you." His fingertip continued on to her belly button. "You make me feel like a man."

Reaching out, she put her hands on his face and tilted it back so their eyes met. "That's because you are one."

She pressed her lips to his, and he kissed her back, licking his way into her mouth. The sensations were achingly familiar, and yet new every time, the warmth and the slick plying a kind of drug that relaxed the tension in her shoulders—and relocated it in a coil in her gut.

"Close your eyes some more," he murmured. "Feel me . . ."

Giving herself over to him, she trembled as he followed the path of where his finger had gone with his lips, kissing her jaw, her throat . . . that collarbone. Her breath got unbearably tight as the whispering nuzzles went between her breasts.

There was a pause. That seemed to last a hundred years.

"Please," she begged.

"Well, when you put it like that, so politely . . ."

Her gasp was loud as he dropped the slow-and-sweet and went right to licking her nipple. He did that again, his tongue laving up the taut tip, and then he sucked her into his mouth. While he worked her, his hands moved to the undersides of both breasts and he pressed them together. Then it was a case of back and forth, from one to the other, the pulls and releases teasing her and satiating her by turns.

All she knew was Daniel. The sensations were so good, grounding her in the present between them, shutting out the world for a short period of time. And he knew that she needed this respite. Sleep was going to be impossible, but this erotic reset? It was going to give her the break she needed.

So she could face whatever was waiting for them on the other side of their bedroom door, on the other side of this intense slice of privacy.

He took his time with her breasts.

When he finally retracted his mouth, she moaned in protest, and he laughed softly. "Lie back."

She obeyed without hesitation—and was gifted with his broad, warm palms on the tops of her thighs. Going slowly, he stroked his way up to her hip bones and rubbed his thumbs over the wings of her pelvis—and then he was parting her knees.

His lips were a soft, searching caress on the inside of one and then the other. Nipping her with his teeth, he licked away the tingle—and this was the way he moved higher and higher to the core of her. In response, she was all liquid for him, the heat redoubling in her sex as he closed in with aching deliberation—

Out of rank frustration, she lifted one leg and let it fall out to the side on the mattress, exposing all of herself to his eyes. His touch.

His mouth.

The air was cool against her, and the anticipation made her lungs burn.

"I'm going to taste you," he drawled.

Except he didn't. He just nuzzled into the thigh she'd angled so wide.

"*Daniel . . .*"

"Hmm?" He lifted his head, lips trailing up and off her skin. "Oh, sorry. You're right. I'm losing focus."

But instead of sealing his mouth on her, his hands went to her breasts, cupping them, thumbing her nipples. And meanwhile, he was still on her thigh—

Rolling her hips, she begged him again. Or at least that was her intention. Some sounds were certainly coming out of her, rising up her throat and hitting the sexually charged airwaves between them—but she couldn't recognize the words. Maybe her hearing was going?

"Now I want you to look at me."

As his voice registered, her lids popped open and she lifted her head.

Daniel was staring up at her from between her thighs, and when their eyes met, he extended his tongue, dropped his head . . . and lapped right up the center of her. Then he went back and did it again. And a third time with the stroke—

Now, he licked all the way free, the sight of his slick tongue leaving her sex sending her right over the edge.

The orgasm swept through her and she let herself feel all of it: The delicious snapping release, the rhythmic pulses deep inside of her, the fulfillment—

He entered her with his fingers, the penetration stretching her. "Keep coming for me—"

"Again . . . ?" she said hoarsely.

"Yes, again. Always—"

Part of that last word was absorbed by her flesh, the vibration teasing the top of her slit.

After that, there wasn't any more talking.

His mouth was busy doing other things.

And she was busy gasping his name.

FIFTEEN

"S O YOU WANT to tell me why you need to know about this?"

As Vishous, son of the Bloodletter, tossed that query over the proverbial transom, he sat down behind his Four Toys and swiveled his office chair away from the bank of computers. Sitting across the Pit's shallow living area, like the pair of them were waiting to be called into a doctor's office—or hell, the school principal's—Xhex and John Matthew were staring at him like they had no intention of opening their mouths to answer the question anytime soon.

Okay, fine, so maybe it was more a dentist's.

V shook his head and reached for a hand-rolled. "Yeah, not how this is going to go. I want to know why you're asking about these murders in Caldwell. You want to stay quiet? Fine. But I'm not finna do shit for you."

John Matthew looked down at his hands as if he wanted to use them to sign something, but was determined to let his mate do the talking. Which meant whatever this was had to do with Xhex. And if she was asking about corpses without their eyes?

Then Rehv was right. She was out in Caldwell killing civilians.

But you'd think that would be the kind of thing the female would remember . . .

In the dense quiet, Xhex sat back into the black leather sofa, the cushions creaking in a biker's-jacket kind of way. As she glanced around, her body was tense, and he wondered if she wasn't going to spring off the couch and start doing laps around the Foosball table—or head into the galley kitchen and help herself to some of his Grey Goose. The latter wasn't going to be a tough target. He'd left a fresh bottle on the counter from having poured himself a little wake-up juice.

Which was what you did when you got a chopped-up text in the middle of the day from an otherwise tight-headed female: *Cn u talk rt now?*

The *bing!* had woken both him and Doc Jane, and courtesy of his *shellan*'s medical career in level-one trauma, and him having been in the Black Dagger Brotherhood for over three centuries, it was insta-wake time, both of them up and fully functioning. He'd texted back a *Yup* and kissed his mate—who was so used to interrupted sleep that she'd been back on the pillow and in dreamland before he'd even pulled on some PJ bottoms.

"Well?" He put the hand-rolled between his front teeth and lit it with a red Bic. "What we got?"

As he spoke through the exhale, the familiar scent of fine Turkish tobacco wafted up around his head, and he brought his ashtray closer. To move things along, he tapped his keyboard, just to remind them of all the data he could be getting for them.

Xhex rubbed her face like she had a vise screwed onto her temples. "I think I might have done . . . some things at work."

V cocked an eyebrow because he felt like pretending he was surprised might get her to loosen up. You know, all *You? Getting violent in a club where humans and vampires hell-bent on making bad choices did drugs and drank alcohol until they went off the chain and needed some consequential learning they maybe didn't wake up from? Naaaaaaaaaaaaaaaaaaah.*

Yeah, he needed his Larry David face for this news flash.

"Can you be a little more specific?"

"It was in the last, say, six months." She glanced at John. "And that's all I know for sure."

"We talking our kind? Or rats without tails."

"Our kind. Them. Maybe both."

172 J. R. WARD

"You don't remember?"

John was the one to answer that with a curt shake of the head.

And then Xhex said, "No eyes. They won't . . . have any eyes."

And the female was known for using the *lys*.

"Okaaaaaaay, I think we'll start there," V murmured, as he swiveled back and fired up his Four Toys. "Let me see what I got on our side first."

Until recently, like within the last couple of years, the vampire population had been on its own. No objective justice meted out for crimes. No place to vet disputes within bloodlines or with neighbors. No mating or birth certifications. But ever since Wrath had finally taken the throne, a system of public records had been established. V and Saxton had created the census table of names, aliases, birth dates—if known—and dates of deaths along with the cause. There was also a Notes section, and he searched under the word "eyes." Because he couldn't remember whether he had used "removed," "lost," or "taken out."

"Lost," like they'd rolled out of the skull?

"What are you seeing?" Xhex demanded as he started reading through the search results.

V took a drag and glanced over to the sofa. "Two a week or so ago. And one—"

"Last night?" When he nodded, she cursed. "What was . . . what happened? With that."

"He was found in an alley off Market." V tapped his hand-rolled as he scrolled down. "Tohr happened to be patrolling that quadrant and he was able to intercede as the police arrived on scene. Ligature marks around the neck, eyes had been removed. Body was taken to our morgue down in the garage and we're still looking for next of kin. There was a human world ID on the guy, but the fake name isn't registered with us."

"So some family is out there waiting for him to come home."

As V moved up to the first of the entries, there was a series of shifting hand positions as John Matthew communicated with his mate.

"The two last week," V said, "were found downtown. Both males. No eyes, ligature marks." He frowned. "Oh, shit . . ."

Xhex jerked forward. "What."

"So this first guy has a reference link to my criminal database." He clicked on the link. "Let's see—okay. Yeah . . ."

"Yeah, what?"

Just as she was getting to her feet, V whistled under his breath. "Looks like you did us a favor."

◆　◆　◆

Going to stand behind Vishous, Xhex looked over his heavy shoulder, intending to read whatever was on the screen. That was a no-go. Her eyes bounced all around the different screens, refusing to light on the one in the center that had columns of information on it.

"This was no male of worth." V scrolled down. "Breaking and entering on his *grandmahmen*. He just robbed her, but the next month, he pulled the same stunt and battered his cousins during the home invasion—and here's some domestic violence against his live-in GF. Twice—no, three times on the DV. Oh . . . fuck."

"What?" She blinked and tried to focus on the words.

As John Matthew likewise whistled in an ascension, V shook his head. "The female didn't survive the most recent attack. The guy was on the run—although what the hell was he doing in that club if he wanted to stay gone."

"What was his name?" she demanded.

"Ero."

"And where was he found?"

"Again, it was Market Street in an alley. Rehv was the one who called him in to us. Apparently some civilians came to him about it."

She thought back to the spring and the confrontation she'd had with Rehv at the club. He'd been right about her grid. She'd been arrogant. And people had died.

Then again, why wouldn't a lack of self-awareness come with your entire consciousness collapsing?

"Do you have a picture of . . ." Her voice drifted off.

Vishous rode his mouse and clicked on something. "Here."

The image that came up was in full color, the flash cutting through the darkness of the night scene. The body was on its back and dressed in clothes that were off-kilter following a skirmish, the arms out to the sides, the boots lax at the ends of the legs. She couldn't see the neck clearly given the collar of the jacket, but the damage to the eyes was nothing you could miss: Empty sockets with not a lot of blood, the removal a clean job.

Like the killer had done it a time or two.

Given the angle of the image, she was guessing it had been taken by a cell phone, and she wondered whether it was Rehv's or from one of the Brothers who'd shown up to deal with the mess she'd created.

V glanced up at her. "You want to go on to the next?"

She nodded in a numb way, and after a series of screen changes, they were back at the first table. This time, she could speed-read, and a riding anxiety made her remember every single word. When she got to the end, she let out a deep breath.

"I want to see the picture."

"Roger that."

The second victim was much the same. Club

clothes, this time lying on his stomach, but the head was turned to the side so that the sockets were staring off at the back exit of some brick building.

"So you've decided to play Equalizer, huh?" V remarked.

It was the same story. A male with a history of extreme violence, multiple complaints from people inside his bloodline and outside of it, who was clearly a danger to vampires and humans alike.

"Don't pat me on the back." She returned and sat with John Matthew. "Not at all."

Goddamn it, she didn't remember ever seeing the males before. "What about a picture from last night?"

"I don't have one yet."

John Matthew put his palm on her back and rubbed her shoulders. She didn't want to look at him, except when she finally did, his face was grave, but not hiding disgust or anything. He was as he always had been, blue-eyed, dark-haired, strong-jawed—steady. At her six. No matter what.

"So I've got a question for you," the Brother said over at the desk. "What the fuck's going on?"

All she could do was shake her head. Back in the spring, she'd been so sure that when her nightmares had stopped—all that waking up on the attack, John having to hold her back, hold her down— she'd turned a corner in a good way, taken a positive step toward the kind of mental health that had always been out of reach for her, no matter how good things were going. Hell, even her aggression had improved at the club. She'd been proud of how much better she'd been tolerating the stupid—

Your grid is collapsing.

"I need a favor," she heard herself say to Vishous. "I need . . . your help at sundown."

SIXTEEN

THE HOSPITAL SMELL was what brought him around.

Later, Gus would amend things into something romantic, but the truth of it was . . . that signature antiseptic-behind-the-fake-Florida scent was the trailhead he followed out of his darkness. At first, he hadn't been able to track what had kindled his consciousness. One moment he was lights-out; the next, he had some awareness, his brain's neuropathways starting to cough up a couple of signals.

And then he recognized the telltale hospital fragrance. *Citrus II Germicidal Deodorizing Cleaner.*

Which, according to the label—that he was somehow able to visualize—met the Occupational Safety and Health Administration's blood-borne pathogen standards for HIV, HBC, HCV, and HAV . . . —

Wait . . . what was he thinking about? Lemons . . . ?

As his body floated along in a buffered state of

numbness, his mind was like a kitten with a ball of string, batting back and forth with the smell thing, the label thing, and the intersections both had with his past. Except where was he in his own timeline? Was he in med school? First year during gross human anatomy? Or no . . . third and fourth year during core rotations when he was actually in a hospital, making rounds of the different departments even though he'd decided when he was ten years old he was going to be an oncologist . . .

How about residency at MGH? Or no, fellowship there? Or when he was a working doctor and a researcher in a lab, teasing out the molecular successes and failures of weaponizing the human immune system against rogue cells, the official names of which all ended in -oma.

Or was it more recently, when he—

As if the cognitive sifting was the choke to Gus's internal engine, his eyes flipped open. Not that he got much from the lid lift. Everything was bright and blurry, like he was in a cloud. Was this Heaven in the Hallmark sense?

Beeping. Behind him.

Oh, he knew that sound. A heartbeat, nice and steady, if a little slow.

So this had to be Earth, and he was the patient, wasn't he? Had he been in a car accident or a—

A blurry face appeared in the indistinct visual

soup, and he recognized who it was because of the crop of blond hair. And then came a voice. The voice.

Her voice.

Catherine Phillips Phalen said roughly, "Oh, my God . . . you're alive."

"Gus is the name," he croaked. "Not God. God's more of . . . a job description."

There was a pause. Then a chuckle. Then something soft and warm, a drop, hit his cheek. A tear? Was it hers . . . was it his . . .

"You really are back," she whispered.

"Where . . . 'd . . . I go?"

"Don't worry about that."

"Feel . . . shit."

"Yes, I would imagine you do."

As much as he wanted to communicate, the conversation was pulling too much energy away from him, his lids drifting back down, his breathing suddenly feeling laborious.

"Don't know . . . happened."

"You're safe," she said. "That's all you need to think about right now."

"Missed you . . ."

There was another pause, and the image of the great C.P. Phalen, in one of her sleek power suits and those fucking high heels that made her legs long as a mile, was as clear as if she were standing in front of him and he was up-on-his-Converse-high-tops and a-okay.

He needed to stop talking—

"I missed you, too . . ." Something brushed his forehead. Her hand? Please let it be her hand. "Don't leave me again."

Had he left her? He couldn't remember. But he knew one thing. There was pain in that steely voice of hers . . . so much pain.

"Okay," he replied to the statement that was really a question. "I won't, Cathy."

◆   ◆   ◆

As Cathy pulled a Kleenex free of a box on the bedside table, she wiped her eyes and reflected on how much she had always hated that name.

Recently, however, she had embraced the honesty that came with it. She had been born in the middle class and had never been anything fancy growing up; so when it had become time to reinvent herself, she had clothed her modest origins in the mantle of Catherine—or even better, the androgyny of her initials, C.P. But now, especially coming out of the mouth it did?

She was ready to get the five letters tattooed on her forehead.

Wadding up the tissue in a fistful of relief, she wanted to touch Gus all over to reassure herself he was alive for real—as if, were she to confirm the warmth of him, it was a predicator that he would stay with her. But that was magical thinking, for one thing. And then there was the horrifying reality that there was almost no part of him that wasn't bruised.

Taking what she could get, she satisfied herself with brushing his temple, his jawline, the lobe of his ear. She told herself he liked her touch. She didn't know whether that was true.

As Gus stayed quiet, his mouth parted and he breathed shallowly. He was clearly drifting off again, and she had a spear of fear that this was it, the final surge of life before he passed. Weren't things always most vivid right before death? She had read that somewhere. That the mortally wounded, the mortally diseased, had a second wind right before the grave came for them.

Would she have one? she wondered. Would he be there for her when she did?

Trying to find solace in the monitoring machine's steady rhythm and lack of alarms, she reminded herself that they were surrounded—literally—by doctors and nurses. All she had to do was open that door and shout down the hall to that great open area of workstations.

The cavalry would come running—

The knock was quiet, and she didn't look away from Gus's face as she answered it with a *Come in.* Out of the corner of her eye, two people registered as they entered, but she was too consumed by the eyelashes that curled up tightly from Gus's shut lids.

Also, she was willing him to reopen his eyes.

"Did he wake up or something?"

At the astonished male voice, she jerked to attention. "Oh . . . hello. Welcome."

As if she were a greeter at Home Depot.

Daniel and Lydia were standing at the foot of the bed, all kinds of shock showing on their faces—this time, for a good reason.

"Yes, he's back," Cathy said to the person they all cared so much for. "Aren't you, Gus. Gus?"

When he didn't respond, toxic terror clawed her in the throat—but then his head nodded up and down on the flat pillow.

Daniel said something. Lydia said something. But the syllables bled into a sound salad she didn't bother sorting into its components . . .

She was not a God person. The whole Christian tradition she'd been raised in hadn't survived her eighteen-year-old emancipation as she'd left that small town for college, and the further and further into the sciences and pharmaceutical business she'd gotten, the more and more of a secularist she'd become.

Yet as her eyes roamed around Gus's misshapen face, she found herself thanking . . . someone up above. The fact that he was alive after what had been done to him?

Miracles go . . . and miracles come. Back.

As her hand went to her lower abdomen, the

hollow loss was in her uterus, and in her heart, profound and deep as any void in the galaxy. But there was a rejuvenation, too. A lifting of the spirit that came when life, previously thought of as unrelentingly unfair, proved that there was more balance than one had assumed. Straddling the two extremes of hope and mourning was a split of emotions that consumed her, and maybe that was why she was thinking about God. Believing in some guy in a white robe standing in a set of pearly gates was easier to handle.

Easier to reconcile.

"When?" Lydia asked. "When did he come around?"

"Just a minute ago." Cathy touched the top arch of his Afro. There was debris in it and she wanted to wash his hair for him. "And only for a moment, but he's in here. He's still with us."

In the back of her mind, some kind of ringer went off—and glancing over at the couple, she focused on Daniel. She had something she needed to tell . . . one of them. She looked at Lydia. Or was it both of them?

"Ah . . ."

As she just stared stupidly, Daniel frowned. "You want me to go get a doctor?"

"He is one." Cathy went back to focusing on the bed. "He's the best doctor."

Then again, it was entirely possible that if the

guy had talked about a plumber, she'd have main-tained that Gus was an expert at PVC pipe instal-lation. Electrician? In the union. Librarian? Worked in the congressional one.

"Is there anything we can get you?"

She lost track of who was talking, but then one of them said it was time to go—

"Wait," she heard herself interrupt.

When the couple looked at her with concern—like they were both thinking of hitting the call but-ton on her behalf—she put her hand to the side of her head. And then . . . she remembered.

"Will you stay with him for a minute?" she asked the wolven. "Please?"

By way of answer, Lydia pulled a chair up and sat right down like she was prepared to wait out a cen-tury if that's what was required.

"Thank you," Cathy said.

"Anything. For him . . . for you."

Cathy put her hand over her heart. And then she indicated the door with an incline of her head, and Daniel followed her out, the panel closing behind them. The hall they were in was private—in the sense that there was no one in it. But perco-lating down from the open area, there was all kinds of talking and walking across the concrete floors. Phones ringing. Machines whirring.

The lab was very much alive. For now.

Like her. Like Daniel.

The financial engine that kept it going was nearly out of gas, however. The money was nearly all gone, and she supposed it was a sign of personal growth that she wasn't worried about that anymore. Or maybe she was just admitting failure.

"This way," she said.

She led him farther down the corridor, and when she got to the last door on the left, she put her hand on the cool panel and stopped.

"You stroking out on me?"

Cathy glanced over her shoulder. "That's a bit harsh, don't you think."

"True. But considering how many people are hanging by a thread around here, can you blame me?"

"No."

Opening the door, she felt her breath get caught, and between one blink and the next, she saw the office not as it was now, empty of all personal effects, but rather as it had been, with Gus's basketball jerseys and sports memorabilia.

Funny, how his things had been windows that looked into a vista she loved. Without them, the space was claustrophobic with its generic furniture and bare walls.

"He really did leave," Daniel commented.

"But he's back now." Feeling the need to rush, she went across and opened one of the side drawers of the desk. "Oh, good."

"Huh?"

Feeling foolish, she held up a Rubik's Cube. "He, ah, he left this behind. The cleaning staff found it in the corner over there. It was the only thing he left behind and I saved it for him."

She stopped herself there because it was kind of a lie. She had been the one to find the toy, but admitting she'd come down here and sat in his chair, and wrapped his fleece around herself, and idly gone through the empty desk, was an admission she preferred to keep to herself.

Daniel's stare dropped to the colorful cube, with its patchwork of primary colors. "I never could do those things. Can't play chess, either."

"You're good at a lot of other things."

He shrugged. "So what's up, Phalen."

"I wanted you to know that the entire facility, aboveground and below, is on lockdown." She idly twisted the levels, the reds, blues, greens, and yellows, shifting around, trading places yet not aligning. "No pass cards, no codes. Entrance granted on a case-by-case basis by guard staff, which I've doubled. And before you ask, all of the men on the shifts have worked for me for the last five years. If they were part of the abduction, they would have struck by now."

"You sure about that."

"At this point, as sure as I can be about anything."

"What else is on your mind."

"Nothing—"

"Bullshit. If you only had to tell me about the security, you could have done it right outside that room. So why are we down here."

After a moment, she put the cube on the desktop, lowered her chin, and stared out from under her brows. "If you insist on accurately guessing my secrets, I may have to break off our friendship."

Daniel chuckled. "You're tougher than that."

"Yes. I am." Unleashing the hatred she'd been sucking down into her chest, she said in a low voice, "We are going to get this taken care of, you and me."

The man's eyes narrowed.

"You know what I am saying, Daniel Joseph."

"Yeah, maybe." That cane was lifted up, as if he were reminding her of it. "You got a staff full of guards who don't have stage-four lung cancer. Why me?"

"Two reasons." With a steady hand, she tapped the toy. "You care about Gus more than they do. And I can trust you in ways I can't them."

"I thought you said that everyone's worked for you for five years, blah, blah, blah."

"I did. But this is . . . different. This is personal to me."

In the silence that followed, Daniel's eyes shifted to the Rubik's Cube. As an expression of calculation sharpened his features, he nodded to himself—as if he'd come up with an idea he thought was a good one.

"Fair enough," he murmured. "I accept the assignment, even if it kills me."

Cathy extended her palm. "I can pay you."

Worse came to worst, she could sell one of her paintings. Or some of those sculptures in her foyer.

"Nah. This is pro bono. 'Cuz I owe Gus—and because I'd decided to go after the fucker who did this anyway."

As Daniel shook what was offered, his eyes gleamed with a darkness that might have scared even her—if she hadn't wanted to see exactly that kind of banked aggression. And this was why she needed Daniel. He was a dying man with nothing to lose, and this would be his final act.

People did their best work when it was their legacy—and as a secondary benefit, she had the sense the purpose would keep him alive a little longer.

When they released their grips, Daniel said, "I do have a favor to ask."

Cathy looked toward the door. "Yes, of course. I will take care of her for however long I have."

Daniel closed his eyes. Then he squeezed Cathy's shoulder, put the business end of his cane back on the floor, and hobbled out.

As the door eased shut behind him, Cathy

glanced around. Then she walked over to the smooth Sheetrock of the wall and touched a solitary picture-hanging hook that had been left behind.

She wanted those framed jerseys back where they'd been.

And the man who owned them back at the desk.

And in her life.

"What do you say, God," she murmured. "What do I have to do to get a prayer answered ..."

SEVENTEEN

AS BLADE GLIDED along the underground polished-stone corridors of the *symphath* colony, he had the hood up on his red robing. With his arms linked over his pecs and his leather slip shoes making no sound, he imagined himself as nothing but a chromatic shadow in the candlelight, a pattern without substance, a transparency the color of an apple.

The mental projection was so resonant, so complete, that he in fact became what he told himself he was.

Nothing.

The transmutation was a practiced shift of his corporeal existence, and as his consciousness retreated behind the vault he created, he thought of the wolven. Her sex was not the right sort for him. He did not favor females. But his attraction went so much deeper than body parts.

His reaction to her was extraordinary because she was extraordinary.

Unlike all the males and men he had ever slept with, he had a kinship with her that was both in the flesh—

Stop it, he told himself.

The illusion needed to be maintained down even into his innermost thoughts in case he met any of his kind. And not just on account of what he was doing. The projection was necessary for there was nothing to be trusted in this labyrinth of ant-like passages, even in one's private quarters—

As he came to a corner he could not see around, he felt a vibration of warning go up his spine, the signal subtle, but the kind of thing that, like his constant preoccupation with the wolven, had to be immediately quelled.

Steeling himself, he followed the curve, and there it was: The male was far older than he, the stride uneven from rickety joints, the back bowed with age, the head tilted at an angle as if the neck couldn't be properly straightened. So the *symphath* was so much more dangerous than one Blade's age. In contrast to the usual course of things, whereby advancing age was associated with weakness, elders were a worse threat as they had wisdom and experience to enhance their manipulative tendencies.

On the approach, Blade made a point to turn his face toward the male. The last thing you wanted to do was avoid eye contact, as the perceived submission could be an invitation to mischief. But you did not want to stare too long, either, as that would be interpreted as aggression and present an interesting challenge if the other was up to it. Thus, among "polite" society—which did not exist herein and was more a term of art referring to the citizenry—there was a perfect interlude of acknowledgment, two seconds or so. After which, if both parties were disinclined to engage, gazes would resume forward facing—

The elder's lingered for a moment too long.

Has my mask slipped? Blade wondered.

Instantly, he halted that consideration. And he could not look over his shoulder to see if the passing had been completed or whether the older other had about-faced and changed his course.

Approaching another turn in the subtly lit passageway, Blade prepared to glance to the right in a manner that was just slightly more exaggerated than the usual motion when one took a corner. Three . . . two . . . and . . .

The pivot on his feet was sharper than it needed to be, his robing swinging with his body—and as if he were checking to see if something had caught his hem, his eyes flicked to his heels.

In his periphery, there was no one.

He needed it to stay that way.

Though he had not been dawdling, he sped up the now, his strides lengthening. He had memorized the subterranean layout long ago, and he needed no refresher as he piloted into the farther reaches of the

Colony. In fact, he knew them even better than the central parts, which he tended to avoid.

His dealings with humans were not exactly disallowed, but he did not need any help with them. Or questions. Which would lead to problems.

When he reached the outer rim of the labyrinth, he promptly turned around—and headed back from whence he came. He was careful to take a random series of inefficient routes . . . and the portal he had actually come in search of took its time in making an appearance. Which was the plan. Still, as he seemed to walk for hours, he began to worry that he might have, in fact, gotten turned around.

No one behind him.

This was good—

Blade stopped short. Turned on his heel.

Ah, finally.

Curling up a fist, he rapped on the polished wooden door. He did not wait for an answer, and opened it wide.

The private quarters that were revealed by a sudden, automatic illumination were a study in minimalism. Unlike this portion of the tunnel, it was a full construction with a proper floor, walls, and ceiling, as well as heating and cooling, electricity, and all the mod cons in the kitchen. But the suite was solely functional, its simple furnishings sparse, hard-angled, and uncomfortable-looking, but classic of the postmodern, fifties era.

Frankly, he hated orange accents on anything, and the wood grain mixed with the chrome was discordant.

"Greetings, cousin mine," he called out. "Wherever are you? You departed your workshop before I arrived to rescue your current project."

Crossing the living area, he came to stand by a closed door just off the galley kitchen. No knocking this time. With his hand on the gun he had hidden in the deep pocket of his robes, he immediately opened things.

The bedroom beyond was dominated not by a bed, but by a high-tech suspension rack, where one's ankles were locked in and one's body could be tilted so that the head became the feet.

"You are still sleeping like a bat, I see."

Blade walked around the contraption and peered into a bathroom that had swimming-pool-blue tile with black accents and a toilet that had been manufactured at the same time as the B-52 bombers of World War II. Breathing in, he did not smell any cologne, shampoo, or soap. No cleaning supplies. No scent of the male at all.

Back out in the bedroom, he went to the closet. There were plenty of red robes hanging on the horizontal rod. Plenty of slipper shoes just like his own lined up on the floor.

Still no scent of his cousin.

The last thing he did before he returned to the

living area was run a forefinger across the top of the *Leave It to Beaver* pine bureau. The stripe that was left behind in the fine accumulation of dust was obvious as a neon sign.

That brutal workshop had not been his cousin's personal residence.

"Where have you gone," he murmured.

Before he left the quarters, he paused and pivoted back around. The only visual chaos in the place was a block of floor-to-ceiling shelving across the room, the books upon the various levels of all different thicknesses and lengths.

He walked over to the collection of tomes, his eyes bypassing the engineering and computer programming titles to search the dark crevices created by the lack of homogeneity . . .

The camera eye was in the lower third all the way on the left, a tiny lens that, if one had not been looking for it, one would have missed it. Motion activated? Probably. Just like the lights.

Squatting down, he stared into the artificial iris. Then he brought his hands up to his hood . . . and revealed himself.

In the last twenty years, as he had been searching for the human labs that had experimented on vampires, he had had the sense that he was someone else's prey, that those animatronic soldiers that had inevitably shown up around his men were in actuality meant for him: The units had never attacked the labs or the scientists. They had found his operatives from time to time, but not with any regularity, and if clashes occurred with his men, the conflicts had been incidental, rather than anything that appeared tactical in nature.

And then the clarifying event had occurred. He had been up on Deer Mountain, falling in love on sight with the wolven Lydia . . . when one of the lookalike cyborgs had found him and tried to kill him outright.

So yes, he was their target.

During his recovery from that bullet wound, he had had plenty of time to think about who he knew who had the resources to create an army out of nuts and bolts, and also the hatred for him that would provide sufficient impetus for such an endeavor. Dear cousin Kurling had come to mind—and in fact, Blade had noted the human alias the *symphath* used in that world in a couple of entries in the database he'd kept with his men.

Kurtis Joel.

Which was how Daniel Joseph had known to bring it up to the wolven.

Within the Colony, Blade had been so careful to keep his little explosive side hustle quiet, but now he was seeing that his hunch about his cousin was confirmed. Kurling had sussed his efforts out somehow, at some point, and abducting the doctor had been a way of closing in on the last of the underground labs.

And how had Blade known where to go for the rescue? He had engineered a little tip owed to him by a male who had sought pleasure of the painful kind. A male who was mated and wished to keep what he enjoyed private.

A male who had given himself over to Kurling once or twice, who knew where Kurling's "workshop" was.

It had been time to find out the truth of his cousin, that which had been suspected pushed into the reality of truth: The reckoning had been long overdue, but Blade had not wanted to know on some levels.

Besides, he had been working too hard to accomplish his goals.

Kurling's motive was obvious. As far as their bloodline was concerned, Xhex had earned her banishment to that lab twenty-plus years ago by associating with a vampire. That Blade was *ahvenging* her? Well, it proved he had a little too much of "the weakness" in him: Half-breeds were tolerated only if they declared their association with what was considered, in these underground environs, the better half of their mix.

To do something to benefit another? Unheard of, in *symphaths*. To defend the honor of a half-breed sibling who had chosen the lesser side of herself to be with? Impermissible.

And his bad choices were threatening the respect and station of his bloodline within the hierarchy of the Colony.

Perhaps his dear cousin had witnessed him coming and going, and had followed. Or maybe there had been some footprint in the sand of his obsession that had been an inadvertent tipoff.

The whys did not matter now.

Reaching forward, he pinched the little lens between his forefinger and thumb. Then he pulled the tiny camera out as if it were a splinter, the wiring coming along until it reached a terminal point of tension.

With a jerk, he dislodged all kinds of volumes as the wire went on a goose chase down the back of its shelf. The scattered thuds as the textbooks hit the bare wood floor were like a tap dancer with heavy feet and no rhythm, and he took satisfaction in the noise and the disruption of the order. Eventually the fragile optic nerve snapped, and he wound up the considerable tail, as well as the ocular head, and put the lot of it in the pocket of his robe.

Standing over the open-faced tomes, he regarded the texts. Unlike the decor and furnishings, the writings were new, going by the drawings of complex circuit systems, the details of computer motherboards, and the depictions of artificial limbs and joints.

Kurling had been smart not to come for Blade in the Colony. That was not a good hand to play in this game, for such intraspecies aggression came with a swift and sure censure from good King Rehvenge.

Indeed, the new regime looked down upon rabble-rousing, and penalties were severe.

Additionally, Blade was a powerful enemy. Outside, on the fringes of the human world—that was a better field of combat. More fun, too, for it added a necessary complication that no doubt Kurling had enjoyed surmounting with his little windup toys.

Alas, the subterfuge was over.

It was time to fight this war out in the open.

May the best male of the bloodline win, Blade thought as he strode back to his own quarters.

EIGHTEEN

ONE GOOD THING about it being mid-November in Caldwell? Sunset came early.

As Xhex re-formed downtown on the fringes of the financial district, the chill seeped through her leather jacket and tightened the flesh of her shoulders and arms. She ignored an involuntary shiver. She would adjust quick.

After John Matthew materialized next to her, they both scanned the environs. The alley they'd chosen was on the narrow side, and there was a buildup of trash running down both sides of the chute, like a river of the shit flowed on the regular and the periphery caught the loose chum to create a shore of soda bottles, plastic bags, and flyaway newspapers. Off in the distance, a deep-throated horn blasted on an overpass leading up to the closest of the two bridges, and off to the south, there was a squeal of brakes, as if the warning sound had triggered an accident in another part of the city.

John Matthew put his hand on her elbow. When she nodded in response, they walked forward.

The Black Dagger Brotherhood had been fighting a war for centuries with the Lessening Society, and the threat to the vampire species had migrated over the Atlantic Ocean to the New World with the race's relocation from the Old Country back in the eighteen hundreds. Courtesy of the tragic continuity, as well as the inevitable passage of time, the Brothers had established facilities to support their efforts all over the urban field of conflict, from safe houses embedded in human neighborhoods to storage units and armories—and most recently, even a soft serve ice cream place.

That serviced Rhage, of course.

Emerging onto Market Street, a wind coming off the Hudson River carried a familiar stink that was muted by the thirty-degree temperature, and they hunkered into their jackets as they headed three blocks farther down, to a set of fire-station-worthy garage doors. The building the panels opened into was a nothing-special that was kept grungy on the exterior on purpose—and she and John Matthew were granted access at a side entry immediately.

Inside, things weren't much warmer or fancier, but they didn't have to be. The arching interior space was all raw concrete blocks, caged lights, and exposed electricals and duct work. Then again, the main attraction was inanimate. The floor space was almost completely taken up by a mobile surgical unit that had always reminded Xhex of the one from *Stripes:* The vehicle looked like an upscale RV, but inside, it had been retrofitted with everything Manny Manello or Doc Jane might need to save a fighter who'd found the wrong end of a gun. Dagger. Rocket launcher.

Vishous stepped out from around the front bumper. The Brother was strapped up under his own black leather jacket, his already powerful body padded by the bulk of the holsters under his armpits and the ammo belt around his waist. In the center of his chest, strapped handles down, were the deadly black daggers he used against the enemy with such skill and ferocity.

"Come on," V said. "I'll take you downstairs."

As her mate nodded, Xhex had an out-of-body experience as they were led over to a steel door in the far corner. After V entered a passcode, the locking bolt retracted, and she caught a flash of copper as the Brother stood aside and she was the first to enter a well-lit concrete and steel stairway.

When they got to the lower level, V stepped forward again and did his business with another keypad. The corridor that was revealed was a short-and-sweet, and she did not have to ask which of the doors was the morgue's.

It was the one that was a meat locker, all stainless steel once again, with a righteous latch and a system of flexible aluminum cooling ducts around the jambs that made it look like an octopus was trying to eat the entrance like a piece of metal toast.

No passcode this time, and no talking. They all knew why they had come and the reason for this visit was nothing that lent itself to casual chatter like how good Fritz's turkey dinner had been back at the mansion, or what anybody wanted to do for New Year's, or when *Deadpool* 3 was coming out.

V did the honors with the release, and there was a hiss as the vaper lock let go. Inside, a shallow receiving room was tiled on three sides by gray and white stone squares. The alternating pattern was anchored by brisk white mortar that burned the eye under the glare of the fluorescent ceiling panels. Then again, the facility had been installed, only what, like, six months ago? No wear and tear, yet.

But as this visit proved, such a depreciation would come.

The bank of refrigerated units took up the whole of the rear wall. Three levels up, six across. Eighteen slots. Which seemed like a lot of vacancies? Then again, at the rate she was killing people, it might only take her a year—

"Fuck," she heard herself say.

"Manny told me it's this one." V went over to the second in from the left in the middle level. "You ready?"

No, not at all. "Yes—wait," she cut in as he went for the release. "I want to do it."

V nodded and eased back.

Unlike all the other individual doors, the one Vishous had indicated had a label sitting in the holder above the latch. Somebody had printed an address on it in black pen: 17th and Market.

Right. Time to . . .

Reaching out, she watched from a great distance as she pulled the lever. There was a sigh of air releasing, and she smelled the flesh immediately, even though the remains were being kept cold. Under her hand, the slab rolled out smoothly, and the body was covered by a white sheet.

Feet first. Was there a toe tag?

Standing by the head, she pulled the covering off the face slowly, and though she had the urge to recoil—maybe so she could throw up on her *hellren*'s shitkickers?—she forced herself to stare down at what she'd done.

He'd had blue eyes. Which she'd wrapped in that red bandana.

And the sockets were clean as a whistle.

Neat job, indeed. Then again, she'd had practice—

In quick succession, she saw other faces, just like this. All male. All without eyes. All . . . dead. But they hadn't been dressed in club clothes. They'd been in lab coats.

Scientists. Humans who had wanted to understand her kind.

Sadists who had enjoyed making things that
screamed and begged for mercy suffer.

In the end, she had slaughtered them all at that
lab she'd been imprisoned in: The ones who had
pumped her full of TB, Ebola, leprosy, and polio to
see what a vampire's body was susceptible to. Who
had tested her reproductive organs. Who had operated on her again and again, just so they could
measure the healing capabilities they could not comprehend.

They hadn't used anesthetic.

And neither had she as she had taken their eyes.

Your grid is collapsing.

Staring into the face of a male she didn't recognize, she had no memory of the killing—and she
didn't get it. She'd already *ahvenged* herself. She'd
killed her captors and burned their little house
of toys down. Now she was happily mated, with a
good job. A stable life.

Why was this happening?

"You know him?" V asked.

She shook her head. "And that's the problem. I
have no memory of him or of doing this, at all."

◆ ◆ ◆

At a little after eight p.m., Daniel got into one of
C.P. Phalen's blacked-out SUVs and sat like a sack

of potatoes in the driver's seat as the garage door in front of him took its sweet time riding up its rails. When the coast was clear, he hit the gas and made the tight turn out of the courtyard between the stone mansion's easterly flank and the heated outbuilding where the woman's stable of vehicles was housed.

He'd used the underground tunnel to depart the mansion because with Blade dropping bodies off on the lawn, he wasn't inclined to take chances.

And also, all the main entrances were locked tight. Thank you, Phalen.

Driving down the allée, he checked the time on the dash. Then looked at the screen of the burner phone he'd been using. The Suburban was two minutes off, and for some reason, this frustrated him as much as a flat tire would.

Which made no damned sense.

Then again, he was studiously avoiding the real source of his—

Fucking Blade. He just had to be the hero, but only on his terms: In spite of the fact that Daniel had called the bastard three times during the day, there had been no courtesy callback. No acknowledgment, whatsoever. Instead? The bastard had made the big show bringing Gus home—and then ghosted out like all he'd done was leave a newspaper on the front doorstep.

The guy just had to be in control. Even though they could have used a hint about—oh, hey, you know, where the fuck Gus had been found, who had done this, and whether the perpetrator was still a threat . . .

Radio silence.

And that meant Daniel was doing something he hated.

Heading down the allée of trees, he stopped at the main gates and waited as they were opened for him. He was glad C.P.—Cathy, sorry—was taking the security shit seriously. He just wasn't sure whether it was going to be enough.

When the coast was clear, he took a right and meandered down the county road some distance. Then he turned around. Meandered back. Walters was so small, there was only the one way in and out, so it wasn't like he could vary his route. There was nobody on his tail, however. No one else out on the road as he turned around at trailheads and on scenic parking shoulders by the mountain stream, before once again heading in the direction he'd been coming from.

He did the bait-and-switch with the compass shit four times, or was it five . . . ?

It was like pacing, except in a car. SUV. Whatever.

Putting the burner faceup on his thigh, he glanced down to see whether there were any calls or texts about twice every ten yards of asphalt. Which was stupid. The ringer was on—

Annoyed with himself, he hit the radio, got fuzz, turned on Sirius, which happened to be trained on the blues channel—hated the twangy Muzak, switched to '70s on 7 in honor of Gus.

Man, that doctor had taken a lickin' and was still kickin'.

It very easily could have gone the wrong way. But last Daniel had heard, dinner had been ordered and Phalen's private chef, who had all the personality of that guy with the soup from *Seinfeld*, had been making chicken à la king like the entrée was better than a blood transfusion.

Screw the crash cart, eat this, St. Claire.

It was all good, though. Showed how Gus got through everyone's shell, whether they wanted him to or not.

On that note, he thought of Phalen leaning over that hospital bed. Was she even aware of what emotion was showing on her face? The love?

He didn't know if she'd even care, actually—

Ding! Ding! Din—

Even though he'd been waiting for his alarm to go off, the sound made him jump, and he slapped at the phone to silence the thing. Perfect timing. Up ahead, the headlights illuminated a break in the pine trees as well as a sign that read "Eagle's Nest Ridge Trail." Easing off onto the dirt parking area, he went in far enough to get the long-bodied Suburban well out of the way. The forest provided plenty of cover from the road proper, and again, who the hell was going to be heading up Deer Mountain in November? At night?

Unless you were a fucking *symphath*, that was.

When the dashboard clock read 8:43, and his phone said it was 8:41, he cracked his door and slid down to the ground. His feet were numb as they accepted his weight, but his legs were strong, and after he shut things back up, he zipped his jacket to his throat, hit the remote to lock things, and walked forward. Under his boots, the gravel crackled and made him think of popcorn on a stove, the old school Jiffy Pop stuff. And off to the right, a soft burble of water suggested the riverbed that the road followed was close by.

The path he was looking for, the one that led to the rushing water, presented itself, and he was careful not to slip and fall when the embankment started on a jagged descent. Grabbing on to branches, he kept himself upright and emerged at the rocky shore. Ahead of him, the gently flowing current gleamed as it moved peacefully along, and he looked both ways. There was cloud cover overhead, and he was glad for it. His clothes were dark and he wanted to blend in as much as he could.

Heading to the left, he shambled downstream, wondering how far to go. A rotten picnic table on a flat-backed boulder answered the question, and as he came up to it, he imagined salmon fishermen sitting on the gap-toothed top, casting translucent lines into spring-flood rushes. Following the ghost of their example, he planted his bony ass on the upper deck, and rested his boots on the seat panel.

He checked his phone again. "Come on . . . ring. Fuck—"

As if his impatience had played operator, the burner let out an electronic *brrrrrrrrrrrring*, and he snatched the cell right up into position.

"We're both still alive," he said roughly, by way of greeting. "Who'da thunk it."

There was a long silence before a male voice said, "Is this really who I think it is?"

"Yeah, it is." He brushed a stick off his pants. "How you doing, Rubik?"

"Ah, I'm good." Another pause. "I'm . . . well, I'm surprised to hear from you."

"Yeah, I figured. But remember that favor you owe me?"

After another pause, there was the sound of a throat getting cleared. "Yes, I do. Of course I do."

"I wasn't sure whether you'd kept this phone."

"Always, Danny. Ah, what can I do to help you? Do you need money—a place to stay or—"

"Nah, it's nothing like that, but thanks, my man. I'm just going to send you some pictures."

"What . . . kind of pictures?"

"Nothing that'll get you in trouble with the law. I know where you work, I'm very aware of where all those brains of yours have taken you. I just need you to tell me if you've ever seen something like this before."

"How do you know where I work?"

"I went up in this world, too, as it turned out." Daniel lowered the phone, and did the deed. "Okay, they're going through. It may take a little bit. I'm in the sticks."

"What happened to you, Danny? I mean, if you know where I ended up . . . where did you go?"

For a moment, the past came rushing back, and the memories were crystal clear. After Daniel's mother had jumped off a bridge to get away from him and the life they were living, he had been left alone at fourteen. Fuck foster care. And besides, learning to survive on the streets had been a training and proving ground for what lay ahead for him in the military—and then later in Blade's happy troupe of troublemakers. *Oh, the places you'll go?* Yeah, he'd seen a lot, and not much of it good—and didn't that make someone stick to themselves.

Unfortunately—fortunately?—every once in a while, in the midst of his own survival-of-the-fittest drama, he'd found himself drawn into someone else's problems.

Like that of Rubik Cube, and his little sister, Annie.

Tim was Rubik's real name. No last name. He'd

been a runner for a mob bookie because he was a human calculator who'd also been able to keep every one of the clients' bets and outcomes in his head.

No pesky paper trails.

No clue how Rubik and Annie had ended up homeless, but one night, Annie had been attacked, and Rubik, at five feet eight inches and one hundred and forty pounds soaking wet in sweats, hadn't been fast or strong enough to defend his sister.

Daniel had been.

He'd saved both of them from the pimp who'd decided a fifteen-year-old Annie could be put to better uses than in the rotation of women's shelters she'd bounced around while her brother had survived sleeping out.

"Hello?" Rubik prompted. "Are you still there?"

"Yeah, sorry." He snapped back to attention. "And to answer your question, I've been here, there. Everywhere. You know the drill."

"Oh, okay—hey, they've come through—hold on."

There was a rustling. Then Daniel could have sworn he heard a soft gasp. After which, he ripped the unit away from his ear as a crashing sound blared into his brain.

Like the phone on the other end had been fumbled and dropped.

"You okay there, Rubik—"

"Where did you get these?" came the breathy demand.

"So you've seen something like it before? What can you tell me about—"

"This is proprietary technology. There should be no photographs of this unit *ever*—but the background isn't my facility. I don't understand how you have this outside of my team at MIT?"

Annnnnd there it was.

Talk about your success stories, Rubik had gone from the streets to the highest echelons of education: The shit with Annie had scared him so badly, Rubik had quit it with the mob, and gotten the two of them into the proper foster care system. Only one year for him, but he'd used it wisely, acing his GED classes, writing a helluva essay, getting a full ride to MIT—where he'd stayed for the last almost two decades. And Annie had ended up okay, too.

Daniel only knew about all the what-next because eighteen months after Rubik had gotten off the street, just before his own eighteen-year-old b'day, the guy had made a point of visiting their old haunts, finding him and . . . thanking him.

Rubik had made a promise to repay the favor someday. And vowed to keep a phone with him for the rest of his life.

Rubik cleared his throat. "I just . . . my workspace is in lockdown. Every one of my team is sworn to . . . I don't understand . . ."

As the stuttering continued, Daniel had to shake his head at how weird fate was. He hadn't thought of his old street friend in years, but the idea had come to him while he was in Gus's former office and Phalen had picked up that cube. And he had remembered the phone number. And the boy on the other end, who was now a man, had still kept to an agreement between street kids.

All things considered, he was surprised he hadn't thought about it before. Then again, he'd been a little busy dying.

Daniel interrupted the panicked stream of consciousness coming through the connection. "Look, clearly you have your own kind of problems, and I appreciate they're a big deal for you. But right now, I need to know if there's anybody else making these cyborgs, Tim. And then I'm going to have to ask you to put your issues on pause, and talk me through a couple of things about its operation."

"You . . . wait, you have one of my units?"

"I do." As there was another stretch of silence, Daniel shook his head, even though they weren't on FaceTime. "No, I can't tell you the hows and whys of anything. You're better off not knowing, trust me. I just need to know . . . how do I turn it on?"

NINETEEN

B ACK AT CLUB Basque, Xhex sat in her office alone and listened to the bass line of the music pumping through the concrete walls of her little slice of privacy. The rhythm was like a heartbeat, reverberating through the building, pulsing across the floor, vibrating up through her chair and the desk. Though she wasn't consciously aware of tracking the rhythm, she noticed that every time the song switched, she looked up from what she was doing and waited to find the new tempo.

Not that there was much variation.

In front of her, the laptop she used to monitor the feeds from the security cameras was open and she was leaning forward toward the screen—but like that could make this hunt-and-peck go better? Then again, nothing could improve the experience of searching black-and-white images of people for the mutilated gray face from that cold slab. Still, there was something hypnotic about watching the humans churn by, their individual characteristics of coloring, height, and weight, blending into an anonymous mash-up. She decided her detached ennui must be how actuaries felt, the forest subsuming the trees—

And there he was.

"Fuck," she breathed as she slowed the video speed down.

The male she'd killed the other night had the kind of swagger that went with an exaggerated pride in one's low-hangers, and that arrogance carried over into the proprietary way he looked at the females around him. He had a buddy with him, a sort of not-quite-there who had a clear case of hero worship going on: While the male was assessing his options, his pal was far more focused on his idol, that weak chin and rapt eyes locked on a guru who didn't seem to give two shits about him.

As time passed, and they moved around, she had to flip between cameras to keep the male in view— and she knew the moment he ID'd his prey. The arrogance slipped and the aggression came out. No more jocular neutral. Now he looked like he wanted to eat something.

Someone.

The target was a small blond human woman— at least, Xhex gathered she was a human because of the way he tight-smiled in front of her. So that the fangs in that mouth didn't make an appearance.

It didn't take long before the pair were dancing,

and his hands traveled to places the woman clearly didn't feel comfortable with, her body always moving back, his always moving forward. As soon as she could, the woman shook her head and broke free of him—but he followed.

As Xhex viewed the interactions, she dubbed in the lines. *You're so pretty, baby. Just one drink. Sorry, I can't fight it. I want you, but I respect you . . . nah, don't worry, he's just my boy. C'mon, I'll buy you a drink.*

The woman ended up over at the bar with the male, and when her friends came across to check in, the vampire shooed them away with a flirtatious floor show.

"Superficial charm," Xhex growled. "You sociopathic sonofa—"

And there it was. The spike of the drink. The move was so smooth, only a practiced eye would have caught it, certainly not a woman who was treading water next to what she assumed was a guy who was attractive, but coming on too strong: He waited until she'd taken two sips, then he pointed out to the dancing throngs in front of them—and as her face turned in that direction, he stretched his arm behind her and dropped something into the open plastic glass.

His friend saw it happen . . . and, yeah, the smirk. That fucking you're-my-hero smirk.

Chinless was in on this game.

As a wave of nausea crested, Xhex rubbed her eyes and cursed: On the backs of her lids, all she saw was that suave drugging on repeat, the extension of that arm, the drop, that punk-ass smile on the other male's face. It was like being in a live action horror movie where she wanted to yell at the character on the screen.

Refocusing, she checked the time counter in the lower corner of the screen.

The woman's affect changed about ten minutes later. All of a sudden, her posture was looser, and she stopped looking over toward her friends, stopped squirming as he put his arm around her, stopped . . . twitching like she was trapped and couldn't find the way out.

And then came the exit. The two males led her down the hallway, past the bathrooms . . . and right out into the darkness.

Xhex stopped the footage. Then switched to another screen. Scrolling down the incident reports for the previous night, she knew what she was going to find and it just killed her. She was supposed to be keeping people safe . . .

The log entry was the third up from the bottom: A police report of a rape, filed this morning, by a woman named Samantha Hoste who claimed she'd been drugged, taken out to a car, and forced to have sex with two men. Afterward, she was rolled out of the backseat and left under the bridge, in the frigid night.

The description of the perpetrators was spot-on.

So when did the second part happen, Xhex wondered. *When did I step in?*

A sixth sense sent her back into the security footage, and she went to change camera feeds—

There she was. Standing at the head of the hallway. Looking down to the exit the males had taken the woman through. The expression on her face was so intense, it was a wonder the force of aggression didn't knock her out of her boots. She even took a step forward—

T'Marcus caught her, tapping her on the shoulder. There was a quick conversation—

"I remember . . ." she said aloud as she watched herself. "The altercation in the wait line last night."

It felt good to be able to recall a concrete event from those hours: Two men who had been posturing out in front of the club had ended up brawling it up, and though her bouncers had separated them, one of the assailants had popped a knife and used it on the other guy. EMS had been on its way. The police, too.

And Xhex was the contact for the club.

So she had gone to deal with everything— but if she hadn't? Maybe the woman would have been spared . . .

Had she done a bad thing? Really? Then again, that wasn't the point. Her total amnesia was the problem—because what if she picked the wrong victim some night?

Like that new hire, for fuck's sake.

Refocusing on the gray-toned footage, she watched herself look back down to the exit one last time. After that, she turned and walked off with T'Marcus.

Xhex stopped the feed and leaned back in her chair. What about the bastard's buddy? Had she killed him, too? Her head started to pound as she glanced to the screen again. The last thing she wanted to do was spend even a second more with the security feeds, and the fucking cameras, and this choking sense of failure she had going on.

But she was not going to find any resolution until she saw her own actions.

This time, when she resumed scanning the footage, she was tracking herself. She followed herself around for—how long was it? Hours, for sure, the counters in the corner of the screen ticking by in a blur as she fast-forwarded: There she was, dealing with the fallout of the stabbing in the wait line, handling the police, fielding other issues with her staff—

And then she went here, to her office.

Before she entered, she looked around, as if she didn't want to be followed. Then she ducked in. And that was that because there weren't cameras in here.

Three minutes, twenty-one seconds. That was how long she was inside here. When she reemerged in the video, she had her leather jacket on, and she was decisive in her movements. She strode down the hall and out of view—so time to switch feeds to the one that was in the northeast quadrant of the interior's open area.

Resuming the tracking from another position, Xhex continue to follow herself, noting the way she moved, with head down, shoulders straight, and lower body in a confident, pointed stride. As she made her way through the dwindling number of patrons, there was plenty of space, no reason to pivot around humans in her way . . . as she closed in on someone.

It was so clear that she had a finish line, her gaze never wavering—and she even ignored T'Marcus when he tried to approach her: The bar. She went to the bar . . . to a pair of masculine figures, one tall, one short, both with dark hair.

The male who had drugged that woman turned around like Xhex said something to him. And those eyes of his went to the floor and traveled back up her body.

He smiled as if he were ready for another fun time.

Xhex left with the two males a mere four minutes and twelve seconds later.

Sitting back once again, she stared at the footage

she'd frozen. It was of that back door by the bath-rooms, the one he'd used to take the blond woman out earlier in the evening.

The one she was using to lure the males into the darkness.

She must have killed his friend, too . . . but where was the other body . . . ?

No one had reported anybody missing yet. Vish-ous had checked that back at the Pit. But those kinds of things could take a little time to develop, depending on who the shorter male had lived with and what kind of job he had. People weren't always missed right after they disappeared.

And if Chinless had been left for dead some-where outside? Even if it was cold, or overcast, a vampire body would go up in flames as soon as day-light arrived, nothing but a scorched spot on the asphalt remaining.

She could always go to the location where Tohr had reported finding the male whose remains were in the morgue. Maybe there was a burn mark some-where around there. Maybe there wasn't.

The details weren't the issue anymore.

The question was . . . what she did about herself.

TWENTY

U P UPON THE summit of the mountain called Deer, Blade stepped out of the hidden cave. Breathing in deeply, he smelled only pine trees, fresh earth, and a frigid humidity in the air that suggested snow would be coming. The cold was biting, his robing protecting him not by much, and as the gusts coming up the elevation pushed at him, his hair waved back from his visage and his core body temperature was drained.

Not that he minded.

Off in the distance, a howl crested through the night, and after a moment, a reply came from across the valley. Behind him, an animal—likely a deer, given the mountain's assigned nomenclature—was being quiet about its movements. He tracked the thing nonetheless out of habit. Out of his own nature.

As he considered what he had done on behalf of the wolven, a rare moment of peacefulness settled upon his shoulders and he told himself to enjoy it. The sense of easing would not last, and heeding that truism, he drank the calm in and tried to hold it in his soul. Soon enough his mental torment would return.

Ah, brain chemistry.

The self was the most dangerous deceptor. This was something that *symphaths* knew to their core, and most others were willfully blind to, and that disconnect was why his kind were so dangerous. Thoughts and feelings were levers to be pulled by words and deeds, and the output was a product of design.

Thus why he had moved out of his quarters at the Colony.

And taken his most precious possessions with him.

Glancing back to the fissure in the rocks, he knew his kind would never find him here. For all the time *symphaths* spent under the ground, they detested nature. Living here? Out in the wilderness? They could not fathom why anybody of their constitution would volunteer for such a thing, even one who existed on the fringes of their bloodline.

Thus he had packed what mattered upon his body and dematerialized out from one of the Colony's disguised entrances. The cave, with its natural spring-fed basin, had been the only place he had considered. He was well aware that it was someone's abode, but the abandonment of the space had been clear the previous time he had been in it, the scent of its wolven occupier faded, dust accumulated on the storage trunks and the bedding platform alike.

Concerning matters of housekeeping, he thought of the finger he had drawn across the bureau in Kurling's quarters—

Another howl sounded out to the west. And . . . yes, there was the other answer.

Closing his eyes, he thought of Lydia, and pictured her human-ish incarnation, with her tall, strong body, and her hair with its streaks of blond, and her eyes, those beautiful golden eyes, which were lycan-like even when she was not in that form.

Her nature was dispositive, no matter the skin that clothed her.

As he thought of the ways she had stared at him, over the short course of their vivid association, he reflected that even when she hated him, he relished any moment that her gaze was upon him. And as he considered the way she had looked at him the night before when he had returned her missing friend to her? Yes, he preferred that best, even if shock had tempered her positive regard.

In light of this, he resolved that it would probably be best not to fool himself. For all the valid, survival reasons that this remote location could be chosen by him, the truth behind his decision to camp out here was about her, not him.

He knew in his gut she would find him here. Just as she had done before.

The cognitive dissonance she would be struggling with the now—why had he returned Gus? what had happened during the evacuation? did Blade know who was behind the abduction?—would drive her to him, and she would come here because it was the only lead on his whereabouts that she had. And he would take the audience eagerly, even if it was answers she sought, rather than he himself.

In this fashion, Xhex still could not argue that Blade was seeking the female out. Free will, after all, was the engine that drove everything that was subject to choice. What fault of it was his if the wolven came unto him—

A sudden rustling close upon him spun his attention around—and Blade palmed his gun and pointed it in the direction of the branches that had moved.

This time, it was not a deer.

Given the lack of scent, but the very clear presence, he instantly condemned his reverie. If it was one of those cyborgs—

All around him, as if some cue had gone off, wolves began howling. Not a volley any longer, now it was a chorus of many positions, the calls mixing and harmonizing, the rising and falling of each individual throat getting lost in the music of the clans.

Blocking out the beautiful calls, he trained his

ears on a crackling of dry sticks. "Be of care," he called forth. "I am armed."

With narrowed eyes, he searched the pine trees, sifting through the fluffy boughs and stout trunks. It was only the sound of an approach, however. No form—which made no sense.

"Halt," he ordered. "Lest ... I ..."

Blade's voice drifted off, his words consumed by the howling that was amplified by the valley's acoustics.

And then he was no longer alone.

The entity that emerged from the coniferous shadows was made of silver moonlight and mountain mist, though there was none of the former ... or the latter, for that matter. The apparition seemed female in nature, though he wasn't sure that applied; it was more an energy source, floating above the raw earth, yet causing sound as if there was weight upon the feet. Certainly its face was that of an old woman, and her long gray-and-white hair cascaded down her shoulders to dissolve into a translucent, glowing aura of light. For clothing, a buckskin skirt and beautiful beaded shawl hearkened back to the First Nations tradition, and he smelled a fragrance of meadow flowers and fresh water.

"What are you," he blurted.

"Good evening to you," the entity said, in a voice that reminded him of a birdcall melody.

Had the wolves stopped? He could not tell. She consumed his focus.

As he lowered the gun, he was not sure whether he was choosing to, or if she was willing his arm down. "And to you as well," he mumbled.

His knee-jerk polite response struck him as ridiculous. Whatever the purpose of this appearance, he was not mistaking it as wholly benign. As a *symphath*, his first instinct was always to assess risk, and the way he did so was to read the grid of whoever was before him.

This "harmless old woman" had no grid.

There was nothing to read.

◆   ◆   ◆

As Daniel parked the SUV back in its garage berth, he waited where he was behind the wheel as the panels descended. He supposed it was overkill, the whole driving off and talking down by the river. Especially given the threat that was out there. But with all the monitoring equipment around Phalen's castle, there was no way the call wouldn't have been recorded.

Nobody needed to know about Rubik.

When things were locked in place, he popped his door open and there was little difference in temperature between the roasty-toasty inside of the Suburban and what he stepped down into. Then again, Phalen had an expensive stable of vehicles.

Nobody wanted their Aventador to get a chill.

Walking by the other Suburbans, then the fleet of Mercedes—and finally that Lamborghini—he stopped when he got to his Harley. Reaching out, he ran his fingertips over the handlebars, and as he closed his eyes, he remembered Lydia leaning back on them and staring up at him . . . hungry. For him—

An odd pressure at the front of his hips made him look down. But it wasn't any kind of phoenix-from-the-boxers shit. His hand had moved over his dick and was sitting on the thing like his palm was expecting some kind of high five in return—and God knew that wasn't going to happen . . .

But didn't they have medications for this kind of problem?

It was hard to say when the idle passing thought transformed into action, but the next thing he knew he was underground and walking down the connector to the main house—and when security cleared him to enter the mansion's basement, he went to the elevator.

He didn't go up to the living areas. He went down even deeper, into the earth.

When things hit bottom and the doors were retracted by the monitoring folks, he stepped out into a bald white corridor hung with double mirror'd panels. As he plugged his cane into the floor and started forward, he noted the drains that were set every fifteen feet or so—and he imagined the stern-faced men on the other side of the glass, all of whom were training their gun muzzles on him like his ass had a target tattooed on it.

Clearly, the holes in the floor had been installed to make cleanup easier. In case things got bloody.

At the far end, he was cleared one more time, and then he finally got access into the lab. A vault-thick partition slid to the side, and there it was, the open area with all the workstations, the boardroom with its soundproof glass walls off to the left. No reception desk. If you needed some-one to help you find your way, you didn't belong here, and if you didn't belong here, you wouldn't have made it this far.

As he headed for the way back, most of the staff was gone, just a couple of researchers staying late, their backs hunched as they arched over micro-scopes or laptops. He didn't mean to stop halfway along, but he did. There were five rows of eight workstations, so forty large steel tables were bolted into the concrete floor, the collection of lab stuff like microscopes, test tubes, and monitor screens varying—no doubt depending on what they were working on. A couple even had beakers on hot plates like in some eighties high school movie.

They had produced that Vita-12b here. The miracle drug that might, or might not, save thou-sands of lives.

And he was supposed to have been the first patient.

Squeezing the head of his cane, he recognized he was using it as a crutch—figuratively, that was. He'd been alarmed at how his energy had faded after the bike ride to Gus's place, and he'd picked the thing up again on a just-in-case. Fortunately, he was feeling not as shitty now. As Gus had said he would. Immunotherapy was not a benign treatment when it came to side effects—for Daniel, at any rate. And though his cancer was now being allowed to progress at its own pace, the ancillary issues he'd had with the failed treatment were backing off—and it was like leaving a suck-ass destination, driving away.

Save for that collapse after what was for him a Herculean task with that bike on the highway, his strength was coming back, and he was being reminded of who he'd been. Mentally sharp. Physically strong(er). Healthy(er) . . .

Of course, the resurrection wasn't going to last.

And that was why he'd come down here, wasn't it.

Getting back with the walking, he pivoted on one foot and restarted for the patient rooms. Things were going well . . . until he came up to a closed door that he told himself he should not open.

Did he really want to ask a man in Gus's kind of shape anything other than "How are you feeling, my guy?" or maybe "What can I get for you?"

So what the fuck was he doing, showing up on the doorstep, looking for—

The door swung open, and a white coat came out with a phlebotomy carrier of tubes filled with Gus's blood. As the panel began to ease shut, Daniel got a full view of the patient. The man was sitting up in the hospital bed and glanced over.

Daniel lifted his hand in a wave. Like an idiot.

And then things were closed again.

A muffled "Hello?" permeated the divider. After which, more loudly: "So you're just gonna wave and walk off?"

Cursing, Daniel entered the room. "Sorry."

"S'all good."

Over on the bed, the good doctor was staring out through bloodshot eyes, and seemed to be holding his head carefully on the top of his spine as if he were worried if he moved too fast, he was going to lose something. Like maybe his dinner. But his face was settling into a pattern of bruising that wasn't getting worse, and the swelling did look a little better—

Gus frowned. "You okay?" When Daniel just blinked, the man said, "Listen, if you got bad news, drop the headline right now. I don't have the energy to wait for the whole article."

"No, no—it isn't like that." Daniel cleared his throat. "And hey, you're sounding . . ."

"Good, right? I had a shower. I got fresh scrubs on. I'm ready to run a marathon."

"Yeah, you do look . . . good."

"You lie, but I'll take it."

There was a pause, and Daniel glanced around. "Can I get you anything—"

"What's on your mind, big guy?" When Daniel hesitated, Gus slashed an impatient hand through the air—then winced, like his shoulder had hurt in response to the movement. "You think I can't read you? Come on, after everything we've been through."

"You got some recovery of your own to do. You don't need to worry—"

"I'm ready for a distraction. Trust me."

Daniel opened his mouth. Closed it.

In the silence that followed, Gus crossed his arms over his chest—then grunted a curse and dropped them back to his sides. "What do you want to know?"

Daniel paced around the bed. Made like he was checking the vitals' monitor—not that he knew shit about the graph of heartbeats or the numbers off to the right. "I, ah . . . I'm really sorry about what happened to you—"

"Stipulated. I'm really sorry you got cancer. What's on your mind?"

After a moment, Daniel said, "I have a question about medication."

"Oh."

As he put his palms forward, all crap-shit-sorry,

the cane clonked on the foot of the bed. "Ouch. I mean, fuck. Now isn't the time—"

"No, no, I'm glad, actually." Gus went to push himself up a little higher on the pillows—and then obviously rethought the idea. "I'm ready to think about something else. What we got?"

As Daniel tried on a variety of dip-the-toe-in-the-water responses, he told himself he needed to drop his pride. Like his doctor hadn't seen him in pretty much every compromising position possible?

"I . . . want to ask about the little purple pill."

Gus's bandaged eyebrow went up. Or tried to. "Prilosec?"

"Is that what it's called?"

"You having indigestion?"

"No? I mean, no."

Tilting his head to the side, Gus demanded, "What body part is the problem."

Daniel took a deep breath. Then pointed to his crotch. "I want to know how to get this working again. And if I have to run the risk of an erection lasting longer than four hours, I will happily take myself to any ER if it happens."

TWENTY-ONE

U P ON THE mountain that was called
Deer, Blade's eyes remained fixated on the
ghostly entity before him. He was not sure how to
defend himself. The gun was going to be useless—
indeed, bullets only worked against corporeal targets. He could run, but he knew without further
information that he was not going to beat whatever
it was in a footrace. And dematerializing? He was
certain that was not an option without even trying.

He was too scattered to calm himself sufficiently.

A static charge was upon the air, one that ema-
nated from the old woman, and it was not merely
agitating the molecules of oxygen, it was in him.
The effect was a heightening of his sight, his hearing, his sense of smell, and that information load
funneling into his brain was creating a buzzy
chaos: The pine boughs were too clear, each needle
among the countless numbers a green knife piercing him, the trunks made of sandpaper, and the
loose stones on the ground a tactile nightmare,

even as he did not touch any of them. Additionally, the perfume that the entity carried was roaring in his nose, as if a meadow in spring with a rushing river beside it was actually inside his sinuses.

And then there were the howls in the air. The wolves' voices entered his ears and echoed into a cacophony that redoubled until he wanted to cover his head to block it all out.

So no, there would be no dematerializing. He was locked in to whatever was happening next.

"I am glad you came," she said in her voice of birdsong. "Your long journey ends up here, and I sense you are ready for it all to come to its conclusion."

The nape of his neck tightened, sure as if a hand had landed hard upon it and was gripping with the strength of a warrior.

"I do not . . . know what you're talking about."

Some *symphath* manipulator he was. He was not playing chess with her, choosing his words carefully, engineering an outcome he would patiently execute and then enjoy. No, he was on his back foot and then some, stumbling over his words, grappling for logic, lost in his surroundings.

"Yes, you do know that to which I refer." The smile was calm and ancient. And yet he was not reassured. "But then destiny transcends words, does it not. It transcends everything."

"Why . . ." He cleared his throat and indicated

the fissure in the boulders behind him. "Is this your . . . home? The cave?"

"You are welcome to take shelter in it for however long you wish. The male who resides there is on his own journey and far from the mountain."

"Oh."

"I saw what you moved in earlier."

Blade's left eyebrow started twitching, the spasms causing his vision to disco. "I was not aware I had an audience."

"I didn't intend for you to know my presence." More with that smile. "You brought your most precious possessions. You take care of them so well."

There was no replying to that. Absolutely not. "I shall move out—"

"Not at all. You are precisely where you are supposed to be. Where you are needed." The old woman looked over to the rocks. "And you have what you need. For what comes next."

"There is no next. I am merely here on a little vacation."

And now seriously reconsidering what he had thought was a private place where he could hide out, determine his strategy against his cousin, and come and go from this base camp as he hunted his prey.

"You are trying to impress her," the entity said, "but you have at your disposal the ultimate prize to present unto her."

"Her? I am afraid you have confused me with someone else."

Now that kindly face registered an authority. "I do not get confused. And you know exactly to what I am referring. You are better at caring for others than you wish to acknowledge, and if you love her as you believe you do, then the decision is an easy one, is it not? Would you not give all of you to the one you love? Sacrifice yourself for them?"

Blade slowly shook his head back and forth.

"Yes," the entity said. "You would. And you have. All these years, avenging your sister. You have lived no life in service unto her—and you have sought no glory for yourself from her. She is blind to your virtue, and that is your business. It is also your preparation for the true sacrifice that is coming."

"Again, I think you've confused me with someone else."

"As you wish. Free will is a force in this world. So you will believe what you do—"

"Who are you? The Scribe Virgin?"

The entity laughed, and as she did, her silver hair seemed to move around on its own, an extension of her mirth. "No, I am not her. She is . . . let us say, we are of relation."

"I do not understand any of this."

"Your understanding is not required." That face, so beautiful even with its lines, grew serious. "The wolven has been shown that you are her future. Give her that. In your heart, it is what you know is right—and the answer to the question you have been asking yourself is yes, there is."

"I have no question," he said in a voice that broke.

She regarded him with the telltale sadness that came with pitying a stranger. "Yes, there will be a compensation for your altruism. You will get what you have sought for all your nights."

"I do not know what you are—"

Now there was laughter. "You asked for me. You prayed for guidance. Did you think someone was not listening? You came up here to my summit, and you stared into my valley, and your heart called out in your torment. So I am here." That smile returned once again. "I wish you the very best—and remember, you have everything you need with you. Even if you lied to yourself about why you brought it."

In between one blink and the next, the old woman was gone, and the instant she disappeared, the howling cut off in midstream, as a door would shut on a sound.

Heart pounding, mind swimming, Blade let his head fall back and just tried to breathe. Up above, the clouds had parted in a perfect circle, an oculus created directly over him, certainly by the entity's strange energy. And now that she had departed, the weather pattern was reclaiming the aperature, and as he regarded the stars twinkling and winking down at him, he felt like they were mocking him—or perhaps he was making everything personal because he felt like the core of the universe had just done a drive-by on him.

And that did make a male feel of special importance.

Whether one appreciated the effort or not.

And he did not.

When the heavens were once again fully obscured, he turned away and sought the cave's entrance. Passing through the rough-hewn corridor with its tight angles and tighter squeeze, he orientated by touch and thereafter emerged into the belly of the space. He had lit a candle upon arriving earlier, and paranoia made him search the bedding platform, the trunks of clothes that were not his own, the old dresser . . . the spring-fed basin in the back.

He was alone, but that was of no reassurance a'tall. If that entity could emerge from out of nowhere outside, there was no reason she could not find him in here, or anywhere. And though she had not been aggressive, he felt as affronted as if she had put a knife to his throat. To his *symphath* sensibilities, the amount of information she had on him was alarming—and the kinds of things she knew were utterly devastating.

"And I was *not* praying."

On that note, he went across to the table set

back upon the rock wall. The candle he had recently lit with his mind was in a holder layered with the melted wax of many previous uses, and he wondered what struggles the rightful owner of the cave had endured . . .

Next to the fragile source of light, there was a collapsible plastic cage with a screened top. And beside that rested a small container, about the size of a ring box.

Lowering himself down to a wooden chair, he arranged his robing with a precision that was not required. "You are my most precious possession."

Inside the cage, the albino scorpion showed no reaction. Then again, she was used to him, and had turned to look at him as he had appeared in her window on the world.

She was not the only one of his collection that he had taken with him, but she was the most important—

You are better at caring for others than you wish to acknowledge.

"Shut. Up."

And yet he could not deny the evidence of that truth. All he had to do was think of those glass cages back in his private quarters and all his careful cultivation of the scorpions therein. For years.

Back when the Princess was alive, she had tasked him with the care and breeding of the arachnids with which she had been obsessed. The post had been titularly a demeaning one, intended to humble him for the disgrace that his bloodline had suffered at his sister Xhex's behavior.

Indeed, following her forced departure, there had been a campaign against all of them, and there were none who went untainted by the degrading treatment. The immediate family had been most affected, but ultimately any who were related came under the pall—which was why he was so certain of Kurling's ultimate intent. If the male could prove what Blade had been doing, and then brought back Blade's head on a stick? Then the male might well rescue himself from the pall—or even be revered.

Rehvenge's "new era" could only change so much.

"Old habits die hard, my love," he said as he stroked the glass with his forefinger. "Do they not."

The scorpion was tiny. Barely bigger than a wasp. And as he considered what was in her stinger, what he had engineered through careful breeding over the previous two decades, he reflected on his uncharacteristic attraction to Lydia.

He may fuck males. But he had always loved deadly females—and like his scorpion, that wolven was a killer.

Unlike Lydia, the arachnid could do something else.

For Daniel.

The ghostly entity had it correct, and he wanted to hate her for the prescient knowledge—in addition to the invasion into his privacy: Unfortunately, having had his interior debate revealed, he now could not ignore the dilemma he had been trying to force down into the basement of his consciousness.

As the keeper of the scorpions, he had been witness to how the Princess had used their venom for all kinds of things: Skin toning. Pain control. Pain infliction. Paralysis. She had had a strange obsession with the elixir, as she had called it, and she had had him test it on himself . . . and on others.

Of whom some had been humans.

The fact that he had ended up doing to those rats without tails what had been done to his sister had seemed like an appropriate karmic payback to the inferior species: There he was, tracking underground labs and destroying them—while he was experimenting on humans himself. That period in his life had not lasted very long, however. Rehvenge had taken out that triple-jointed female and all her sick perversions.

Which was what happened when you thought a male like that was a toy you could play with forever.

In the aftermath? Blade had stayed with the scorpions . . . and all the knowledge he had gained remained with him. Including that which he had regarded as wholly irrelevant.

Some of those humans had had cancer. That had been . . . cured.

As vampires and *symphaths* did not get the dis-

ease, there had been no benefit to the discovery—
and he never would have believed then that that
throwaway would mean something in his life.

Well, potentially mean something. That was devastating.

Picturing Daniel, so weak and ailing, Blade knew
that he was running out of time to emerge as the
hero he had no interest in being—and not in terms
of delivering his cousin's head on a stick as a show
of revenge, which was what Lydia thought she
needed from him.

Indeed, the future she wanted so badly with her
mate was in his reach, and his alone.

"But what is in it for me?" he whispered to his
scorpion. "Nothing."

No, that wasn't true.

Suffering. That was what he got in return, and
as pain was a destiny through which he was already
slogging, he rather held on to the notion that if that
man of hers died, Blade might have a chance with
the wolven. And God knew, he was more than willing to be patient and wait out her mourning.

A new mission, to replace the one with the labs
that he had completed.

He infinitely preferred that future as opposed to
living in a world where true love blossomed next to
his heart's gravestone.

"Fuck that," he said bitterly.

A *symphath*'s first interest was always their own,

but no male wanted that lonely outcome—and as
he shook his head, he knew that he was not going
to stray from his course. He had brought his favorite arachnid with him only because, having revealed
himself to Kurling's camera, his personal quarters
might be in play, so to speak, and though losing
some of the others would be unfortunate, he would
not be devastated.

His favorite, however, he could not spare. Nor
her court of daughters.

And she and her direct offspring would be safe
here, while he assassinated his cousin. And then
they would all wait up here on the mountain whilst
nature took its course with one Daniel Joseph.

That scorpion was not here to help Lydia's one
true love survive his dreaded fucking disease.

Not at all.

TWENTY-TWO

The King's Audience House
Caldwell, New York

WRATH, SON OF Wrath, sire of Wrath, sat back down in his armchair in front of the fireplace in the Audience House's main room. As soon as his ass hit the cushioned seat, George let out another big shake, his damp ears flopping on his head with a slapping sound, his tail whipping Wrath's leathers, his paws doing a stompy-stomp on the carpet.

"That was a good roll outside, huh," Wrath said softly.

As he put his dagger hand down, the golden bumped his head into his favorite palm, and Wrath stroked the wet locks that hung down like hair off George's ear. God, he loved everything about the dog, even the old rug smell when things were wet. And though he wanted to spend the next fifteen minutes oochie-poo'ing with his best boy—one, that was not something he did in public, and two, the sooner he got through tonight's calendar of audiences, the faster he could get home to his *shellan* and his son.

And then oochie-poos-in-private could happen.

Some things, you only wanted your *shellan* to know about.

Ready to get on with shit, Wrath reangled his face so he was "looking" out into the room. "We ready for the next one or what."

Over to the right, Saxton cleared his throat, and there was a creak as he got up from his desk chair. "Ah, yes. And I believe I will excuse myself—"

Wrath narrowed his eyes behind his wraparounds. "You all right? What's going on—"

"Oh, no, Sire. I am very well indeed. It's just . . ."

There was a hesitation, and Wrath could imagine his solicitor looking in the direction of the two brothers who were on duty tonight. Qhuinn and Sahvage had been pairing up on schedules lately, the two falling into a team that was proving very effective out in the field of Caldwell's downtown— and then also here, with these civilian meetings. The rule was that there had to be two brothers in the room, and two more on the premises, at all times.

It was the reasonable thing to do, set up by Tohr, who was the most reasonable of all of the Brotherhood.

And it chapped Wrath's ass like a bike seat.

"Somebody better get fucking talking," he commanded. "Why is my lawyer recusing himself."

There was a brisk knock, and after Sahvage barked out a yup, the scent that entered what had once been the house's formal dining room was not exactly a surprise—but it wasn't expected, either.

"Rehvenge," he said. "What we got."

The King of *symphaths* was always welcome. But this was not a friendly little hi-how're-ya: There were no greetings by the brothers, and Sax being prepared to leave? The only conclusion was that some kind of shit had hit some sort of fan, and everyone else knew what was going on but—

"Saxton, you stay," he ordered.

"My lord . . . ah . . ."

And then two other people came in. As soon as their scents registered, he cursed. This was not going to be a run-of-the-mill civilian dispute. Nope. John Matthew and Xhex shouldn't have been in this part of town at this time of night: The former was supposed to be out in the field, and the latter was in charge of security for that club down on Market—a full-time job and then some.

Plus what do you know. The tension in them both thickened the air, an astringent tang that changed their normal scents.

"Go," he said in a low voice to Sax.

"Thank you, my Lord."

There was a shifting of fine clothes—the male bowing—and then the solicitor took his leave faster than a coin in a slot, the double doors being closed quick.

"Whatever it is," Wrath announced, "I'm down. Just spit the shit out."

In the quiet that followed, he imagined all kinds of eyeballs shifting around as the group that remained decided who was going to draw the short stick and drop the bad news. He had the sense that Qhuinn and Sahvage might be in on it, too, because they started pacing, the pair walking back and forth along the windows at the far side of the long space—

"Somebody better start fucking talking. *Now*."

At his feet George sat up and put his big, boxy head on Wrath's thigh. The golden was supposed to help with the lack of sight going on, but over the years, he'd shifted into the emotional support animal crap. Which Wrath didn't need. He took care of himself.

His dagger hand went to that soft fur, and as he stroked things and fiddled with an ear, his blood pressure eased up a little, his temples not pounding so much—

"I killed three people. Maybe four. Maybe . . . more."

As Xhex spoke up, Wrath angled in her direction, relief rolling through him. That was her goddamn job, wasn't it? Then again, if the unaliving had taken place as part of her employment, there would be no need for all this.

"What were the circumstances."

"It was at the club." The female cleared her throat. "They were ... dangerous to my customers."

"And?" Wrath drummed his fingers on the arm of his chair. "What's the problem. You handled your business with some humans. As long as you covered your tracks, there's not a problem—"

"They were vampires. They were ... us."

Wrath's brows dropped under his wraparounds. Okaaaay, now he got it. "Have the families been notified."

"The identity of the most recent one—well, 'ones,' probably—hasn't been established yet—"

Rehv spoke up. "All of the males had documented histories of violence and criminal behavior. They fucked around and found out. That's what it is."

Nodding in agreement, Wrath asked, "When did this happen?"

"About a week ago." Xhex came forward, and there was a thump-and-rattle on the floor in front of Wrath. "And then a week ago. And ... last night. So I'm turning this in."

Flaring his nostrils, he noted the scent of gunpowder. "It's not my birthday. What's with all the weapons."

"I'm disarming myself," the female announced, "and whatever has to happen to make this right— I accept."

Wrath opened his mouth to tell her to come-on-get-fucking-serious.

But then he thought of Saxton leaving. And slowly closed his piehole.

For the majority of his adult life, he had walked away from his birthright—birth demand, really. It wasn't like he'd volunteered to be the son of his First Family parents, and after watching them get slaughtered in front of him as a young, he had bolted from his responsibilities. And that had been true both in the Old Country, and after he came over here, to Caldwell.

Meeting his Beth had changed everything, and year by year, he had pulled the species back together, revising the Old Laws, establishing order, resuming traditions.

And that meant that whereas in the not-so-distant past, Xhex offing a couple of assholes who were hurting other people wouldn't have been an issue—now? He'd made rules about homicide. What kind of leader would he be if he bent them in favor of somebody he was close to?

A bad fucking one.

"I'm going to have to get V to look into the deaths," he said in a low voice. "I need to follow the procedures I've set up."

"I'd expect nothing less." Xhex cleared her throat. "I imagine it's going to take him some time, so I'm going to go away for the duration. And again, whatever you decide, I will accept."

He believed that. He could scent her intention. But there was something else.

"What aren't you telling me." When there wasn't an immediate response, he shook his head. "You're gonna want to get it all out right now. Trust me."

There was another long pause. And then, in a reedy voice, "I have no memory of the killings. None . . . I literally had to go through Basque's security footage to find out when and where I intercepted the last one."

There was a sharp whistle and then some soft brushing noises, and Wrath kept quiet as John Matthew communicated with his mate using ASL.

"He, ah . . ." Xhex murmured something—and got another whistle in response. "John wants you to know that the male . . . the male I killed last night drugged and raped a woman he met in the club."

As Wrath became aware of a loosening of his own tension, he had to cop, at least to himself, that he wanted there to be a good reason for it all. The amnesia? He didn't fucking know about that—but as long as there was a justification?

Except he couldn't go very far down that route. In this situation, he was the King, first and foremost, and a person second. His feelings could not come into play. And if she was going off, with no memory? As some kind of vigilante?

That was going to be a big problem for everybody.

"Are you okay?" he asked.

"Yes," Xhex said roughly.

Well, that was a "No" if he'd ever heard one. "Can you talk to Mary? One of the other therapists at Safe Place, maybe?"

"I'll be fine. This is the first step . . . I have to take."

He wanted to tell her she should stay put in her own damn bedroom back with the rest of everyone. But if she was killing and blacking out? Fuck, what the hell was going on with her.

"We need to be able to get in touch with you," he said.

"I'll have my phone."

He pictured her glancing at her mate—and remembered what the female had looked like before his eyes had failed him entirely. Xhex had always been a tough piece of work, and Rehv had used her as an enforcer and his head of security when he'd been in the club and drug racket. After he'd stepped away, she'd gone to work for Trez, who'd taken over all the businesses.

Wrath could imagine what she'd done to those males.

Frankly, he was surprised there was anything left over.

"We're going to take off now," she said. "You're busy."

"Never too busy for you. Or him."

"Thank you," came the choked reply.

He wasn't surprised when the pair of them left quickly. They were clearly hanging by a thread. He also wasn't surprised when Rehv stayed behind.

"What the fuck is going on with her," Wrath demanded of the king of all *symphaths*. "And how can we help."

◆   ◆   ◆

As Xhex bolted out of the dining room, she was dizzy and disoriented. Neither was a surprise. Standing in front of the Great Blind King, laying out her shit, with a duffle full of deadly guns and knives—and her *lys*—between them, she felt like everything that had started back in the spring had come to a head.

For the hundredth time, she relived that vivid memory of Rehv in the billiards room of the Black Dagger Brotherhood mansion, telling her that her grid was collapsing, that she was in trouble, that she needed help. If she hadn't fought him then, maybe . . .

It doesn't matter now—

John stepped in front of her. As he started to

sign something, she did the best she could to track the positions of his fingers and his hands, but she couldn't follow any of it. She was still back in that elegant, if rather empty, room, staring at the last purebred vampire on the planet. Sitting on that otherwise run-of-the-mill antique armchair, Wrath had been an overwhelming presence, one that turned any piece of furniture into a throne. With his waist-length black hair falling from a widow's peak, and his cruel, intelligent face zeroing in on her as if he could see, he was the force to be reckoned with that he always was—and she'd been tongue-tied as soon as she'd entered his audience room.

Yet she could feel the respect he had for her. Under the hard surface, there was an even harder core—but he liked her, and she had the sense that he wanted to do what he could for her.

He would bend nothing in her favor, however.

Xhex looked over her shoulder at the closed doors. Rehv was still in there, and she imagined they were talking about what the investigation was going to entail. She had some answers from her own digging, but considering everything else she didn't know and all that she couldn't trust in herself? Who the fuck knew what was going to come out of . . . anything.

She glanced at John. He'd lowered his hands and was staring at her with steady, intense eyes.

"I'm sorry about all this."

He shook his head. Then mouthed, *Nothing to be sorry for. And we stick together. I'm going to ask Tohr for some time off.*

God, where were they going to go? she thought. They couldn't crash in some Residence Inn—vampires, hello. Pulling drapes wasn't safe enough during daylight hours. And she was *not* staying in the mansion. She didn't want to even go back for her clothes.

She couldn't trust herself around those people—and their young. Especially the young.

Hell, she wasn't sure she wanted John Matthew to stick with her. The only thing that reassured her on that front was that he could overpower her—but it wasn't like she had a choice. He wasn't giving her any input into his decision. When she'd suggested that, for safety, he stay at the mansion while she went off?

She hadn't gotten even half the sentence out before a rock-solid fuck-no had come back at her. And when she'd tried to press it? He'd just asked her what she would do in his position.

So that had settled it—

As muffled voices registered, she glanced to the waiting room. There was no one in it, and she found herself wondering whether it was at the end of the night or not. She had no concept of time. Checking her watch, she was surprised it was just after midnight.

Early. But Rehv had cleared the place out for her.

Even the receptionist was gone.

Just as she pivoted toward the front door, Rehv came out of the audience hall, looming in his full-length mink duster. With his cropped mohawk and his black silk suit and black silk shirt, he cut a powerful figure as always.

Except those amethyst eyes were gentle as he looked at her. In response, all she could do was shake her head.

"You were right," she said roughly. "I should have listened to you—"

Rehv closed the doors behind himself and stepped up to her. "I'm not looking to do an I-told-you-so."

"I had no idea. About the grid—my grid."

"I know." Rehv's grave purple stare went back and forth between her and John Matthew. "Listen, I have a place for you guys. My Great Camp is private, safe, and empty. While we figure out what comes next, I want you to go stay there."

Xhex's first impulse was to argue with the male—but come on. Look at how that had gone so far.

"Thank you," she said in a small voice. "I just . . . don't really know what to do here."

He reached out with his free hand, the one that wasn't locked on his silver cane. Squeezing her shoulder, he said, "That's why you let people help."

As her mind started to spin out with all kinds

of crazy things, John Matthew tugged at her arm. When she turned toward him, he took her face in both his palms. With his blue eyes boring into her own, he didn't mouth any words or make any with his hands, but he communicated loud and clear:

I love you. And I am not leaving you.

"What the hell did I do to deserve you," she said.

He kissed her quick. And then it was time to go.

"Follow me," Rehv said. "I'll make sure you get there safely."

Glancing over her shoulder, she got a last eyeful of those closed double doors . . . and wondered if she would ever see any of the males in that room again.

Or any of the people she had grown to love as her family.

Somehow, she felt like this was the end of the road for her. And she knew, if that was true, she was going to have to let John Matthew go, too.

Even though that was going to kill her.

TWENTY-THREE

BACK AT THE Phalen estate, Lydia followed Daniel to a part of the house she hadn't been anywhere near before. And when he checked in at a camera, there was a longer than usual wait . . . in front of a vault door that belonged in a bank.

Why were they going into C.P.'s safe room, she wondered.

"So you did see Gus?" she said as she leaned back against the wall and covered a yawn.

Daniel nodded. "When I went down to the lab, I thought you might be there."

"Instead, you caught me napping."

"You make it sound like a sin." With a gentle brush of his hand, he moved a strand of hair back from her face. "It's midnight. Most people are sleeping now. Besides, it's been a lot—I should have let you rest."

"No, I'd rather be up." She turned her face to his palm and nuzzled him. "As for Gus, he's doing really well, don't you think? Physically, at least."

As Daniel lowered his hand, his face tensed up. "You really should rest now, when you can—"

"What aren't you telling me?" Lydia cut in. Then she shrugged. "Look, keeping me in the dark is not protecting me. You're making things more dangerous."

He closed his eyes like he hated where they all were.

"Talk to me. I'm your partner, not another problem you have to take care of."

After a long pause, Daniel nodded and looked at her. "Gus was abducted for a reason, and it wasn't to kill him. If death was the object, they would have just shot him and left the body in the condo. He was tortured for information, and it doesn't take a genius to figure out it was about someone trying to get into the lab—and there was no way Gus didn't give up what he knew. At some point, everybody breaks. Even the professionals trained to withstand that kind of thing."

Lydia's eyes flooded with tears. Wiping them away, she crossed her arms over her chest. "Oh . . . God."

Even though she had guessed, having Daniel spell it out in such bald terms was shocking. But come on. Reality was what it was, even if the details weren't spoken.

"I don't think we have long," Daniel said gruffly. "We need to get ready for an attack—it's coming. I

262 J. R. WARD

can feel it in my bones, and I'm never wrong about
these things."

"How much time do you think we have?" she
said softly.

"It's safest to assume it could come at any moment. And I'm not going to tell you what to do, but
I really think you should go to the mountain."

"I'm *not* leaving you." She took the hand that had
touched her so tenderly. "And I'm not leaving Gus
or C.P."

Daniel took a deep breath. "That's what the
guards are for."

"Then they can guard all of us together."

A hint of a smile teased his lips. "I had a feeling
that's what you were going to say."

"Guess you know me well, huh?"

"Yup, and I'm not going to argue with you. In
the words of Forrest Gump, 'I'm not a smart man,
but—'"

Abruptly, there was a metal-on-metal shifting
sound, and they both turned to the vault entrance,
reaching out at the same time for the latching system.

"I've got it," Daniel said.

And he did. He grabbed on to the handle, and
then sank into his lower body, using his weight
more than strength to open what was clearly a
heavy load.

On the other side was . . . an octagonal room
paneled in what appeared to be stainless steel. A

lighting system was mounted in cages in the ceiling, and the too-bright light reflected off of every angle in the space, creating a high-tech aura.

Wow. And yet could she be surprised?

Only C.P. Phalen would buy a property where the listing included, in addition to 8 BR, 9.5 baths, professional-grade kitchen, detached heated garage, and in-ground pool, a "Counterterrorism Escape and Containment Area."

At least that was what a little plate read on the inside of the doorjamb.

And then she didn't think anymore about labels. It was all about what was inside: On a stainless slab in the center, a human-form collection of nuts, bolts, and mechanicals was orientated as a body would be on its back. The arms were flush with its sides, its legs out from the sockets, the feet splayed wide at the ankles. There were no clothes on the unit, and patches of its skin-like covering were intact in some places.

"Holy . . . crap," she breathed.

The face had been dissected, the fibers that seemed like swaths of muscles pulled off the metal cheeks and put in glass dishes over on a series of shelves, the eyes already gone because Daniel had taken them to make sure the cyborg couldn't function. Parts of the neck had likewise been examined . . . and the chest as well.

There was no heart at the sternum—and she

shouldn't have been surprised by that. She was, though.

It was so . . . human-like, and yet utterly manufactured.

A work of man, not God. A killing machine with no conscience.

"I hate this thing," she said, as she approached it cautiously. "And I keep expecting it to come alive."

Joining Daniel next to the table, she felt a creeping tension at the back of her neck. When Daniel had told her that he'd spoken to a friend of his, she hadn't asked a lot of questions. But now that he'd taken her here? She wondered what kind of conversation had been had.

"Help me roll this fucking thing over?" he said. "Toward us."

Lydia didn't hesitate, but she hated touching the cool metal, and the feel of the flexible wires, and the sticky, corded connections between the "bones." Gripping the rib cage, she dropped down into her legs and shifted backward. The unit was very heavy, heavier than a human of the same size. And as soon as the cyborg was balanced on its side, she started running through scenarios where it suddenly woke up on the attack.

What the hell are we doing? she thought to herself.

With a fumble in his pocket, Daniel took out a

penlight and triggered the beam into the nape area. "Okay, got it. Can we roll things all the way over so it's facedown?"

"Yup."

Sinking down into her thighs again, she circled the torso at the ribs and shoved forward at the same time she flipped it back with a yank. The jerky maneuver worked okay—but it was like tossing a pancake that weighed as much as a sofa. That was slippery. Fortunately, Daniel caught the thing and kept it from falling off the other side onto the floor.

Then he was back at it with the penlight. "Shit."

"What?"

"It's been dissected. There's nothing salvageable. Let's put it back."

On his cue, she muscled the unit again, and as it flopped to the faceup position, the metal clanging was a reminder—not that she needed it—that they were dealing with technology, not anything that lived and breathed.

Daniel stared down grimly. Then he put his hand on the center of the chest, where the heart would have been if it had been mortal.

"This is what's coming for us, Lydia—I know because it's what I would do if I had control of them. If I had a target, I'd send them instead of anything that was mortal." He moved down the body. "These things are a design triumph. They're perfect for fighting. No food, no sleep, no conscience or independent thought. Just a battery source and a set of orders. It's the future of warfare."

Lydia thought back to when she'd faced off with one of them, alongside Blade, up on the mountaintop.

"Let's all leave," she murmured. "Let's just pack up . . . and go."

After a moment, Daniel shook his head. "I think they're going to find us wherever we are."

◆   ◆   ◆

Standing over the mechanical soldier, Daniel reflected on how helpful Rubik had been—after the guy had lost his shit for a while about the mole in his program. With the flip-out in the rear view, Daniel had gotten along with the deeper reason for the call. The favor had been granted—to an extent.

An over-the-burner-phone connection was a poor substitute for Rubik being on-site and getting hands-on with the cyborg. But Daniel's brain was a sponge, and he had retained most of what had been explained.

Unfortunately, with the power plant being so wrecked, there was no way of working with the thing. He'd been hoping to reverse engineer the unit, and send it back to its master with a tracker. A Trojan robot, so to speak.

All that was a no-go, so Daniel was making other plans. Staring into the face of the steel soldier, he began to do mental gymnastics involving risk management and the execution of strategies—all of it so spinningly manic, too manic to truly be effective. Then again, his brain had been centrifuging out even before he came here to try to do something that made a difference.

"Daniel?"

He shook himself back to attention and stared into those whiskey-colored eyes he loved so much. "I really want you to leave here."

"Not unless you come with me."

Her words were spoken softly, but they landed like a holler—because he wanted to talk sense into her. He was almost out of time. She had her whole life ahead of her. Their situation was already a tragedy—the last thing they needed was her getting herself killed in the middle of this mess they didn't create, couldn't escape. And yeah, sure, from a physical strength perspective, he probably needed to go to safety before she did, but he was hungry for an enemy he could fight.

He might be weak physically, but he could still hold a gun. And bullets worked against these cyborg fuckers if you had enough in your magazine.

"I'm not leaving," he said remotely as he stared at all the metal and wires.

"And that's one of the many reasons I love you."

"Because I'm stupid?"

"Because you don't run."

At that, Lydia leaned into him and stroked her hand over his head. Then she kissed him. And kissed him again.

"And I'm staying, too," she whispered against his mouth.

With the rushing buzz of Jack Daniel's on an empty gut, a sudden surge of energy raced through him, and he pulled her in against his chest. Searching her face, with the warmth of her body registering against his own, he cursed. The idea that her vitality, her life-force, would be anywhere near one of those killing machines? He felt like shitting himself.

And that made the anger in him threaten to boil over.

"Come on," he said. "Let's get out of here."

He couldn't wait to get her away from the fucking vault, and when they were on the far side of the lead-lined cylindrical coffin, he shut the heavy panel with relief that struck him as shortsighted. She was right to worry about the unit waking up. He was worried, too—even though he'd now seen with his own two eyes that the lithium battery was compromised, and so was the circuitry that ran up the back of the neck into the CPU.

But more were coming for them. And the fight was going to be brutal because they were just that deadly.

According to Rubik, when the guy had designed the robots, he'd decided not to try to improve on one of Mother Nature's miracles of invention: After five million years of evolution, with the process of natural selection solving problems left and right, why, the guy had said, would he reinvent such a functional platform? And then there was the advantage of it appearing to be a human.

Fit in well. Confuse the enemy.

Rubik had four units that he was working with, refining, testing. So all of his were accounted for. But someone, clearly from his program, had leaked the plans—as well as the sources of materials and know-how, including the propriety formulation of the skin and the programming of the CPU.

The loose lips was a big problem for the secret program, but it was not Daniel's concern—and all things considered, it was nice to turf anything off to someone else. He also told himself that in claiming his favor, he'd done the man a favor in return. Rubik had had no idea that he had an independent actor on his ship.

"We'll figure something out," he murmured. Mostly to himself.

Putting an arm around Lydia's shoulders, he drew her against him, and as they walked down to their bedroom, he tried to ignore the fact that he was split in half, only part of him with her, by her.

The tactician in him was churning with defensive ideas and plans for the attack that was coming— maybe tonight, maybe at dawn. Maybe at twelve noon—maybe at three p.m. . . .

As they arrived at the foyer, he glanced over his shoulder. In that statue alcove across from the front entry, the guard standing at attention, so fit and strong, was a grim reminder that, sure-shot trigger fingers aside, the reality was he really only had thoughts to contribute to an effort he was not welcome to participate in for so many reasons.

He was totally on the sidelines, and not just of any attack, but of everything that mattered . . .

Regardless of what he'd promised to C.P. about going after Gus's abductor.

Regardless of the vow he'd made to himself.

Yet here he was, a husk on fire with aggression that could go nowhere, the burn in his veins making his blood rush . . . a savage hunger enlivening him. This was not the healthy stuff, not the measured focus and determination to get to a goal. What he had now was the unhinged drive of combat, conflict, war.

And he wanted to release it.

Through an expression that was carnal.

At the door to their suite, he stopped and turned his woman to him. Frustration ate away at his internal organs—or at least it felt that way. "Lydia, I . . ."

As he struggled to find the words, she shook her head. "I know. You don't have to say it, just kiss me."

"I can't. Not tonight."

"Why?"

"I don't want to be gentle."

"Then don't be."

He closed his eyes. Things were complicated on the surface, but simple down deep, not that the clarity helped him. "I want to fuck you. Right now—I just want to fuck you. And I can't—"

"You can—"

"I can't!" Without warning, his anger got the best of him and he pounded on the door. "*Damn it.*"

Breaking off from her, he paced around in the hallway, going back and forth like a Ping-Pong ball, his hands on his fucking bald head, his bad-balance, weak body listing to and fro like he was on the deck of a boat, his lungs incinerating from emotion.

Or the cancer.

Or both.

"I'm just so fucking mad at nothing and everything." He wanted to grab on to his hair and pull at it, but there was nothing long enough to grip. "I'm sick of this shit. I can't do anything—it's a *fucking* triumph if I can get on my Harley and leave the driveway. I can't fight for shit, I can't protect you—I'm an old man and I'm useless and I'm *fucking* done with it."

He had no idea what he was saying. So he shut

his mouth, crossed his arms over his chest, and stared at the glossy stone floor, telling himself to get a goddamn grip—

"Don't go silent on me now," Lydia murmured. "You need to let it all out."

"That solves nothing."

"Well, think of it as some exercise. Cardio is good for people, right?"

He looked up again. In the overhead light from the ceiling, Lydia's face was stunningly beautiful, her features soaking in the illumination like she was one of those movie starlets from the forties, everything highlighted and deeply shadowed at the same time. With her hair loose around her shoulders, and her lips slightly parted—because he'd clearly surprised her with the outburst—it was as if she had been properly kissed.

Properly taken care of by a man who loved her.

"I want you," he said hoarsely.

"You can have me—"

"No, I can't—"

"Daniel—"

"You want to know why I went to Gus's frickin' hospital room as soon as I got home?" he snapped. "It wasn't to see how he was doing. I wanted some Cialis so I could maybe get it up for you—and you know what he told me? My heartbeat's fucked up so he 'wouldn't advise it.'" Daniel dragged a hand down his face. "The punchline? That fucking drug is used to improve the effectiveness of some cancer treatments. Ha ha. I'm a fucking outlier only when it bites me in the ass."

As her face tightened in commiseration with his disappointment, he had a fresh wave of anger that he was putting her through so much shit.

"I'm sorry . . ." He rubbed his eyes and then closed them again. "The last thing you need is me going off the deep end. But I feel like I'm already dead and I—"

"Look at me."

"—don't know what I'm doing, what I'm saying—"

"*Daniel.*"

"What." When she didn't answer, he had no choice but to glance over. "I . . . —"

His breath caught. She had taken her fleece and shirt off, and was standing before him bare-chested and unapologetic about it, her breasts bathed in that light, her nipples standing out in stark relief.

"Fuck me, Daniel," she said in a guttural voice. "Now."

TWENTY-FOUR

JUST AFTER LYDIA and Daniel backed into their bedroom and kicked their door shut, Cathy walked down to her study and closed herself in her workspace. As she glanced around at the austere decor, she thought, Christ, would it kill her to add a little color. In a rug, maybe. A fricking throw pillow.

A damn bouquet of flowers?

Annoyed with herself, and so many other things, she went to her desk and sat down. Out of reflex, she leaned over the glossy top and checked her reflection.

"Holy shit."

As opposed to the perma-composure she had always cultivated, her hair was a floppy mess, all kinds of blond stalks shooting off in all kinds of different directions. Running her hands through things, she tried to put some order into her follicles, but really, the stuff growing out of her head was just half the problem. The bags under her eyes were something you'd have to check at TSA, and the lack of makeup really let the sallow cast to her skin shine.

She was clean; that was about all she had going for her—and it was going to have to be enough.

Sitting back, she wrapped Gus's fleece around herself and crossed her legs. She needed to check her email, but she knew what she was going to find there. She needed to check her phone messages, but she knew what she was going to find there. She needed to . . .

Start wrapping things up.

Glancing around again, she'd always intended to die here in this house: This was supposed to be her toe-tag property. For most people, that was an old-age thing, but not for her. Still, that had been the plan. The banks, however, weren't going to let that happen. The debt she'd taken on was attached, like its own kind of cancer, to any asset she had—and as with metastasis, it had spread through her stock portfolio, this real estate, the equipment in the lab, her cars, the art. She had pushed her leverage as far and as hard as it could go to buy herself time to run the lab with all of its employees and expenses. Each day and night was another advancement in experimentation, results analysis, and new compound ideas, even as Vita-12b had been the real horse to bet on.

So much had been riding on that initial human test, and the fact that she'd been prepared to do it herself had been a kind of poetic justice, a money-where-her-mouth-was moment. Except then the pregnancy had happened, and Gus had left the company—and everything had gotten even worse after that.

She had never once considered leaving the drug to any child she might have or had any second thoughts on those documents she'd signed. The compound really was Gus's, the result of his brilliant mind and all his hard work. Besides, she had done some very ethically questionable things in pursuit of her business goals.

Contaminating her baby with all that had been a wrong-foot-start that she hadn't been interested in.

Putting her hand on her belly, she felt the ache in her heart kindle up. The sorrow and emptiness behind her sternum were on a rheostat, she was discovering, flaring and subsiding depending on what her focus was at any particular time. But they were never not there—

A light flashed underneath the desk's plane of glass, and she closed her eyes and shook her head. Then she reached under the lip, pushed a button, and a seam opened on the expanse. Like Cinderella's glass slipper on a tufted pillow, the black office phone presented itself as a gift, its base rising up. There was no sound associated with the incoming call, just the light. She hated ringing.

On the digital display, instead of numbers, the word "BLOCKED" appeared.

She didn't want to answer things, but she reached out and picked up the receiver. "Gunnar, it's the middle of the night."

"Getting closer to dawn, actually, for you."

"How's the weather in Houston." She swiveled toward the long windows even though there was nothing to see out of them. "Or did you have something else on your mind."

"Must we play these games," he said with a sigh of defeat.

"Apparently."

It was their typical banter, yet neither was putting much effort into it.

"What can I do for you?" She rubbed her temple as it began to pound. "And before you ask, no, I still don't know where Gus is."

The lie was smooth off her tongue. Then again, she had been posing in front of business competitors for the last decade and a half at the negotiating table. Hell, her whole life was a front.

"I have to say, I'm not sure why I'm calling."

"Then I'll help you out." She let her head drop back on the chair's padding. "You're going to behave like a superior asshole, I'm going to call you on your shit—"

"Must you be so crass—"

"—and we're going to end with me having the upper hand and you steaming as you hang up on your end."

"That is *not* how things go."

"The fuck it isn't. Sorry, 'fudge.'"

There was a period of silence, and she imagined the man—dressed in his European-cut suit, with his tie right up to his throat even though it was late—grinding his molars as he sat in an office every bit as streamlined as her own. The picture of irritation was so satisfying, she wanted to go another couple rounds of prognostication peppered with cursing calisthenics.

And how's that for a mouthful—

"You were right."

Cathy blinked. Then frowned. "I'm sorry, what did you say?"

"I am not repeating those words. I have no idea why I am saying them in the first place."

"Well, this is a surprise. And if you keep up with the compliments, I'll add you to my speed dial."

There was a shuffling sound, as if Rhobes were rearranging himself. "That was not a compliment. Merely a statement of fact."

"I'll take it as I wish—and you're wasting that holier-than-thou expression with your eyebrows up along your hairline. This isn't a Zoom call."

"I despise you, Phalen." Except there was a

chuckle behind the statement. "And the reason you were right is that the car was in the garage."

"I'm sorry." She sat forward. "What?"

"I endeavored to send an attorney to Dr. St. Claire's condominium so that the employment documents could be signed and notarized. You remember, that gentleman works for me now?"

"I despise you, too," she muttered.

"Yes, I am aware of that. At any rate, I had emailed and phoned Dr. St. Claire late that evening to arrange such a visit. Having received no response, I was concerned that you were working your feminine wiles on him."

"FYI, I was not." Gus had turned her down the one time she'd tried to kiss him. "And Dr. St. Claire does not go against his word. If he told you he's with your company, then he is."

"I hope that your high opinion of his loyalty holds out if he returns. When he returns, rather." Tension tightened the accent in that deep voice. "In any event, I found your accusation quite maddening."

"Which one? That you're an asshole? As you say, that was a statement of fact."

"I shall take it as *I* wish, Phalen."

She had to laugh a little. "Fair enough. But all kidding aside, what are we talking about here?"

"Dr. St. Claire's car. You accused me of lying

about its location, and then insinuated I was the abductor myself."

"I don't think I insinuated the latter. I was pretty up front about it. But I'm very sure you weren't personally the one taking him out of that condo. You probably don't even buy your own suits. So you would delegate any kidnapping to—"

"That is quite enough, thank you." A string of quickly spoken syllables suggested Rhobes was cursing in German. But then he got his control back. "After I could not reach St. Claire for a protracted period of time, I sent a representative to his home."

"Representative? Again, is that what you're calling those henchmen you use?"

"And you employ—what do they call them? Boy scooters?"

"Scouts," Cathy said. "And now I'm picturing a Vespa wearing a sash of camping patches right now, so thank you for that—"

Rhobes cut her off briskly. "The representative was the one who informed me of the car's location— and after I enjoyed your conversation ever so much, I attempted to reach him. For the last twelve hours, I have been unsuccessful."

Interesting, she thought. So whoever the guy was was either a deserter or had, in the words of Daniel Joseph, woken up dead. Unless Rhobes was lying again to cover his tracks—which seemed a more reasonable conclusion than him admitting to a person he considered a professional enemy that one of his private guards had gone AWOL.

"Maybe his phone is charging," Cathy hedged carefully.

"Do you honestly think we have not been to the man's abode," Rhobes muttered. "He had worked for me for about two and a half years. His credentials were impeccable, even if he was . . . a bit dodgy, shall we say. These private for-hire guards are a bit of a black market, are they not. I am aware you know to what I refer."

Cathy remained silent for a moment. "What can you tell me about him?"

Not that she expected Rhobes to say—

"We have had no problems with his employment—"

"What's his name?"

Now it was the man's turn for a pause. "I am sorry, all employees in that sector are kept confidential."

"And yet you're supposedly sharing HR details with one of your competitors."

"These circumstances are rather unusual, do you not agree."

Drumming her fingers on her desk, she found herself nodding. "Actually, I do agree." Then again, they were both running underground research labs. Their version of business-as-usual was anything but, just to begin with. "Any chance the guard went by the name of Kurtis Joel?"

Daniel had brought up the name when she'd had him witness the Vita-12b documents. And if there was any possibility that—

"How do you know that name?" Rhobes blurted.

"Is that your employee?"

"No comment. Now answer me. How do you—"

"No comment."

There was yet another long moment of quiet. And then Rhobes said in a low voice, "Be careful, Phalen. And I mean that not as a threat, but as a recommendation for self-protection. You know what happened to my lab in Pennsylvania. If that were to happen beneath that house you live in? No one would survive."

"You're something, Rhobes. I'm not sure what surprises me more—the fact that you honestly sound like you mean that or the sadness in your voice. Are you saying you'd miss me?"

"No comment."

"Look at you, going soft." She found herself smiling again. "You might not be so bad after all, Rhobes."

"The truth is, Phalen, I rather like having a competitor like you around. You keep me on my toes. May I ask you something?"

"Sure." At this point, what did she care. "And I think I know what it is."

"Oh?"

"I gave Vita-12b to Gus because it's really his. That compound is his work. I just provided him with a safe place and the resources to develop it. I'm the catalyst, but I'm not the creator, and I guess . . . I want to go out knowing that it is where it belongs."

"Out? Phalen, are you retiring, then?" The surprise was not hidden in the slightest. "I realize that I may have been a bit aggressive with the talk of your financial difficulties, but surely you know that bankruptcy is just the first stage in fiscal recovery. With your contacts and reputation, you can turn all this around. I myself have had my difficulties, from time to time. It happens."

Cathy took a deep breath. Funny, she was almost tempted to tell the truth. But in the end, she knew that was not wise. No one outside of Gus, Lydia, and Daniel knew about her illness. Well, those three and her medical team.

She cleared her throat. "I just think I'm going to pack up my dolls and dishes, as my mom used to say, and move on to something new."

"Well, good for you, I suppose. Although imagining you doing anything but what you are now seems like a waste. In any event, I shall keep you posted concerning any developments with Dr. St. Claire, and I expect you to do the same for me."

"Roger that, Rhobes." When the man did not immediately hang up, she said, "Something else?"

After a moment, the man murmured, "There was one strange thing about that bodyguard."

"What was that?"

"He only worked at night." A dismissive sound percolated over the connection. "But I suppose that was just a personal preference."

TWENTY-FIVE

As GUS GOT into the lab's main elevator, he wasn't sure where he was headed.

Nah, that's a lie, he thought as the doors shut and he hit a button on the panel. He knew exactly where he was going, he just didn't want to think about it too much.

When nothing moved, he punched the button again. And then many times—

Things finally got rolling, and the ride up out of the earth to the house level was a slow one, slower than he remembered. To pass the time, his brain toyed with his last ascent in this Otis box. When he'd headed home that night, he'd known he wasn't coming back to work here anymore, and that had struck him as kind of shocking. Little had he known what would be waiting for him at his condo.

And now here he was, the prodigal researcher returned—

A muscle spasm gripped the hamstring on his left leg, and he cursed as he switched his weight to

his other foot. When that got him no relief whatsoever, he tried shaking things out—and that just
caused him to lose his balance and bang his sore
shoulder into the brushed steel wall. Fucking hell,
talk about your deck-chairs-on-the-*Titanic* situation. It was probably way too soon for him to be up
and around, especially without a crutch or a cane.
If he'd been just any patient he was treating? He'd
have slapped every available wrist and ankle with
slip-and-fall risk bands.

But that was the beauty of being your own doctor: You could suck at your trade and not have to
worry about malpractice. If he passed out or went
into a vertigo spiral and cracked his head open on
this slick, hard floor? Who the hell was going to
sue him—

Bump. Bing.

There was another pause. Like he was being vet-
ted in some new way by the security types. And
what do you know, the shame that washed over him
made him want to vomit—

Whrrrrrrrr.

As the doors opened, he looked up and wanted
to apologize to all the guards who were staring back
at him from the camera that was mounted in the
upper left-hand corner. But that was stupid . . .

Before memories he couldn't bear to go back
to threatened to derail him, he stepped out and
breathed in deep. It had been a lifetime since he'd

been in C.P. Phalen's black-and-white house. Or at least it felt that way. But as he walked forward into the foyer, the stupid modern art sculptures still looked like a waste of money to him.

The judgey conviction was a bit of a relief because it was familiar, and right now, everything about him, except for the most basic timeline of his existence, was veiled by an amnesic fog. Sure, he could recall the born-here, schooled-there, lost-his-sister-when, soldiered-on-how stuff, but even those big tentpole things, even the childhood loss that had shaped his entire career in oncology, were all stereo instructions, no emotion tied to anyone or anything.

An autobiography that hadn't been written well—so the reader just didn't give a shit.

Maybe that was why he was up here in this stone fortress decorated by Magnus Carlsen. He was seeking the only thing that made him feel . . . anything . . . when he thought about it.

Heading to the left, he told himself to turn around, go back to his hospital bed, etc. etc. etc. But all that good advice was just a frontal lobe reflex, nothing that he took seriously and certainly nothing that caused him to pivot back around.

And then he was standing before a closed door, and remembering when he'd opened it without knocking before—and what he'd seen on the other side: C.P. Phalen and the blond guard.

Well, first C.P. Then the guard in the private bathroom, looking like he'd had an orgasm—or three—that he'd really enjoyed on his goddamn lunch break.

Fuck.

Curling up a fist, Gus felt like a total fool as he—

The doors opened automatically, triggered by some switch in that weird modern desk C.P. used, and as the study was revealed, his eyes shot to where the woman of his dreams was sitting.

"Areyouokay?"

Three words, four syllables, the lot of it spoken on a oner as the lady of the house bolted upright from her chair.

As Gus stared across the formal room, he stalled out—not because he couldn't remember why he had come or what he wanted to say. On the contrary, everything became too vivid.

Especially because she was wearing his fleece. Still.

Gus's heart rate quickened. Although that was probably not good news, for so many reasons. "Ah . . . you got any Coke still?"

C.P. blinked, like she was translating something that wasn't making any sense. And then she nodded. "Ah . . . yes. But are you sure you need to be—"

"I'll help myself. Thanks."

Crossing the study, a buttery soft blanket registered under his feet and he paused to look down.

Sure enough, he wasn't wearing shoes, and for a split second, he was concerned that he hadn't noticed until now. Then again, hey, at least he wasn't flashing her his ass because he was in a hospital johnnie. Scrubs were almost real clothes, FFS.

Over at the bar, he opened the mini-fridge that was kitted out to look like the rest of the glossy black cabinetry, and as he palmed up one of the red cans, he wondered idly what was in the rest of the compartments.

The crack of the opening was loud, and as he turned around, C.P. Phalen was back sitting down, her hand resting on a black office phone that seemed as though it might have extra powers: Landing the space shuttle if NASA ran into problems of the Houston variety. Solving *pi* to twelve billion digits.

Bringing back *The Office* for a reunion season with the full cast.

"Gunnar called just now," she blurted as she fiddled with something under the lip of the desk; abruptly the phone disappeared, as if it were sinking under the surface of a liquid abyss. "I didn't tell him you were . . . you know. I mean, he's your new boss, so I figured you'd probably want to call him yourself."

Or not, Gus thought as he took a sip.

"Damn, this stuff is good."

"I keep it in there for you. In the house—and the

lab, too." She looked down and seemed not to know what to do with her hands. "What are you thinking as you stare at me like that."

"You look like hell."

She laughed shortly, but not at all in a ha-ha-that's-funny kind of way. "Go figure. And you're not exactly ready to run a marathon yourself—how are you even out of bed? Does Lipsitz know you're up here?"

"Yeah, he does." And that had been a fun conversation. "I'm going to leave in the morning."

Those eyebrows crashed down as she shot a glance at him. "You're not well enough to go anywhere."

She was right, of course. He was on the verge of a collapse standing here on this nice rug—which he imagined, if he did go down, would offer a good cushion and wasn't that fortunate. But the Coke was helping.

He told himself it was helping.

Okay, fine, he couldn't feel his legs, and his entire body was not seventy percent water, but seventy percent pain impulses. His anger and his panic were like gasoline in his veins, however, and though the engine of his will was battered, it couldn't help but turn over.

"You don't need to worry about me from a malpractice liability standpoint," he said. Because, hey, he'd already compromised her location to an enemy of hers. How could any lawsuit compete with that? "I advised myself it was okay to come up here—and I don't work for you anymore, so no workers' comp risk, either."

She mostly hid a wince. Mostly. "It's not safe for you outside here."

Taking a deep breath, he heard himself reply, "It's not safe for anyone inside here. I told them everything—" As his breath caught, he took another sip, but there was no getting anything through his tight throat. "I am so sorry—"

"No," she cut in sharply. "You do *not* blame yourself. Am I clear? No matter what you said, it doesn't matter. I've been a target for most of the last decade by all kinds of bad actors, and that was before you even came along. I'm a big girl. I can take care of myself."

His eyes blurred with tears and he looked away. "I tried not to tell them. I couldn't fight—"

"Stop. Right now."

When she didn't say anything else, he glanced back over. Her stare was totally direct, and for a moment, he was reminded of who she really was. Yeah, sure, the hair was no longer sculpted, and that crappy fleece of his was standing in for one of her power suits, but the inner steel was still there.

Hell, he almost felt sorry for whoever was taking her on.

"I've taken care of us here," she said. "Nothing

short of a nuclear bomb is going to breach this facility. Heal yourself by letting go of the guilt, okay?"

Gus blinked. A couple of times.

Well, jeez. Put like that? If she wasn't . . . the most perfect woman he'd ever met, he didn't know who else lived up to that standard. Too bad she was pregnant with a dead man's baby, and prepared to die bringing that other man's infant into this world. Assuming she lived even that long. Her disease was really advanced, not being treated, and very soon, the symptoms she was no doubt fighting off by sheer willpower were going to take over: The body always won over the mind at the finish line. No matter what a person told themselves as they rounded their final lap.

"Look, I just wanted to tell you something before I left." He took a drink of the Coke like it was whiskey and might give him some courage. "I'm going to rip up those papers you sent over to me. About Vita."

Her eyebrows bolted up. "Why in the hell would you do that?"

"I don't want something for nothing."

"*Nothing?* You made her. She's yours."

Gus thought back to as recently as a week ago. When he'd thought Vita was theirs. "You need that drug more than I do. Take it, sell it to Gunnar if you want—or someone else. I'll be fine. There are other things I can work on for him. Besides, he hired me without knowing what you did—"

"I'm not going to let you do that."

"You don't have a choice."

"So you give her away. Do whatever you want."

Did C.P.'s voice just crack and she tried to hide it? He wasn't sure.

"No," he said. "You put the money in all along, and you're bearing all the debt. Sort your finances out with it and, you know, leave something . . . to your baby. They're going to need it in this world."

Especially if you're gone, he thought.

"Anyway, that's all I came to say." Well, that and the apology she refused to accept, for being tortured and blabbing like the wuss he was. "Take care of yourself, okay?"

With a jerky swing, he turned around and headed back for the door as fast as he could. Which wasn't that fast. When he finally got to the black panels, and he reached for the knob, he had to look back. Even though it was a bad idea.

She was still sitting behind that desk, her face a mask, her eyes unblinking as she stared over at him.

He focused on what she was wearing. "You look good in navy blue, you know that. Not as severe as all that black." He opened things and told himself he needed to get gone before he said something stupid. "Anyway, Lipsitz is going to give me a ride—"

She bolted to her feet. "*Gus.*"

Looking across the distance that separated them,

he thought—not for the first time—that he was willing to die for her.

And if things went the way he was going to make them go? He probably was going to, and he was okay with that. Over the past three years, he'd thought he was living for the work he was doing on Vita.

Not true. He had been living for C.P. Phalen.

"I understand you want to go," she said, "and I don't want to be harsh about this—but for fuck's sake, they almost killed you. You think they're not going to want to finish the job?"

Yup, he sure as hell had done that math. And as she confronted him, he couldn't tell her what his real plan was. But he had to protect her.

There was only one way to do that.

"I lied," he told her. "You don't look like shit. You never could. Then again, the inside of you was what I've always loved best about you."

With that, he left her . . . taking the last Coke he'd ever have with him.

TWENTY-SIX

AFTER DANIEL KICKED their bedroom door shut, he kissed his wolven so hard, she stumbled backwards—but she was nothing if not light on her feet. And as she caught her balance and wrapped her arms around him, that was exactly what he needed more of.

Melding their mouths once again, he took them all the way over to their bed, and as she fell back against the mattress, he covered her with his body, pushing his way between her legs, shoving an arm under her so he could hold her even closer. Goddamn, this was good. His tongue was in her mouth, and his free hand was going for her breast, and his hips were rocking against her—

It was hard to say when . . . things got hard.

And not as in difficult.

He was so busy just swallowing her moans, and feeling her undulate under him, that he didn't even notice when the softness of her core started to cushion something at his pelvis. A ridge. A length—

Daniel slowed down. Pulled back. Pulled off.

And looked to the front of his pants.

Well. This was . . . *"Fuck."*

"What's wrong—are you—what . . ."

As her words drifted off into stunned silence, he was pretty sure she saw what had captured his own attention.

"You know," he said, "all things considered, it shouldn't be that surprising."

At that, he looked at his beautiful wolven, with her lips so red from his hard treatment, and her hair tumbling over the pillow, and her ribs pumping in a way that jogged her breasts, the tight nipples bouncing.

She was, after all, the hottest female anything he had ever seen.

"Fuck, we gotta move," he heard himself say.

Like there was an expiration on the erection? But shit, in case there was, he wasn't missing this chance to—

"Oh, my God, yes," she blurted. "Fast!"

The scrambling that followed was about as romantic as tearing the clothes off someone who needed urgent medical treatment. As Lydia started yanking off her pants, Daniel's own hands shook as he attacked the button on his fly and frantically wrenched down his zipper. Then he shoved everything down as far as he could.

He had to touch it.

Reaching for his pelvis, he had a thought that this better not be a dream. This better not *fucking* be a dream—

"Ohhhhhhh, yeeeah . . ."

Nope, this was real. And shit was stiff enough to do the job. And he even had feeling in the damn thing—the friction registered and so did the lightning strike in his balls that came afterward.

"Lydia—"

As he glanced over, his wolven was tossing her bottoms away like they were on fire, and then she grabbed for him, yanking him off-balance—

Daniel went right back to where he'd been—except this time, there was nothing between them and he had something he could work with. He wasn't even worried it wasn't as stiff or as thick as it had been before. He was a miserable beggar who was not going to be choosy about this gift.

"I love you," he said as he went for her mouth.

"Daniel, I love you, too—"

He true-north'd himself with his hand, and the instant her wet heat registered on the tip of his erection, he shook with anticipation. He was a virgin all over again, while also knowing what his woman liked and needed—the best of both worlds?

Sure as fuck was.

His hips knew exactly what their one job was, and before he could think of anything else, he thrust into her sex—

They both cried out, and he might have teared up a little. He didn't know, he didn't care. He was pumping now, deep and deeper still, in a rush, in a panic—because what if this ended—

"Daniel—I'm coming, oh, *Daniel*—"

From a distance, he heard his wolven cry out again, but he was too busy going into himself, measuring the crest of an orgasm as it intensified, feeling the sensations of pressure in his sack, hinging his lower spine so he could move faster and faster still. He was aware that his lungs were burning, but it was anticipation—

And fear.

Fucking please, he prayed. If he never asked for another thing in his life, *ever*, just let him come. He wanted to be in this moment once again with the woman he loved, to share the carnal so they could both go to the divine, to transcend the earthly suffering he had been wallowing in and fly, freely—

And that was when it happened.

Her sex contracted around his, pulling at him, milking him, and he had a moment of infinity, a suspension between everything that was so frantic, and hungry, and needy, and desperate—and the float that was on the other side of the rise.

He needed this like he needed the cure that wasn't coming for him.

That he wasn't going to get—

The first ejaculation racked him, whipping his body straight, every muscle in him seizing up—and then the next came. And the next—

He started crying.

As his body did what it had been built to do, as he filled his female up, he squeezed his eyes shut, buried his face in her fragrant neck, and let the life inside of him go into her. Was it joy? Yes. And sorrow, too.

But mostly . . . it was gratitude.

For one prayer finally being answered.

✦　✦　✦

Underneath her man, Lydia dug her nails into Daniel's back. The feeling of fullness, of completion, was overwhelming, and so was the release she was finding—and continued to find—because he was coming inside of her. And as he lowered his head into her, she smelled his tears and held on even tighter.

It was all so unexpected.

Closing her eyes, she arched up into his chest. She was naked except for her socks—because why bother with them—and he still had his hoodie on and the strings in front were digging into her breasts and she didn't care in the slightest.

The union was everything in the whole world, the surging of his body into her own, the stretching sensation of his erection going deep, the way her thighs were spread open and he was between them and they were—

Her orgasm kept rolling, and she went with it, trying to record every single slide and penetration, the way he kicked in her, the gasping—hers, the moaning—his . . .

This was a gift she had never dared ask for because he had been enough for her, just the way he was.

When they finally stilled, Daniel rolled to the side and took her with him, and he hugged her close, his hand stroking down her spine and cupping her hip, locking them together like he didn't want them ever to part. She knew how that felt.

He lifted his head and wiped his face. "Sorry I'm sloppy—"

Lydia smiled and kissed him, tasting the salt. "Never apologize. Especially not after that."

They were still joined, and she moved her leg up a little higher so that the fit was even better. In response, he kissed her, stroking her lips with his own. Then kissed her even more deeply. As his tongue entered her, she sighed and gave herself up to the sensations.

After a little while, he eased back. "I don't think I've got a second round in me. But considering the first was a shocking surprise, I'll take what I was given and be grateful for it."

"Well, I'm grateful for having been taken."

He laughed. "Are you now."

The good ol' days, she thought. This was . . . like it had been.

The temptation to get lost in sadness vibrated under the bubble of her happiness, but she tamped the darkness down, praying that her will to hold it in place was strong enough.

She smiled into his eyes. Such beautiful eyes, she thought.

"You are quite a man," she murmured.

"Am I now."

"Yes, you are."

They lay there for what felt like an eternity, and the peacefulness was a water level nourishing a dry lake bed.

"Hey," he whispered, "can I ask you something?"

Lydia nodded. "Anything."

"Will you marry me?" As she felt herself jerk in surprise, he shrugged. "I know that I'm supposed to be on one knee, and it's supposed to be at sunset, and we're supposed to have a photograph so you can post online—"

Lydia kissed him and said yes at the same time, and then they were laughing.

"It's why I took you to the apple orchard," he said. "I thought it was pretty romantic. I don't know, we don't have beaches up here, and even if we did, November is November. But those trees, you know. I thought in the spring when you went by them they'd be in bloom and you'd remember that I loved you."

Lydia's smile slipped a little. Slipped a lot. "I will always know you love me. Always."

"My wolf . . . my beautiful wolf."

They kissed again, but this was different. It was a vow, not a start of something sexual or a way to finish off a session of making love.

"I should get you a ring," he murmured.

"I don't wear them?" She flared out one of her hands. "I like to be able to change at will, and I would hate to lose it."

"I know something else then. We can go—"

The knock on the door was not shy. And then a familiar voice: "You guys up? I need to talk to Daniel."

As Daniel sat forward, Lydia tucked the covers under her armpits and did the same. "Gus—"

"Gus?"

The door opened wide and there the doctor was, up on his feet, dressed in blue surgical scrubs, looking like himself. Well, almost himself. The swelling and the bruising were still on his face, and he hung on to the doorjamb like he was not completely sure of his ability to stay standing.

Daniel yanked the duvet over his naked body. "Hey, are you okay—"

Gus put an arm over his eyes. "Jesus, when am I going to learn not to walk in on people—"

"No, it's okay," Lydia said. "But why are you out of bed?"

"Does everybody *have* to ask that?" the guy muttered. "And I'm sorry I interrupted—"

"What do you need," Daniel demanded. "Whatever it is, I'm there."

Gus lowered his arm, looked at them both, and then focused on Daniel. "I need you to teach me how to shoot a gun."

Lydia lifted her eyebrows. "Why would you . . ."

But then she looked at the side of his neck, where there was a burn mark—and figured, maybe it was for personal protection. And who could blame the man?

"Yeah," Daniel said grimly. "I can do that."

TWENTY-SEVEN

I T WAS RIGHT at dawn that Daniel stepped out the back of Phalen's house. As he took a deep breath, his lungs threatened to cough on him, but he exhaled quick and told himself not to get ahead of things. Then again, it was in the nature of knuckle-headed men to bust a nut and feel like Paul Bunyan.

Which would make him a model for paper towels, he supposed.

But come on, it had been how long?

"You ready," he said as he glanced over his shoulder.

Gus St. Claire didn't look all that ready. The guy had on a black parka from the stock the guards used, and it was okay in the shoulders, too short in the arms. His boots were likewise on the lend from the supply closet, and as he stepped out onto the back terrace, he lifted them up funny, like a dog with booties strapped on its paws.

"Yeah, of course." Gus zipped the puffy jacket up his chest to his chin. "I was born ready."

The way his eyes bounced around the back forty suggested he was in an internal debate with himself to the contrary, but it was hard to know whether he was worried about being out in the open or if it was more what they were about to do.

Maybe it was that he was counting down to a departure from this fortress of relative safety—and was uneasy about it.

Leaving was a dumb idea, of course. But hey, stones and glass houses and all that: Daniel wasn't exactly a poster boy for being sensible. Otherwise he wouldn't be out here in the cold with his lungs, would he.

"Come on, Doc," he said as he started off. "We'll take it slow."

Not that there was an option to go fast-wheeling. Both of them were dragging, and though Daniel wouldn't have wished so much as a hangnail on Gus, it was nice to not feel like he had to apologize for his own snail's pace.

After they crossed the flagstone terrace, they hit the dead lawn and rounded the winterized swimming pool. On the far side, they started into the meadow. The thing had been mowed one last time before the frosts had started, so short of watching out for gopher holes, the going wasn't so bad.

Overhead, the sky was a dull gray, and the gathering light of day wasn't making much of a difference when it came to illuminating the landscape.

Daniel didn't mind the relative darkness at all. He preferred the shadows, and instinctively, he searched the pines in the distance, and the open field, and the house behind. He'd made it clear to the guards that they were going out together, and explained what they were going to do. The uniformed types hadn't liked it. *He* didn't like it.

But there wasn't a gun range inside the house or the lab, and Gus was determined to go home—and maybe this little tiptoe into the world of firearms would prove to the guy exactly how foolhardy it was for him to leave right now. Did the doctor really think he could come out here, shoot at a couple of tree trunks, and be qualified when it came to self-defense? No fucking way. Hopefully how hard it was going to be would make Gus change his mind.

And as for security, there were cameras everywhere, guards on standby—and outposts in the forest that were manned. They would be safe . . .

Fine, safe-ish. And if this kept Gus on-site? The roll of the dice was worth it.

"So this is where you came out to smoke?" Gus asked as they continued tromping through the short field grass.

"Ah . . ." Daniel glanced over, and as he flushed, he thought it was amazing how you could be a full-ass grown man and still feel sheepish when you got caught doing dumb shit. "How'd you know."

"Lydia told me about it." The doctor nodded

to the forest line that was still a ways off. "I figure out here is the only place you'd get any privacy—plus you seem to know exactly where we're going."

"It was stupid."

"Quality of life, not quantity."

Daniel laughed in a hard burst. "I coughed the whole time, so it was neither of those."

"Old habits die hard. You don't need to apologize to me."

"Even though I gave myself lung cancer?"

"I don't judge." The man shook his head, his dark eyes shifting over. "Your DNA let you down against an environmental toxin that, yes, is avoidable, but plenty of people get cancer without engaging in risk factors, and plenty of people engage in risk factors and live to be ninety-five. It's just the luck of the draw. Like everything."

"You're a wise man, Doc."

The grunt that came back at him could have meant a lot of things: pain from walking, stress from everything, modest agreement that he was a Mensa candidate.

When they reached the trees, Daniel entered the way he had before, through a natural gap between a stand of birches and two oaks. The going got easier because the underbrush was kept in strict control during the growth season so that the monitoring of the property was more effective.

The navigational props he'd set for himself were

intact, the sticks that were crossed or laid at specific angles on the ground, the branches that were hung in the V's of trunks, the rock that was set in the cradle of a root, all precisely where he'd left them last. He tracked the directional cues on a parallel process, part of his mind making sure he didn't trip and fall with his unreliable feet, the other half ticking off the progression of markers.

Gus was talking the whole time, his chatter a release of nerves, and who could blame him. Fortunately, the conversation—about the weather, and the college football playoffs that were approaching in a month, and what he liked with his Thanksgiving turkey—was not the kind of thing that required robust responses.

Meanwhile, Daniel was looking for signs of disturbance. Footprints. A pattern of broken branches. His makeshift trinket map fucked up because the points of orientation had been so subtle that they wouldn't have been noticed and avoided.

There was none of that.

But come on, like whoever had abducted Gus wasn't savvy enough to camo their presence?

The fucker had been here already, though. Had to have been.

It's what Daniel always did before infiltrating a site.

"Here we go," he announced as they stepped out into a clearing of sorts.

There was a fallen maple right down the center of the break in the trees, and he remembered sitting on the downed trunk and trying to smoke and drink a little Jack. Really pathetic, if you thought about it.

"Have you ever held a gun before?" he asked, even though he guessed the answer.

Gus shook his head. "Not unless an arcade counts."

"It doesn't. Okay, let's start from the beginning." Daniel unholstered his nine millimeter. "There are three rules. One, assume all guns are loaded. Two, don't put your finger on the trigger until you're ready to shoot. And three, don't point a gun at anything you aren't ready to destroy."

Gus glanced down at the weapon. Looked back up.

"Repeat what I just said," Daniel prompted.

"Am I being graded?"

"Yup, and the F gets me shot while I'm trying to teach you."

The three rules were spit back at him like Gus had had them drilled into him all night long. Then again, the guy was a genius, right?

"Good." Daniel put the weapon flat in his own palm. "This is a nine millimeter Glock seventeen, Gen five. There are seventeen rounds in the magazine—"

"Wait, can you show me first? Like how it works?"

Daniel nodded, slipped off the safety, and front-sight-focused on a tree trunk about twenty yards outside the clearing. As he inserted his forefinger and found the trigger wall, he took a slow, easy breath. Settling a little deeper into his stance, he drew in another relaxed inhale.

Then he swiveled his head toward Gus, met the guy's eyes, and pulled the trigger. The *pop* and *thwack* were a quick one-two, and the doctor's mouth went slack.

"How did you do that?"

Daniel lowered his arms. "Practice and muscle control—"

"Whatthefuckisthat—oh, *shit*—"

As Gus recoiled and jumped back, Daniel wheeled around and pointed the gun in the direction of whatever had gotten the man's attention— but when he saw the pair of glowing yellow eyes, he immediately slipped the safety back into place and returned his weapon to its holster.

"It's a g-g-goddamn wolf," Gus sputtered. "What are you doing—shoot it!"

"No," Daniel murmured as he got down on his haunches. "We do not shoot wolves in my family."

As soon as he lowered himself, the beautiful gray and brown female broke her hiding spot and trotted over, and God, he could feel himself smiling throughout his whole body as he held his arms wide.

He should have known his Lydia would watch over them.

His female was protective that way.

◆   ◆   ◆

Confronted with the prospect of being eaten by a wild animal, Gus was kinda done with the whole shitting-in-his-pants-terrified thing. In fact, he'd been born un-ready for the sort of adrenal assaults he'd been enduring lately. A man of science, who liked controls and facts, was notfuckingequippedto-dealwithgettingtornapartbya—

As Daniel went down close to the ground, like he wanted to make things easier on the wolf when it turned him into a Big Mac, the massive, one-hundred-twenty-pound predator . . . trotted over like a pet, ears floppy, jowls loose, tail swinging back and forth. And when that idiot opened his arms, the predator went right to him, rubbing its face on his chest, in his neck, on top of his head.

"What . . . the . . ."

On his side, Daniel was all about the Steve Irwin, stroking the powerful flanks, sinking his fingers into the fur, smiling like the pair were all reunited-and-it-feels-so-good.

". . . fuck," Gus finished.

"She's here to protect us." Daniel looked up from the animal. "She's our best line of defense. With her nose and her ears, we have nothing to fear out here."

At which point, the wolf angled "her" head toward Gus. With that tongue lolling out of those fangs, it was hard to reconcile the I'ma-eat-you with the lapdog routine—but you couldn't argue with the fact that the animal had had more than ample opportunity to chew Daniel's face off. And his arm.

Maybe one or both of his legs—

The wolf refocused on Daniel and took his sleeve gently between her front teeth. Then she sank down onto her haunches and started tugging.

"What are we doing?" Daniel asked as he stood up.

The wolf released and went to the place in the clearing she'd come out of. Then she pawed at the ground.

"Okay, we're coming," the guy said.

"We are?" Gus muttered.

As Daniel walked off, Gus looked around—and considered his options. He had two choices: Stay out here, alone, in the woods—where there were either more wolves that weren't friendly or the guy with the fucking sodium thiopental back to finish the job—or follow along after a man with a gun who knew how to use it and that carnivore who had a politician's way with people.

"How the fuck do you know she's not leading us to a buffet table—where we're the entree," he groused as he started to follow.

The rhetorical was answered as Daniel's hand

rested on the back of the wolf while the pair went along, winding their way around trees and shrubs, a rock or two, a deer stand. They were in such sync, you'd have sworn they were ballet partners, but fortunately for Gus, they didn't put on the speed. The going was measured, like the wolf knew she was in charge of two people who weren't so great on the balance side of things—or endurance, either. And when she finally stopped, Gus was relieved to lean against the trunk of a tree and just breathe.

As the animal fixated on something on the ground, Gus rubbed his face—or tried to. As he bumped into his swollen eye, he winced and dropped his arm. The good news was that the cold air was wonderful in his lungs and on his cheeks, and he could feel that he was getting stronger physically, seemingly by the minute.

He was going to need it when he went back to his condo . . . and waited for that fucker to come for him again.

Please come finish your job, he thought as he stared up at the gray sky. Because surely his captor would check for his body and find it gone?

Provided Daniel taught him a few things, first.

Refocusing on the wolf and the man, he said, "Whattya got?"

"A set of footprints." Daniel pointed to what looked like any other square inch of the forest. "Side by side."

The wolf was shaking her head. Looking around. Shaking her head.

As Daniel's eyes also did a roundabout, the guy nodded. "And no tracks. They start here, like whoever it was had been dropped from above. And there's something in the tread of the boots."

Gus wandered over and glanced down. "Serial numbers?"

"No, like fresh . . . sawdust—"

"What?" Dropping into a crouch, Gus narrowed his eyes. "Oh, my God. That was the smell."

"What smell?"

"When I was being . . . whatever'd . . . ah—" Sweat broke out across his forehead and down his chest, but he did his best to kick off the reactive anxiety. "There was this smell in the air, I couldn't place it at the time. But it reminded me of my grandma's—Pine-Sol."

Sure enough, inside the tread pattern, there were lemon-yellow flakes . . . of fresh shavings.

"Except that is the real thing, isn't it," Gus murmured.

Daniel glanced up. "You know you can't go home now, right." The guy pointed to the prints. "That's going to be waiting for you."

"Which is the idea."

Daniel blinked like he was sorting through various responses and weeding out the ones that didn't completely emasculate the other half of the conversation he was having. "No, you're too valuable to waste on a vigilante mission you're ultimately going to fail at—"

"It's my life, Danny boy—"

"Yeah, and it's mine, too," the man snapped. "You're my fucking doctor. I need you even if I'm a hopeless case, and so does C.P. You want to deal with your misplaced guilt over something you couldn't control? Do it by sticking around and helping us the way only you can. You're more useful to us alive than dead."

Gus felt his eyes start to water. "This is all my—"

"Fault? Because you volunteered to get kidnapped and tortured? Explain to me that math." Daniel jabbed a finger across the cold air. "You stick with us—and you'll get a chance to make your amends by helping us in the grim homestretch we're both facing. That's the way you deal with the self-blame. Not running off and getting yourself killed—unless you think twenty minutes out here is going to turn you into a sure-shot? Because I guarantee it won't."

The fantasy of being all vigilante and drilling that bastard with the accent in the center of the forehead began to fray. Especially as Gus measured the exhaustion that had crept up on him courtesy of their little stroll.

And he thought he had the energy for a gunfight?

"They're coming after me, though," he said.

Daniel glanced down at the footprints and then looked at the wolf beside him. After a moment, he shook his head.

"No, I don't think so. I think . . . there's a bigger picture, but I just can't see it. Yet."

TWENTY-EIGHT

"CLOSE ENOUGH TO noon," Lydia said as she hit the brakes. "'Come back in two days.' For God's sake. It's just stupid games, anyway."

As she punched the P button on the Suburban's dash, she looked out at Eastwind's house and wondered why she was bothering to turn off the engine. The sheriff was toying with her, and besides, now they had Gus back and alive, right?

She thought of the footfalls she'd seen in the forest when she'd been in her wolven form.

"We need to play this out," Daniel said as he opened his door.

"So he should pick up a phone and just call us," she groused. "He's a sheriff, not a king. What's with the royal visit bullcrap."

"In small towns, that's the way it goes."

Cursing under her breath, she got out and waited for Daniel to come around the hood of the SUV. Even after the tromp through the forest, he'd still left the cane behind, and she was relieved to see he was walking so much better. His color had improved, too—and not just because he was flushed from the chill in the gray morning.

"This won't take long," he said.

"It better not."

As she faced the house, she was distracted by all her rank pissed-off—so it wasn't until she was almost to the front door that an eerie tingle went through her spine. Stopping, she tilted to the side so she could look through the windows on the first floor. Everything was dark inside.

"What's wrong?" Daniel asked.

"I don't . . . know." Backing up, she leaned away so she could see upstairs. "There's something off."

Heading up to the entry, she had been prepared to pound with her fists—instead, she used the lion's head knocker.

Bang, bang . . . bang.

Shaking her head, she murmured, "I've got a bad feeling about this—"

Right on cue, a white car made a quick jog onto the long drive and came racing down, dust kicking up behind its rear tires. As the sedan skidded to a halt, the driver's side door, which was marked with a decal that read "Hanson & Honeywell Realtors," was thrown open.

"I am so sorry I'm late." The young woman tripped over an untied sneaker as she launched herself out from behind the wheel. "I'm Sarah—

Gary Honeywell's my dad? Oh, wait, the message said you're not from around here so that doesn't matter. I was about to teach a spin class when you texted. I do it downstairs at the church? Noon today. Peg's taking over—"

She stopped. "I'm rambling. Sorry. I do that. But here, I'll show you the house right now."

As she hipped the car door closed, she patted at the messy brunette bun on top of her head. She was wearing blinding yellow Lululemon tights on the bottom, and for a split second, all Lydia could do was wonder what the top half was like. Fortunately, things were covered with a ski jacket.

Then she snapped back to attention. "See the house? We're not here to—"

Daniel stepped forward and put out his hand. "We just got here ourselves, so don't worry about it."

"Oh, thank God." Sarah-Gary's-Daughter shook what was offered. "I really appreciate it. I just moved back to Walters. I went to SUNY Platts-burgh and I graduated this past June—well, I had to make up one class this summer—"

She stopped herself again. "I'm doing it some more, aren't I. Okay, refocus, refocus—so come on in." The girl smiled, flashing beautiful teeth. "You guys are the first to see this place, and I don't know your situation, but if you're serious about renting, I'd jump on it. There aren't many houses in Walters like this one.

"Three bed, two and a half bath." After fishing around in her pocket, she took out a key and unlocked the front door. "And there's the barn in the back meadow as well as that detached garage over there."

At this point, Lydia's ears stopped working as she tried to look around the woman's shoulders as things opened—and as soon as she was able to get into the living room, she didn't pretend and play a role. She strode through the rooms—and knew Eastwind was gone. The sparse furniture was all in the same places, the beautiful Native American textiles hanging right where they'd been, the kitchen neat as a pin. But as she inhaled, there was no fresh scent of the sheriff.

He must have left in the middle of the night, soon after they did.

Even though the speed with which she surveyed the house wasn't going to change anything, she hurried upstairs, taking the steps two at a time. She hit the big front bedroom first, the one with the en suite bathroom, and everything was tidy, the queen-sized bed made, the towels in the loo folded neatly over rods by the shower, a faint whiff of Windex and Pine-Sol lingering in the hot, dry air—

A hissing sound made her jump. But it was just the radiator under the windows that faced the main road.

"What the hell are you doing, Eastwind," she muttered as she went over to the dresser.

Of course all the drawers were empty. And the closet was free of even hangers, nothing but a solitary dowel stretching from one side to the other.

Just as she was pivoting around to check the other bedrooms, something caught her eye. An envelope. On the bed stand closest to the door. As she went over to it, the strangest feeling of déjà vu went through her.

The fact that her name was on the front was almost not a surprise, and her hand shook as she reached out. It was heavy and thicker than it appeared, and as she opened the flap with her forefinger, her heart started to beat hard.

Things beat harder as she eased out the letter that had been folded around—

"What the hell?"

The stack of twenties that feathered down to her feet made no sense, and she gathered them up and put them on the little table so that she could read the handwriting. There wasn't much, but she could hear the words spoken in Eastwind's deep voice:

> I've stayed too long. But I was waiting for the next steward. Take care—and if the radiator in the living room stops working, just kick it a couple of times. It'll come back on. Tom

Lydia reread the four sentences over again. And then tried them out for a third time, only stopping when she heard footsteps ascending the uncarpeted stairs.

"—have kids? No? Well, Walters is a great place to live. Everybody knows everybody. Hey, do you do spinning? No? Well, it's great exercise—"

The realtor stopped short in the bedroom's doorway and smiled. "Oh, hi! I was wondering where you'd gone. Great place, isn't it?"

"How much is the rent," Lydia asked hoarsely.

"Eight hundred and forty. That's what the owner said he wanted."

"Um . . . who owns it? This house, I mean."

"I'm afraid he didn't want to say. I mean, we all know him, he was the—sorry. He doesn't want anyone to know."

Lydia cleared her throat. "Did he explain—did he say why? I mean, is he going somewhere? Or did he just not like the . . . house. Or something."

Man, she was a sucky liar.

The young woman looked back and forth between her and Daniel. Then leaned in like she was afraid the room was bugged. "He said he was relocating? Frankly, we all find it a little sus. He's only ever been here. Why would he leave?"

"Where to," Daniel said casually.

"He didn't say. But I think there's a story." Abruptly, the young woman put up her hands in surrender and shook her head. "None of my business, though, and my dad'd kill me if I go blabbing my mouth. Here, let me show you the rest of the upstairs."

◆ ◆ ◆

This was going to go fine.

As Cathy stepped into her mansion's main elevator, her heart was tap-dancing in her rib cage and she had a fine sheen of perspiration above her upper lip. There was a momentary pause while she was cleared for descent—because in days and nights like these, everybody got cleared, *everybody*—and then, when things got going, she entertained a brief fantasy about Gus St. Claire. She imagined that, having been reunited with his coworkers at the lab, he would be so struck with a longing to return to the place where he was needed most, wanted most . . . that he would rip up that employment contract with Rhobes and tell her he was staying for the rest of his life.

Okay, fine. The rest of hers.

When the bump announced her level had been reached, there was another pause, like the elevator was gathering the strength to open its doors. In that period of stasis, she closed her eyes and pictured the way Gus had always strode through the aisles of the workstations, everyone else in a white coat, him in a concert t-shirt featuring the Grateful Dead, or Pink Floyd, or maybe Peter, Paul and Mary, his Afro framing his face and shoulders, his body moving so confidently.

Bing!

At the sound, the doors parted, and as she caught a whiff of mechanicals, floor polish, and disinfectant, her gut rolled.

Stepping out, she tugged at her black suit jacket, and as her weight settled on her high heels, her balance wobbled a little. Her Achilles tendons had ached for the past few days while she had been in flat shoes, but now that her feet were artificially arched again, they were quiet, the position they'd grown used to reestablished. Cathy couldn't say she felt the same as she walked down the screening hall with the double mirrors. Her clothes were not constricting in the slightest, as she hadn't been eating well, but the makeup felt like she'd spray-painted her face, the outer corners of her eyes tickling because of the liner and the mascara. Oh, and her hair was frozen in place, the swoop like a sculptural effect instead of anything that grew out of her head.

The *clip-clip* as she marched down the polished concrete floor was the metronome of her life, and the Armani suit was her uniform, and the look was that which she had cultivated and perfected a decade ago. In the past, the illusion had been skin-deep, going right down into the core of her. Now? It was window dressing that she was hoping would give her some false courage: The cramping in her lower belly was a constant reminder of what she'd lost, and the creeping exhaustion she felt like she was battling harder every day was a marker of what was coming—

What if Gus had already left the property?

She'd known as soon as he and Daniel had gone out into the woods at dawn. She'd been upstairs in bed, not sleeping, when her monitoring system had gone off. Sheer terror had thrown her over onto the laptop that lay open beside her, and she had felt no relief as she'd watched the pair walk across the field.

What if he just strode away without a goodbye?

But come on, she'd told herself. First of all, it was a helluva trek back to Plattsburgh on foot. Secondly, there was no getting over the perimeter wall—no easy way, that is. And finally, Daniel was sensible. He understood the reality of what they were all in, maybe even better than Cathy herself did. He would talk sense into the good doctor.

And they had come back, the pair of them.

Whereupon Gus had gone down to the lab.

Their lab.

As she was cleared for the last time and the lab's main door was opened, she entered the cavernous area of workstations. Researchers looked up and nodded at her—then promptly went back to whatever they were doing, and their focus was something to envy. She felt so scattered and scrambled that she wondered how in the hell she had done all this: Hired these people away from jobs that were on the up-and-up, found this facility and renovated it for her purposes, created a drug that had real potential thanks to her head of R&D.

Then again, she hadn't been where she was now when the journey had started.

And of course, for all her efforts, the lab had cost her everything. Literally.

The fact that the enterprise needed to be wound down was a reality that she couldn't ignore, and she had to get started with that right away.

Tick-tock with the clock.

As she entered the hall of patient rooms and examination spaces, she had a flashback to her and Gus planning everything out, from those workstations, to the cold storage units, to the organizational chart with the employee positions and the reporting lines of authority. She could remember them walking down here, and him shaking his head at the bald concrete and empty, cave-like space.

Where the hell did you find this place?

I have my sources. And it will work.

And it did. For a time.

When she reached the doorway to what had been his office, she hesitated before she knocked, and she thought about the elevator's pauses. Then she got with the knuckling.

No answer.

More with the rapping, and then she leaned into the door. "Gus? I need to talk to you."

He'd left his patient room, and she knew without checking there that that hospital bed would be
empty. Having gotten up on his feet, he would not
go backwards. Not unless it was a medical emergency, and she would have heard about that.

"Gus?"

When there was still no reply, she pictured him
stretched out on the bare floor by the desk. He'd
done that sometimes when his body's need for sleep
had finally trumped that incredible mental engine of
his. She'd never understood how he could find anything REM-related without so much as a pillow—

She pushed things half-open. "Gus?"

Shoving the door all the way wide, she told herself she was making sure he hadn't had some hor-
rible complication. This was a medical necessity—

"Shit."

Cathy backed out of the empty office quickly,
and then stalled in the hall. She hadn't seen him
among the medical staff in the workstation area,
and the boardroom with its glass walls had been
empty.

When she started walking again, she went back
out to the open area and hung a sharp left to go all
the way down the far side of the lab. In the distant
corner, a steel door marked "Authorized Use Only"
loomed even though it was no larger or thicker than
any of the other fire exits—and when she punched
at the bar, she felt her entire body tense up.

On the other side, the small, square room glowed silver from all the stainless steel, glass, and overhead lighting—and Gus's living, breathing presence was a not-like-the-others in the midst of the technology and mechanicals.

He didn't even turn around from the cryobanking unit.

And after she stood there for what felt like an entire year, she cleared her throat loudly—

"Christ!" he barked as he spun around.

As their eyes met, her hand went to the base of her throat. "Sorry. Didn't mean to startle you."

"Oh, yeah, no." He took a couple of deep breaths and looked her up and down. "Going somewhere?"

She studied his face as if it were tea leaves and she knew anything about predicting the future. "I thought you were leaving."

When he just shrugged, she nodded to the unit with its warning signs and the fingerprint-locked release on the jamb. "You thinking of taking her with you? You're allowed, of course—we're just going to have to get you an ice chest."

As the venting system hummed at a deeper volume, like the compressor had kicked in, he exhaled like she annoyed him. "I told you, I'm ripping up that contract and you're keeping Vita—"

"That's actually what I wanted to talk to you about. Can you take some of the staff with you?"

Gus shook his head as if to clear it. "What?"

"Rhobes and you are going to need researchers familiar with Vita, and everyone here was trained by you—"

"Are you hearing anything I'm saying, or as usual, is it the C.P. Phalen show—"

"—so it's not like you need their résumés—"

"—and to hell with everybody else—"

"—alsoIcanbeyourpatientonenow."

She spoke that last sentence real quick because she was determined to show no emotion. But as he just stared at her, she realized she might have overplayed the velocity.

"You're in charge," she tacked on. "Of her. So you can give her to me. At Rhobes's."

The wave of exhaustion that visibly went through him seemed to take a couple of inches off his height, and as he started shaking his head again, he brought up a hand like he wanted to rub his face—before he grimaced and abruptly dropped his palm as if he remembered there was nothing but bruises there.

"Look, I'm not going through this with you again—"

"I'm not pregnant. Anymore. I lost the ba— I miscarried a couple of nights ago." Putting her hands on her hips, she looked around at the high-tech everything and tried to draw some strength from the clinical nature of it all. "So your rate limiter is gone."

Gus stared at her for a long moment. "Are you okay?"

"Oh, yeah. Absolutely. I was thoroughly checked out. An ultrasound was performed and there is no residual tissue—"

"Are you okay," he interrupted with more volume.

"Yes. I'm fine."

When he just continued to stare at her, she started talking about something, anything. It could have been Rhobes's location down in Houston, or maybe transferring Vita-12b. Maybe she'd switched it up and was talking about world peace. Basic arithmetic. Who the hell knew.

"Stop," Gus said, putting his hand out like he was on a crosswalk and his job was ensuring schoolchildren didn't get mowed down in traffic.

"I'm fine."

The sharp edge to her voice was directed at him. At herself. At the whole world, and the dumb luck of biology—dumb bad luck, in her case. And for godsakes, if he didn't stop looking at her like that, she was going to have to leave. It was as if he saw all the way through her, right down to the cramping, which seemed to be ramping up like her now-empty uterus knew it was the subject of conversation . . . right down to her sad, pathetic, broken heart.

"I'm really sorry," he said softly.

Cathy looked away, and holy hell, she was glad her makeup was waterproof. Blinking fiercely, she tried to find her voice so she could brush off the concern.

Finally, she said, "I'd really appreciate it if you weren't nice to me right now. Thanks."

TWENTY-NINE

W ELL, ISN'T THIS a surprise," came the brisk welcome. "A BOGO that shows you two worked it out."

As Daniel stood on the front step of a little cottage just off the main rural road, he still couldn't remember the older woman's last name. Apparently, his chemo brain had taken things as far as it was willing to go by filing her away in the memory banks as "Candy the WSP Receptionist." That was all he had.

Well, that and the fact that he didn't want to rehash the last time he'd been here, and the blowup that had come with it. But that was all in the past, and hey, Candy was right. He and Lydia had worked things out. Thank God.

"I just need to ask you something," Lydia said to the woman. "Do you mind if we come in?"

Candy, whose hair was on the pink side of "natural redhead" at the moment, backed up and indicated the way inside with a hand that had red-

and-green-polished nails. "C'mon in. I got coffee, and leftover pie. That's it 'cuz I'm going food shopping today in Plattsburgh. Daniel, how're ya."

The Brooklyn accent cut all the syllables up into sharp corners, and the last part was not a question that required much of a response, but rather a statement to show that she cared about how he was.

"I'm good," he murmured as Lydia's forward progress faltered. For a very good ho-ho-ho reason.

"Oh . . . wow," she said as she looked around at the decor. "You outdid yourself this year."

"Looks great, doesn't it." Candy shut the door. "Takes a while to set up. But I was inspired—plus now that the WSP is shut down, I have time on my hands to do it right."

The parlor was covered in Christmas, from the tree all tinseled up in the corner, to the Santa statues and nutcrackers, to the collection of themed teddy bears that took up most of the couch. All of the knickknacks and figurines that had been there before had been replaced with ones that were in the holiday spirit, but none of that was the highlight.

A model train track had been laid down on the carpet, the twin stripes of rails running a sweep throughout the room, passing under chair legs, swinging through a couple of tables, and going around the tree. Currently, the locomotive was chugga-chugga-choo-choo'ing by the front of the fireplace, and of course, Santa was the conductor in the bright green engine, and Rudolph was riding on the cherry red caboose, and in between, the open boxcars of presents and real candy were actually pretty damn quaint.

As he knelt to inspect a bridge made of Tootsie Rolls, he said, "I saw this up for sale a couple of weeks ago."

"I couldn't resist."

Daniel glanced over at Lydia. "Candy's another QVC lover."

"Oh, that's right." His wolven went over and perched on a sofa cushion that was three-quarters teddy bear. "You two have that in common, don't you."

"Never pegged him as a shopper," Candy said with a shrug. "But people surprise you. Now, who wants coffee?"

When they both shook their heads, the woman went over to a recliner, sat down, and shifted a set of needles linked by a pink square of stitching into her lap.

She pointed with the project. "You can move the bears, ya know."

Lydia smiled awkwardly, like she was anxious to get started but didn't want to be rude. "I'm okay."

Daniel likewise sat down amid the sea of teddies, and he did move a couple. Onto his lap, as it turned out—because where else was he going to put them, he thought as he picked up his feet so the train could pass by. As Lydia did the same with her boots, he decided this was a new kind of low-impact aerobics.

"So what we got?" Candy's hands fell into a sequence of moves that she clearly was well familiar with, the needles making a little clicking sound. "And don't make it too hard. It's too early in the day to think too much—"

"I need you to tell me what you know about Thomas Eastwind."

The woman looked over sharply, her hands freezing in mid-stitch. Something about the way she stopped moving so completely brought into hard focus all that bright red hair, and her Santa's elves sweater with its silver and gold accents, and her bright green polyester pants. But make no mistake. As those eyes narrowed under all their blue shadow, the calculation in them was about as homey as a shotgun.

"Whattabout him."

Again, not a question that was looking for an answer—especially one that involved any urging her into making a statement about the man.

"You've known him for a long time." Lydia sat forward. "Haven't you."

"Not really."

Shaking her head, Lydia said softly, "I can't tell you why this is important. But you've got to help me."

Candy put her knitting aside, stood up, and walked out.

"This is going well," Daniel muttered as he played with one bear's ears.

The sounds of rustling in the kitchen percolated out to where they were sitting, a refrigerator door opening and closing, cutlery knocking into a plate, something being poured. When Candy came back, she had apple pie with ice cream on it and a cup of steaming coffee. The mug was orange and black, and shaped like a pumpkin. Clearly a holdover from October's decor.

As the woman sat down again, Daniel remarked, "So you don't do Thanksgiving?"

"Nah, that's for families and I don't have any really." She forked up some of the apple pie and put it in her mouth. Then she immediately went to the satellite ice cream scoop for a chaser. "I'm a Christmas girl 'cuz Santa comes to everybody. And just let me eat this in peace first, 'kay? Then we'll get to the Eastwind shit."

Maybe they were finally going to get something from somebody, Daniel thought as he lifted his feet up to accommodate the train.

Man, he was tired of wild-goose chases, he mused as he discreetly glanced over his shoulder. Through a gap in the lace curtain, he saw a second of Phalen's blacked-out SUV sitting at the head of the driveway, on the rural road. The damn thing looked about as subtle as a grenade on a teacup's saucer.

As he refocused on Lydia, he didn't mind the obvious presence—not that he expected any trouble. Walters was a quiet little town, but even people who lived in quiet little towns had cell phones and 911. If whoever was coming for them had any brains, they wouldn't try something in broad daylight.

Candy went through the pie the way she did her conversation, with no dawdling and no fuss. She also didn't seem to worry about things like the careful rationing of ice cream and pie or regular coffee sips to balance the palate. She just got the job done, and then put the clean plate and fork aside and wiped her mouth with a paper napkin she took out of the pocket of her handmade sweater.

"He came here," she said.

As Lydia jerked to attention, Candy nodded. "Yesterday. Told me I should expect a visit from you."

"You're kidding." Lydia looked across at Daniel. Looked back at the woman. "How did he know I would—"

"I don't know, and I don't care. He just informed me that I was to tell you to move into that house and take over from him."

"Yes . . . he left me a weird note about that and some money?" Lydia shook her head. "But I'm not going to be a sheriff—"

"He's not talking about the law, Lydia. And don't pretend you don't know what he means."

Candy stared across the room as the train came back around by the couch. Once more, Daniel lifted up his feet first and then Lydia did the same, and then the choo-choo headed back toward the tree in the corner.

"Listen, you don't need to waste time trying to bullshit me," the older woman said quietly. "You're different, just like he was. I knew it from the moment you walked in the door at WSP and applied for the position as our head biologist. But hey, I believe people are allowed their privacy, especially when it's about stuff I don't understand."

Daniel ran a hand down his face and checked on Lydia. She had lowered her eyes and was churning her hands in her lap.

"It's okay," Candy announced. Like she was declaring that a new law of physics worked within all existing rules of time and space. "I won't say nothing. B'sides, who the fuck would believe me? 'Cuz you're right. I've known that SOB for forty years and he hasn't aged one day. Meanwhile, look at me. I'm turning into a goddamn Golden Girl—"

"But I don't know what he means. Take care of what—"

"I didn't like him." Candy held up her hand like she was swearing on a Bible in court. "Not because he was evil, but because he lied to everyone, and expected to get away with it. He thought we were stupid and didn't notice things. Well, I did. I just kept my mouth shut about it."

"The mountain," Daniel breathed.

When both women looked at him, he only focused on Lydia. Studying her face, he felt as though pieces were fitting together. Finally.

"He wants you to take care of the mountain," he heard himself say. "He's giving it to you, the place you love the most. The place . . . where your people are. That's your future, Lydia."

At that last part, he could feel himself getting teary. And yet it was okay. If he had to leave her, at least he would know she had a higher purpose, one that would serve her as much as she served it.

"Ding, ding, ding," Candy murmured. "Somebody get this man a jelly donut."

◆   ◆   ◆

Oh, God, she'd lost the baby.

As the news sank in, Gus didn't believe C.P.'s "I'm fine" declaration for one fucking minute. It was why the woman had put her business clothes back on. It was why she couldn't quite meet his eyes. It was why her hands were trembling.

It was why she was blinking like that.

She was as far from fine as he was, and having learned of her loss, there was a curious deflation on his part. He had hated that she was pregnant, and

not because she couldn't try Vita-12b. No, it had
been a reminder that she had fucked someone else.
Which had been real damned petty on his part—
but at least he didn't feel any relief at the news.

Maybe he was turning over a new leaf when
it came to the woman, finally putting aside all the
things he felt that he needed to. For his own sake.

I'd really appreciate it if you weren't nice to me.

"What kind of mother would I have been anyway." Her voice cracked and she coughed it back
into order. "I mean, come on. And that's before you
toss in the cancer. And as for Vita-12b, I don't have
anyone to leave a legacy to, so that's why you are
taking her. It . . . I mean. The drug."

"I don't know what to say—"

"You don't have to say anything. Just take your
staff with you. I'm going to have to shut all this
down in the next week or so because I can't afford
to pay them anymore, and you know you're going to
want the continuity of work. Rhobes will hire them
all. They're the best of the best, right? And then
you'll have me as your patient one. If you'll have
me." She held her palms up. "I have nothing better
to do with the end of my life, and nothing to worry
about, either. The banks and the creditors can fight
over what's left, split it up, write off the rest. And
I'll coast out having finally been useful."

"What if you live, though," he said remotely.
"What if she cures you."

"We both know there's a toxicity issue that has to be sorted out. With my advanced cancer, you're going to have to hit me so hard, there's no way I'm going to make it for long. But you'll be able to prove it works, and you'll learn things that will help you help other patients. In that, I have a future. Of a sort. Right?"

His eyes drifted over her face, and he remembered the first time he'd seen her in person. He'd read about her in the papers, but the photographs hadn't done her justice—and it wasn't her facial features or the Ice Queen window dressing, either. It had been her eyes, so hard and sharp. No softness in them at all.

It had made him want to find out if there was anything in there, behind the curtain of control.

"What." She crossed her arms over her chest. "Will you please say something? And if you're trying to compose a nicely worded brush-off, I'll tell you right now, I'm your best chance. I have the right markers, and you know it. Besides, we were on this track until . . . things happened and you said you wouldn't administer the drug."

Gus opened his mouth. Closed it.

"Jesus," she snapped. "Will you *say* something?"

"I don't want to kill you."

At that admission, she didn't miss a beat. Even stepped up closer and put her hand on his upper arm, like she was consoling him. "But don't you get it? I'm dead anyway. Let me do something good on the way out—that's . . . what the baby was for, when it was with me. Gus, we were on this path. We just need to get back . . . on the path."

He returned to the moment he'd told her she was pregnant. She'd been to MD Anderson for regularly scheduled scans and assessments, but they'd neglected to pay any attention to the results of the hCG test they'd given her—probably because so much had been going on with her cancer.

She hadn't believed him, so they'd tested again in-house.

"Why can't I seem to leave you," he said roughly.

Her eyes flared like he'd surprised her. Then she whispered, "You don't have to. Leave me, that is."

THIRTY

AS DANIEL SPOKE up, Lydia felt a strange shimmer come over her, and because she didn't know what else to do, she picked up a random bear from the collection and cradled the thing to her chest. The plushie had soft black fur and a red Santa suit on, and as she dropped her face forward, she knocked his white-trimmed hat off.

"I think you should take over from Eastwind," Candy said.

"What does that even mean," Lydia mumbled.

Even though she knew: The man's voice came to her mind, sure as if he were beside her and whispering in her ear: *Nothing happens on my mountain without me knowing about it.*

"You're going to need a job after—" Candy steepled her red-and-green nail tips. "Well, everyone needs a job, don't they."

Lydia looked at Daniel.

He was staring at her with a somber expression, and when he started to cough, he was quick to shut the throat spasm down, covering his mouth with his hand, as if he didn't want to remind her of what she couldn't forget.

"You were protecting the wolves before," he said. "So just keep doing that—and maybe add a couple of acres. You love it up there anyway. That's your joy."

You're my joy, she thought.

Still, deep inside of her, her wolven self prowled against the cage of her will, wanting out right now, so it could go home up on the elevation, smelling the pine and feeling the earth underfoot.

The mountain had always been her solace. But if she went there, just because Daniel died and she needed a place to bury her grief? She'd end up hating the place.

"No," she said as she forcefully got to her feet. "And I'm sorry we bothered you. We have to go now."

Candy's blue eyelids narrowed. "You can't run from what's going to happen to him—"

"Are you really talking about Daniel like he isn't even here?"

"—and you shouldn't try to. It just wastes what time you have."

As Candy fell silent, it was on the tip of Lydia's tongue to deny everything. To say she wasn't running. To point out that it wasn't possible when she was sleeping next to Daniel every night and worrying about him every day—no matter what else was going on.

Except she wasn't fooling anybody. Not even herself.

And as she thought of that *symphath* in the red robes, and how the light of dawn had found him and flashed, brilliant as a nuclear bomb, she felt her soul crack.

"I can't think of what comes next," she said roughly. "I have no future. Only the present."

Becoming aware that she had a crushing hold on the bear, she put the toy carefully back in its place and brushed off her perfectly clean pants.

"I'm sorry we bothered you." Hadn't she already said that? "I mean—"

"You didn't." Candy got to her feet, too. "I still got to have the last piece of pie, and I wanted a coffee anyway. So, where you guys headed next? Grocery shopping? Or does that Phalen woman have half a Price Chopper airdropped into her front yard once a month—does she actually feed all those guards of hers? Not that I don't get why someone would want them around. If I were a younger woman, I'd have admired the view, if you know what I mean."

Candy was talking her way to the door, like nothing of any significance had been discussed, and as Daniel started following her, Lydia looked back at the Christmas tree. It was an artificial one, and collections of ornaments were grouped together on the branches: Disney princesses in holiday-themed dresses in one quadrant, traditional bulbs in another . . . and there was a whole section on cats. The lights were blinkers. Some white, some colored.

Six weeks until December 25th.

She couldn't fathom thinking that far ahead.

As a cold swirl circled her legs, she jumped and stumbled back—but it wasn't some evil portent or metaphysical intruder. It was just the door getting opened and the weather coming in like a dog sniffing around.

And hey, at least it got her out of the way of the train that Candy had set up with such great care.

Lydia floated out into the weak noontime sun, feeling like it was the middle of the night. At the end of the driveway, there was a second black Suburban, sitting like a Doberman that needed to be fed. The guards had followed them at a not-at-all-discreet distance, and overhead, drones buzzed on the periphery. As she regarded the protection, she had the sense that the tenacity of the men in those uniforms wasn't so much that they were running interference on any potential threats, but rather they were monitoring to make sure there were no security breaches.

"You guys take care of yourselves," Candy said from the front door.

"You, too," Daniel responded—even though he wasn't looking at the woman, but rather focused out on the rural road.

Lifting a hand, Lydia murmured, "I'll see you soon, 'kay?"

"Yeah, sure," Candy said. "Anytime. You know where to find me."

It was hard to turn around, and walk to the SUV. She felt like she was never going to see the receptionist again, although whether that was paranoia or prediction, she wasn't sure. Neither was a great way to feel.

Back at their Suburban, she got behind the wheel, and when the doors were shut, she glanced across the console.

"I have no idea what to think. About anything."

Daniel's face was grave. "Do you want me to drive?"

No, I want you to be well, and for me to be back at the WSP, worrying about nothing more than wolf migration and breeding seasons.

"No, I can get us home. Back to Phalen's, I mean." She pushed the start button for the engine. "And then . . . who the hell knows."

THIRTY-ONE

WAITING WAS ITS own special kind of torture, Daniel decided as he paced around Phalen's sleek, anonymous mansion.

Following an afternoon of toe-tapping and twitching, and a dinner that had been made with care but tasted like something that had come out of a truck stop vending machine, he'd started making rounds of the house. The route he established took him from the kitchen and private eating room, down by the library that was all closed up, past Phalen's study, and into the bedroom, where Lydia was sleeping.

And back. And again. And again.

He told himself that at least he was getting a little exercise.

He told himself that the improvement in his stamina was a good sign.

He also ignored the shortness of breath, the way his right leg dragged, and how his stomach couldn't decide whether it was hungry or nauseous.

His mindless gerbil activity had persisted even after Lydia had gone off for a snooze, and the kitchen had been shut down for the night. After Phalen's obnoxious chef and his skeleton crew had left, it was just the guards and him. He had no idea where Gus and their hostess were. They hadn't shown up to eat.

He hoped like hell the good doctor had stayed on the premises. There were three exits the guards let people in and out of: the front one of the mansion, the one that went out to the parking area for the lab, and the subterranean tunnel that headed out to the garage. Everything else was barricaded. So if he'd left, someone had to have let him go.

And driven him away.

Not an Uber, either.

Gus wasn't the only one with departure on his mind. After dinner, Lydia had talked about going out to run the mountain. Daniel had sensed her restlessness as if it were his own, and he knew that she needed to let her wolf free. More than that, maybe she was safer there on the elevation. She was certainly faster on her feet—paws—than those robotic soldiers.

Not that she could out-bolt a bullet.

In the end, though, she had decided to stay put, probably because she was worried about him. And he decided it was okay because at least he knew where she was, currently lying down on their bed.

She was exhausted, and he hated that.

Maybe he'd been wrong to say what he had about Eastwind and the mountain . . . and her.

As he arrived at the foyer he looked at the sculptures set with a museum curator's eye on the black-and-white-tiled floor.

"So much money wasted," he muttered as he went over to one of the blobs.

Putting his palm on the abstract form's bulges, he smacked it like a horse's rump—because God knew the thing was big as a Clydesdale. The smooth marble was cold, and he supposed he had to give the artist credit. Lot of work to get rough stone to look like it was melted cheese.

On that note, he kept going across the checkerboard floor, and as he came up to the next major piece in the open space, he pulled another ass-smacker. This time, the sinuous form was painted with some kind of sealer that was so thick, there was no way of judging what the underlying structure was made of, and so shiny, he could see his own reflection.

"Helluva mirror," he murmured as he cleared his throat and ran a hand over the new growth on his head.

Continuing on, and ignoring a sudden exhaustion, he nodded to the guard in the alcove, got no response at all—and thought about Candy the Receptionist's nutcrackers. All this guy needed was some gold piping on his uniform and a funky hat, and he was a prime candidate to bust some nuts.

In a figurative sense.

Bored of his established route, Daniel went to one of the library's French doors and popped it open. On the far side, there was nothing but darkness, a shaft of light piercing in and carving a visual slice down onto the—wait for it—black carpet.

'Cuz the shit could only be that or white in this house.

As he entered the long, narrow room, he could smell the old books, even though he could only see the shadows of the shelves that ran up the walls. Considering how antiseptic the rest of the house was, he wondered why C.P. had the collection of first editions, given that they seemed to fly in the face of her shiny-and-new vibe. Then again, they were probably good investments?

Man, he was really getting tired. Maybe he needed to head to bed.

Closing himself in, he kept the lights off because the big plate glass windows that marked the far wall became portals for monitoring the back meadow. As he went to the view, he searched for shadows moving around the winterized pool. Then wondered what exactly he would do if an attack occurred.

Other than call for the guards.

Still, he'd rather figure that one out, even with

his limitations, than be here waiting. And thinking of those boot prints that had appeared out of nowhere in the forest.

It was very possible something other than a human was stalking them—

"Daniel?" came a distant call.

"In here," he said over his shoulder.

Lydia opened the same door he had, and as her body was silhouetted by the light streaming in from the foyer, his instinct was to block the view of her with himself. But before he could get into position, he remembered that all the glass had a reflective coating on it. No one could see her from the outside.

Still . . . "Come in, but close those doors, would you?"

"Sure, but what are you doing in here?" she asked as she stepped in and did as he'd requested.

"Oh, not much." With all the light cut out once more, the visibility improved. "Just watching the night sky. There's a moon tonight."

"You're stargazing without me, are you?" Her voice was warm. "Hey, where are you . . ."

He wished he was merely looking at the heavens. "Just follow the sound of my voice."

As she closed in, he covered a little cough with his hand and glanced over his shoulder. Outside, there was nothing moving in the back of the property, no shadows zeroing in on the house, no outright attack marshaling on foot or from the air—

"Oh," she said as she bumped into him. "I'm sorry."

Putting his arms around her, he shook his head. "Don't be. I don't mind at all."

With the curves of her body registering, he swept his hand up her spine and found the tie in her hair. Pulling it free, the waves swung down and they were a little damp, smelling of her shampoo.

"Mind if I kiss you?" he murmured.

"Mmmm, please."

She was the one who brought his mouth downward, and as their lips fused, he moved his hips into her own. He had no idea whether lightning was going to strike twice, and he told himself that his getting physically aroused shouldn't matter. There were many things he could do to her—

The hardening was both natural and normal—and a total fucking miracle. And she felt it, too. Her lower body moved in closer, and the sound she made, of hunger and satisfaction combined, juiced him further.

As they continued to kiss, the darkness was erotic as fuck; it meant he felt her even more—and he backed them both up, orientating himself with his hand extended out and batting at thin air. When he found the table he was looking for, the one that ran down the back of one of the silk sofas, he laughed deeply in his throat.

Thank you, Phalen.

Courtesy of the woman's relentless minimalism, there was nothing on its surface. Which was fucking perfect. He lifted Lydia by her waist and set her on the lip. Conscious that this was a semi-private situation at best, he didn't want to waste time, but as he got back with the mouth-to-mouth, he was aware that no one knew what tomorrow was going to bring. So he had to savor this.

Taking his hands down to her breasts, her knitted sweater was a soft cushion over her contours, and he couldn't help it. He had to taste her. Easing her back a little farther, he pushed the folds up, and she had no bra on—so as he went down with his lips, there were no barriers. Sucking on her nipple, she groaned and linked her hands behind his neck, pulling him closer, closer . . . closer still.

She was wearing leggings, and they melted off her thighs as he pulled them down—

Outside in the hallway, voices volleyed back and forth, some kind of casual conversation burbling along, and his head whipped up. There was nothing to see—unless someone opened something. And talk about opportunity. The room had, like, three sets of doors that broke up the wall-to-wall shelving. He might as well have chosen to do this in the frickin' boardroom down in the lab . . .

"They're moving on," Lydia whispered.

"Good." He palmed her breast and rolled his

thumb back and forth over the tip. "I want to finish what we started."

Lydia gasped and then laughed softly. "I am not shy, but I'm not exactly an exhibitionist, either."

"Do you want to go back to the bedroom—"

Thump. Thump.

The sound of one and then the other of her shoes hitting the floor was her response, and he smiled into the velvet void.

With hands that were surprisingly steady, he finished the job with her leggings and got right in there with his pelvis, pushing into the space she made for him. Their lips re-fused, and the slide of her tongue against his, coupled with the way she rubbed her core against the front of his jeans, made him go for his zipper.

The last thing he was going to do was come in his pants.

What a damn waste that would be.

On that note, his numb fingers performed their job admirably, and he thought about the way rarity made everything more precious. The fact that he didn't know whether this was his last time meant that he was going to especially savor every penetration and all the sounds she made and the way she felt beneath him.

But the fact that the rest of the household was on the other side of those frickin' doors meant he had to hurry the hell up.

Palming his arousal, he went in, and brushed her sex with the head of his cock. Up and down. She was so slick and hot—and he trembled, for all the right reasons, as he entered her. That first stroke in was always a revelation, and the feel of it went straight into his brain. After that, his body took over, his pelvis pulling back and pushing in.

Under him, Lydia was holding on, and then she shifted herself on the tabletop and wrapped her legs around him. Rocking into her, the familiar build was an exquisite anticipation, but there was going to be no release for him yet.

She came first.

Always.

THIRTY-TWO

L YDIA FELT AN orgasm coming for her and she welcomed the sensations. Daniel was deep inside of her, and his penetrations were getting faster and faster. With her legs wrapped around his lower body and her spine arching into him, he was all she knew, all she felt.

And the lights being off blurred the distinction between memory and reality.

Was this the past? Before everything had gone so tragic? Or was it the present where she was trapped by it all?

Because she didn't know, she was free to choose—so she clung to the illusion that a reset had occurred, that the nightmare had been woken from, that her life was continuing as it had been in the spring, the future assured in the way it was for mortals . . . with blindness to fate making it seem like there was a long runway to live out day and nights and make plans with the one you loved.

Squeezing her eyes shut, she parted her lips and held on. "I love you . . ."

Something was squeaking under them, probably her butt, although the table they were on was steady enough—still, if she'd been thinking clearly, she probably would have suggested they move onto the floor. Or, better yet, do this in their bedroom.

Except she wasn't into the thinking thing now.

Holding on to Daniel's shoulders, she knew he was getting close. So was she—and then she toppled over the edge of the world first. As the release flooded her senses, she cried out Daniel's name, and that seemed to be what brought him his own orgasm.

As he started to fill her up, she stilled so she could feel all of it, the pumping, his breathing in her ear, the way her body absorbed what he was giving her.

Heaven, she thought. *This is my piece of heaven.*

When he was finally spent, they just lay there, exchanging gentle caresses and murmurs that were quiet and loving.

"Tell me something," she said. "How are you so good to me?"

"I'll put that right back on you." She felt his fingertips on her forehead, her cheek . . . the side of her neck. "My wolf."

"Will you come to bed with me now? I don't think I'm going to be able to sleep, but I'll bet we can figure out how to pass the time." When he hesitated, she said, "Please. I need to be with you."

"That's all you gotta tell me."

As he retracted from her, she closed her legs and got to her feet. "Oh, crap, it's dark in here. I have no idea where my leggings are . . ."

There was the sharp sound of a zipper and then—"Wait, I think I've got them."

As she felt something soft and springy get passed into her hands, she performed some contortion moves to get the Lululemon back in place— and probably put them on backwards. The sweater was easier. She just pulled it down, then moved her foot around the carpet in search of her shoes.

After they were once again ready for prime-time viewing, so to speak, Daniel walked into the void and she heard his hands tapping at the books on the shelves.

"Found the exit."

When he opened one of the doors, the light that flooded in blinded her, but as she went over to him, her retina recovery was fast—and as soon as she stepped out, she checked her clothes situation.

Well, what do you know. Everything was front-facing, and properly arranged on her body.

Walking side by side, they went all the way down the hall, and at the end, he stepped ahead and opened their bedroom door for her.

"I'm going to take a shower," she said. "Care to join—"

She stopped as she caught him making a discreet

grab for the doorjamb to catch his balance. After the last six months, he'd gotten good at hiding any lulls in his energy level, but she knew his tricks well.

"You need to go warm the bed." She forced a smile. "I won't be long."

Daniel nodded and cleared his throat. "I'm good with that. And don't be long."

As he wagged an eyebrow, she thought that maybe, this once, she'd misjudged him. Maybe he was okay and she was merely looking to find weakness because it terrified her.

"I'll just shower," she repeated for no good reason.

Heading for the bathroom, she was almost inside the marble enclave when she glanced back— and froze where she was. Daniel was inching over to the bed, his face tight with pain—or maybe he was having trouble breathing? And when he got to the edge of the mattress, the way he gingerly turned himself around and slowly lowered his body down made her chest ache.

As he stretched out and put his head on the pillow, his eyes closed and he released a long breath. The cough at the end was like a curse.

She knew she should turn away so he didn't catch her staring at him with what was undoubtedly a worried expression. Except he didn't look at her.

He just lay there, breathing.

"Daniel . . . ?"

His lids whipped open. "Wha—what, are you all right? Lydia—"

All of a sudden, he struggled to sit up, his hands paddling at the duvet, his face going pale as he started to pant and try to catch his breath.

Then everything went haywire. The coughing spell came on him in a series of full-body spasms, like he had been holding it in and couldn't control the reflex any longer.

The blood went everywhere, speckling his gray sweatshirt, the splatter so dark against the fibers it was as if the void back in that library was something he had taken down into his damaged lungs— and had to expel.

"*Daniel.*"

THIRTY-THREE

LONG AFTER NIGHT claimed the Adirondack Mountains, Xhex went to a set of double doors that had been handmade and set in their frame in 1874. Behind her, a crackling fire set on maple logs threw out heat not just from its flames, but from the massive lake stone hearth that ran up half the entire wall of the great room. There were lamps throwing out calming light in the corners, including one that had a taxidermied porcupine posed on a stump as a base, and another that was made out of a woven basket. There was also an old desk with a strip of Persian rug as a blotter, and a collection of antique glassware gleaming on shelves that were mounted around a center window of leaded panes.

Not that she could see out of the hand-blown panes. Heavy velvet draping covered every portal to the outdoors.

The Victorian-era Great Camp had been built

by humans hell-bent on escaping the summer heat in New York City—and also because it had been *de rigueur* for a certain class to own wilderness getaways. She had heard the stories from Rehv, about how there had been steamboats that came up from the base of the long, thin lake, carrying people and supplies to their recreational locations, and before that, the waterway had been one of the strategic military routes used by the French and the British during the battles for control in the mid-eighteen hundreds.

As she threw her back into the effort of opening things, she braced herself for the cold—and that was a smart move. The air was so dry and frigid that her sinuses burned and she hurried to put on gloves even before she re-closed the heavy painted panels to keep in the heat.

The porch that faced the lake was a good forty or fifty feet long, and in the warmer season, it was furnished with wicker seating areas. Now the expanse was bare of everything: chairs, tables, and even that plastic goose lamp that glowed like a ghost.

There had been good times on this porch, she thought . . . back when she and John Matthew, and some of the other Brothers, would come up here and hang out with Phury, Cormia, and the Chosen. She'd particularly liked it when Zsadist had brought his guitar and sung during the moonlit August nights.

"Voice like an angel," she murmured.

As she tried to remember her favorite tune, the one that he always closed with . . . something by Sting? Or was it U2? . . . those evenings seemed so far away that it was as if they were stories told to her by someone else as opposed to something she had lived.

How had everything come to this? she wondered. Turning in her weapons. Taking herself out of Caldwell for the safety of others.

"Fucking mess."

Walking down the porch, she stared out to the lake. There was a moon just cresting over the mountains to the east, and its illumination drew a line on the water, the stripe flickering on top of the waves.

John Matthew had left first, because she had insisted he go out into the field. What else was he going to do? Sit and stare at her?

She wasn't dying.

Besides, where she was going . . . she wanted to be alone.

Stepping off the porch, she walked across the lawn. The grass was nothing like the lush, chemically enhanced carpets down in the Caldwell suburbs. Up here, the blades were thin as needles, and just as fun to sit on. The lack of rain, but mostly the regular frosts that had started up in late October, had pulled the green out of everything, so all you had was a pale five o'clock shadow on the hard clay ground.

She paused at the head of one of the stone walkways that wound down to the water. The house had been set up on a cliff, because back when it had been built, prospective homeowners had had the pick of the lots—and man, had they called this site. The view was a dramatic, perfectly centered framing of the mountains that dropped down to the basin of clear water, like an artist had carved the landscape just so Hudson River School painters could have both realism and symmetry.

The vista really should have calmed her.

She needed a number of deep breaths and shoulder rolls before she could dematerialize, and as her molecules scattered, she had a vague worry that there would be no reunion of her components. Then again, even if she was fully corporeal, she wasn't all together, was she.

When she re-formed, she was at the base of Deer Mountain, on the main trail. The fact that she didn't bother to hide herself behind a big tree, but instead popped out of thin air right in front of anybody who'd been around? Not good. And as she got to hiking, she told herself the protocol slipup had been intentional because the temperature was north of a meat locker, and who the hell would be out here?

But that was bullshit. She hadn't even thought about some human who might be hardcore-ing for their wilderness YouTube channel seeing her *poof!* into existence—and recording the damn thing.

It was the one rule that the vampire species and the Lessening Society agreed on.

No human involvement, unless it couldn't be avoided. And then if it couldn't be avoided, you needed to clean that crap up.

Xhex glanced around.

Then again, considering everything else she was fucking up lately, this was a minor infraction. Besides, no one was actually out here.

Nobody human, that was.

As a shiver went through her, she crossed her arms over her chest, her leather jacket creaking from the cold. Without her usual holsters on, there was too much room inside her coat, the sartorial equivalent of clipping your nails, she supposed.

"I've got a journey, huh," she muttered as she scanned the trees that crowded up to the cleared trail. "So here I am. I'm starting. I'm walking."

With visions of Dustin Hoffman in a white suit pounding on a taxicab hood, she trudged onward, ascending at first gradually and then with greater angle. She remembered the first time she had done this—and John Matthew had been forced to reveal himself.

There was no one with her tonight.

And unfortunately that continued to prove true. No matter how far she went, or how intently she searched the pines, the old woman with the strange aura failed to show up.

It seemed ironic that she was trying to seek out that which she had totally denied back in the spring. Then again, life had a sick sense of humor, and people who were at rock bottom didn't have the luxury of getting fussy with their opinion of reality.

You have a disease of the soul. If you do not cure it now, it will destroy you.

Between one blink and the next, she saw eyes staring up out of a bandana, eyes that she had taken without any conscious knowledge of having done so. Then she pictured that body on the slab at the morgue.

The energy is trapped just beneath your flesh. Unless it is released, once and for all, you will never be at peace.

"But how?" she said to the pine trees. "How do I release it? Ah, come on . . . throw me a fucking bone."

You must, child. Or you will die by inches . . . and take all you love down with you. To stay where you are is a death sentence.

"What am I doing? Please . . . tell me."

There was no reply, and goddamn but she

wished she hadn't wasted her time arguing with the entity. Instead of getting answers, she'd only wanted to fight with everything she hadn't wanted to accept.

Now, when she needed guidance most, all she had were her own useless thoughts, scrambled and tormented.

And her own useless company.

Or so it appeared.

◆ ◆ ◆

As Xhex marched up the trail like she was heading to her own execution, Blade tracked his sister through the pines, making sure that he stayed downwind and behind her. He was also careful to monitor her vicinity. That male of hers, John Matthew, was bonded, and he had big friends, so there was a chance that there were members of the Black Dagger Brotherhood nearby.

It wasn't that he couldn't handle them. He had too much on his mind to be bothered—and the fact that Xhex had shown up tonight, while he was already wrestling with so much, was just fabulous.

Exactly what he needed.

Her mood seemed no less sore than his own, however. Walking up the main trail, she stopped regularly, but not because she was taxed physically. She was in prime condition, a true specimen of a female, capable of feats of strength and cunning that made her just as deadly as any male.

No, she halted from time to time because she was searching for something, and he wondered what would bring her here with such dark expectation.

Then again, her grid was in shambles. The collapse that had been threatened had in fact occurred, the three-dimensional structure of her emotions and her consciousness utterly disbanded. Something had happened since he had seen her last— and so recently, too.

You are better at caring for others than you wish to acknowledge.

Shut up, he thought back at the voice of that "old woman."

Memories of the entity, or whatever it was, had dogged him since the moment the thing had supposedly departed. To the point where he felt hounded. Pursued. Even though there was never aught in his wake. Indeed, he had left the confines of the cave shelter after darkness had arrived to try to find some peace—and his sister's path up the mountain had intersected his winding way down. As if things had been planned.

Or mayhap "inevitable" was the word.

It was hard to know when he made the decision to allow his presence to be known, but at some point, halfway to the top, he stepped in some distance behind her. As his strides were slightly longer than hers, the gap between them was gradually closed as the ascension progressed.

And yet Xhex persisted in her forward orientation, her attention remaining upon what was before her and off to the sides, but never what was in her rear.

The absence of a reaction—or any awareness at all—struck him as alarming. After which, it dawned on him that she was, in fact, totally alone.

"Xhex."

The instant he said her name she pivoted, her hand pushing into her leather jacket and fumbling around for something.

"Do not shoot me," he said, assuming a bored tone.

You care for things more deeply—

"Shut. Up."

Xhex stopped with her searching, her dark brows slamming down over her gray eyes. "I haven't said shit."

Gritting his teeth, he forced a smile. "That was not intended for you. And are you . . . unarmed?"

He hadn't noticed before, but there was no scent of gunpowder on her. Which was not her normal course of things.

Alone? With no personal protection? Where the *fuck* was her mate—

"Then who's it for," she countered. "And what the hell are you doing following me."

No surprise she left the weapons question unacknowledged. And he told himself it was not his place to worry over her.

He did not believe that lie, however.

"You came to the mountain, sister mine. I was already here," he intoned grimly.

She glanced around. "So you think you own all this now?"

"No, but if you're accusing me of tracking you, I have every right to point out the fact that you arrived where I reside, not the other way around."

"Your home is the Colony."

"By birthright, so is yours."

Xhex shook her head. "No, I was escorted out of there. Remember?"

He opened his mouth to answer with something flippant, something appropriately distancing and arrogant. But as the moonlight filtered down through the pine boughs, he saw not the illumination for what it was. Rather, he saw fragments of that old woman, as if her shimmering essence had been split apart, yet not diminished.

Shifting his eyes back to his sister, he felt as though he were standing at the lip of a great fall, one that he had been teetering on for quite some time. For . . . over twenty years.

"What," Xhex snapped.

When he could not speak, she threw her hands up and pivoted away from him. "I'm done with your games—"

"I have never forgotten."

His sister slowly twisted back around. "What did you say."

He cleared his throat. And yet his voice was no stronger as he repeated, "I have never . . . forgotten why or how you left the Colony."

THIRTY-FOUR

*E*VERY TIME *I get out . . . they keep pulling me back in.*

As Gus ran for the patient room he'd recently been treated in, Al Pacino's voice banged around his head, but one of the better scenes in the worst *Godfather* movie was promptly forgotten as he shoved open the door and flipped into doctor mode.

The patient on the bed was not a surprise.

The options for treatment were going to suck.

And given the amount of blood on the front of that gray sweatshirt, there was a whole lot of nothing good going on.

"What happened," he asked Lydia as he pushed one of the staff out of the way.

Even with the three or four medical types circling the bed, removing Daniel's clothes, hooking up leads, the woman was right by her man, and going nowhere. She was clearly scared to shit, her face frozen in terror, her hands shaking as she kept pushing her hair back over her shoulder. But someone was going to have to forcibly remove her if they wanted to reach that left side.

Which, at the moment, they didn't need to.

"He started coughing," she said, "and he couldn't stop—and then he just lost consciousness. I called down here and they came with a stretcher and . . ."

As she trailed off, he glanced at the monitor. Oh . . . *great.* Oxygen stats were in the cellar. Blood pressure was way too low. Heart rate was in the high 180s, trying to compensate for both.

"I need oxygen, stat, and let's get some blood." Maybe Daniel had an infection somewhere and was going septic? Except the downturn had been a little fast for that. "When he's stable, I want to do some imaging—and could someone gimme their stethoscope."

That last command was followed fast, and as soon as he'd plugged his ears, he took a listen—

"What is it." Lydia leaned in. "What are you— why do you look like that?"

Well, because the poor bastard's lungs were full on one side. Not that he was going to talk about that until he had a plan—

The door to the room opened wide, and yup, there she was: C.P. Phalen, still in her tough-guy armor. And as she stepped inside, he fought back his emotions.

Not now, I do not need the distraction—

But instead of interrupting or causing a further

disturbance—or even looking his way—the woman stayed quiet and just went to stand by Lydia. And as she put her hand on the shoulder of Daniel's better half, Gus shook his head and wished like hell that Phalen wouldn't keep surprising him. The calm compassion was going to be a help.

"What's happening?" Lydia demanded. "Is he going to—what can we do?"

A mask with positive flow oxygen was strapped on Daniel's face, and Gus stayed still as he looked at the monitor. "Come on," he murmured. "Let's see some better numbers."

As he waited, he could feel the presence of everybody else in the room—where they were standing, how they were moving, whether they were talking, if they were silent—but all that was a distilled awareness. Daniel was his sole focus, everything else fading away into a buffer zone that he could call on if he needed, but that, if it wasn't immediately relevant to the survival of the patient on the bed, he could completely disregard.

Fuck. The numbers were not improving. Oxygen stats remained in the low 80s, and heart rate continued to spin out.

Time to up the interventions or they were going to lose the man.

As Gus started barking orders, a split of consciousness happened—most of his mind remained trained on his professional duty, yet a vital part of him got sucked back to when he'd been strapped to that chair and getting tased by a man whose face he never saw and whose motivations had been evil. He just remembered that accented voice talking to him, and the pain wrecking his will to protect this site.

And the woman who owned it—

From out of nowhere, Gus's brain coughed up a missing piece of what had happened to him: Suddenly, he remembered being carried by someone— carried . . . across the field outside of Phalen's house. He must have come around for a moment or two because he'd become aware that he was being brought back to the estate.

By a man in a red priest's robe—

"What was that, doctor?"

Forcing himself to fully engage, he communicated a second round of instructions. As medical staff followed his directives and things got really busy over Daniel's body, Gus glanced across at C.P. Phalen. She was staring at him, and there was an accusation in those eyes.

Then again, they hadn't left on a good note.

He'd told her no. That he wouldn't administer the drug to her. After that, shit had gotten critical and she'd ramped it up with a shrug and a drawl that had lit his temper like a flare.

Fine, you're ripping up the contract? I'll just get someone else to give Vita-12b to me.

At which point he'd informed her that he was going to keep the goddamn contract intact. Like he was a twelve-year-old sassing a teacher by defiantly eating all the paste.

It had been a fantastic conversation, and after she'd marched off, he'd had the cold comfort of knowing that he'd won.

Now, as she glared at him, he thought of the red-robed stranger who had come and gotten him, who risked their own life to get him out—and bring him to where he was most likely to survive. It must have been one of her guards. Who decided to do one last mission before he took his oath to the Catholic Church and cardinal'd himself.

If that man, that savior, hadn't come? Gus would be dead.

As he thought of Vita-12b, and all the lives it might save, he knew he had to try it on a human. That was the next step. But not on C.P.—and yes, he was letting his personal feelings get in the way of her freely given consent.

Snapping back into the present once again, his last thought on the matter was how in all cases, it was best to be objective.

Emotions were the worst kind of complication in life.

Especially when shit got critical.

◆　◆　◆

Up on Deer Mountain, halfway to the summit, Xhex was certain that she hadn't heard that right. Even though her brother had said the words twice.

Although to be fair, it wasn't so much his syllables as the tone of voice that had shaken her. And then there was that pause, like he'd had to gather himself to continue speaking at all.

I have never . . . forgotten why or how you left the Colony.

Called forward by all the things she didn't comprehend, Xhex walked over to him, the sounds of her boots over the loose gravel of the trail loud in the silence.

"I don't understand," she heard herself say.

As she realized what she'd spoken, she wanted to take it back. That was not what she'd intended to lead with. Blade was never someone anybody should trust . . . yet the way he was staring over at her made her narrow her eyes on him in a way she never had.

And then she realized what it was. The whites around his irises were pink. And there was a perfectly formed blood-red teardrop just under one of his eyes.

"Are you crying," she breathed. Because she could read his grid . . . and she wasn't sure whether she could believe what she was seeing.

What he was choosing to allow her to see.

He was devastated by inner turmoil—and it seemed to be somehow all tied to her? How was this possible? Except she couldn't deny how—and why—the three-dimensional structure of his emotions was blazing with energy.

His grid was glowing bright as the sun.

With pain . . . and regret.

Blade shook his head. Cleared his throat. Brushed under his eye with impatience and rubbed the blood away between his fingertips.

"I watched you go that night, sister mine. I watched . . . the van go. And I knew . . ." His voice cracked again and he put his hands up, covering his face. "I knew where they were taking you, and what was going to happen to you. And I let you go. Oh . . . fuck—I am—"

As he stuttered over his words, a bizarre inner calm came over Xhex. It was the strangest thing: All of her thoughts quieted, the chaos she had been struggling with like a snow globe settling after a shaking, her mind clearing from the confusion that had plagued her . . . for decades, it felt like.

Abruptly, her brother's rambling came back to her ears.

"—I tried to get them out. I tried to save them because they were you. They were . . . you . . . but . . ." When Blade dropped his hands, blood was running down his face, the true tears of a *symphath* so rare that they were indeed squeezed from the marrow. "They were dead. They were always . . . dead . . ."

Xhex blinked a couple of times. "I don't understand what you are telling me."

The words that came out of him next were halting—and she wasn't sure what she said in return. But as streaks of moonlight flickered over his red-washed face, the strobing created by the wind teasing the pine boughs, a picture emerged that took her breath from her.

Labs. Explosions. Rescues that were recoveries because it was too late.

Vengeance. Taken out on those who had hurt her, whether or not they were directly involved with what had been done to her.

As the truth of what her brother had been doing for the last two and a half decades hit her, she was vaguely aware of a wolf howling off in the distance.

And the call was answered by another.

And another.

Abruptly, a chorus of wolves she could not see began to sing to the night, and oddly, in the cresting and falling of the harmonies, she heard something that she not only understood, but felt like was directed to her.

Believe. Believe. Believe . . .

"I'm sorry," she stuttered. "I still don't . . ."

After a shuddering breath, Blade seemed to pull

himself together. As if he knew he was not going to have a second chance at their conversation.

"I went to the labs."

"What labs . . ." Although why did she have to ask that?

"The ones that you were in," he repeated. "The underground facilities with the humans and the experimentation. I tried to find you. For years."

"You went . . . looking for me?" she mumbled.

"For years. And after I heard you were out, that you had gotten yourself free, I went to Caldwell and located you in that club, Screamers. It took me a good year to track you down. But I had to see for myself that you were okay."

"You went to that club?" She had to have him repeat everything because the recasting of reality that was required to take what he was saying as truth was so vast, so deep, that she had to be sure. "The club I was working in?"

"Indeed, I went with some regularity. I never intended for you to see me. I blended in, and you were not looking for me, so I passed among the crowds you were hired to control." As the sounds of wolves rose in volume, he had to speak more loudly to project over the din of the howling. "By then, I had already taken out five of the underground labs looking for you, and it occurred to me that I must finish the job. Even if you hated me for all the right reasons, there were other people's sisters out there.

Other people's . . . brothers. Sons. Daughters. I did not save you . . . but I could *ahvenge* you and make amends to others, even if they never knew it or understood my motivations. Even if you never did."

Xhex put her hands on her head as her heart pounded and she got dizzy. "You went after the labs . . . for me?"

"I wanted . . . to be forgiven. By you, by my own conscience. I should never have let them take you. I knew what our bloodline intended to do. I should have warned you so that even if you couldn't have gotten out before the van came, you could have been prepared and escaped en route. I should have . . ."

Jesus, she wished like hell the wolves would shut up. This was the most important conversation she was ever going to have with one of her relatives, and the lupine community had decided it was time to tune up their sirens—except then she thought of the ghostly entity, the older female that Xhex had come to seek.

She had engineered this.

And though the entity was not visible, she was here, somewhere, in and among the pines. That was why the wolves were singing. She was of them somehow . . .

"Blade," she interrupted her brother.

As he stopped talking, she stared into his face. They had similar coloring, the pair of them . . . and she had thought that was all they had in common as half-breeds, both of them part of an experiment to mix the blood of *symphaths* with powerful vampires to see if there was an evolutionary advantage.

Back some twenty years ago, when she had begun seeing a vampire, she'd been viewed as compromising the integrity of the research—and there had been a fear, never expressed, that the program had all been a very grave mistake. Their bloodline hadn't wanted to be punished for what had been a heretical idea to begin with, so she had been sacrificed for the protection of her family for a number of reasons.

"How many of these . . . labs did you close down," she said.

"All of them."

Xhex leaned forward onto the balls of her feet. "I'm sorry, what did you say?"

"Every one of them," came the rock-solid reply. "I took them all out—well, except for the one under us now, and Daniel tells me they do no experimenting on your kind. So I am leaving it be."

"You closed down . . ."

"All of them. It took me over two decades, and it does not feel like enough."

The male's face seemed to change shape for her, the features at once familiar and yet completely new.

"You did that for me?" she whispered.

"It was the only way to make amends."

All around, the howling continued, becoming

even louder still, if that were possible. And that was when she saw it, over in a clearing by a stream . . . a wolf that was like no other, a silver lupine form who was watching them as if in approval.

Finally, she thought, as she raised her hand in greeting.

As Blade caught the direction of her focus, he glanced over to the side of the trail. And then he said the strangest thing: "It's her."

Xhex did a double take. "You mean . . . she came to you, too? Up here?"

"An entity like none I had ever seen before. An old—"

"—woman," Xhex finished. "With a message."

"Yes, did you—"

"She told me I had a journey and that my only hope was for me to start on it or die." Xhex glanced down at the ground, and saw that her brother's boots and hers were toe to toe. "A journey . . ."

To this spot here. Right here.

Her whole adult life, she had been meant to come here, to this spot on the trail that led up the mountain, to . . . her brother.

She looked at Blade. Over twenty years. All the labs. And he had never said a thing to anybody— a wise survival skill up in the Colony, but something that would have gotten him help if he had told the right people in Caldwell. But that hadn't been the point for him, had it.

The Federal Bureau of Genetics, she thought. Blade as Daniel's boss. The work that Blade had gotten humans to do with him because he'd needed backup that no one knew about.

Because all that had been his journey.

And now they were both here.

Xhex reached up to the slick cheek of her brother. Swiping her forefinger down the red tears he cried, she retracted her hand and turned her fingertips around.

After a long stretch of silence, she streaked her own cheeks with his blood. "I . . . forgive you."

All at once, the howling stopped, and the silence of the night returning was such a shock, they both jumped as if the void were a loud noise.

And then Blade refocused on her, his eyes gleaming with the red wash of his emotions. "You do not have to."

"I know." Xhex put her hand on his shoulder. "I forgive you. Now forgive yourself and let it go. We both need to . . . let this go."

As she spoke the words, a soaring feeling buoyed her body sure as if her feet had left the ground, and all at once, a rushing sensation in her head burned—but not in a way that hurt. It was like a reinflation.

"Your grid," Blade whispered with wonder.

The embrace that followed happened naturally, the both of them stepping in together, and as Xhex wrapped her arms around Blade's heavy shoulders, she felt as though they were cocooned in a peace that was tangible. Protective.

Healing.

A journey coming to a peaceful end.

They stayed together for the longest time, the cold air not touching them, the moon bathing them in soft light. And when they finally parted, they each stared at the other. Then she laughed a little.

"Well. That happened."

Blade laughed as well, then looked around—and recoiled.

"She's not there anymore," he said, pointing to the spot in the trees where the ghostly gray wolf had been.

Xhex went back to the night she had come up the trail for the first time, and had found the old woman. She had never thought it would lead here, to her . . . beginnings. But maybe that was the thing with healing. If only the surface of a wound reknits, the injury festers as an infection. Only by going deep, to the very source, and clearing the base of it all, could health be restored.

Family had betrayed her . . . but family had *ah-venged* her, too.

"I guess her job with us is done." Xhex glanced down at her body, then patted at herself to make sure this wasn't a dream. "With me . . . with you."

When she looked back up, she had to know. "Blade . . . about my grid . . ."

There was a long moment. And then her brother slowly smiled. "The rebuilding is happening, as we speak. I can see it plainly, so no, you are not deluding yourself."

"I can feel it." She touched her ribs again and her head. "I swear I can."

"Good. I am glad."

As a smile stretched her mouth—it didn't stay put. Just as he could read her grid . . . his was obvious to her, and the stress remained.

Only this time, it was unhappiness, not regret.

And she knew what it was about.

"You've got to leave Lydia alone," Xhex said roughly. "If not for her own good, for yours. You don't know the hell where I've been in my head, my soul—and we don't need two people in the family there."

Blade took a deep breath. "Family."

"Yeah. Family who looks out for each other. And if you keep holding on to the thing with that wolven, what happened to me . . . is going to happen to you."

THIRTY-FIVE

T HINGS WENT DOWNHILL *so fast*, Lydia thought as she sat at the bedside.

Daniel had been fine in the library, and then he'd gotten to their room, collapsed on the bed, and started coughing up all that bright red blood. And now, as she found herself in the midst of a throng of medical staff, with all kinds of drugs being pumped into him and vitals monitoring that was going badly, she couldn't grapple with where they were. How was it possible that he'd been doing so well—hell, they had had sex, *twice*, for godsakes—but then all of a sudden, he was slipping into a coma?

But come on, like making love was a physical fitness test.

"I'm right here," she said roughly as she stroked his dusting of hair. "I need you to stay with me—"

"*Lydia.*"

The sound of her name, so close by, and spoken so insistently—like she hadn't heard it a couple of times—made her jump and glance up. "Gus . . . ?"

"Hey, honey." The doctor got down on his knees in front of her, his bruised and swollen face a reminder of how much other people were suffering right now. "Can you focus on me for a sec?"

She nodded, even though she wasn't sure she could look away from Daniel for even that long. "What can we do?" she asked. "Please ..."

"He's had a bleed in his left lung from a bronchial arterial breach inside one of the tumors. Remember how I told you this could happen?"

"He's had them before, though. Why is he ..."

"The bleeding's under control and he's better, right? You can see, he's breathing more easily and he's relaxed. Look at the monitor, no alarms going off."

She glanced to the screen behind his head, with all its numbers and the mountain ranges of his heart rate. "He's had that happen before. So why ... did he collapse?"

"His oxygen got low because of the coughing, but we're supporting his breathing and he's stable now, and I need you to start breathing again yourself." As she began to well up, Gus put his hand on her shoulder. "Listen to me, I've got him, okay? You can trust me."

"But then what. What happens tomorrow. What happens ..."

When there was no getting control of whatever took him down. When one of his mets invaded a vital organ and his liver stopped working or his—

"We're staying in the moment, Lydia. And right now, he's okay, and that's where we are. We're here—"

"But what does it mean," she cut in as he pointed at the floor tile. "For the long run."

Stupid fucking question. That had already been answered by those scans they had done a week ago, the ones that showed Daniel was riddled with disease.

"We're just going to keep making sure he's comfortable, and keep after the—"

"He was doing so well." She grabbed on to Gus's arm like it was a lifeline. "His strength was back, he was walking better, he was—"

She looked to the hospital bed like she expected Daniel to sit right up and start ticking off the fact that he'd had a pair of orgasms, he'd driven the SUV, and he didn't need his cane once he'd recovered from that breakneck Harley ride on the highway . . . except of course, there was no awareness on his part—and no possibility of any kind of response that she could see: Behind the mask that was forcing air down his throat, he showed no signs of consciousness.

"The immunotherapy was really hard on him," Gus said gently. "And when we took him off of it, and gave him the nutrients and fluids he needed, there was a resurgence of energy. Well, we're going to keep him here as long as we can by supporting his organ function and making sure he's comfortable."

She thought back to the spring—and some of the Facebook groups she'd joined when she'd tried to find information and support.

"It was the last flare," she heard herself say.

"I'm sorry?"

Lydia cleared her throat and went back to stroking Daniel's face. "I saw some posts online that . . . in the last stage, right before the failing, there's often a short period where things are kind of normal. Or normal-er. Like, they come back and have some good days. A bloom in the fall."

When Gus didn't say anything, she glanced over at him. "You've heard of that, too?"

"Every case is different."

"That's such a doctor response."

"It's also true. Lydia, as much as you can, I need you to try to remain calm. We've seen him out of this acute episode, and tomorrow, we'll reassess what our longer-term options are."

"You already told me we're out of them." Her voice went flat. "Unless you think we can give him Vita-12b."

Gus's face grew tight. "That isn't what he wants."

"No . . . it isn't." As she stared at Daniel, willing him to wake up, she felt like her soul was dying with him. "He doesn't want to suffer anymore."

"And it's an untested substance," someone said.

C.P. Phalen. That was who had spoken. And as Gus looked across the room sharply, Lydia moved from the chair to the bed. Stretching out next to Daniel, she laid her arm gently over his chest, and tried to take some reassurance from the fact that he was breathing on his own. Even if the hiss of the oxygen mask was a reminder that he wasn't completely independent.

"Daniel," she said in a voice that cracked. "I'm right here . . ."

◆   ◆   ◆

Up upon the mountain called Deer, Blade stood before his sister, his sense of what was real and what was a hope-created fantasy becoming suddenly, inexplicably, one and the same—and considering what he was, that was an unexpected confluence on so many levels. Optimism was to a *symphath* as sociopathy was to the well-adjusted—but oil and water were mixing. Had mixed. And *prima facie* evidence that the impossible had occurred was the fact that Xhex's grid was reknitting, reforming, quadrant by quadrant, right in front of his own eyes.

And her advice about the wolven was spot-on, too.

He did need to leave Lydia Susi alone.

Shaking his head, he closed his eyes. "I don't think I can."

"You have to—"

"Let me ask you something." He refocused on his sister, squaring his shoulders and shifting his weight. "Do you know how you feel in this moment? The relief? The grace? The near miss that ended well as opposed to badly?"

"Yeah?"

"If you could give this to another who suffers . . . would you do it? If you loved them?"

"Of course."

"But what if it cost you the very core of yourself."

Xhex frowned. "What are you talking about?"

He glanced back at where the entity had been, in its wolven form. "The old woman told me that I am Lydia's future, but not in the way I wish I was."

"She is in love with Daniel."

"Yes, and he is dying—and that, I am afraid, is what I can fix." As his sister's eyes widened in surprise, he had to walk off a little because he could not hold inside his skin the emotions within his heart. "If he dies, I could comfort her, and that is something to build on—"

"First off, I hate to break it to you, but she'll love him forever even if he's dead." His sister put her dagger hand over her heart. "And I know this because if anything happens to John Matthew, there's no one else for me."

Blade thought about it for a moment. "Interestingly, that rather helps."

"But I don't get it. What can you 'fix' for Daniel? I mean, mind control is one thing, but advanced cancer? That's not the kind of shit you just will out of someone's body."

"Oh, it is not his will that I have at my disposal."

Xhex stared at him, clearly nonplussed. "You have a . . . cure? For *cancer?*"

"It is not without a sacrifice, however."

Silence stretched out between them. "Do you love her," Xhex said. "Truly, really, love her, without motivation, without ulterior interest."

He thought about the wolf, staring at him with those golden eyes, so deadly . . . so beautiful.

"Yes, I do."

"Okay, then. What else in the universe is more worth sacrificing for than . . . love. If you really feel like that for her, and you know you can save that which she cares for the most? The answer is simple. Love is giving everything you have, even if it hurts."

But what if it destroys, he thought.

And yet . . . his sister was right.

After a long moment, Blade bowed deeply. "Thank you. That is most helpful. And may I tell you that I wish you all the best, you and your male. Now, if you will excuse me—"

"Where are you going?"

He exhaled and glanced around. "To get my proverbial doctor's bag, sister mine. Good evening."

He did not walk off. Rather, he dematerialized. After all, when a plan had been decided, a resolve locked into the marrow, one did not wish to dally on foot whilst time was of the essence: Although he had never consciously been one for feats of heroism, he would feel rather cheated if Daniel Joseph, his former operative, lover of who Blade feared was the love of his life, died on the cusp of his rescue.

Lydia's favored future cut short by biological failure, when there was a far happier resolution on the verge of reaching her beloved.

And there was another reason he wanted to dematerialize instead of go on foot. It appeared as though he was turning over a new leaf of virtue, and he didn't want the other half of him to sabotage it by a trip-and-fall, engineered by the *symphath* in him.

One should never trust a *symphath*, even when one was such a thing.

Re-forming up on the summit, he strode toward the fissure in the boulders and turned sideways, shuffling through the tight squeeze. As he emerged in the cave's belly, he went over to his scorpion's cage.

She was so perfectly constructed, her white segmented body tiny, yet with all of its component parts. To get her attention, he tapped on the side, and as she turned to him, her stinger flexed over her back.

Though he had not wanted to admit it, he had come to think of her as a daughter of a sort. He had raised her, nurtured her, cultivated her.

And now . . . he was going to have to kill her.

To save a man who was going to end up ruining his life.

THIRTY-SIX

I N THE END, Cathy could not stay down in the lab. For one, Daniel's acute medical episode was a promise of what was waiting for her, and she found that disturbing. Though her cancer was a quiet invader at present, sneaking into crevices in her lymphatic system, in her organs, in her blood, soon enough it would become unavoidable in all its manifestations—and then she would be in a hospital bed, just like Daniel, all kinds of people trying to artificially re-create normal functioning with medicines and procedures that might or might not do the duty, for a short period of time.

But the other reason she had to leave was that being around Gus when he was doing what he did best was an exercise in masochism. Everything about him made her feel alive, from the way he took control of everything and everybody to how good he was with Lydia when it really counted.

Plus she still wanted to scream at him.

As she stepped off the elevator at her house level,

she went right for her study. She didn't know how long it had been since she'd eaten anything. She didn't care. And she wasn't sure about the drinking thing, either. Also didn't care.

But as she sat down behind her desk, she was tired of the cramping. Was the process of miscarriage ever going to stop? As if she needed the reminder.

Sinking back into her chair, she measured the distance to her private bathroom, and felt like it was miles instead of feet—and though it made her a total diva, she really wanted to call someone to go into the medicine cabinet over the sink and get her the bottle of Advil in there. Maybe she'd make them bring her a sandwich, too, on the theory that the abdominal discomfort might be hunger pains?

It wasn't hunger pains.

In any event, she stayed where she was to punish herself. As the torsion in her now-empty womb went into another round of tightening, she took it as a physical manifestation of her foolishness. To believe she could have been a mother? Ridiculous, and not because of the cancer. Just like she'd told Gus, she was not—

The beeping noise was subtle, but it was the kind of thing that might as well have been a grenade with the pin out, bouncing right onto her glass-topped desk.

Someone had entered the property. Or . . . some*thing*.

With a shaking hand, she triggered the release for her computer, and the unit appeared before her on its rotating base. Signing in, she was quick to access the security system—

And there it was, in the camera feed for the backyard: A lone figure was walking through the field, closing in on the rear terrace. Whoever it was processed slowly, and was solely focused on the mansion—

It was the man. Who had brought Gus back. The one with the robes.

Outside in the foyer, footfalls sounded in a rush.

"No!" she said as she burst up. "Wait!"

She was shouting as she ran out and down the hall. "Stop!"

The guards who had assembled and were checking their weapons turned to statues, like they were a postmodern exhibition commenting on the nature of war.

"We need him," she said. "Subdue him if you have to, but do *not* kill him."

Her head of security nodded curtly. "Yes, ma'am."

From all around, a quiet whirring permeated the house as the window reinforcements came down over every square inch of glass, and at the same time, the men marched out the front door, fanning to the left and right in some kind of formation they had no doubt practiced in person as well as theory. Then the main entrance slammed shut and locked itself.

She rushed back to her study, and shoved her face to the screen.

Her guards moved in perfect sequence, guns double-handed and up in front, beams of light and red laser sights focusing on the solitary man.

Who merely halted and put his hands up.

The red robes, and the striking face, were exactly what she'd seen on the previous feeds from the night Gus had been brought home—

All at once, her guards froze, as if they were a unit with a single brain. And then the roles were reversed. Now the figure was the one who was closing the distance.

"What the hell are you doing?" She tapped the computer screen—like that was going to help wake the guards up? "What the fuck are you …"

Her voice drifted off as the man in the robes walked through the lineup of uniformed, weaponed guards, and as soon as he was on the other side, the squadron turned, reholstered their guns, and followed him in a little line. Like they were ducklings after momma.

The red-robed figure walked to one of the sets of doors of the back terrace. And then her head of security went to the keypad—and punched in the access code. Of course he was denied entrance, because everything that had happened in that field had been seen by the security detail inside.

But as he tilted his head and spoke into his

shoulder communicator, the red-robed figure looked up and cocked an eyebrow at the camera. Like he couldn't fathom the delay.

Cathy told herself to stay put. But then she remembered him bringing back the man . . . she loved.

Without thinking, she burst up and ran back out of the study. Triggering a hidden door off to the side in the hall, she entered the master code, the one that nobody but her knew, the one that did not require secondary approval. As the seal breached, she jogged a short distance, pushed a panel release, and jumped free to land on the terrace.

Alerted by the noise, the man in the red robes turned around, and as curls of cold air swirled about him, it was as if he were about to take flight.

"Who are you," she asked.

"Forgive me," he said in a heavily accented voice, "for my trespassing. But I am here for Daniel Joseph. Is he in?"

Cathy shook her head. "I . . . what?"

"Daniel—"

"No, I got that. I just—who the hell are you? And you brought Gus back. And—"

The man glanced over at her head of security and gave a nod. Without any hesitation, like a trained dog, the guy she had hired to coordinate everything in a time of conflict and chaos backed off some.

And took everybody else with him.

"What have you done with them? What are you—"

"Worry not, I have come in peace." The robed figure indicated the lineup that was retreating. "And I figure you would prefer those back inside?"

"Who . . . are you."

"As I told you, I am a friend who has come in peace . . . who has something Daniel Joseph needs, desperately."

◆   ◆   ◆

Lydia's first clue that Daniel might possibly be coming around was a tightening of their entwined fingers—except then she wasn't sure whether she had shifted her grip or if it had been him. Lying beside him in the hospital bed, she listened to the beeping that was not quite even and then reminded herself that there was no alarm going off. She might not understand what all the monitor was showing, but she knew when there was no screaming noise.

Gus was right, no alarm was good.

"Knock knock," she whispered as she stared at Daniel's eyelashes as they rested on his cheek. Then she filled in his response. "Who's there. Feisty. Feisty—no, that isn't right. What was it again?"

The joke totally derailed because she couldn't remember which part came next, and was confused about the punchline—and besides, as she had lost her partner in the back-and-forth, what did it matter anyway.

And this was pretty much what the rest of her life was going to be like ... without Daniel.

"I love you," she whispered as her eyes teared up. "What am I going to do without you?"

What she really needed—what *they* needed—was a miracle—

The door to the patient room swung open, and at first, all she saw was red—and her brain misinterpreted both its placement and its source: For a split second, she thought Daniel had somehow bled out. But why would what belonged in his veins be upright and standing in the doorway—

"Blade?" she asked as she sat up on her elbow.

"May I come in?"

The question was so formal, so out of place—because hello, he shouldn't be here—that she nodded reflexively. "What are you doing in our lab?"

And that was when she saw C.P. Phalen standing behind him. The woman was looking fragile, her eyes wide and confused, her hand going to her temple and rotating as if her head was aching from trying to grapple with what was going on.

"He's got something," the woman said in a stilted way. "For Daniel."

Lydia glanced at Daniel. Then she disentangled herself and swung her legs over the edge of the bed. "I don't ... understand."

Well, wasn't that the theme for the night, evidently.

Blade came a little farther forward. "I have a cure for him."

As the words, in that accented voice, hit the airwaves, they went into her ears. But they made no sense.

"I'm sorry, wh—"

Gus barreled into the room, half his face covered with shaving cream, a razor in his right hand. The doctor was shirtless, the scrubs on the bottom half of him hanging low on his hips, his well-defined torso flexing with muscle—and marked with bruises.

"What the fuck . . . is going . . . on . . ." His words trailed off. "It's *you*."

"Good evening, Augustus." Blade bowed at the waist. "You're looking better than when I saw you last."

"You . . . were the one who got me out."

"I did."

"You sound like him," Gus said remotely. "Your accent."

"Yes, I have a similar one to him. But I am not he who hurt you."

"You know who did, though."

"Yes, I do." Blade inclined his head to Gus. "That is not why I have come, however. It is your patient whom I have sought out. I have the solution to his little problem."

Gus's eyes narrowed. "The man does not have a little—"

From out of a pocket in the robe, Blade presented a small glass box, about the size a pair of earrings would come in. From Lydia's vantage point, it was hard to see what was inside—

Blade looked at her, and her alone. "If you want him to live, I will give her to him."

"What the *fuck* are you talking about," Gus snapped.

"She will cure him." Blade's eyes were steady and sure as they held hers. "His cancer will be gone, over a period of weeks. As if it never was."

Gus started talking to C.P. Phalen in a hard, cutting voice, the word "security" getting used a number of times: *Where is security. When is security coming. Why did security let this crackpot in—*

Blade ignored the commotion. And so did Lydia.

"He will be as you knew him then. The man he once was. That is what you want most in the world, is it not."

"What is . . . it," she whispered.

The *symphath* in the red robing stepped even closer to the bed, and she made sure she kept herself between the two, protecting Daniel with her body.

"She is a love of mine. I bred her."

It was a scorpion. In the little glass box . . . an

albino scorpion stared out through the portable prison, its tiny pincers and curled stinger so small, Lydia had to squint.

"Her venom is the way to kill his cancer."

Lydia's chest constricted as all her breath left her. "A . . . cure?"

"Yes. She is a very special member of her breed, and her sting works in humans, for their disease of the cells. It will cure him—as long as we get it into him now. If he becomes much sicker, he shall not be strong enough to handle it." Blade held out the little box to her. "If you want him back . . . I will give her to you."

"Why would you . . . help us?"

Blade's eyes traveled over her face as if he were memorizing her features. And then he said, with evident sorrow, "I have my reasons. That is all you need to know."

"I don't trust you."

"Allow me to show you how I am so certain."

Without warning, her mind became filled with images that were like memories, except they were about events she had never seen or experienced. She saw . . . decades of . . . things, all around the scorpion and its venom . . . and people. And it was from the point of view of someone . . . else . . .

Blade, she thought. These were Blade's memories. When the deluge stopped, she put her hand to her temple and tried to rub away the ache that had sprung up there. Just as C.P. had been doing as she'd walked in.

Gus spoke up, loud and clear. "This is insane, get the fucking guards and—"

"Give it to him," Lydia snapped. "Right now."

THIRTY-SEVEN

ABSOLUTELY FUCKING *NOT.*"

As Gus laid down the law—because someone clearly had to be reasonable in the middle of this shit show—the man in red turned to him.

Before the guy could start blabbing, Gus put his palm up. "This is bullshit. There are *so* many reasons I'm not going to allow you to have my patient stung by—"

The smile that came back at him was cold. "You are not involved in this business."

"The hell I'm not. I'm his fucking doctor."

"Then why are you getting in the way?"

"You come in here, with a goddamn arachnid in a bug box, making like you've got a Nobel Prize in your palm, and you're accusing *me* of getting in the way? And spare me any hocus-pocus, Google doctor talk. When it comes to cancer treatment, that kind of venom is only a facilitator. Chlorotoxin is not a compound that actually kills the tumor cells. It just helps our modalities get to where they need to be—when appropriate."

"Ah, but I told you," the man intoned. Like he was the voice of God or some shit. "She is a very special member of her species, cultivated over generations for—"

"Just give it to Daniel," Lydia said sharply. "*Now.*"

Gus pivoted around. The poor woman was leaning over the bed, her hand gripping Daniel's, her eyes rapt as a convert's—and he told himself not to lose his temper completely while Daniel was lying there two inches from a coma, and C.P. Phalen was doing absolutely nothing to stop this, and Lydia, as a grieving partner, was getting seduced by a snake oil salesman.

Scorpion venom. Administered by a sting. Was *this* where they were all ending up?

"Okay, everybody has to leave now," he announced. "Lydia, you don't need this distraction—"

"It's not a distraction!" She turned to the man. "Blade, I believe you! This explains everything. I saw the light at dawn that means you are my future, but it wasn't in the way I thought it was! You save Daniel and you *give* me my future—"

Stepping between them, Gus went on man-to-man defense, putting his hands out in front, prepared to shove the red-robed SOB from the room. "I'm going to ask you one more time to leave. And then I'm going to take you out by your asshole because nobody else seems to—"

Before he could get any further, he was forcibly picked up and displaced out of the way. For a split second, he thought it was Daniel, somehow back on his feet. Nope. It was Lydia, and she was stronger than he was—and not just because he was still healing.

Pinning him against the wall, her eyes glowed with a yellow light so bright, he felt the burn in his face—

The wolf. From the forest.

The conclusion came to him with a certainty that made no sense. Yet for some reason, it was clear to him that she was . . . somehow . . . what had come out to find him and Daniel. Who had taken them to the footprints. Who had protected them through acreage.

And she was prepared to kill him if he didn't get the fuck out of the way.

That was also clear.

Her voice, low and threatening, threaded into his ears with the growl of an animal: "This doesn't involve you."

Gus shook his head. "He doesn't want Vita. What the fuck are you doing putting poison into his—"

The explosion registered from someplace off in the distance, the loud *boom!* muffled, but the detonation close enough so that a quaking hit the patient room like a ton of bricks. As a crack spidered across the ceiling and then ran down the wall, the hospital bed rolled around, and a table rocked on its legs. All at once, he and Lydia and C.P. threw their hands out for balance, while the man in red sank down into his thighs and held that little glass box to his chest.

In the aftermath, as dust filtered down from overhead and alarms started to blare everywhere, "Blade" looked over at Gus, then indicated Daniel with a nod of his head. Calmly. As if he'd expected the bomb.

"It will work. My scorpion will save him—"

Popping sounds now. Out in the corridor. A scream.

The door to the patient room opened, and a guard leaped inside, clearly to give them an update. Except . . . no. There was something wrong with him—in the center of his forehead, a small, sooty black mark was precisely triangulated between his eyebrows. And before Gus could look too much at the smudge, the man collapsed to his knees and fell face-first into the tiled floor.

The back of his head had been blown off.

"You have to do it now," Blade announced. As if some guy hadn't just dropped dead of a gun-shot wound right in front of the group. "He's come for me."

"Who's come?" C.P. demanded as more shooting was traded out in the open area.

"The man who abducted you," he said with a nod to Gus, "is actually trying to kill me. He must have seen me approach the house. I am afraid, in retrospect, I could have been far more discreet. It's a bit of a family dispute, don't you know."

What, like someone hadn't shown up at fucking Thanksgiving?

But whatever. The reasons didn't matter at this precise moment.

The attack everybody had been waiting for . . .

. . . had finally arrived.

◆   ◆   ◆

"Barricade the door," someone said.

"Get his gun—" somebody else chimed in.

"What are you doing—"

The voices talking over each other, along with the sound of a bomb going off, were partially what woke Daniel up. The other half of it was a sixth sense that Lydia was in trouble: More than the noise or the evident panic, the inner core of him came alive to protect her.

As he forced his eyes open, he couldn't understand what was happening: It looked like she was standing in front of Gus and seemed to be holding him against the far wall. Meanwhile, Blade was off to the side, dressed in one of Candy's Santa robes, apparently, and Phalen was by the foot of the bed, a hand resting at the base of her throat like she was either going to throw up or scream—and was trying to stop the reaction.

Distantly, he heard the unmistakable exchange of gunfire.

"Weapon," he mumbled. "Get the guard's weapon."

Well. What do you know. That had been *him* talking a moment ago, spitting out good advice about securing an available gun. Too bad everyone in the room was arguing with each other and didn't hear him.

As adrenaline flooded his system, Daniel shoved the oxygen mask off and put everything he had into a holler: "Get that goddamn service weapon!"

His yelling got their attention, but before anyone could react, another explosion went off, and this one was closer than the first. With more dust floating down from a crack right above his bed, and the stench of burning plastic coming through the HVAC system, he knew they were all going to die.

Unless they got out before this attack—which he had known *all* along was coming—reached the patient room.

"Help me," he said to Lydia.

The second he reached for her, she backed off of Gus and rushed over. "*Daniel*—"

"Listen to me," he told her. "You have to get out of here. This room is a deathtrap with no escape—"

"I'm not leaving without you!"

Rumbling, somewhere near. Like a load-bearing wall was collapsing. "Then take me with you, but we gotta move."

"Let us go then." Blade bent down and stripped the guard of his gun—and a knife. "With speed."

Daniel glanced over at the man. And then started ripping things off of himself, IVs, wires, blankets. "Take one side of me, will ya?"

"I need to be able to shoot—"

"I'll do it," Gus muttered as he lunged for the pillow and ripped the case off. "But let me wrap your vein up. You're losing blood already."

After he tied off the inside of Daniel's elbow, Lydia and the doctor humped him to his feet, and it was a bad shuffle to the door.

"Where's Phalen," Daniel said just as they were going to step out.

"I'm right here," the woman answered from behind. "And we need to go to the northern tunnel. It's the best access point I can get us through. Left. Go left."

Out in the smoke-filled hall, Blade led the way because he was the one with the weapons—a gun he'd evidently had with him plus the dead guard's. Phalen, meanwhile, brought up the rear, and she was good with the navigation, steering them down the corridor in the opposite direction from the open area where the workstations were. Where the shooting and the explosions were.

Fuck. Researchers and medical staff were dead or dying . . .

At the end of the hall, there was a steel reinforced door, and Phalen elbowed her way forward to enter a numerical sequence on a keypad. For Daniel, everything was a blur, but he was aware enough that as they filed in and closed the heavier barrier behind their group, he thought they might have half a chance.

The tunnel ahead was lit with low-energy ceiling fixtures, the illumination dim and blinky, as if some of the power sources had been attacked or at the very least threatened by what had been detonated. He did what he could to keep up, but soon enough, Gus and Lydia were holding all his weight up by his armpits, his bare feet tickling the cold concrete floor.

At the far end was another steel door, and Phalen went ahead again.

He wasn't sure where they were going to come out, but if they couldn't get to a vehicle, they needed more weapons and a good barricaded position—

"It's not working. Goddamn it, the master code's not working."

He glanced around Gus's bare chest. The woman was viciously stabbing at a keypad, the little red light in the corner persisting every time she hit the # key.

"*Fuck,*" she said as she wheeled back around. "We're trapped—"

Yet another explosion vibrated through the earth, and he looked up overhead. The sprinkling of concrete dust was not good news—supports were weakening throughout the subterranean lab.

He glanced at Lydia. She was terrified, but keeping it together. Gus was the same, his eyes bouncing around, but his grip steady. God, Daniel hated that he was so physically weak and they had to carry him—

"I shall go back and ensure all of your safety."

As Blade spoke up, Daniel narrowed his stare on his old boss. "You can't hold them off. You know what's out there, and it's not human."

"As I said, I am the one they want." The man held out the guard's gun, handle first. "Take this, Daniel. You are the only one among them who knows how to shoot—"

Phalen snatched the weapon out of the man's hand. With a quick series of shifts, she put the nine millimeter through its paces, checking how many bullets were in the magazine, cocking it, taking off the safety.

"No, he's not the only one."

Blade chuckled. "I beg your pardon, madam. Hold your position. I will attempt to get them out of the lab."

"How," Daniel spoke up.

"They will follow me. You all are incidental—"

"How do you know that?" Daniel held on to his

Lydia a little more tightly, and thought about what he and Gus had found out in the forest, those footsteps that came from out of nowhere. "There are a lot of different people down here."

"My cousin is the one who has invaded this facility. If I leave, he will be forced to follow. Then you may come out."

Daniel cursed under his breath. Maybe the guy was right, maybe he was wrong.

Either way, they didn't have many choices.

THIRTY-EIGHT

B EFORE BLADE DEPARTED the group, he focused on the wolven. She was standing by
her male, supporting him in so many ways more
than just the physical, his arm draped over her
shoulders, her body strong enough to hold him on
his feet.

Going over to her, Blade held out his hand. "This
is for you. Do with her as you will."

The female went still and glanced down at the
glass container. For a moment, he thought she was
not going to take his gift, but then she snatched
the scorpion from his palm. As her fingers brushed
his skin, his blood rushed through his veins, but he
knew that he was the only one who felt anything—
and a now-familiar sense of weary sadness made it
easier for him to turn away and start running.

She did not thank him. Or if she did, he didn't
hear it.

"Wait," the blond woman called out. "I need to
spring the lock for you."

The owner of the lab was mercifully light on her feet as she joined him, and when they reached the portal through which they had entered the tunnel, she was quick with the passcode. After a pause, during which he knew they both held their breath ...

The lock released, and she looked up at him. "Fuck it. The master code is seven-nine-two-one-five-five-one. Use it on any keypad. Good luck—and thank you."

Blade inhaled deeply through his nostrils, confirming, even through the smoke, that which had been readily apparent out on her terrace. Leaning in, he said softly, "It will work on you, too. Be well."

He did not look back as he stepped out, but he made certain that the portal was re-secured before he faced off at the remarkably dangerous hallway: If Kurling or one of his machines happened to pass by the head of this offshoot, and utilize their super-keen eyesight, Blade would be a sitting duck, nothing but rooms with flimsy doors offering a momentary cover.

Dematerializing in this environment was not advisable, as it was too dangerous to re-form when one was not certain of obstacles. Besides, he was too amped up to concentrate.

Ditching his red robes, he was fleet of foot in his combat garb as he put his back against the wall and headed down past the room Daniel had been in, zeroing in on where alarms were going off and fresh smoke was curling up. As the lights overhead flickered, the strobing effect made his vision dance, but he got to the end with alacrity. Stretching off to the left, the vast open area of equipment and work-places had been hit with some lower-end explosives, the kind that were more noise than structurally damaging. They had certainly laid waste to the previous order, however, the blown-up equipment, shattered glass, and puffs of fire making it look like an action movie set after the final showdown.

There were moans, too, of injured staff members.

Unfortunately, this was only beginning—and at least one or more stairwells, somewhere, had been properly bombed. That was the only reason they could have felt such shock waves in that patient room.

Hurrying on his way, heading to the right, Blade's nose stung from the chemical burn—

The robotic soldier came out of a boardroom made of sheets of glass, and Blade had the advan-tage of first sight. Raising the muzzle of his gun, he let off one round directly into the thing's chest, the bullet entering the torso—but barely having any ef-fect other than to announce Blade's presence.

The return fire was instantaneous, and accurate to a rattling degree. As Blade ducked, a bullet went into the wall right where his head had been.

No torso, big-target aiming for these things.

As another bullet sizzled by him, Blade had to ration his counter-firing as he jumped behind a support column. He could spare only one trigger pull in response, and the humanoid ducked easily, the lead slug penetrating through one of the floor-to-ceiling glass panels, the entire wall shattering and crashing to the ground.

Which brought the other soldiers unto him in an efficient fashion.

The units came from every direction, and Blade broke cover and bobbed and weaved to avoid getting shot. Still, something went into his shoulder, but he ignored the blaze of pain—and given that he didn't know the layout of the lab, there was no strategy to his route as he kept going.

All he wanted was to draw everything away from that hallway.

As he passed the elevator down which the blond woman in black had taken him, he thought his assailants' strategy of trapping everybody underground was a good one. Bombs made noise and attracted attention, and the small town might not have had much on population, but there were people who would have noticed an aboveground altercation with this many pyrotechnics.

Down here, anything could happen. And with the elevators disabled and the stairwells compromised? And those cyborg soldiers having no pesky sense of self-preservation?

Kurling could wait anyone out.

On the far side of the elevators, he jumped over the dead body of one of the guards who had escorted him and the blonde down herein. And another who was gravely injured. Bullets continued to flash by Blade, pinging into the walls, skipping across the concrete floor with sparks, some more hitting him.

He kept going, and when he made a turn and an "EXIT" sign appeared over a steel door, he knew his instincts had been right. Clandestine labs needed fire escapes, not for building code purposes, but as a practical consideration, and every one he had ever been in over the last twenty years had had more than one satellite escape.

As he came to a halt, the footfalls of what was pursuing him were the heartbeat of his demise, but he felt no fear. He concentrated on the keypad and punched in the code the blond woman had given him.

"Come now, come now . . ."

Just as he caught a major whiff of his own blood, the dead bolt gave way, and he punched at the bar. The second steel weight opened, he slipped through, re-shut things, and listened to the lock re-engage.

A staircase, good lighting, and fresh air greeted him, as if he had entered a luck lottery and come out a winner. Plenty of those units had seen him go in here, so they knew where he was—and that meant Kurling was going to order a takedown and put all his resources into the effort. Pulling clean oxygen into his lungs, Blade's thoughts began to fragment, likely from the blood loss, but he couldn't let his concentration slip. He needed to give himself a flight's worth of head start before he let them close in—

The steel door was blown off its hinges directly in front of him, the panel flying at his body, only his quick reflexes sparing his life as the *woof!* of the shock wave tossed him to the side and the heat singed his eyebrows and hair.

Without missing a beat, he spun for the stairs and took them two at a time, his left leg hindering his ascent—whilst down below soldiers that had the advantage of not needing oxygen to power their muscles came after him at breakneck speed. Thinking of Lydia, he ran even faster because he needed to survive a little longer, so he could draw the fight farther away from her. As the zenith of the ascent was reached, he struggled to punch in the code to free the lock—

The release took many seconds longer than he'd wanted, and he had no idea what he was getting into when the door was finally able to open—

He burst out with gun forward and head swiveling, as he made sure the stairwell's exit closed and locked behind himself.

It was another hall, in another structure. And the air was dry, and smelling of concrete.

A basement? he thought. Likely of the home.

He chose right for no reason at all, and looked for cover as he went along. There were a number of closed doors—

Boom!

As the robotic squad blew another door off its jambs, the banging sound as the steel panel ricocheted off something hard echoed through the hallway. Continuing on with his limp, his breath burned in his lungs, and that left leg seriously lagged. He must go faster. He was prepared to get into a shootout, but he wanted more distance if he could get it and some cover.

As he reached yet another door, something teased at the edge of his consciousness, but he didn't have time to allow it to come to full cognitive recognition. He entered the passcode, endured an interminable wait, and hit another stairwell and exit.

And then he was back in the house proper. He could tell by the scent of fresh oranges and dishwashing soap—but he was not where he had been let in before.

A kitchen, he thought as he tracked the scent.

Rounding a corner, there was stainless steel cabinetry everywhere, as well as ovens, gas burner ranges, and refrigerators that were professional grade. Crossing the red-tiled floor as quickly as he could, he kept going, emerging out the other side into a small private eating area with a round table. From there, he entered the foyer with the statues, and paused to look back. As there were no immediate sounds of a chase coming for him, he glanced down to assess his wounds.

They were all superficial ones.

Those soldiers with the perfect aim, once they had identified him, had not tried to kill him. And that was when he realized that he had thought he was leading them. Instead, they had chased him . . . here.

Soft laughter percolated into the space and he pivoted sharply.

At the base of the primary stairway, sitting on the bottom steps, a male with a face that was nearly identical to his own was smiling.

"Did you have a good workout, cousin?" Kurling drawled.

THIRTY-NINE

W E CAN'T STAY here. The air quality is getting worse."

As Daniel spoke, Lydia glanced down at him. They had come back to the point at which they'd entered the smoky escape tunnel, and to take the pressure off his legs, she and Gus had sat him on the concrete floor. In the unreliable, on/off lighting, she tried to judge his vital signs by how pale his face was and how often he blinked. Which was nuts.

And of course he wasn't doing well. How could he be?

Gus coughed and paced back and forth. "He's right. Besides, there's nothing out there anymore. No more shooting, no explosions—"

"That we can hear," C.P. cut in.

The woman was standing off to the side of the door Blade had departed from, that gun in her hand held with a relaxed confidence, her eyes locked on the latching mechanism like she expected things to open at any moment.

426   J. R. WARD

The air was getting thick with smoke that had backed up into the ventilation system, and though it was nice to think the quality was better down on the ground where Daniel was, she knew his lungs were vulnerable—and she herself was getting light-headed.

They had to somehow get out of the lab, if they were going to survive.

"We'll go out and clear the area," she heard herself say. "She and I."

The protests from the men were immediate— but as she met C.P.'s eyes, the two of them were in perfect accord: Daniel couldn't run, and out of the three of them who could, Gus was best able to keep Daniel alive.

There was just one thing that needed to be said before she went out there.

Lydia glanced down at her hand. The glass box with the little holes in the top was warm from her holding it, and the creature inside prowled around, pincers working like it was practicing the moves it planned to use as soon as it got a chance to get loose.

With grim intent, she looked at Daniel.

In response, he put up his own palm. "Go. And be careful. I'll take care of the scorpion."

His voice was as grave as she'd ever heard it, and she knelt down, staring into his eyes earnestly. "I believe Blade. I don't understand him, but I believe him. It's your choice, though. When this is all over."

Daniel reached up and stroked her face, his thumb lingering on her lower lip. "I will love you from the other side—"

"Don't say that—"

"—because you're claimed forever mine."

It happened so fast. One moment, he was taking the box from her; the next, he released the scorpion and placed the thing right at the base of his throat.

"No! What are you doing!"

Lydia's voice echoed around as she went for the deadly arachnid—which was stupid considering she wanted him to take the venom. Just not here, not now—

The sting was immediate, and Daniel gasped as if he'd been shocked by electricity—and his body certainly reacted as if there were volts going through it, his legs kicking out as his head jerked back and hit the wall behind him with a sickening thump.

"What the fuck are you doing!" Gus barked as C.P. also shouted—even though it was too late.

The scorpion was tiny and fast, and it marked its trail down the electrode pads that were still stuck on Daniel's sunken chest. Three stings? Four?

Lydia tried to catch the thing, but then she stopped with that because what if she got stung? Ripping off her fleece, she used the folds of the pullover to brush the arachnid off his skin. But that didn't work. In the end, the scorpion chose when to go, skittering off into the shadows.

And then she didn't think about the damn thing.

Daniel's body started contorting, his lips peeling back off his teeth as he writhed in agony. In a sickening bloom, sweat broke out all over him, and his eyes started to roll into their sockets, only the whites showing.

"What did you do . . ." She fell down beside him. "Oh, God, Gus—"

The doctor dropped to his knees and checked Daniel's pulse at his wrist. Then he looked to the steel portal. "I need an EpiPen . . . and I don't know what else, but none of it is in this fucking hallway. Jesus! He's insane—"

"*No*," Daniel gritted out as he jerked his head up, his hands like claws as he lifted his arms. "I want this . . ."

Lydia put her face into his. She wanted to yell at him, she wanted to kiss him, she wanted to pray—

His eyes focused on her. "I want . . . to go out fighting, not failing. Fighting . . . for us . . . not dying by a disease."

Tears flooded her vision. It was the very essence of him, wasn't it. He was a warrior, a man of strength. And he was right, dying while hooked up to tubes on a fadeaway by inches was not his way.

But, oh, not like this. Not here. Not—

Gus pressed two fingers to the side of Daniel's

straining throat. "He's going into anaphylaxis, I have to get that EpiPen. Right now."

Lydia didn't think a thing of it. She closed her eyes.

And shifted into her wolf form.

◆   ◆   ◆

As Gus's patient went into a seizure at the same time a catastrophic allergic reaction started to get rolling, he thought things couldn't get more out of control. He was wrong.

One minute, Lydia Susi, a woman he had known in the kind of deep and intimate way tragedies tended to forge, was exactly who he had always been cognizant of. The next . . . she was . . .

Going through some kind of transformation that he had never seen before.

And would never have believed if he weren't seeing it with his own eyes.

The change in her physical body was the source of myth and nightmare, a wolf emerging from the confines of her human form, arms and legs turning into limbs with paws, face altering into that of a canine-snouted profile, fur covering the nakedness as her clothes were split and fell away.

When it was all over, Gus thought once again of being out in the woods with Daniel.

"Jesus . . . Christ, I was right," he breathed.

She was the wolf.

He looked at C.P. And when she was only staring with a remote expression of awe, he realized she had known all along—

A strangled wheezing sound refocused him on Daniel.

"I need my bag," Gus said. "It's in the patient room."

"We'll get it," C.P. responded.

Standing by that door, a gun in her hand, and her eyes shining with a war-like light that suggested she was ready to shoot at anything that moved, he thought, for the millionth time, that C.P. Phalen was the most incredible woman he had ever met. And next to her, the wolf—Lydia???!—was likewise ready to roll, its jowls crinkled with aggression like the thing was already biting something.

"You have to stay here with him," she said. "You're the best medic we've got if he needs CPR."

When, Gus corrected to himself.

"I agree," he muttered. "But wait."

Rising to his feet, hysterical laughter, the kind that meant a person was totally losing it, bubbled out of the terror-congestion inside his chest. And before he knew what the hell he was doing, he marched over, grabbed Phalen around the waist, and yanked her against him.

After a split second of shock, she yielded, her body easing into his own, her right arm—the one with the gun on the end of it—rising to rest along the top of his shoulders.

Gus bent her back, like he was dipping her while they danced.

"I've wanted to do this since the moment I first met you."

With that declaration out of the way, he kissed the ever-living shit out of the great C.P. Phalen, crushing his mouth to hers, licking his way into her, holding her against him even though his ribs were still broken. But fuck it. Fuck everything.

When he pulled back, he stared right into her eyes. "If we make it out of this alive, I'm taking you out, woman. And I'm paying."

Phalen laughed in a short burst and blinked away tears. "We'll split the check. But I'll let you get the door for me."

He searched her face and prayed he would see it again. "Deal."

And then fun time was over.

As he righted her balance, she looked down at Daniel. A bright-red flush was spreading up his neck from the stings, and his lips were swelling. Down on his chest, his ribs were pumping in an uneven way, and one of his legs was kicking sporadically.

"Is there anything else you need?" she asked.

He described the location of the go-bag in the

patient room. And he nearly pulled her back as she turned to the keypad and started to enter the numbers.

She was going to die out there.

Or maybe they would all be killed, picked off one by one.

"Be careful," he said to her.

She looked over her shoulder. "I'll be back."

Like she was the Terminator or some shit. Then again, as she punched open the door, and she and the—wolf?!—disappeared into the thick smoke, he almost felt sorry for their enemy.

As the panel slammed shut, he got with the program.

And returned to his patient. "Daniel, hang on. Just breathe with me, okay . . ."

FORTY

O UTSIDE IN THE hall, Cathy glanced down at the wolf next to her as it dawned on her that the thing might not recognize her as a friend. But Lydia—assuming the woman was in there somewhere—apparently had some control over the beast, because it wasn't going after its partner on their Hail Mary mission. In fact, the enormous timber wolf had put itself in front of her as it lifted its nose and sniffed the air—which might have been thick with smoke, but that clearly had some information that was relevant, going by the attention getting paid to the milky waves of chemical stink.

"This way," Cathy said.

But the wolf was anticipating the direction, padding forward, continuing to stay directly in front. Keeping the gun up, Cathy anticipated the door to the patient room she was looking for as if she could manifest it—and then there the thing was, sure as if it had heeded her call.

Pushing the panel open, she led with the gun,

the strobing lights from the compromised electrical system making everything even harder to assess.

The wolf stayed in the hall, as a guard.

The good news—and, man, they were overdue for some—was that the air was much clearer here, and she went over to the supply cabinet above the stainless steel sink in the corner. The black bag was exactly where Gus had said it would be, and she yanked the surprisingly dense weight out. A set of handles dropped down, and she looped them over her shoulder, tucking the carry-on-sized duffle under her arm.

She heard the growling just as she returned to the door.

And then she heard gunshots.

"Fuck," she muttered.

But she wasn't leaving Lydia—or the wolf, and the wolf, whatever the wolf—out there unde-fended. Slipping out past the jamb, she expected to find the animal right there, but it had moved positions. Battling the smoke, and trying not to cough so that she gave her position away, she tracked the sound of that low, menacing purr all the way to the end of the hall—

The destruction of the work area was nearly total. The place had been demolished by bombing or gunshots or both—and as she looked across the lab stations, she couldn't see anything moving. Up on feet, that was. There were bodies writhing on the ground. Guards. Medical staff. People she knew, had worked with, had hired. Had trusted.

Where the hell was the wolf—

The gun muzzle came out of nowhere, and it was right at the level of her head, so close she could smell the munitions powder.

Cathy shifted her eyes to look at the soldier. The empty stare she met was a dead giveaway that it was one of those machines. That and the fact that the skin tone was too even, no capillaries or flush enlivening that pasty white countenance.

"Give me your weapon."

As the command sank in, between one blink and the next . . . she was back in the tunnel with Gus, his strong arms holding her, her weight hanging in the air, his mouth on hers, their bodies finally together.

As last thoughts went, it was not a bad one.

"Fuck you," she spat as she swung her own weapon around.

As triggers were pulled, the attack came from the side, the wolf flying through the smoky air as if from out of nowhere, its tackle taking the machine at just the right moment: The bullet meant for Cathy's skull went flying off to the left, a pinging sound ringing out.

After which there was the temptation to just pull her own trigger again and again.

Except the wolf was busy, fangs flashing, heavy

body dominating the ground game, such that it was impossible to get any reliable target. The cyborg soldier still had its weapon, though, and as a bullet rippled past Cathy's ear, she ducked and covered her head. Like that was going to help—

As a yelp cut through the struggle, a second attack unit appeared, and now was the time to discharge bullets. Aiming for the broad chest, Cathy started shooting and kept at it, the force of her bullets' impacts halting the robot's progress and then driving it back.

But that momentum ended abruptly as her magazine emptied.

She didn't have anything to reload with.

Yet.

Ducking into the smoke, she ran forward instead of back where the tunnel was, scrambling between the workstations in a jagged fashion, crunching over glass, jumping over bodies that her mind simply refused to process. She needed to find one of her guards. If she could just locate one of them, they'd have backup magazines on their tool belt—

Pop-pop-pop!

As a fresh wave of gunshots rang out, she tucked herself in behind one of the counter setups. Praying that the wolf was okay, she—

Remembered what the workstations were stocked with.

Opening the cabinet below the sink, she scanned what was under there. Then pulled the knob on the set of double doors next to it—

A light came on inside the storage unit, and the lineup of glass jars and beakers was labeled clearly: There were a lot of skulls and crossbones on the containers.

"Thank you, God."

Reaching inside, she took out a clear yellow liquid that was marked with so many warnings, it might as well have been in an opaque jar.

"Okay, you can do this. You can . . ."

Her breath was sawing in and out of her mouth, and her hands shook, and as she looked down at herself, she saw that her pantyhose had ripped, there was blood on her knees, and her skirt was covered in dust and smudges.

In an odd flare of pride, she realized she had done all that running in fucking heels.

And Daniel was right. Like him, she had a terminal diagnosis, but she didn't want to go out on a morphine drip in a hospital bed, just fading away.

Fuck that. She wanted to go out with a bang.

Jumping up, she hauled back the container of liquid nitroglycerin, a substance so unstable that the slightest impact could cause it to explode. Then she waited—

The cyborg emerged from all the swirling, noxious smoke like a wraith, its frozen face locking on her and showing no emotion at all as it triangulated its gun muzzle and got ready to take out its target.

"I love you, Gus St. Claire!" Cathy screamed as she let loose with the beaker.

And braced herself to be blown apart.

FORTY-ONE

U P ON THE first level of the house, Blade
was taking a little rest.

Well, not really. But his weight wasn't on his feet
anymore. Which would have been nice given his injured leg, he supposed.

Too bad it was all on his arms.

As smoke from the destruction below percolated
up through the ventilation system, Kurling's cyborg
soldiers had subdued him quickly, and he hadn't
been surprised to be strung up from the banister
of the stairway, his arms over his head, his toesies
dangling in his shoes. His cousin had performed
none of the work. Of course he hadn't. Kurling was
a gentlemale of the prime order, and thus had had
one of his mechanical minions bring over a settee so
he could watch the hog-tying comfortably.

The *symphath* was still sitting there, composed
as someone listening to a concerto, his legs crossed
at the knees, one hand propping a slight lean to the
side.

"I truly do not know what is worse," the *symphath* murmured. "What your sister did to disgrace us, or what you did to *ahvenge* her."

Blade shrugged. Or tried to. With his arms in their current position, there wasn't much shoulder movement available to his biomechanics.

"That's a bit"—he took a labored breath—"like wondering whether you . . . are lazy or just incompetent."

Kurling laughed softly. "That is a weak taunt."

"I am a bit . . . compromised . . . at the moment."

"True. And I shall forgive you for that. But not anything else."

The male rose to his feet, and tugged his black combat sweater down so that it was smooth over his chest. There were guns at his hips, but he had not taken them out. Of course he hadn't. This operation, like cleaning his quarters or preparing his own food, was beneath his efforts.

No, he was saving the glory for himself. The dirty work, for others.

"How did . . . you find out," Blade asked as his cousin came in close. "About me and the labs."

"I followed you one night. I couldn't understand why you were disappearing with such regularity. At first I assumed that your sister's lower standards had infected you and you were forging relations with a vampire down in Caldwell. But you were not, were you. You were out in the field. In the mountains. By the sea and in the desert. I must commend you for your thoroughness. You were quite effective."

"Why'd it . . . take you so . . . long."

"For things to come to this?" Kurling shrugged easily, sure as if he were showing off his freedom of movement. "Well, firstly, I needed my own army. You used humans, I wanted to improve on that, and it took me some time to gather the necessary contacts. You inspired me to start looking into the underground, actually. It's amazing what you can buy, what secrets are available to the highest bidder. These units"—he indicated the soldiers that were standing all around like radios ready to be turned on, or laptops prepared to be booted up, or cars itching for a driver—"are the future of human warfare. It's just going to take those rats without tails a decade or two to get the technology cheap enough and the squabbling over rights settled. Issues with you aside, we in the Colony will of course need to have our own stockpile of these weapons, and I have a production facility going already. Further, some of the technological problems the humans hadn't quite worked out needed to be solved. Battery life is such a difficulty."

"My heart bleeds for you," Blade muttered.

"Oh, it will."

The knife came out from behind his cousin's

back, having obviously been nestled in a holster there. And the blade was solid gold, the precious metal gleaming.

"This is your weapon, cousin." Kurling held the thing up. "I stole it from your quarters two years ago, but you never noticed. You were too busy being weak—do you have any idea what would have happened if the Colony found out you were *ahvenging* your whore of a sister? Who fucked a vampire? She brought shame upon the whole of our bloodline— especially those of us who have led our lives in the right and proper way. I have no mate, no prospects, no life because of her, and then you"—the tip was angled forward—"*you* do something even worse. *You* are going to get all of us killed. Rehvenge may have reset some of the rules, but the Colony has its own underground and the assassins will come for each one of us. *You* must be eradicated for the rest of the bloodline to survive."

Blade's belly pumped in and out as the point of the gleaming golden knife came to rest against his naked abdomen.

"And as long as I kill you, the infection can be controlled. The rest of us will not be tainted by your inexplicable actions—"

"Not . . . inexplicable."

"No? What else would you call them? Xhexania brought shame to your immediate family, and after she was dealt with appropriately, you go off and destroy the very thing that cleansed our bloodline of her infection? I cannot fathom why you would do such a thing."

Blade stared into eyes that were the color of his own, and thought for an instant of the two of them as youngs, playing outside one of the disguised kiosks that fed into the Colony's maze of subterranean tunnels.

Now they were here, enemies by circumstance and action.

"Because I am not like you," he heard himself answer. "That is why I did it. That is why it is anything but inexplicable."

Kurling blinked as if the response was as confusing as the deeds that had been done in the name of love for a sister who had been treated unfairly by those who should have stood by her the most.

"Well, enough with the catch-up, cousin," the *symphath* said. "Let us commence this so that we shall both get our due."

With that, the knife was driven in hard, the gold cleaving through clothing, skin, and organ, smooth as a surgical strike.

And then came the twist.

As Kurling jerked his fist, the knife bored a bigger hole through Blade's lower abdomen—

His scream ripped through the foyer, echoing throughout the house, the acreage . . . the whole world:

"Xhexxxxxxxxxxxxxxxxxxxxxx."

If Blade was going out, he wanted his beloved sister's name to be the last thing he uttered—

In his delirium, things that couldn't possibly be true seemed to happen—

This was *not* possible. There was no way that the doors of the mansion exploded open and the very female he had called out to burst through curls of smoke as if she had answered to her name.

Except it *was* his sister. And she was not alone.

Warriors, strong of back, with black daggers strapped, handles down, to their chests, flooded the foyer and engaged with the animatronic soldiers, the fighting propagating like an immune response to cancer in an otherwise healthy person.

Xhex went right for their cousin.

And in his surprise, Kurling was no match for her.

Then again, Kurling would have been no match for her even if he had been prepared. She overpowered him with her better skill, taking him to the ground with a smooth and ready move, mounting him and pinning him in place with a strong arm and a grip on his throat.

How she got control of the gold dagger, Blade did not immediately know. But perhaps Kurling had retained his fierce grip, and then extracted it as the weapon of his choice as he was attacked. But however the transfer happened, the blade was relocated from his abdominal cavity to her palm.

And she wielded it with brutal efficiency: As Kurling tried to bat her superior strength away, she took his eyes.

First the left.

Then the right.

Popping them out of their sockets with the tip that was marked with the blood from Blade's veins.

As he started to lose consciousness, Blade was in terrible pain . . . but there was a smile on his face.

The death he had always wondered about had come for him finally, all those narrow misses as he had snuck around the human world and fought to defend that which he had failed, culminating in this final mortal calamity.

He was good with how he was leaving the earth, however.

He had taken care of things far better than he'd cared to admit, in the words of the silver wolf.

And in return, his sister had not just come for him, she had brought her mate and the Black Dagger Brotherhood with her.

Wasn't family divine.

FORTY-TWO

WHEN HER WOLVEN side was in charge, Lydia was not much more than a backseat driver, able to offer suggestions as to actions, but unable to control things.

And in this wartime scenario, she had little of value to add. Her wolf was a predator with practice, and really, how could she improve on that?

As the artificial soldier battled against the attack waged against it, she just went along for the ride, swirling around with her other side as fangs were sunk into limbs that had metal bones and wires for ligaments, but that were nonetheless subject to being torn apart.

Not even the electrical shocks slowed her wolf down—

The explosion was off to the left, and it was so loud and forceful, the ground battle was paused as the wolf and the soldier briefly reoriented awareness toward the sound.

Car parts, everywhere.

Not car parts, really, but metal shrapnel flying so fast that there was no time to duck—and the distraction was something the soldier recovered from quicker than the wolf did. The flip-over came without warning, and as Lydia became aware that she was now staring out of the wolf's eyes at the ceiling instead of the floor, she knew her other form was in danger of losing this battle.

And that was when she remembered Daniel rolling the unit over and checking the back of the neck for the power source.

If there was a way she could disconnect the battery from the motherboard? But she was going to need her human side to do it.

And another distraction . . .

As Lydia attempted to regather the reins, her wolf did not want to relinquish control of their joint system. She won, however, by sheer force of will. Then again, when you needed to get back to your one true love with a medical bag, you had strength reserves you didn't normally access.

As the shifting occurred, she knew it was a long shot, but it was all she had—

The change was not as smooth as it usually was. But that didn't matter, and beneath the cyborg, she transformed into her human incarnation.

Which made the fucking thing freeze. Like she had broken its brain.

With its dead eyes locked, expressionless, but

clearly confused, on her female face, she had a split second to get something, anything she could, to use as a weapon. Shoving her hands down to the cyborg's waist, she furiously fumbled with whatever was there—

The gun seemed to find her grip instead of the other way around, as if the nine millimeter wanted to put an end to this whole thing as much as she did.

Lydia was not a confident shooter. She wasn't sure how the safety worked. She only had one hand.

But the image of Daniel seizing up on the floor of that concrete hallway, with Gus empty-handed beside him, gave her some kind of core knowledge in weaponry she'd never had before.

Pop!

It happened so fast, she wasn't even sure what she had done. But as the side of the soldier's neck blew out and the thing collapsed on her, she stared at the gun in wonder.

Then she kicked the bucket of dead bolts off.

Panting, prepared for anything, she glanced at the cyborg. It was so completely almost human that she had an odd communion with the fucking thing. Lydia looked human on the outside, too. But at least her window dressing held a conscience that no artificial life ever could—

Her arm swung the gun around without a conscious thought as a figure she hadn't noticed emerged from the foggy, nauseating fumes.

C.P. Phalen looked like something out of a *Jack-ass* movie, her hair and face singed with soot, her Armani uniform all out of whack, one heel broken, the other stiletto cocked to the side as if her ankle had been dislocated.

Under her arm, cradled against her chest, was a medic bag that was as debris-covered as she was.

In a bored, exhausted voice, the woman said, "If you shoot me after all of this shit, I'm never having you or your man as a houseguest again. Ever."

◆   ◆   ◆

In the emergency exit hallway, Gus had Daniel out flat with the man's head cocked back at an awkward angle to free up as much airway as he could. He had two fingers on the side of Daniel's neck, and as long as there was that too-fast pulse, no chest compressions were needed. It was only if things went still that he would double-fist up, and start pumping.

The initial round of spasming paralysis had passed, and now the limbs were lax. And as one side of Gus's awareness calculated the infinitesimal chances that Phalen or Lydia would come back alive—much less with anything he could use to help the man—the pharmaceutical researcher in him was wondering what the hell was going on with his patient.

Daniel's skin had gone white, all over his body: As a Caucasian, he hadn't had a lot of melanin to begin with, but now it was as if vitiligo had taken him over. The only color anywhere on the chest or arms came from moles or the occasional freckle, and the flesh was cold to the touch, like all surface circulation had ceased.

And then there was the hair thing.

The dusting of hair on his forearms was falling off, or sloughing off, if Gus ran a hand over the limb. Likewise, on the scalp, all of the follicles seemed to be releasing, the post-chemo regrowth fuzz drifting off.

Except Daniel's heart was still beating, and he was breathing—in a wheezing fashion, it was true, but there *was* respiration—

"Ah! Fuck!"

As Gus yelped, he brushed frantically at his leg, and in the back of his mind, he was glad no one else was around to see him sissy-scramble away from the scorpion that had crawled up onto his thigh.

Courtesy of his flipout, the thing went flying and landed on the concrete floor. And when it just sat there for a second, like he'd stunned it, he grabbed for the container and put the glass box over the arachnid.

The confinement seemed to reorient the thing, and the scorpion started pacing around, like she was ready to sting again.

"No worse for wear, are you," he murmured as the creature pivoted toward him and seemed to meet his eyes. "And don't look at me like that. Did you see what happened when you envenomated that guy? I'm not looking to be white, thank you very much—"

The steel door of the tunnel swung open, and Gus didn't bother trying to protect himself. It was either the two women he most wanted to see in the world. Or it was death in the form of something with a gun.

Or maybe a wolf who was hungry?

Whatever. He was too shell-shocked after everything—

"Daniel—is he alive?"

The words didn't really compute, but the sight of Lydia Susi emerging buck-ass naked through the smoke, blood streaking from minor wounds, plaster dust in her hair, kind of made sense.

And then he saw his Phalen.

Catherine Phillips Phalen looked like hell in a handbasket, and the fact that she was walking on the side of her ankle was something he was going to have to take care of. If he got the chance.

As Lydia dropped to her knees by Daniel and shifted his head into her lap, Gus's dream woman walked up and set down the med bag right beside him.

"Is he going to live?" Lydia asked. "What's going on with him?"

Gus forced himself to snap to attention. "If I— ah, if I could get him out to a patient room, I could probably find out. But right now, as far as I can tell, his vitals are steady—for the moment."

"We cleared the place," she said. "Before we came back here. The remaining two soldiers, we took care of them. So we can go out there again."

As she focused on Daniel and started to murmur to her man, Gus looked up at Phalen. "Hi," he said stupidly.

"Hi."

She pushed at her hair. The stuff had been burned off in places, and he worried about a raw patch on her cheek. It was at least a second degree, maybe a third degree'er.

"You know something . . ." she murmured, "I've had a helluva day at the office."

He started to smile. "That's what they make Coke for, honey, why do you think I drink it all the time?"

When he reached up for her, she kneeled by him and rested against his chest like they had been together for years.

Then again, they had been partners for three years, two months, eleven days . . .

Gus checked his watch and said against her mouth, "And seventeen minutes."

He knew this because he had been counting on her.

All along.

FORTY-THREE

Y OU'RE AWAKE AGAIN."

As the condition report was presented to him, Daniel wasn't so sure about that. But he knew who was talking to him. Then again, he could probably be dead and still recognize his Lydia's voice.

Opening his lids, he had a thought that he was tired of playing patient—but then all he saw was her smile. She was so blindingly beautiful, in a way that had nothing to do with how she looked. She was glowing from the inside—and by some miracle, he was still alive to be warmed by her.

"You are"—he cleared his throat with a little cough—"a sight for sore eyes."

She started blinking away tears as she kissed him. Then she eased back, and he was able to orientate himself. He was in a hospital bed—but not in any of the ones he was familiar with down in the underground lab.

"Where . . . are we?"

"Cathy's bedroom."

He rolled his eyes. "She's changed her name again."

"This time it's sticking—"

"IsGusokay?" he asked in a rush.

"Yes." She stroked his face. "And Blade made it through as well. Gus had to operate on him in the middle of a battlefield in the foyer. But he's doing well, and so is Xhex. She's with him now. She hasn't left his side, actually. She showed up at just the right time with just the right kind of friends."

Daniel frowned, and tried to piece things together properly. When that effort didn't go far, it dawned on him that—

"You've told me all this before, haven't you." As she nodded patiently, he remembered other things . . . explosions, escapes . . . "My memory's sketchy."

"It's okay. Gus says everything will come back, we just have to give it time."

Daniel took a deep breath. And then another. And braced himself for a coughing jag. When it didn't come, he frowned.

"What time is it?" he asked.

"Eight o'clock-ish."

"In the morning."

"No, at night."

"Oh. How long's it been since the attack?"

"A couple of days."

"Oh," he repeated.

Glancing down at himself, he discovered that there was an IV in his other arm and beeping from somewhere behind him, all common things to him. He also had the joy of a catheter. But something was different.

Lydia . . . was different. She was glowing in a new way, an aura of some kind of emotion he couldn't remember her having before turning her face and her hazel eyes into something that seemed almost dreamlike.

"What day is it?" he asked.

"Thursday, December first."

All at once, he went to sit up. "What? That's more than a couple of—how long have I been out of it?"

She didn't stop him from going vertical. She didn't warn him to calm down. She didn't call out for Gus or a nurse or another doctor.

She just stared at him with those glowing eyes.

"Why are you looking at me like that?" he said slowly.

With a little laugh, she brushed away another round of tears. "Knock knock."

"Okay, now's not the time for jokes, Lydia. I don't get what the hell is going on—"

"*Knock knock.*"

"Who's there," he snapped, aware he was being an impatient ass, but come on. After all the shit that had happened—like, fifteen fucking days ago—he was not in the mood for games.

"Cancer free," she said.

"What?"

Lydia took his hand again. "No, the proper response is 'who.'"

Daniel blinked. A couple of times. "Who . . . is cancer free."

"You."

In the quiet that followed, he tilted his head. "I'm sorry, what did you say . . . ?"

"Blade was right. Whatever is in that scorpion's venom? It's a cure. Gus is over the moon, and I guess he and Cathy are going to partner with some big pharmaceutical company down in Houston to develop the compound and figure out how to make it in a lab. That scorpion sting has a revolutionary, tumor-targeting chemical in it that starves cancer cells. They can't access any energy, and anything that doesn't have energy dies."

He took another deep breath. And another. Then put a hand over his chest.

"It takes time," she said gently. "But everything inside of you is reducing. They've been doing regular imaging up here—and the results are irrefutable. And guess what, Cathy took the venom five days ago. She's having the same experience. They don't know if it will work for all cancers, but for you two, it's a miracle, and that means for other people, it will help as well."

"Cancer . . . free? Have you told me this before?"

Lydia shook her head. And then laughed a little. "They told me to wait until you were further recovered, but I just can't hold it in anymore. And I get the shock. It took me some time to get used to it, too. I can assure you, though, you're cured."

"I don't . . . understand. Am I dreaming?"

Lydia shook her head again. "No. This is real—"

"*Oh, God.*"

Hard to know if that was a prayer to keep him awake and to believe in what he was hearing or if it was thanks to a higher power . . . or if it was just a pair of words that humans uttered when they don't understand a shocking truth.

What he did understand? Down to his core?

Was the feel of his woman as he pulled her up onto the bed, onto him: Lydia was warm, and weighty, and very corporeal, and as his emotions overflowed and he began to shake, she held him fiercely. Because that's what your partner did when you were splintering apart.

They held you together.

Squeezing his eyes closed, he couldn't breathe—but this time, it was for a good reason. Gratitude flowed through him, and it was like an antiseptic to the sorrow he had carried for the last six months, cleaning him on the inside, scrubbing out the grief and terror and loss, the pain and side effects, the self-blame and the guilt over what he had put Lydia through.

"It's okay," she said hoarsely. "Just let it all out. I've got you."

Pulling back, he touched her face and found him-self thinking back to the moment they'd first met. With a vivid clarity that gave him hope his memory would indeed come back fully, he remembered being shown into her office at the Wolf Study Project. She had been wiping down her desk with Lysol, scrub-bing at something like it was contaminated, like her elbow grease was going to save the world from what-ever bacteria she was so worried about.

The instant she had looked up at him, she'd had him.

He'd refused to acknowledge this, of course, be-cause he'd had a job to do, a mission to complete—and falling in love with a woman, who later turned out to be a wolf, while they ran from artificial in-telligence mounted on Terminator chassis, as vam-pires rallied around them as allies, and some guy in a red robe, who was a romantic rival but turned out to be a friend, delivered a lifesaving drug pack-aged in an albino scorpion at the last minute to give them their future back . . .

"I mean, fucking hell," he said. "You just can't make this shit up."

"What?" his Lydia asked.

"Never mind." He started to smile. "I'm not going to question good fortune."

"Neither will I."

EPILOGUE

Three weeks later . . .

"THIS IS WHAT you want?"

As Gus tossed out the question, he looked around the library's collection of first editions and seriously questioned his buddy's fiscal prudence. "Cathy's giving the whole place away—and all you want is this sofa table?"

Daniel put his hand on the glossy top. "Yup. We'll take this."

"You sure you don't want one of those?" Gus nodded out to the foyer. "I mean, those sculptures are . . . great. Well, they're worth a bank, at any rate."

On that note, the team of movers tilted a dolly and started rolling out one of the melted-cheese-marble lumps.

"We don't have a lot of space in Eastwind's old place. And you guys are already insisting we take an SUV."

Gus refocused on the man, and maybe it was the doctor in him, maybe it was the researcher—probably it was just the human—but he couldn't help but measure the change in the last thirty days.

The height was the same. The dark hair, skin color, and the moles on the side of the throat and the jaw and that one on the temple were the same. Voice was the same.

No, it was stronger.

And yet for all that remained unchanged, it was a new man who stood in front of him. Daniel Joseph was a good thirty pounds heavier, and gaining every day. His balance was spot-on, his movements fluid and balanced, his body resuming a normal course of functioning. The improvement was even in his face, too, his cheeks flush with healthy blood flow and his smile ever-ready.

His eyes were different, though. For reasons that were not well understood, the pigment in his irises was draining out, the rings around his pupils so pale now, they were nearly indistinguishable from the sclera—

"There you guys are—Daniel, are you sure you just want that table?"

Gus's body started to turn to the voice before he had a conscious thought that he wanted to look at his woman. But it was like that with Cathy. She was a destination for him even when his physical form wasn't traveling. Part of it was everything they had been through with her looming illness, the touch-and-go and coming goodbye wiped off the board by a miracle he was still deconstructing on the science side.

He was going to figure that venom out, however. And then he was going to bring it to the world.

With Cathy. And Gunnar Rhobes, their new partner.

"Yup, only the table, he's telling me." Gus put his arm out to the side. "I tried to sell him on one of the sculptures, but it's a no-go."

As she fit herself against him and looked up, he pulled her in for a kiss. Ten days after Daniel was stung, while the dust was still settling after the attack, Cathy had been stung. It had been ludicrous. No clinical controls other than him shitting bricks and being ready with all kinds of crash-cart/epinephrine support.

Oh, wait. He'd swabbed her forearm with alcohol.

He'd never forget her lying in that hospital bed, eyes locked on his, a peaceful expression on her face. She'd been rock solid. He'd been a mess as he'd held her hand while that man with the red robes had placed the scorpion on her skin. Right before the strike, two things had gone through Gus's mind: One, that the foreigner with the accent and the calm surety was all that made him hang on to his emotions—and in this, he was seeing himself through the eyes of his patients: He'd been that guidepost for others so many times.

Now a stranger he didn't understand was it for him.

The second thing he'd thought of was that this

was how modern medicine had started, people using what was available in the environment to help themselves survive. The vetting had not been in a laboratory. It had been out in nature, the trial and error coming at a high cost when the dice roll went against you.

"Where have you gone, Gus?"

The soft words were punctuated with a stroke on his cheek, and he came back into his body. He'd been prone to fits of drift for the last month, his brain vacillating between trying to catalog what reality now looked like and flying off into all kinds of molecular chemistry. But again, he was going to figure out why the venom worked, and then he was going to synthesize it in the lab, and then he was . . .

"Hi," Cathy said as she waved her hand in front of his face. "You're still gone."

Yes, he was. But one guaranteed anchor? Looking at her. She was like Daniel, refreshed with health, her cheeks flushed with good circulation, her lips a natural pink, her eyes also lively, and paling out like Daniel's. Courtesy of not leaving the compound, her short blond hair was growing out, the roots showing dark, and she was trying to decide whether she was going to keep the light color or not—and wasn't that a nice preoccupation. As she'd said, if all you had on your mind was what was growing out of your head? Life was—

"Life is so good," he murmured. "I get lost."

Cathy looked at Daniel and the pair of them shared the stare of survivors. Although her physical status hadn't been anywhere near as declined as his, she had been braced for a long road into her grave—and the knowledge of that approaching descent had been a stressor that had aged and depleted her. With them both freed of that burden? Not just health had returned.

"Anyway," Daniel said. "Just this table, and thanks."

Gus pushed up the sleeves of his Army green *M*A*S*H* sweatshirt. "I'll help you get it into the car."

They each took one end, and Gus did the backing out. As they crossed the foyer, Cathy ran forward and intercepted a pair of movers, pointing them to the back of the house so they didn't forget something. Then she fell in step again.

Outside, December's icy night was a slap in the face, but the snow-covered landscape was an apology for the sting. The pristine drifts were like the abstract marble sculptures the movers were packing into the black-on-black eighteen-wheeler. No commercial company for Cathy. Even after all this time, Gus had no idea how she pulled so many dark-market things out of thin air, but she seemed to have access to some kind of billionaire's Craigslist where everything was super discreet, no questions were asked, and service didn't come with any smiles.

As Gus humped the table out, there was no har-har, we're-in-this-with-you-boys to the profession-als. Hard to compare a four-legged with a little top to a polished frickin' bolder, but there was a sense of satisfaction as he and Daniel stuffed the freebie into the back of the Suburban.

As Daniel hit the button and the rear door auto-matically closed, the man jacked up his jeans. "So we'll see you up on the mountain?"

Gus checked his watch. "Yup. Gettin' close. You ready?"

"More than ever before in my life."

"Amen, brother." The two clapped palms and jerked in for a clutch. "And then we'll meet in Houston."

Daniel passed a palm over his short hair. "New Year's Eve."

"The four of us."

"We're looking forward to it. New phase."

Cathy came forward and the two murmured to each other. They were in a special club, one that didn't necessarily exclude anybody else, but that had an inner circle of understanding that no one but survivors shared. Gus was glad for them. Miracles were great and all, but they didn't go *tabula rasa* on shit. The past stalked each one of them, a panther in the shadows thrown by the bright light of hope and health and excitement for the future.

Over time, maybe things would feel more solid. In the present, the slope they'd all ascended sure as hell felt slippery and gravity seemed very greedy.

But sure as shit, they were grateful to be at the summit.

Daniel opened the driver's side door, gave them both a final wave, and got behind the wheel. After a flare of red taillights, the engine came to life, and the Suburban skirted the moving semitruck and trundled down the allée.

"Come on," Cathy said as she slipped an arm around him. "We have a wedding to get dressed for."

He looked down at his woman. "You're really going to let me wear my Converse All Stars?"

"It wouldn't be right if you didn't."

◆   ◆   ◆

Blade knew the moment that she was back on the mountain. He felt the disturbance in the molecules of the already brisk wind, even through the rock wall of the cave, and his only thought was . . .

Please, no.

Sitting on the bedding platform, he knew the reason she had come, but as he checked his watch, he saw that she was early—and he worried that he was going to have to congratulate her and pretend that he was fine. That everything had worked out as it should be. That the future was bright because it was assured, and optimism was the sun that out-shone the moonlight.

The reality was that he was sitting here in his red robing, like a young scolded for bad behavior, his hands twisting with torment in his lap.

Because her hello was his goodbye.

As the footfalls in the tight throat of the cave grew louder, his emotions got turned up even fur-ther in volume. For a male, and a *symphath* at that, he found the inner quaking very unpleasant, but when the center of the chest was affected, one had no choice except to ride the wave. The truism of "everywhere you go, there you are" was never more apt than when the wolven you loved was going to mate another—

Blade jumped to his feet. "Oh, it's . . . you."

As Xhex stepped into the open area, she crossed her arms and then eased into a lean on the cave's granite wall. With her gun belt on, and the knife strapped to her thigh, she was as close to being in wedding attire as any fighter was willing to get.

At least she was not in white, he thought with a surge of fondness.

"Expecting someone else?" she murmured.

But that wasn't really a question. His sister knew who he'd thought it would be.

"Here early for the festivities?" he asked. "Is your *hellren* with you?"

"He's on his way." Those wise, gunmetal gray eyes dropped to the bag that was by the end of the bedding platform. "Going somewhere?"

He nodded. "I rather thought I would take a vacation."

"Where to?"

"Here or there. Everywhere."

After a stretch of silence, she shook her head. "You're not coming back, are you."

A lie would be easier, but he owed her better than that. "No. But I think my presence is best . . . in other places."

"Were you going to say goodbye?"

"To her . . . or you."

"Both. Either."

Blade bent down and picked up the bag. It was not that heavy. He had been given some clothes by Daniel, and indeed, he was currently dressed in a pair of the man's blue jeans and a parka that was very warm and soft. The wardrobe donations had been delivered by the doctor, Gus St. Claire, who, having operated quite competently on Blade's abdominal perforation on the black-and-white marble flooring of that foyer, had become a bit of a friend: During Blade's recovery up here, following his transfer from that house, the two had enjoyed fine conversation about a variety of topics.

He would miss that.

Focusing properly on Xhex, he resolved that he would miss a lot of people, and opening his mouth to speak, he . . . found he did not have the words.

"It's okay," she said softly. "I don't take it personally. And I'll tell her when she comes up here."

"What will you say?"

"What you would have, if you were here."

As their eyes met, he knew she was reading his grid. He did not return the imposition. He already knew that his sister was healed—he could tell just by the way she held herself with such calm ease. She was truly at peace. Finally.

Funny, he had intended to *ahvenge* her by blowing up all those labs. But the true balance had come not from the explosions, but from her knowing the truth of what he had been doing. That loyalty and revenge had brought her back.

"Are you going to leave me a way of contacting you," she asked.

"If you need me, I will know."

"How."

He touched the side of his head in salute. "I shall keep in touch . . . somehow."

She didn't believe him, of course. And that was okay. Reality did not need to be believed to be lived.

"The wolven's going to want to thank you," Xhex said. "For everything."

"And I would rather have my eyes plucked out of

my skull before I must endure such an exchange."
As his sister arched her brow, Blade smiled a little.
"'Tis quite unpleasant, both experiences."

"Yeah. For real."

There was an awkward pause. And then she
dropped her hands to her hips and rubbed her
palms on her leathers as if they were damp.

"I want you to know something." Her voice was
low in volume, strong in tone. "It's a two-way street,
between you and me. If you need anything, you
gotta let me know."

Blade's heart skipped a beat and he made a show
of looking at the natural spring in the rear of the
cave. The bedding platform. The storage trunks and
the table with the candle on it.

"I rather thought you'd prefer to never see me
again."

"No," Xhex said. "That's not what I'd prefer."

"Well." He cleared his throat. "Isn't that quite
lovely. Now, if you'll excuse me, I must be going."

Bending at the waist, he bowed to her, and then
he walked forward. As he passed by her position,
there by the passageway's entry, he thought perhaps
she would reach out to him. She did not. And thus
he processed, alone, through the narrow confines of
the way to the great outdoors.

Emerging, he took a deep breath and felt a
burn in his stomach. But it was not bad. Indeed,
his healing had progressed quite the thing, and in

another week, he would have no residual effects whatsoever.

Physically, that was.

With one last glance around, he expected to see the silver wolf off to the side, looking satisfied with herself in all that she had engineered. Then he closed his eyes and—

"Blade—wait!"

As he turned, Xhex raced out of the cave's entrance, and the next thing he knew, she was hugging him hard. He did not hesitate to return the embrace.

"Take care of yourself," she said roughly.

"You, too, sister mine." He squeezed his eyes closed. "You . . . too."

◆   ◆   ◆

Lydia arrived up on the mountain's summit wearing white winter-weight hiking pants, a white turtleneck, and a white parka. Even her boots, which were snow-rated and waterproof, were white. Socks and long underwear, too.

She'd driven Candy's car—which had previously been her own—up the back trail, and parked it a bit away from the magnificent clearing that provided the view of the valley. As she got out, the cold nipped at her, and she welcomed the burn in her cheeks, the way her eyes watered, the hum in her sinuses.

It just felt good to be alive. And she was excited for what was going to happen soon.

The guests would be arriving in just half an hour—Daniel, too.

She had come early.

As Lydia walked forward, she heard rustling in the undergrowth, and then the howling started. The sound made her heart sing further, and she stopped, let her head fall back, closed her eyes . . . and thought of Eastwind.

She had moved into his house with Daniel.

And she was taking over from him. Whatever that meant.

Well, so far, it meant that she and Cathy were reopening the Wolf Study Project. With that hotel starting to do business across the valley, and the ever-present threats from people being on the mountain, her beloved wolves needed protecting now more than ever—and she was just the person to do it.

As Eastwind had had his sheriff's badge, so she had the WSP, a perfect camouflage for her sacred duty to the mountain and the lair of the wolven.

Maybe she'd stay forty years like he did. Maybe she'd find someone to take over earlier than that. But either way, for however long she was here, she had a job.

And hey, so did Candy. The receptionist had been thrilled to be asked to come back to work.

It was too bad that Gus and Cathy had to move down to Houston, but they didn't have much choice.

The lab was all ruined, and the mansion had painful memories of so many medical staff and researchers dying in the raid. Somehow, the deaths had all been covered. Lydia hadn't asked any questions. That part of the human world wasn't her business, anyway.

The important thing was that they had the venom. If Vita-12b had shown some potential, it was nothing compared to what that scorpion had given the world.

And she had her Daniel back—

It was just as Lydia arrived at the cave's hidden entry that her nose caught a scent, and she followed it deeper into the earth. As she stepped out into the living space, she wasn't surprised at the female who was sitting at the little table.

Xhex smiled. "Hey, it's the bride-to-be."

"Hi." She looked around. Even though there was nowhere anyone Blade's size could tuck behind. "Has he . . ."

"Yeah, he's gone."

A sting of pain went through her chest. "I wanted . . . to thank him."

Standing up, Xhex tugged her leather jacket down and smoothed her hands over her short hair. "And he wanted you to know that he's happy for you both, and he's glad Daniel's okay. He wishes you all the very best things in life."

"That's very kind of him."

"He's a very kind male. In his own way." There was an awkward pause . . . then Xhex nodded to the passageway. "Now I guess I better go start the fire."

"Xhex, is your brother . . ."

"Going to get over you?" The smile had a sad tilt to it. "Do you want me to be honest or make it easy on you?"

"Honesty, please."

The female shook her head. "No, he's not. But he's at peace with knowing your future is secured."

Lydia remembered seeing that flaring light so close to dawn surround the male. "I owe him . . . everything."

"So love your male right. That's all you need to do. Blade'll survive—I'll make sure of it."

"Then I know he really will be all right. Thank you."

Xhex smiled and nodded to the passageway's exit. "I'll see you out there."

When Lydia was alone, she went over to the bedding platform and stared down at the indentation where someone had been sitting. The *symphath*'s scent lingered in the air, but she imagined, in a month, certainly two, there would be nothing left of him.

Except for his legacy—

"You're not rethinking this, are you?"

Lydia looked over her shoulder with a smile. "Never."

Daniel was wearing all black, from his boots to his own turtleneck and parka situation. In the previous couple of weeks, he'd been rebuilding the muscle he had lost, in the on-site gym. His hands remained on the numb side because that side effect from chemo was permanent, and he did take a nap every now and again, but everything else was returning to him, his energy, his balance . . . his sex drive.

"We can do this somewhere warmer," he murmured as he came to her and put his hands on her waist.

"No, I want us to say our vows here. This mountain is our past, present, and future."

He glanced around. "Hey, you think someone might let us have a honeymoon here? That natural spring back there is a hot tub if I've ever seen one."

Running her hands up his his pecs, she no longer measured his ribs, or worried about his blood levels, his blood pressure, his respiration and heart rate. He was just Daniel, without the disease.

The thing she had prayed for.

"You know something," she murmured. "I saw my grandfather right before I left the house just now."

"What? I thought he was—"

"I don't mean to freak you out. His ghost does that sometimes. He just shows up—and I was . . .

comforted to see him this time. I feel like he was blessing us. It meant a lot."

Daniel tucked her hair behind her ears. "I would have liked to meet him."

"He would have approved of you. Very much."

"Because I'm a trained killer who can protect you?"

"Yes, and you're also in love with me."

"Very much." He kissed her. "Very, very much . . ."

The mouth action started reverently, but it didn't stay that way. As if Daniel were making up for lost time, he had been making love to her every chance they got—and she was more than happy to oblige. She wanted him, too.

Always—

Lydia inched back and checked her watch. "How has twenty minutes gone by already? People will be waiting for us."

"Yeah, and I guess I better save something for the honeymoon, huh."

"I'm not sure who we need to ask to use this cave—maybe we should just apologize if someone else shows up?"

"Deal." His eyes roamed her face. "So Blade is gone, huh."

When she nodded, he shook his head. "No goodbye. That bastard."

"Xhex knows how to get ahold of him. Or at least . . . I hope she will."

"Only if he lets her. He's . . . complicated."

"And a lifesaver."

"Yeah, I did not see that one coming."

They kissed a little more, and then they were walking through the passageway together. When they stepped out, all they had to do was follow the chatter and the laughter—and the flickering light from the campfire.

And there they all were, standing around the logs that were crackling and throwing out warmth: Cathy and Gus. Xhex and John Matthew. The snippy chef who had made a beautiful cake. The staff of the mansion, who were all relocating down to Houston. Candy, who, in a red-and-green ankle-length wool coat, and hair that was Christmas-tree green and gold, was standing at attention, prepared to conduct the ceremony.

The group was so busy talking among themselves that they didn't notice the intendeds off in the shadows, but that was good. Lydia wanted a moment to soak it all in.

Eastwind should be here, she thought—

And there he was.

"Holy crap," Daniel murmured with a start. "Are you seeing that?"

Just outside the glow of the firelight, an old woman and the former sheriff were standing side by side, the two of them ethereal and beautiful, made of moonlight. As they joined hands, it was as if they were joined in many other ways, and were welcoming Lydia and Daniel into the club of happily mateds.

"I am so lucky," she said as she teared up. "How are *we* this lucky?"

Daniel was quiet for a while. "I don't know. But we shouldn't waste this moment. Or any other."

"I agree." She took her future husband's hand. "Let's not keep our friends waiting."

As they both went to take a step forward, and the wedding party turned to greet them, the wolves started howling again, and the old woman and the former sheriff disappeared into the night air. But they were never far. Lydia knew that deep in her bones.

Your true allies, the ones who kept you right and had your back and loved it when your life was going well, never left you, even when they weren't right next to you.

And sacrifices made for the right reasons were never wrong.

And true love never died.

Just before they got to the circle, Daniel stopped, and patted down his parka. "Oh, you gotta be kidding me. I forgot my vows. I wrote them back at our house and left 'em next to Eastwind's old Barca-Lounger."

"Don't worry about it." Lydia smiled up at her man. "Just tell me how I feel."

"Oh, that's easy." He kissed her again. "I love you, Mrs. Joseph."

"Well, I think that'll do very nicely, Mr. Susi." She patted right over his heart. "Very nicely indeed . . ."

ACKNOWLEDGMENTS

WITH SO MANY thanks to the readers of the Black Dagger Brotherhood books! This has been a long, marvelous, exciting journey, and I can't wait to see what happens next in this world we all love. I'd also like to thank Meg Ruley, Rebecca Scherer and everyone at JRA, and Hannah Braaten, Jamie Selzer, Lauren Carr, Sarah Schlick, Jennifer Long, Jennifer Bergstrom, and the entire family at Gallery Books and Simon & Schuster.

To Team Waud, I love you all. Truly. And as always, everything I do is with love to and adoration for both my family of origin and of adoption.

Oh, and thank you to Naamah, my Writer Dog II, and Obie, who is now a WD in training. They work as hard as I do on my books!